# In the Himalayan Nights

by

## Anoop Chandola

Savant Books
Honolulu, HI, USA
2012

Published in the USA by Savant Books and Publications
2630 Kapiolani Blvd #1601
Honolulu, HI 96826
http://www.savantbooksandpublications.com

Printed in the USA

Edited by Zachary M. Oliver
Cover Design by Helen Babalis
Author photo courtesy of Harminder Phull of Beautiful Moments
Photography

13-digit ISBN (EAN): 978-0-9829987-0-0
10 digit ISBN: 0-9829987-0-8

# Dedication

This is for Prasha and her Dada's *gita* drummers with a resounding note: Religion and nationalism beat other disorders in leading humankind to harm's way.

# Acknowledgments

I thank Sudha, my wife, for working through all the incarnations of the manuscript. For their timely technical help I thankfully appreciate these family members: Abhinav, Neeti, Neha, and Varun. Varn, my son, deserves thanks for his assistance on several key points of the manuscript. I thank DanaRae Pomeroy, Vonda Lee Morton, and Stephen Fahl for leveling the battlefield of the initial draft by their editorial work. Thanks to Prof. H.S. Bhola for cheerfully reading the initial draft with his positive evaluation. Zachary Oliver, editor-in-chief, makes me humbly grateful for his professional and professorial editing of the final manuscript. Helen Babalis deserves a thousand-word appreciation for her meaningful cover design. Words are not enough to measure my Himalayan appreciation for Dr. Daniel Janik, the publisher, for caringly treating and daringly highlighting such a volume of misdiagnosed darkness.

# Table of Contents

In the Himalayan Nights

This novel was inspired by the author's field work on the Himalayan "Holy-War" dance story coming from the age-old *Mahabharata*, the second longest epic of the world (over one hundred thousand verses in Sanskrit).

# Chapter 1

# The Possessed Woman's Question

*What is here is out there. What is not here is not anywhere.*
*—Mahabharata*

Lashing out from under her wildly disheveled hair, Goda's red darting eyes glowed as they caught the firelight. She shook her head in large circles with an intensity that demanded attention, focus. Accordingly, a silence gathered among the onlookers. It was a silence which elongated an evening teetering towards the creeping darkness of night. Sensing the arrival, the onlookers gasped. Everyone's eyes were fixed on Goda. Fearlessly, she stretched her quivering hands out, letting the raging flames lick her fingers. A spell was cast. Possessed, this strange petite woman, or the thing that had entered her, gathered her trembling body and released the moment with a torrent of violent, abandoned screaming. She lunged, grabbing at the drummers.

"Five men took turns with me and other women! Why?! Tell me why! Tell me why the heroes of this war…!"

Even the crackling of the burning logs seemed to surrender before the primal display which had pulled from deep within Goda. As her questioning echoed across the heads of the onlookers, she began to gyrate in a sacred war dance. All remained suspended in the moment, the space between day and night. The only sound was that of the drummers uttering, in Hindi, a traditional prayer to welcome the arrival, "*Jai ho, Mata*! *Jai ho, Debi*!" (Hail, Mother! Hail, Goddess!). No one danced. All eyes were trained on Goda.

I noticed a man reach into the fire. As he grabbed a glowing-hot iron ladle from the bonfire, I whispered to my wife with concern creeping into my throat. "Apparently he understood her movements. He has been prepared all along for this moment."

"Yes, but I hope that he understands what she is asking for." Tula whispered in return. A worried look danced across her face along with the shadows from the fire.

Goda grabbed the ladle by its handle from the man and waved it at those nearest her, daring them to come closer. With a fierce growl, she licked the red-hot scoop. A wave of smoke flowed from her mouth. A gasp moved through the crowd. With buckling knees, Goda's eyes rolled back in strange ecstasy.

"Quick, ghee!"

A plate with some sacred material, including a ghee lamp, appeared. Having collected her balance, Goda, again, began her odd gyrations. With her lips pulled back and the red-hot ladle held with her teeth, she smeared the ghee (clarified butter) on her elbow and rubbed the hot metal on her bare skin. I heard the sizzling.

Quickly whispering to Tula, "I want recorded evidence," I left her side and scrambled closer with my camera.

"Why?!" Goda shrieked lividly, wildly striking out, turning the still glowing ladle into a dangerous projectile aimed carelessly into the crowd.

And then, I remembered how many religious people object to having their pictures taken.

*Whack!*

A dog whimpered a pitiful cry. We snapped at the sound. In her dazed frenzy, Goda had narrowly missed her husband's head and hit a dog instead.

"Oh, poor thing!"

"Aiyah! She hurt the poor animal!"

Hearing the dog making unearthly noises from the pain, Tula and I both winced. A young boy quickly poured water over the poor dog's smoking fur; the smell crept into our nostrils. Goda's eyes filled with tears and smoke; we noticed her glancing toward her husband at least twice while in the trance. Nervously, she pulled at her plain green blouse and ordinary yellow *sari*.

"Oh, my god..." an open-mouthed Marla, my graduate student and a champion of animal-rights, exhaled. Both Marla and Jennifer, my other graduate student, looked on, aghast. They had come for research, but this was far more real. Snapping out of her daze, Marla asked the question on everyone's mind.

"Is this staged? It doesn't look faked, but we've never watched this kind of possession before."

"I could be in jail for allowing such performances on my lawn."

I punctuated my students' thoughts, recognizing the severity of the moment. I was deeply concerned for everyone's well-being, not to mention the success of our project. This was the first possession during our set of performances; I had no idea or experience with which to gauge Goda's manifestation. Yet, I had thought I had made it clear that no dangerous displays, proofs of possession, would be asked for during this performance.

The man shrugged defensively when I shot him a look in warning. "Goda's sincerity had to be tested. She was supposed to lick the red hot ladle."

"Do not encourage such risks!"

Turning to my wife, I exhaled and shrugged to release my lingering frustration. The thought which had worked its way into my throat finally voiced a tired and deeply concerned realization.

"I wish the whole event was just a show."

"Our project is quickly becoming somewhat unique," Tula grinned nervously.

"Yeah, what was supposed to be another staid academic venture," I replied, catching her humor, "has begun to transform into a bizarre adventure. It looks as if we had better prepare ourselves for eighteen strange *Himalayan nights*."

Shaking our heads in wonder at the shivering intensity of the preceding moment, Tula and I turned our attention to Goda, who was just emerging from her trance. And as this slim, petite middle-aged woman, an untouchable, awakened, the moment engaged and all of the onlookers sharing it exhaled. The spell, thus broken, released time. The evening began again dissolving into the advancing darkness of night. The drumming resumed, the dancers stirred and began to move.

In the gathering shadows, I found a moment to reflect. Goda's scary scream, it seemed to me, must have been directed at her husband, Magnu, who had appropriately earned her anger. Tula had told me in the final moments of the trance that Goda was a partner in a polygamist marriage. To make matters worse, Magnu's second wife was Goda's younger sister, Chunni. Earlier that day he had told Tula, I would find out later, how his father-in-law had made a simple request of him, during his wedding to Goda.

"Take Chunni along," is all he had said.

While officially Goda's husband, there was no marriage ritual between

Magnu and Chunni. Without thinking much about it, Magnu reasoned that the wedding ritual with Goda had extended to Chunni, too. But, and more importantly, the intention of his father-in-law was exceedingly clear.

To Magnu, that is.

In her notes which I would read after our adventure was over, Marla referred to Magnu's marriage with Chunni as an extra-marriage. Marla also noted in her analysis of this relationship: *Most marriages in this region of mountains and rivers are endogamous, but endogamous marriage with two women—polygyny—is not a recognized pattern here.*

I had advised the girls in an earlier discussion that endogamy is less commonly practiced in Dehradun than in the upper Himalayas. Also, a man having two or more wives was difficult to find now anywhere in this region, as were polyandry practitioners. Jaunsar, an adjacent section of Dehradun, was a notable exception. It was known to be the home of a woman with several husbands—all brothers.

A shortage of women in this section of the country was given as an explanation for this practice. But the practitioners are also said to believe that they are following in the much older tradition set by the Pandavas, the triumphant clan remembered in the timeless saga, the *Mahābhārata*. In it, the five Pandava brothers shared the beautiful Draupadi as their common wife.

Marla, still visibly shaken by seeing the stray dog injured, asked Puran Singh, the historian Thakur brother and companion in our research team, "What was Goda complaining about?"

"Goda's suppressed voice blew through Draupadi's spirit. But, interestingly, in this possession, Goda spoke in Garhwali, not Hindi."

After translating all of Goda's Garhwali laments and screams, Puran offered us a few thoughts as context. "Goda is complaining about our holy heroes, just ours…and don't feel bad for her act. As a bigamist's woman, she has every reason to heal her past. Her husband is not a true lover, even if he builds for her a Taj Mahal."

Finishing his thought with this obtuse comment, Puran stopped talking as the two drummers started playing a short rhythm consisting of the beats 1, 2, 3—twice. This folk rhythm corresponded to the 6-beat rhythm of *dadra* in Indian music. In Western music, this rhythm is known as the beautifully elegant dance of the Waltz. As it filled the air with the promise of the cool night, this new beat refreshed all who shared the moment.

I smiled as I beheld the beautiful scene around me, smelled the bonfire smoke, watched the dancers, and savored the gathering chill. I whispered as much to myself as to my group, "I'm so grateful and excited to be here, especially this time of year. And, with my birthday and Christmas coming up, this trip is the perfect gift."

Hearing me, my wife smiled warmly at me. She had been supportive of this investigation, having had no idea of what we were going to uncover on our way. We were only just at the beginning of our adventure, a few days into our experimental juxtaposition of the ancient with the modern. Despite my excitement, I noticed that Jennifer and Marla were deep in thought, nodding their heads to the pulse of the drums. Excited from what we had already seen and at what was still awaiting us, I didn't interrupt their reflection. There would be time enough for us to discover our own conflicts.

The circular war dance, the *Pandau*, that which we had come to observe, seemed very exciting around the huge bonfire during this wintry Himalayan night. Gathering momentum, the drummers, Bijlu and Daphra, were singing their *git* in Garhwali, "*Jai jai bola he mera Pandau!*" (Say victory, victory! O my Pandavas!). They were praising the Pandava brothers, calling the great warriors after whom the dance was named. Their voices were deep; the beat was martial. Our hearts should have felt the energy.

Yet, not everyone's heart had lightened.

"Dumb, dumb, dumb," Jennifer whispered after she reflected on Puran's final translation of Goda's statements.

"Dumb, dumb, dumb," Marla repeated with eyes fixed to the ground.

I thought they were imitating the drums.

Turning to Marla, Tula wearily shook her head, understanding the emotion permeating my students which had lingered ever since Puran had made his comment about the Taj Mahal. She took a moment to address the young ladies.

"You are right. With her statement, Goda was trying to fight an ugly tradition. Not only ugly, but dark. It ignored the ordinary folks and glorified those men whose marital mores civilized folks would not adopt today. Some of them would certainly be in jail for these behaviors."

Goda had communicated much of her heart with Tula during their earlier interview on the matter of her marriage; Tula felt that, at this juncture, it was important to Marla and Jennifer to share some of the context of that discussion.

Flipping pages in her Steno pad, Tula related that, during the interview, she remembered scribbling and circling one of Goda's strongest statements: *I wanted to kill my husband when he brought my sister along.* She showed us the page; the words jumped off the paper.

Still waving the page, Tula went on to explain that, in her notes, Goda had detailed that her mother was beaten by her father for voicing opposition at the extra-marriage. During the interview, Goda had said, "For women, untouchable men are no different from other men. My husband was, and continues to be, a *bhainchod*."

This comment was the maximum vent that we noted from Goda. For Jennifer and Marla, I translated without adding anything, except an uncomfortable look. I kept my eyes on the ground.

"My husband is a sister-fucker."

Listening to my wife, Navin Singh, the sociologist and the other Thakur brother, smiled at Marla as he spoke to us, taking the discussion in another direction. He explained, "Draupadi thought she would, alone, be Arjuna's wife, because it was he who, alone, won her by holding the big lemons, at least in the Garhwali version of the *Mahabharata*, on the tips of his moustache. Interestingly, the Sanskrit version features fish instead of lemons."

Nodding in agreement with the classic confusion trapped inside every translation, Puran punctuated his brother's comment, "Regardless, Draupadi was forced to accept the five Pandava brothers as her husbands. Some holy men told her that it was fate that she do this, that this was predestined by divine will."

I added, for Marla and Jennifer to consider in their research, "But the *Bhagavad Gītā*, considered as part of the *Mahabharata*, has no mention of the marriages of Arjuna or Krishna. There, they appear to be very austere men, believing in the control of senses. My father firmly believes the setting of the *Bhagavad Gita*. For my father, for example, there was no *Mahabharata* fight during the *Gita* discourse. It took place in the middle of the two armies. Arjuna became depressed when he saw the two armies ready to fight. Krishna counseled Arjuna right there. His counsel covered eighteen chapters. Dad reads one chapter of the *Gita* daily after his bath and before breakfast. He even cries sometimes in the middle. For him, it's not a myth; it really happened."

Continuing, I quoted my dad in my best imitation of his voice and devout mannerisms, "It's not inconsistent; it's not incoherent; and it's not a metaphor."

I paused to adjust my jacket against the chill, watch the drummers, and let my words sink in for Marla and Jennifer. And, perhaps, for me as well.

His attitude to all of this had long been a sticky point in our relationship. Dad had no idea how my Sanskrit teacher, Shastri ji, debunked the myth of the *Gita* discourse as having occurred in the middle of the two armies. I didn't have the heart to tell him and risk eroding one of the great loves of his life.

This love of his: the 18-chapter discourse which has come to be known as the *Bhagavad Gita* is in verse. It's a song: Bhagavan's Song. Bhagavan, or God, is Krishna. There have been other Krishnas, but only the *Mahabharata* Krishna is Bhagavan.

"Did your father really believe that one could kill his own relatives and teachers after hearing the great *Bhagavad Gita*? Could he do that?"

Marla asked me this, referring to the ending of the twisted drama of the saga. My response was succinct.

"My dad believes it was a dharma war."

"A dharma war? A war of fairness?" Marla translated out loud, pushing back the hair from her eyes. "The *Gita* discourse has a clear disconnect. It shows no impact. Its placement in the original story is nonsense, questionable."

She paused, letting her comment linger momentarily in the air before emphatically launching into her judgment.

"Your father is a PUDI."

Our group knows Marla has coined this acronym to describe a "person under devout influence."

Before I could shape my reply or a defense of my father, Jennifer interrupted, "Bhagavan and Arjuna are clearly male chauvinists!"

*Oh, that kind of nonsense.*

Like Shastri ji, I thought of the comment's anachronism. My great teacher had emphasized one more salient point to keep in mind, reminding us of its importance as we move forward.

Objectivity.

The Thakur brothers, interestingly, looked very rational during this exchange. In the beginning, I had some doubts about their objectivity, even though one was a historian and the other a sociologist.

"What do you think of this war's heroes in light of the *Gita*?"

I put this question to both of the Thakurs in an effort to reign in Jennifer's undisciplined analysis and to switch the discussion's energy.

"Ask the drummers. They will sing the war and its heroes. It's their call. They decide who is a hero and who is not. In this place and during this ceremony, the story is not only told; it is manifest. Jennifer and Marla might want to keep that in mind when researching here."

Puran said this with a friendly wink toward the girls.

The Thakurs shared a knowing smile with me and nodded, silently agreeing on the importance for objectivity.

After letting the silence settle for a moment, Puran punctuated his point with a well-placed and foundational comment for any researcher looking into the great subjective realities of human culture.

"We must watch carefully to ensure that, in our thinking and in our behaviors, we don't alienate people on the basis of their superstitions."

Navin nodded his head as he looked at me and quoted a proverb in Hindi in support of Puran's comments.

"*Ap ki bat danke ki chot jaisi hai.*"

It translates powerfully: your statement is like a big drum's bang.

During this last exchange, Abdul moved closer to me. Though he was among the honored guests at the event and a chosen member of our research team, he had been quiet so far. In spite of his good college education and successful business, he had appeared, to me, to be less intellectual than the Thakur brothers. Apparently, he had overheard my concerns as he said in Hindi, "*Mera waham bhi sun lijiye* (Please listen to my superstition, too)."

After saying this, he took me aside and said in a whispered voice, "I have no identity conflict. Some think of me as an outsider and some see me as an insider. Whatever. Please tell these girls about a mantra which has seemingly discovered me."

"What is it?"

"I am whispering because a mantra's secrecy is sacred. You know; I have been trying my best to help these two girls. But a mantra is traditionally only given by a holy learned person. I am not such a person, but you are. You are Mr. Archi Rainwal, a Brahmin, a Ph.D., and a professor. You are the one to give them this mantra."

"I will give it to them and I appreciate your help. You are so prompt and punctual. Dad says you don't work *on time*, but *ahead of time*."

"Pandit ji is so kind...So, here is the mantra..."

But he stopped abruptly, shaking his head and changing tactics slightly. "I will also provide a little background for this mantra. It was revealed to me when Goda was under the influence of Draupadi's spirit. It is for women only. That is why I can't meditate on it."

He rolled his eyes around and slightly coughed. Nobody was close to us. Still, he spoke in suppressed voice with closed eyes, "The mantra goes like this: Rally against the daily holy roly poly, *Jay ho Devi.*"

With a straight face, he opened his eyes with folded hands and said with a smile beginning to curve on his lips, "I'm glad to see you are still unshaken. This mantra is fiery and potent..."

Bubbling up, I couldn't keep my laughter in check, even though he sounded so poetic, so serious. His plan, I felt sure, was to make me laugh. Sure enough, his serious façade crumbled into a playful guffaw.

With my mood lifted, I thought to myself about how much I appreciated this jolly and helpful young man.

Whispering, he continued after I stopped laughing. "Look, I am serious. Goda is an uneducated woman. If, without any mantra in her trance, she can shoot a burning question like that...then we, men, won't have to wait long to feel the heat of educated women in the open. And men will begin to melt in that maddening heat."

Now, beyond just jovial, he sounded prophetic, too.

In a normal and spontaneous voice, I responded simply, with complete transparency as our comments were once again swallowed by the intense drumming filling the night air.

"Seriously, Goda's question feels more like the tip of the iceberg."

# Chapter 2
# The Team, the Time and the Territory

*When they apportioned the Purusha, how many ways did they partition him? What about his mouth? What about his two arms? What about his two thighs? What are his two feet called?*

*His mouth was the Brahmin; his two arms were made the Kshatriya. His two thighs the Vaishya; from his two feet was born the Shudra.*

*—Rigveda: Purusha Sukta*

Just a few days earlier, before Goda's possession would become seared into our memory, our nine-member team had kept only the regular *Pandava* folk dance in focus during our initial meeting at our Dehradun residence on Rajpur road. That meeting was held on an ugly and overcast day. Everyone was expected to come for that meeting informally and according to his or her convenience, preferably around 10 A.M., but at least before lunch. We had folding chairs and a few tables set up to hold this planning meeting. My goal was to foment an action plan and allow for the process to unfold.

Earlier, I smelled brahmi oil, sandalwood incense (and the scent of roasted cannabis seeds?) emanating from the handbags of Marla and Jennifer as they opened my office door to put away their music cassette tapes. The girls had brought some western rock music to Dehradun on homemade mix-tapes—Bob Dylan, David Bowie, and Peter Frampton were a few of their favorites—and the girls enjoyed these on our house stereo occasionally to get psyched up for the days ahead. On this morning, Led Zeppelin's popular song "Kashmir" drifted through the house, perhaps indicating the girls' enthusiasm for our folkmusic project.

Although my wife, Tula, and I had been living in Seattle, we'd returned to my family's home in Dehradun, in India's Garhwal Himalayas, to study the *Pandau*, a traditional dance with music accompanied by a drum ensemble.

My objective was to show the connection between the *Mahabharata* heroes and modern men. More specifically, I wanted to juxtapose the ancient and contemporary heroes of the Garhwali region, so, the focus of our study was the *Pandau*, its strange name emanating from the Pandavas—the primary characters immortalized by the ancient epic, the *Mahabharata*. It is the ancient story which relates the tragic and complex events of the war between the Pandavas and Kauravas which continually inspire humanity to engage in the conversation of self definition.

Quietly, I also wanted to explore the hypothesis that the *Bhagavad Gita* is actually unrelated to the *Mahabharata* and was just cleverly folded into the epic by clever, less-than-truthful authors just trying to pen a good story. This question, also, I hoped to answer with my observations of the *Pandau*. Alone for the moment, I sat quietly with my thoughts for a while before everyone would arrive for our meeting.

Eight months before I returned to Dehradun with our students to begin our project, I picked up a newspaper on 24 March 1977: DESAI WINS! Morarji Desai, the new prime minister, hated anything coming from the West, especially from America. His predecessor, Indira Gandhi, had lost the election, mainly because she had enacted the infamous "Emergency Rule," thus suspending democracy.

*Democracy is a product that came to India from the West, especially from America. Unlike Desai, Mrs. Gandhi loved Dehradun and its East-West mixture—the double-roti culture*, I wrote in my notes to share with my students later and smiled at the playful metaphor inspired by my stomach, which had very much enjoyed all of the delicious food during the first few days of this trip, a sort of homecoming.

The round flatbread of India is *roti*. Western bread, called *double roti*, is also very popular in Dehradun. Some Indians think that this bread is called "double" because of its puffed up, large size. They seem to be unacquainted with the word sandwich, which is prepared with two slices, hence many have come to use the word double to describe the Western-style bread. *Double roti* looks really puffed up when other enjoyable items are inserted in between the two slices.

Now, eight months later, in Dehradun on the first of December 1977, I jotted in my binder: *Our team also reflected the sandwiching of Western and Indian lifestyles. Nine of us, with multiple interests, were involved in the organization and completion of the study. Both our drummers and their mentors wore shirts and pants that showed Western influence, yet they were assembled to present the oral history of India's traditional heroes. Like my wife, my two American students alternated between Western clothing and the traditional sari-blouse combination.*

I looked up when Marla and Jennifer came in. Both wore beautiful *sari* and sterling-silver Indian jewelry, their beautiful western hair braided in Indian fashion. As usual, they resembled polite and lovely young goddesses. Marla said, "Namaste, Rainwal ji" while politely pressing her palms together in respect.

Jennifer followed Marla in similar fashion, "Good to see you, Dr. Rainwal ji."

These were my American students. They had taken my course on the great Indian epics. Marla was working on this region's folklore for her Ph.D. while Jennifer was exploring any appropriate material about the local folk heroes for her Master's thesis.

Tula, after completing her Ph.D. dissertation, had published several articles on Indian temple rituals. Being a native of this region, Tula had easy access to any temple. Now, she was interested in the local polygyny and polyandry—the practices of one husband with several wives, and one wife with several husbands who are brothers, respectively. In fact, she had already begun the process of meeting and interviewing as soon as we had arrived in Dehradun, possibly before even recovering from the long travel just to get here. Intrestingly, just a few days later, I would find out that Goda was featured, along with her husband, in these early sets of interviews. These interviews would come to light after our first possession experience.

"These practices in this region are now almost on the verge of extinction," I told the two American girls, who had their own questions related to the local polygamy.

Their fieldwork also included a discrete exploration of sensitive issues like women's abuse, animal cruelty and caste discrimination, all sanctioned by religion. But their supreme research question was: *Are polygamists really holy?* Noticing that they had more to say, I waited before offering my reply to their first question.

"Animal sacrifice is still my pet project. I despise animal abuse even more now that I see it practiced here so casually in public. But I'll keep my animosity toward abuse low-profile so as to not offend local customs," Marla said in Hindi.

I replied in Hindi, "Your Hindi is pretty good, so I'll introduce you to my dad's friends, Abdul and the Thakur brothers, to help you when you need to understand Garhwali."

Garhwali is a Central Pahari language spoken interchangeably with Hindi in the region. Having access to the language would profoundly deepen these students' level of analysis of the upcoming *Pandau* ritual and of all the realizations patiently awaiting us in this place, here in the shadows of the Himalaya.

"Jennifer, you so seldom take notes," I gently teased in Hindi.

Jennifer smiled. Born and raised in Surrey, England, she'd moved to the United States after high school. She spoke British English, American English, and Hindi. I knew nothing more about her background. Unlike Marla, she knew much less about India. So for her sake, I sometimes repeated things that Marla already knew.

"Puran and Navin are the Thakur brothers; they and Abdul are local men who serve as mentors to the drummers, and will explain the dances and answer the myriad questions that arise, as well as tell us stories about real people of their time who became folk heroes, much like the *Pandau*."

The girls were all ears so I continued, "Navin and Puran are Hindu and belong to the *rajput* caste. This word refers to the princely class, so the man from this class is respectfully called *Thakur,* or 'lord'."

I wanted to offer them some context to the traditional Vedic class system, often called 'the caste system' by Westerners. The castes are defined in four groupings: the Brahmin, Khsatriya, Vaishya, and Shudra. Each has a distinct role or purpose in traditional Indian society. Any understanding of India must advance out of an understanding of this system as this is the way people had been taught to think about themselves for thousands of years. And, so, I continued my explanation.

"The rajputs are considered Kshatriyas, or part of the warrior class. Tula and I, in contrast, are Brahmin. We are considered as the priestly class, also called the *pandits* (pundits), 'wise'."

Skipping ahead, I pushed on to the next group, "Vaishyas are considered to be the business castes. These three comprise the so-called higher castes. The fourth class, Shudra, is low and its members have been mistreated as untouchables. Shudra, like people born in other castes, are not able to change their class. Everyone is considered to be a member of his or her class by birth."

Circling back to the Thakur brothers who had agreed to participate as members of our research team, I gave some background information to help my students further conceptualize the expertise and support these individuals might offer. "These excellent individuals, cornerstones of our research team, the Thakur brothers are also graduates from the famous Banaras Hindu University. They come with strong academic credentials and a deep awareness of this place. Both in their fifties, Puran, the oldest, is a historian and Navin is a sociologist. They are *Pahari* people, mountain people. They are Indian, but with some Tibetan features. The Thakur brothers run an export business of the famous *basmati* rice of Dehradun."

I still had their attention, so I told them about our other support member. "Abdul's background is interesting. He's a college-educated man and runs a store of fancy clothes—Indian and Western—in Dehradun. More importantly, he's Muslim, as his name indicates. He was orphaned as a child. A rich Pahari Brahmin couple adopted and raised Abdul as their Muslim son."

His physical features indicated that he was not a Pahari; he clearly looked like a common brown man of north India with Pahari behavior. I checked my watch, thinking that Abdul's addition to our group would be interesting as he was such an uncommon individual: born an orphan, raised as Pahari, committed to Islam.

"Abdul will be here shortly."

Tula, a resident of the region, explained to the girls, "Our plans have been laid out carefully. Dehradun is spread across Doon Valley, between the higher Himalayas in the north and the lower Siwalik Hills in the south. The valley is very close to the sensitive militarized borders with Tibet and Nepal, yet not extremely far from New Delhi. The climate is generally temperate, mild to cool by day, chilly to cold at night. Don't research or roam in the border hills or temples without the trusted guides we've engaged, especially after nightfall. Generally, avoid police and military. Keep your passports safe here at home. Most people up here are genuinely friendly and helpful, but follow smart personal safety and avoid talking passionately on politics or religion till you know the person a little bit first. Communist troops nearby occupy Tibet and a communist movement here in India's top military and intelligence city is trying to undermine democracy, so you don't want to be perceived as agitators, okay?"

Identifying some of our agreed-upon perspectives which we had used to design the research experience, I added, "Our dance sessions are open to anyone. There are no invitations required, no fees, no appointments, and no dress codes. No questions asked about gender, religion, language, region, *jati* or caste. All dancers are treated as equal."

Further emphasizing our research goals, I continued, "One of my goals in writing about the project is to get outside, objective opinions to compare with my own."

Jennifer nodded and smiled as Marla spoke for both of them, "OK, we'll keep our ears open for those too, and we're willing to play some role in the war dances."

"Good," I ventured, "I'll also dance on occasion, but frequently drop out to make notes of the thoughts that come to me while dancing. I anticipate that my field notes will be based on a combination of observation and participation. In addition, I'll gather information on real people during my own free time. I'll include even people whose participation doesn't make sense. And then there are casual visitors, some desirable and some undesirable. I realize that life is full of contradictory or inconsistent sets of things!"

I told Tula and the girls my strategy, reading it roughly from my notebook prepared months earlier: "I'll use no tape recorder, except to record the drummers. My notes and the stories will be gathered informally. Convention and format are unimportant. It is the information that is critical. There will be occasional gaps."

Fortunately, Marla said, "I share your interest in the local heroes." She smiled at me before continuing, "Between the two of us, we'll be able to compile some powerfully compelling stories."

Shifting the energy, I updated my now-excited students, who shared an interest in musicology, about our low-caste untouchable Himalayan drummers. Our other guests hadn't yet arrived; therefore, this was the perfect time to outline some of the more technical data concerning our planned research environment. Besides, I had Marla's and Jennifer's focus on the project and on the academic work ahead for the time being.

"We've scheduled nineteen to twenty days of dance sessions in order to cover the eighteen-day war of the *Mahabharata*. This circular dance could have more than one pair of drummers together in one single session. Normally, one pair of the drummers is used: one plays the big double-headed barrel drum, the bass *dhol*, and the other plays the small timpani-shaped drum, the high-pitched *damau*. The drummers hang them around their necks. The *damau* is beaten with two sticks. The *dhol* is beaten with one stick on one side and with fingers and slaps on the other. The *damau* can be played independently, but not the *dhol*."

The Thakurs and the drummers arrived on time. After greetings and introductions, I complimented them on having been a big part of planning this excursion.

"A large part of my interest in you is because your *Pandau* dance contained innovations. As an example, the traditional test for a possessed person, one who became possessed during the dancing, could be dangerous. So, a man possessed by Bhima would be considered his true spirit if he will eat mud. Furthermore, he might be expected to chew the scorpion plant, which causes blisters and excruciating pain. I want no such risks. There is no health insurance for the project."

Both Thakurs assured me, "There'll be only risk-free tests to determine the status of any hero."

The drummers, Bijlu and Daphra, nodded their heads.

We saw Abdul coming with hands folded to greet us. He quietly sat behind the drummers.

Our academic project was planned and built on equality while we were back in the USA. Yet, upon our arrival in India, my traditionalist Brahmin father had modified these plans to meet an additional layer of needs. I'd rented a large house and expected to host these gatherings elsewhere, but my parents had demanded that our whole entourage come to stay with them during the course of the study. This is how the event came to happen at my father's house.

"Your mother and I will eat inside," Dad said to me. "Our cook made careful arrangements to assure our dietary and religious requirements are met."

This would keep my Brahmin parents satisfied. They still believed in the caste system, headed by the Brahmins as priests. I was grateful to my father. He, with help from the Thakurs, Abdul, and the project funds, had assembled the drummers, who were grateful for the opportunity. In addition to what were, to them, luxurious accommodations and meals, he gave them more money (from the project funds) than the average Indian Administrative Service (IAS) officer earned as a monthly salary.

We informally adjourned the meeting and ate a delicious curry-rice lunch right there, as arranged by our great cook, Bhag. During lunch, we talked about the logistics of the forthcoming first session.

Nobody anticipated then the possession of Goda and the question she would leave hanging in the air just days later.

The next Sunday, Daphra and Bijlu, our drummers, gave us a surprise visit. They had not yet occupied their new accommodations. They were accompanied by their three male relatives—all in their early to mid-thirties, like Bijlu and Daphra. All of them had umbrellas as the morning was cloudy and a rainy Sunday was imminent.

Two of them asked me, "Could you please hire us as an extra pair of drummers?"

The other one was better dressed up than the others—clean-shaven like the drummers, but with clean white shirt, pants and shining shoes, as if going for a job interview. The drummers called him *Guru*.

"Sorry."

They looked at me, waiting for an explanation.

"I know that a big dance could use more drummers simultaneously. But my project's size neither needs another pair, nor do I have the budget for them."

"I am just an observer with these relatives of mine." The fellow called Guru responded, explaining his presence there, without even blinking his eyes.

"For a living, I do clerical work," he explained.

Bhag followed Tula toward us and served snacks on the verandah where we all sat at a round table. We talked mostly about Pahari food. Guru complimented Bhag's culinary skills with class and attention to detail.

"Thank you for these tasty wild asparagus *pakoras* and lemon-sesame *chutney* that you obviously prepared fresh in addition to the spicy tea—very appropriate items for a day like this!"

At that, Tula joked, "Some of my Indian friends in America swear that such a classy vegetable like asparagus does not grow anywhere in India, that asparagus is a Western thing. Some of them tasted asparagus soup for the first time in New Delhi's 5-star hotels. I have a hard time convincing them that Paharis have been eating the classy *jhirna* for ages."

"Yes, most Indians eat cheap potato *pakoras* and don't know that the potato came to India from America." Guru added his comment with a big laugh. "And, many here are convinced that the cosmos creator, Brahma, came from Narayana's navel. And that Brahma's mother tongue was Sanskrit."

Playing along with Guru's adventure into a socio-religious critique, Tula didn't lose any time in responding in her own pithy manner.

"I am convinced. The first son of God had no mother."

We all looked at each other, enjoying the irreverence and playfulness of the moment in this new place with these new people.

Softly to Guru, Bijlu interjected in a low voice while we were laughing at Tula's response, "*He Guru, tin Barma ki utpati ta thik samjhai, par ya allu ki utpati tin ham sani kabbi ni sikhai!*" (Hey Guru, you explained the origin of Brahma all right, but you never taught us this origin of the potato!)

I was momentarily curious about why Bijlu reacted like this, but I didn't have to wait long for an answer; the look given as response when Guru blinked at him with his lips together in response was revealing in many ways.

Feigning disinterest, I kept my thoughts to myself

Bijlu's remark was in Garhwali instead of Hindi, which we had been using. Obviously, Guru must be Bijlu's close junior relative as he used the singular pronoun *tin*—meaning "you"—a variation of the most informal *tu* "thou." And yet, the senior relative expected the junior relative to teach... strange. I didn't want to dwell like this on this trivial matter too long, though, and miss the fun part of our snacking.

After the tea party, our guests all left.

About twenty minutes later, Guru came back. He apologized for his return.

"Sorry, I forgot to pick up my umbrella."

His better-looking outfit made me more and more curious. A clerk has to live on bare subsistence level and yet has to maintain a facade of classiness. But I didn't want to engage him in any talk. I didn't want to give him any other opportunity to ask me for work.

Just then, Bhag came out with his umbrella and asked him if he would like more tea. Shaking his head as a polite rejection of the offer, Guru put his hand in his shirt pocket, took out some money, and slipped it into Bhag's shirt pocket. To my surprise, Bhag took that money out and returned it to Guru, forming his response in Garhwali.

"*Na, na, bhaut dhanyabad*" (No, no, much thanks).

Guru did not insist further, but his face showed some sort of irritation despite the formality and politeness showed to him. He began to walk toward the gate with his face down. I accompanied him. He broke the short-lived silence and looked up toward me with a dry smile.

"I wanted to tell you something because you are an educator. We need your help. Please come down from your academic Himalayas to the plain public level in order to inform and reform. We have entered the modern age of information and are ready to explore into even Space for future living..."

I interrupted him, "Thanks for your thoughtful consideration. We have come here to learn from your relatives, the drummers. They are our Buddha."

"Of course, you will learn a lot from them. But I wanted to talk about something else. First, about the actual Buddha, who teaches us that everything passes. However, some things pass very slowly. We have to make a conscious effort to change some things faster; otherwise, we will never be prepared for the future into which we rush. Regardless, it was so nice of you that you ate food with us. I realize that your cook has made separate arrangements for your parents."

He paused, continuing to show no smile on his face, "The humiliating religious behaviors of the *savarnas* forced many *asavarnas* to convert to other religions. Ambedkar's conversion to Buddhism is a recent example. He was a politician turned preacher. But, as a member of an oppressed class myself, I have a different view. Religion will never give salvation; secular democracy will. Our goal is to prove that."

I was baffled more by his usage of Sanskrit words for "high castes" and "low castes" than by his comment as a whole.

Furthermore, I was stunned even more deeply when he stopped momentarily in the middle and looked straight and with focus into my eyes. He had stretched his palms up and had quoted a famous text from the Western tradition.

"Following Socrates, the unexamined beliefs are not worth practicing." He moved his head horizontally at the same time, watching me for my reaction. When I offered none, he continued. He clarified his perspective with gathering passion in his voice.

"I understand no one can examine and control all the circumstances. We can, however, examine and control those circumstances which cost us nothing. You may not demolish temples that discriminate against the untouchables, but you can eat with the untouchables in your home. The xenophobia of higher castes is controllable. It actually is not even their fear of strangers. What they fear is their own untouchables, the *dalits*."

Then, he added his Hindi sentence with an authoritative touch in his tone, like a stern warning, "*Profesar Sahab*! *Bachche ke sath bap ko bhi sikhaie: Dharm hatao, gyan bachao.*" (Mr. Professor! Please teach the father, too, along with the child: oust religion; save knowledge).

Quietly, I nodded my head.

Letting the moment linger for a moment, he opened the gate and paused. Before moving through it, he left a final thought.

"It's important to emphasize this in our general education: Religion leads to regression, knowledge leads to advancement. You should tell your parents, too, not to repeat history."

He folded his hands, raised them, and said, "*Namaste.*"

I responded with folded palms only and closed the gate behind him. But, before walking away, he turned around again as if a final thought had just occurred to him.

"I didn't mean to downgrade Dr. Ambedkar's roles. It was wonderful to talk to you. I will try to meet you again. How long are you going to stay here?"

"Not much. I may be forced to cut short."

"Why?" He came closer and leaned over the gate, looking me in the eyes.

"The Dehradun police headquarters made a mistake. They wrote the wrong month in my visa expiration date. I have requested them to extend it, but you know how arrogant and incompetent they are!"

"This is a serious matter of behavior. As I told you, some behaviors, like circumstances, can be changed at no cost. Every top government service has the word *Service* attached to it. Indian Administrative Service, Indian Police Service, Indian Foreign Service and what have you. They begin to behave like bosses without realizing that their role is to *serve*... Anyway, I will try to be in touch with you as soon as possible."

"*Namaste,*" he said a second time, and walked away.

I noticed some irritation on his face. Maybe his irritation showed because I didn't formally reciprocate his appreciation for our interaction. He might think we had talked, but he had lectured me. I thought lecturing was *my* job. Regardless, he certainly had assigned a lot of homework for me to wonder about his views.

In particular, his opinion about Dr. Ambedkar's roles surprised me. His view reminded me of Mark Twain who wrote, "I am quite sure now that

21

often, very often, in matters concerning religion and politics a man's reasoning powers are not above the monkey's."

When I came back, I saw Bhag waiting for me. He offered me an explanation as to why he had refused the tip from Guru.

"That man tried to give me a tip. He is an IAS officer. But I am a *rajput*, so I could not accept a tip from an untouchable."

According to the caste system, Bhag was correct; such an action would be an upheaval in social order. Guru's behavior in that action was nothing short of a rebellion against the accepted and institutionalized social norms permeating Indian society for thousands of years.

Interestingly, this man, Guru, had understood how to work through Socrates' Greek quote from its English translation "the unexamined life is not worth living." No wonder. In India, it's normal to study any great non-English material through its English translation. But how many know the Greek word "xenophobia" and its English translation "fear of foreigners"? Of course, an IAS officer shouldn't have any such problem. Nobody can pass the toughest government job test of India, the IAS examination, without having an excellent command of the English language. But an IAS officer may not have the slightest idea of how *Socrates* is pronounced in Greek as Indians follow the English pronunciation. English rule still dominates.

Nevertheless, it is fascinating that an Indian IAS officer, hailing from an untouchable class, understands how to use Socrates' wisdom. Bhag wouldn't get it. My parents wouldn't get it. And the *Mahabharata* heroes would never have gotten it.

Delighted, I wanted to chase this strange government officer called Guru by his colleagues and shout in exaltation, "Thanks to the achievement of India's fledgling democracy! Kudos goes to its affirmative action and to its IAS officers!"

I was euphoric, yet speechless. This man, Guru, had truly touched some place inside of me which had wondered what would come of the India once it emerged from these turbulent times.

A few minutes later, I told Tula about the whole episode and asked her, "Should I tell my parents exactly what the IAS officer told me?"

She looked puzzled as she advised, "Maybe not."

"What if Guru comes later and asks me how my parents reacted?"

"Then, try to modify somewhat like this: Guru, the government administrator, is looking forward to seeing a knowledge-based world order instead of one built on religion-led rules. This would not offend them, I guess."

But, did Guru really mean this? Shouldn't I tell them verbatim what he said? My academic training gave me halt.

Worse, I would never have the guts to tell them what Mark Twain wrote. I would hate to modify Mark Twain's extraordinary wit. Mark Twain was not just a great satirical writer, but a great antireligious *guru*, too. This IAS officer didn't look simply to be just a government administrator either; he sounded more like an unofficial *guru*, more importantly not just one on a fundamentalist mission to "flatter the faithful and insult the infidel."

More thoughts kept cropping up in my head. The thought, *what if Bhag's information is incorrect?* kept nagging at me. I raised this hypothetical question with Tula.

She responded with her eyebrow raised, "But you are not going to verify it, though." She punctuated this comment with a salient point, one which cut through my questioning and passed my enthusiasm for India reincarnated as in Guru's vision.

"Even if he is not an IAS officer, he certainly talks like a highly educated and rational man, not a garden variety PUDI. He still can come back with our drummers. He can still meet your parents, who will find him, not an IAS speaking of a new India, but as an untouchable speaking the unspeakable."

"Then, he is likely to be addressed by my traditionalist parents with those traditional words which are now politically incorrect, some legally punishable," I mused.

"So, you must do everything to keep him away. Right now, you would be better off to forget your meeting with him altogether and concentrate on planning the first session."

"But, that does not guarantee that government agents would not create any obfuscation ahead. You must remember throughout that our project is known to the locals as supported by U.S. funds—some will suspect CIA funds—being spent in the sensitive borders of India and China. Doesn't it look a little suspicious that, of all the regions available in India for our study, we just happened to choose the one city most bristling with military and intelligence headquarters? Heck, Nixon wanted to bomb India just a few years ago during the Bangladesh movement. India is still under threat by hawks in the U.S. and China; our nearby India-China border is sitting over a highly volatile military-political fault line. A very different and probably atomic *Mahabharata* could be provoked between these modern-day cousins."

The next day in the afternoon, Bhag entered my little office room and told me, "Sir, a police officer is here to see you."

"A police officer! No kidding? Great. Just what I need. Is he with handcuffs? I've never been cuffed before."

I struck my head with my palm.

"There goes my project. Someone must've made a mountain out of a molehill—I am a U.S. citizen. Richard Nixon's legacy haunts my project. Dang it!"

"Bhag, I tell you... my students, Tula, and I will all be suspected of spying around a lot in this sensitive region. That's why my visa date was changed; it was on purpose. Their 'misunderstanding' was not my fault."

As I was absorbed in apprehension, the officer entered my office and gave me a salute right in front of Bhag. I stood up and simply said, "*Namaste.*" He handed over an envelope to me and said, "Our Sahab sent me to give you this envelope. He will try to meet you again."

With a quick salute, he left the room.

Somehow, despite my shaking nerves, I opened the envelope. I was ecstatic. "My visa was extended, Bhag!" Not only was the promptness of Dehradun's police headquarters welcome, but also the courtesy of hand delivery totally beyond my expectations. "And politeness! I've never been saluted by a police officer before—and twice in a row!"

Yes, Guru was right; some behaviors can be changed at no cost. Regardless, I am not going to tell my parents what Guru said— or, maybe, at least, not until after the project is over.

# Chapter 3
# The Judge

*The Lord said: The four-class stratification has been formed by me in accordance with quality and work. Know me also its creator, yet non-doer and unchangeable.*

*—Bhagavad Gita 4.13*

Our drummers had many heroes, but none could compare with Judge Sahab, as they called him. They had their folk theory about the man, but it was the Thakurs who told us during our next meeting that, "His full name was Jag Tarak Tiwari and he was a very successful attorney, capable of putting on a grand show. He was a folk hero, as much as Mahatma Gandhi." But with a big difference, as the Thakurs pointed out, "After the Buddha, the greatest man India has brought the world is Gandhi."

Although Jag and Gandhi were both lawyers, Jag had no room for clean living. As the Thakurs objectively explained, his village, Daya Gad which translates as Mercy River, was located on the bank of a rivulet and had all the features that made for a grand show. For his brother and sister, he was like the embodiment of a Daya Gad god. They loved his money as God's gift. Although Jag wasn't a religious leader, he could have been; Jag's family was Brahmin, the priestly class. Every morning, he took a dip in the rivulet, and said a short *sandhya*, a set of mantras to God, which he devoutly followed with a couple of verses from the *Bhagavad Gita*.

Following breakfast, usually a big *paratha*, the stuffed fried bread, with a spicy sauce or *chutney*, Jag would ride his horse to Pauri, about four miles away, where he had a second house. He often stayed there with a cook, a horse, and a groom. Here was his library with rows of books. In addition to various legal tomes, there was Sanskrit and English literature. There were world-famous authors, such as Ptolemy, Machiavelli, Nietzsche, Rousseau

25

and Dostoevsky, among others.

Jag valued modern knowledge far more than prayers. He was a law graduate of Calcutta University and deeply impressed by the Bengali intellectuals. The Thakurs said he had a well-known saying: "The Garhwalis live in the highest region of the Ganga and the Bengalis at the lowest, but the intellectual achievement at the two altitudes can be detailed as an inverse ratio."

"This is true," Puran acknowledged before offering us an explanation. "The Gods of Garhwal, the *Deva Bhumi* or the 'Land of Gods,' kept us Garhwalis low. We prayed to them for thousands of autumns with no response or opportunity. The mortal judge, on the other hand, wanted to invest in higher education for us, for the Garhwalis. He paid all of our college expenses, allowing us to study at the renowned Banaras Hindu University."

Navin explained that their father, Bodha, had been Jag's gardener and their mother, Rithi, did household chores in Jag's big village house.

"But why," I asked, "do the drummers consider Jag Tarak Tiwari such a hero?"

"Tiwari ji's fame started during his first year of law practice," Puran said. "He won a murder case for an adulterer. The defendant stabbed the husband of a female adulterer with a Himalayan dagger, a *khunkri*. He was quite drunk at the time. Tiwari ji managed to get the man off. Since all of this was unusual for this area, it became an event worthy of a song for the drummers."

Shaking his hands to slow down Puran, Navin interjected, "You need to understand some of Tiwari ji's biography, first. A few months before beginning his practice, his family insisted he marry a woman of their choosing, saying it was time he settled down. The woman was from a wealthy family and the dowry was as appealing as the idea of marriage. Lila, the girl, could neither read nor write."

Sensing value in Navin's digression, Puran interrupted. "There was nothing wrong with her brains. However, traditionally, girls aren't believed to need schooling."

Shaking his head, Navin continued to elaborate. "Although she wasn't literate, she was very attractive and sophisticated. She was unhappy about her husband winning the murder case and setting free a man who'd, in her estimation, committed two crimes. A year later, Lila became pregnant.

26

Unfortunately, both she and the baby girl died during childbirth. Two years later, the lawyer's parents arranged a second marriage. Murli, the second wife, gave him two daughters, Tara and Jagati, beautiful and healthy girls."

Navin paused for a moment before changing directions with the story. "By this time, Tiwari ji was one of the most successful lawyers in Garhwal and very wealthy. He decided to take another wife and arranged to marry Surama on his own. Their first child was another girl, but three years later Surama presented him with a boy, who was named Durlabh, in recognition of the 'difficult achievement'."

Puran interrupted again. "During the delivery of Tara and Jagati, there were rumors the midwife was having an illicit relationship with the lawyer. This time, during the delivery of Durlabh, no such rumors were heard. This time, the midwife successfully refused his nocturnal overtures."

Puran also stopped, recognizing the need to elaborate on a cultural custom of the place, "One thing you must understand is that in these hills, the newborn and mother usually live together in a separate room with the midwife. All of them are considered untouchables for ten or eleven days. After this period, the naming ceremony is done, which purifies the baby and mother. The midwife remains untouchable and cannot eat with the upper castes."

Satisfied with his explanation, Puran continued, "Durlabh's naming ceremony was celebrated in his hometown of Pauri. Although small, the town was the administrative headquarters of Garhwal during British rule. Our mother has told us much about it, as it was the highest celebration that ever took place in the Garhwal Himalayas. Normally, one priest would have officiated, as is required to worship any number of deities and perform any Hindu passage rite. But Tiwari ji believed in pomp and show; he asked for there to be three priests present at the ceremony. The local British administrators were invited to attend the ceremony, which took place in the lawyer's beautiful garden, where tents, tables and chairs had been set up. These administrators later rewarded him with the job of judge."

Navin took up the tale, jumping in excitedly at what he clearly considered to be a formative memory. "We were young boys, but we were also there. The British Deputy Commissioner attended the ceremony. Pahari sweets were distributed. Most of the adults had whisky and rum, though we heard some had local wild bhang, the Himalayan marijuana, in their drinks, as well. Each drummer got a bottle of rum." He grinned conspiratorially at the recollection.

"The musical aspects of the ceremony were important for the drummers. Their involvement in the celebration was traditional. An international flavor was added by the playing of the Scottish bagpipes. Such playing, with a pair of two local drums, *dhol* and *damau*, had become traditional. The British army had introduced their highland instruments. The resonating drums paired with the bagpipes make any event audible for miles around."

Puran continued with his eyes wide, painting a picture of the judge's propensity for the grandiose. "Four pairs of drummers and three bagpipers in Durlabh's ceremony made above normal noise. Two granduncles of Bijlu and Dahpra were one of the pairs among the drummers chosen for Durlabh's ceremony." He made hand gestures holding up numbers to show how the regular ensemble had been magnified for the occasion.

"The other kinds of musicians in this ceremony were the *baddis*. The *baddis* are more or less nomadic drummers, who are easily available without invitation. The male *baddi* plays the *dholak*, a barrel-shaped drum hung around his neck. The female *badin* or *badini* provide the dances. Both sing popular folk songs together. They can create new songs, including songs of praise and worship of folk heroes."

Punctuating all of this, Puran pointed out, "All these developments made Jag more and more of an epic-power hero. His glory, not only as a relatively young judge appointed to the District Court by the British administration, but also as performer of an unprecedented birth celebration, culminated into a praise song which became wildly popular in the region, courtesy of the *baddis*."

Jennifer asked them if the *baddis* played the same kinds of drums used in the performances we were to witness during our project. Showing an interest in the story of the judge, Marla, always interested in shamans, asked if the *baddis* also participated in other rituals.

Puran, exhibiting patience with the questions, answered in the negative to both and offered a further analysis to clarify the digression. "The shamanic drummers play the *daunr* and the *thali*, which are not the same kinds of instruments used in these praise songs."

The *daunr* is a small double-headed hand drum, beaten with a stick on one side and slapped with the hand on the other. It can be substituted by another small double-headed drum, the *hurki*. This drum has strings attached to its heads which can be pressed to produce varying pitches. The *thali* is a metal plate, usually made of brass. It is beaten with a stick.

Puran explained, "No shamanic drummers were invited as musicians because the drums they played were not associated with high ceremonies such as passage rites. Their drums were mostly used to invoke a trance in a person in order to cure an individual possessed by a ghostly spirit or god. The drummers, in these ceremonies, praise the deities and scare away the ghosts. This naming celebration did not need these kinds of drummers."

Moving into a different analysis, Jennifer then made an interesting point that was as applicable to the naming celebration we had just heard about as it was to our planned research experience. It was a comment that was right to follow from our discussion concerning the socio-religious worldview indicative of the caste system.

"Our drummers and the ones in these stories have been labeled as untouchables. Am I correct in understanding that they were present and continue to be present to glorify the story of those who victimized them? I find it very strange that they would drum up the heroism of the bigots. Why don't the untouchables rebel? Why does nobody think of their plight, at least in modern times?"

Luckily, the Thakur brothers showed no signs of discomfort at discussing the topic, sometimes repeating the same information in different words. Surprisingly, Marla seemed to be familiar with much of it and was absorbed elsewhere. But Jennifer had genuine questions.

I said to my wife, "Jennifer shows keen interest in the historical background of untouchability."

Jennifer asked questions less often, so she took very few notes. Thus, I jumped at the relatively rare opportunity to serve her better.

Noting my willingness to add context to her perspective, Jennifer asked, "The community of drummers belongs to the castes which were designated after India's independence as 'scheduled castes'?"

"Yes," I replied. "Traditionally, they were called *Dom*, or untouchable castes. Higher castes of this region—the Brahmins and Rajputs—would not allow them to enter their kitchens or temples because they consider the 'doms' to be low castes."

Jennifer then asked, "Mahatma Gandhi used a holy and respectful name for low castes—*Harijan* or God's people, right?"

"Correct, but untouchables resented this term," I explained. "Instead,

29

they used the word *silpkar* or artisan, because they were and continue in many cases to be artisans. They also accepted the other current word *dalit*, which translates as oppressed, because that has been the nature of their experience." Sanskrit *śilpakāra* 'artisan' is pronounced *silpkar* in Garhwali.

Jennifer got my point, "They understood that Gandhi's fictive name *Harijan* didn't make them lovable to the *savarna*, the higher castes."

Nodding my head from her quick synthesis, I explained further: "Later, Bhimrao Ambedkar became the major voice for the rights of untouchables. He was an untouchable himself, yet he was one of the best-educated lawyers of India. He became one of the framers of free India's constitution. Gandhi's worship of an imaginary 'loving' God did not impress Ambedkar much. So, he revived a Godless religion: Buddhism. Such a revival had never happened in modern times before this."

Puran heard us and interrupted with a light-hearted reference to Gandhi and Ambedkar, "I always thought that those two lawyers were very superstitious."

His brother, Navin, disagreed with a slight shake of his head, "They were smart. This wasn't simple superstition; they used their religious beliefs as fuel to drive their agendas. But our Himalayan 'low castes' were not fooled. Were the untouchables really God's people? Then why had the higher castes hated God's people for ages? Buddhism had already failed in India. Like any missionary church, it needed funding—cash from low castes! If they had no cash and no power, then how could they be God's people?"

Abdul agreed in part, "Another Indian lawyer, Mohammad Ali Jinnah, the founder of Pakistan, used Islam for power, not for its love. He led the bloodiest *Mahabharata* battle between the cousins—Hindus and Muslims. Neither Hari nor Allah was found in this battle."

I held my tongue, scribbling Abdul's main idea in my binder, as he expanded further taking his analysis to a very personal place. A committed Muslim: on this moral issue, Abdul was just disgusted with both sides.

"Maybe Ambedkar did the same thing with Buddhism. But Gandhi ji used religion to unite people, all people of any faith."

He shrugged for a moment feeling the wave of a thousand years of intolerance wash across his consciousness. Silenced for a moment at the staggering lack of human development, he looked around before continuing with his thought.

"I also thought that Ambedkar, like Jinnah, could have divided India further. Ambedkar wanted a separate country, like Pakistan. He, too, wanted to manifest another revenge for the untouchables—a revenge of thousands of years' repression."

Navin, sensing Abdul's weariness, said, "Yet, with Mahatma Gandhi's influence, Dr. Ambedkar dropped his demand. He dropped Gandhi's God, as well. Gone were the Hindu gods and goddesses, too; their imaginary existence was of no practical use to a landless or homeless untouchable. The Buddha had already done this some 2,500 years ago. He, too, had dropped the imaginary Isha or God of Hindus. But why did he keep the Hindu *karma*? That did not make any empirical sense to our untouchables."

I wrote in my notes under Navin's name: *If a Brahmin priest mispronounces the Vedic mantras he is still an officiating priest. And an untouchable mason cannot eat in a kitchen which he has constructed for that Brahmin priest. The karmic chain does not seem to cause rational results.*

"The untouchables wanted the real ultimate: social salvation," Navin emphasized. "Not simply nirvana after death."

Refreshed, Abdul added, "A considerable number of untouchables became Muslims for social salvation. A mass conversion of Hindus took place throughout the Muslim rule."

The Punjab and the Sindh region, including the old Bengal, became big concentrations of converts. Rounding out the point, Abdul punctuated his point with a very incisive point: "These untouchable converts took revenge in the formation of Pakistan."

Thoughtfully, I joined the conversation with a gentle point meant to add another layer of complexity to our discussion on the connection between religion and politics. "During British rule many converted to Christianity for the same reason, social salvation. The children of our local converts studied at Pauri's elite missionary school, Messmore High School."

This landmark school had put a dent into the theory of lower intelligence held in the hearts of many representatives of the higher castes. I didn't tell my new teammates that many Brahmins, some of them my relatives, literally believed that the low caste lacked higher intelligence.

The Thakur brothers had nice words for the Christian teachers of this school. I knew I would bring this up in the book I was writing, so I penned in my diary: *Even though every class started with a 25-minute Bible Class, its impact was negligible on the first-class education provided by this missionary school. For example, not even Christian students believed in a recent creation of the cosmos. How could anyone create the Himalayas in six days six thousand years ago?! None of my classmates were so dumb as to not know the age of the Ganga and the Yamuna. They knew some of their ancestors lived here before God's creation. They were not untouchable then.*

They knew who made them untouchable, certainly not God. The conquerors who called themselves *Arya*, the "noble" people—they had decreed them so. The ancestors of these conquerors lived in the Caucasian mountains even before God created the world, most probably 3,000 years before Christ was born. But, they had some powerful religious beliefs—quite different from what Christ said much later. They modified their beliefs further when they settled in Iran. Then they invaded the Indian subcontinent from Iran. Again, they modified their beliefs when they won the natives of India just 1,500 years before Christ.

The natives were given the name *Shudra*. The ancient Vedic Sukta says so: The sages divided the First Sacrificial Being or the *Purusha* into *four* parts; the *Brahmins* or priests were born of His head; the *rajanyas* or rulers from His arms; the *vaishyas* or business owners from His thighs; the *Shudras* or untouchables from His feet.

"Is it correct that the Aryan conquerors, who were the first to divide, rule, and sacrifice uncountable people with no accountability, should be called 'noble'?" Puran asked, not looking for a reply.

The Thakur brothers, putatively related to the royal or *rajanya* (*kshatriya*) class, felt very strongly. "Segregation based on skin color started with the ancient Indo-Aryans," Puran said. The reality is that, unlike the first three white classes, the Shudras were black in color or *varna*. This has been the nature of a discrimination fostered in this place for over 3000 years.

"The *Bhagavad Gita's* authors were xenophobic Brahmins. They were afraid of *varna-samkara*, miscegenation. What's so wrong that white Marla, for example, had a brown Indian husband before?" Navin looked at Marla in solidarity before continuing, "No society of this world has suffered so much from this Aryan virus of *varna*. Even now, the Brahmins keep spreading it by *puja*."

I was relieved that my parents were not present when he said this. They always did the *puja,* or worship, by using the sixteen mantras of the *Purusha Sukta*. The *Purusha Sukta* has been the Puja standard.

Interestingly, the Sanskrit word *Puja* came from the black Dravidians' language. The Dravidian puja was later integrated with the Aryan fire worship or *homa*. But the original color-based caste system continued unchanged without any watering-down despite the mingling of language and culture.

"The *Mahabharata* battle has nothing to do with color, though. The *Pandava*s and *Kaurava*s were cousins. All who participated belonged to the *rajanya* or *kshatriya* class." Puran wanted to show that the despicable battle which we had come to observe, to manifest, was, ironically, clean of color bias.

"Bad family relationships led the cousins to fight each other," Navin Singh added.

"So, the undesirable relationships of these classy clans produced heroes?" I wanted to ask my drummers after the session. I had a reason. And, I believed that Bijlu Das and Daphra Das knew that reason very well. Their names clearly suggested that they were no classy or *savarna* castes. Unlike other drummers, they had been called "the Das drummers" by locals.

I said to my wife, "I doubt my drummers' historical understanding." Would they believe me if I told them the Vedic origin of their names? I wondered if I could explain and elaborate the connection for them.

The word *Das* is recognized as having developed from the ancient Vedic word *dasa,* which means "slave." The Aryans fought the people who had the *dasa varna* or the slave color—a dark complexion. In the strange course of time, *dasa* began to also mean "worshipper." In early Indo-Aryan history, the *dasa* people began to serve the higher classes. Later, the worshippers of gods and goddesses were also given names such as *Kalidasa*, or "Devotee of Kali." *Kalidasa* must have worshipped the famous black goddess Kali. Kalidasa is also, interestingly, the name of someone considered to be the topmost author in Sanskrit literature.

I jotted in my notebook: *No scholar has suggested that Kalidasa was an untouchable like Bijlu and Daphra, and these two brothers, who play the dhol and damau, are the focal point of this research, not Kali or ancient Sanskrit authors. The drums these brothers play are sacred. They are used for worshipping gods, goddesses and religious heroes, so the drummers would be honorably addressed as 'Das'—but only on the occasion of drumming. As drumming is the main relationship through which we are connected, we will address them as 'Das ji' throughout these drumming sessions.* The Indian word *ji* is added for respect; it is derived from the *Arya* "Noble." I closed my book after scribbling a postscript: *Drummers of other drums, such as the daunr and hurki, are not addressed in this manner.*

Maybe the Thakurs had already told the drummers all about this. They clearly were aware of the Arya Samaj movement for the untouchables before any of us ever found a moment to discuss it with them.

The Arya Samaj or Aryan Society, founded in the late 19th century, did try to change the *Arya* image. The Society's founder was Swami Dayananada. He had a verbal *Mahabharata* battle with Christian and Islamic clergy and began to convert their followers. Such conversion has a name: *shuddhi,* or purification.

"The traditional Hindus felt offended by Arya Samaj. Purification of untouchables was as an attack on their religion—the *Sanatana Dharma,* the 'eternal religion' given to them through the traditions captured forever in the *Bhagavad Gita.* Bhagavan created the everlasting *Sanatana Dharma,* the four-fold division of the society that has been called the caste system by modern society, only in India. Bhagavan had no jurisdiction anywhere else. Forget that he claims in the *Bhagavad Gita* to be everywhere with his mighty *maya* magical power," Puran explained in a later conversation when the topic arose. Sacrilegiously imitating the pose of the mighty god by twisting his neck with a flat hand up in the air, he playfully smeared the solemnity hinted at in the great saga.

"One of the greatest hoaxes of the everlasting Dharma is that if you are born untouchable, then you must be an untouchable forever. And the Swami had the guts to challenge this hoax. His rebellion was that he wanted to put a new mask over the divisive Vedic face."

Talking stock of Puran's internal struggle, I reflected on my father's comment. He, like many orthodox Hindus, maintained that, "the Arya Samaj is not Hinduism." But, this isn't what came out of my mouth...

"I disagree. Though, you are right, in a way, about Arya Samaj. Its version of Hinduism looks like Christianity and Islam, with no idolatry and just one Parmatma or God."

Clearly in conflict with himself and the espoused framework of his tradition, the Swami held this reformed belief, an influence of the iconoclastic religions that he opposed so pugnaciously.

Without a doubt, there was no simple response available for anyone touched by the argument.

"How would Hinduism remain distinct if it mimics missionary churches like Christianity and Islam?" Dad had asked me this paradoxical question once in a while. In the face of such questions, I always remain silent.

In my mind, though, I reflect on my tenet that the belief in one God or many gods, with or without idolatry, is originally a folk construction, not the kind of idea which is based on scientific research such as that which Einstein brought into the world.

Nevertheless, my father said, "I know that you admired Swami Dayanand, not because the Swami 'purified' many as Aryas and also not because he was trying to make Hinduism into an organized, monotheistic religion, but because he fought for radical reforms. For example, he emphasized gender equality. The Arya Samaj opened its educational institutions to boys and girls and untouchables. And, furthermore, he did this regardless of the fact that the Swami didn't have any children of his own. He was a monk—*brahmachari*."

The institutions he referred to were called the Dayanand Anglo-Vedic schools—institutions meeting the needs of modern times. By hyphenating the word "Anglo" with "Vedic" to emulate the Western ideal implicit in the celebration of multiculturalism, the Swami was working towards the post-modernization idea of "Sanskritization."

Pausing for a moment, I responded respectfully in agreement, "The Swami was a visionary. He helped untouchables. India was listening; just after Independence, the government adopted the concept of *reservation* or Affirmative Action."

Delicately jumping into this exchange between my father and me, Navin said, "That was a necessary legal purification of the untouchables and other subalterns. They suffered from a social apartheid which has been codified in every layer of society and culture throughout many thousands of years." He said this in praise of the contribution of the Swami.

After looking around the participants of that moment, he added, "It's funny that Swami Dayanand, Mahatma Gandhi and Mohammad Ali Jinnah all came from the same *Indian background—Gujarati*. They all helped untouchables…"

In the case of Jinnah, he was suggesting that Pakistani Muslims were converts developed from the untouchables.

Interrupting Navin, Marla commented, "But they all were wrong. The untouchables did not need Islam or Hinduism. They needed modern rationalism." Her comment was indicative of her worldview and followed the pervasive belief of the modern world from which she had developed, not to mention providing an echo of Guru's words earlier.

"The substitution of one religion with another, godless or not, was precisely the mistake Ambedkar made. The untouchables needed rationalism, not Buddhism. Adopting any religion is going back to the dark ages again." Puran agreed with Marla, thus evidencing how deeply his education had sharpened him in Western scientific thought.

After Independence, the Arya Samaj became more active in this region. They began to convert untouchables more vigorously. Such converts would now have a family name, too. Up to this point, the untouchables only had one name—there was no such thing as first name, middle name, last name, etc. Rarely would an untouchable would have one more name, just as he would rarely have more than one room or one piece of land. They even had their separate rituals, quite different from those of higher castes.

# Chapter 4
# Before the War

*Dhritarashtra said: Assembled in the holy field of Kurukshetra for war what did my sons and Pandu's sons do, O Sanjaya?*

—*Bhagavad Gita: 1.1*

"So, here we are, back to Marla's original question: 'Are polygamists holy?'" I said to Tula as we prepared for the evening.

"Marla is sharp, gets facts before passing judgment," Tula praised our student.

"Yes, she has come all the way to Himalaya to get the facts."

I, too, praised her.

Marla and Jennifer had attended my course on the great Indian epic *Mahabharata*. Understanding India's heroes and their all-too-human behavior was vital for my students in order to begin to answer their own questions about Indian polygamy. I typically introduce that course with words to the effect that The *Mahabharata* is the biggest story of the Kurus, the white people called the Indo-Aryans. Pay attention to the characters of *Mahabharata*! As Bible parables and characters set examples for millions of people growing up in the West, the *Mahabharata* and its characters are pivotal to understanding ideals and role models in Indian civilizations. As much as the Bible still influences Western thought, morals, ethics, and law, so too the *Mahabharata* still influences Indian thought, morals, ethics, and law.

"Are polygamists holy?" Marla asked me, symbolically returning to the beginning of her research, after making her customary greeting and situating herself in preparation for the evening.

I had anticipated the question and was ready with a response. "You should be the judge of that after we revisit, as a relevant start on polygamy's role in the region, the famous polygamists of the world's second longest epic that you've already been introduced to. Again, these men are India's most celebrated heroes and role models that we have been taught to respect and sing of since ancient times; these are the heroes of the *Mahabharata.*"

Jennifer had quietly joined us with a smile and wink during that comment. And, when we greeted her, she, too, verbalized her wish, "You told us that there are too many versions of the *Mahabharata.* I want to hear the local version in short." So, I summed it up:

People know here that sage Vyasa narrated the original *Mahabharata* story. Bhishma was the son of Shantanu and Ganga; thus, he was destined to be the king of the Kuru dynasty. However, Shantanu took a second wife, Satyavati. There was one condition Shantanu made to confirm his union with Satyavati: Satyavati's son was to be heir to the throne. This would mean that Bhishma would never have the throne. However, Bhishma agreed to his father's commitment and vowed to remain a bachelor, with no claim to the throne.

Satyavati had two sons: Chitrangada and Vichitravirya. After Chitrangada's death, the younger son, Vichitravirya, sat on the Kuru throne. For him, Bhishma identified three princesses, two of whom became his wives.

Refusing Vichitravirya, Amba declared that she was already in love with another man, a prince. After a verbal quarrel, Bhishma let her go to her lover, who now refused to marry her. Deeply disappointed, she immediately went to the Himalayas to pray to Lord Shiva. It was in this moment that the great family drama, with the conflict with Bhishma at the epicenter of the saga originated.

With Shiva's grace, Amba was reborn as the daughter of King Drupada. King Drupada was frightened when he learned that his new daughter, when she reached adulthood, would be responsible for Bhishma's murder. Concerned, King Drupada exiled the young Amba to a forest. There, she did sacred penance, the result of which was that she emerged transformed. Amba had become a man. Her new, male name was Shikhandin.

In a tangle of events so characteristic of the classic story, Bhishma finds out that Shikhandin had been a woman, that he was the transformed Amba whom he had seperated from her lover. And, though he wanted to end the young warrior before the conflict could come to a head, he had taken a vow not to kill a woman. So, he left Shikhandin to grow.

38

Interrupting myself, I said to Marla and Jen, "Actually, the story contains more details and checkered genealogies."

Vichitravirya, the son of Satyavati from Shantanu, was unable to have a child. Unfortunately, he had to have an heir to continue his dynasty. So his mother, Satyavati, requested another of her sons, Vichitravirya's half-brother —a young man named Vyasa—to be the surrogate father for that heir.

The reluctant sage was unable to ignore his mother's request. He accepted *niyoga*, the surrogate parenthood. It meant that he shared a bed with the two wives of his half-brother. As problematic as this would normally be, Vichitravirya, the half-brother, was dead, so his consent wasn't a problem. His two widows, Ambika and Ambalika, consented and soon potential heirs were born to the family.

Vyasa's son with Ambika was Dhritarashtra. His son with Ambalika was Pandu. By mistake, Vyasa slept with a royal maid, too. Tricking him, Ambalika refused to sleep with Vyasa a second time; she put her maid in the bed instead. Fooled, the Brahmin sage didn't figure out the ruse. From the maid, Vyasa recieved another son whose name was Vidura.

All the sons, Dhritarashtra, Pandu, and Vidura were princes. However, as the son of a maid, Vidura never claimed any part of the kingdom. He could not have; his mother was a *dasi*. But he was the most learned and the fairest man among the Kurus. As the drama emerges in the saga, it was Vidura who was opposed to the emerging family feuds which would come to a head with the conflict brewing among the children of his two half-brothers.

Dhritarashtra, Vyasa's son with Ambika, was born blind because his mother had covered her face while sleeping with Vyasa. But Pandu's mother, Ambalika, didn't make that mistake. Nevertheless, Pandu had his share of problems—he was delicate, sickly and unable to procreate. But he was fortunate: the various prominent gods became surrogates in order to allow him to procreate.

"So," Jennifer asked, "was sickly Pandu the biological father of his five sons, the Pandavas?"

In reply, I made a very succinct point anticipating the common assumption about the conflict which I sensed she was about to make, "This question was moot for the Kaurava's or Dhritarashtra's sons. They did not dispute the Pandava claim to the Kuru kingdom over this issue. The defining conflict would be something much stranger and more human than the question of royal succession."

Bhishma could have claimed the throne; instead, he let his nephew Dhritarashtra remain the official ruler. Dhritarashtra was blind. So, with Dhritarashtra's consent, Pandu, his fragile half-brother, was given the responsibility of adminstering the kingdom. Dhritarashtra and his wife Gandhari had one hundred sons who have come to be referred to as the Kaurava after their common ancestor Kuru. The oldest two sons, Duryodhana and Duhshasana, were big bullies.

The sickly administrator-ruler Pandu had two wives, Kunti and Madri. Kunti's sons by Pandu were Yudhishthira, Bhima, and Arjuna. Madri's sons by Pandu were twins, Nakula and Sahadeva. Unfortunately, Pandu and Madri died early, leaving Kunti to raise all five sons of Pandu. These five sons were called the Pandavas after their father, Pandu.

Unknown to the Pandavas, Kunti also had a son, Karna, born prior to her marriage to Pandu. She only revealed Karna's origin to the Pandavas in the shadow of the looming war brewing between the two sides of the family.

Recognizing a common thread across much ancient literature, Jennifer and Marla grinned when I punctuated the story with my comment, "The Sun has been mentioned as the father of Karna!"

The seeds of war were sown when the eldest Kaurava, the bully Duryodhana, claimed the entire Kuru kingdom. "My father Dhritarashtra is the official ruler; Pandu is only a proxy ruler" was his basic argument.

Outraged, the Pandavas asserted, "Our father, Pandu, ran the actual kingdom, so we deserve some portions of the kingdom."

Blind Dhritarashtra, as the official king, wanted to stop the feud. He declared, "I divide the kingdom in half—one portion for Duryodhana and his brothers, the Kaurava, and another for Yudhishthira and his brothers, the Pandava."

The bully Duryodhana still insisted, "I want to rule an undivided kingdom."

To accomplish this, he used a dice game which his maternal uncle, Shakuni, had fixed. Knowing the plan, Shakuni played the game on Duryodhana's behalf. Yudhishthira, the oldest Pandava brother, played against the cheating Shakuni. He never had a chance.

Quickly, the honest Yudhishthira began to lose. Soon, Yudhishthira wagered his brothers and lost. Then he wagered their common wife, Draupadi. Tragically, he lost her to Duryodhana. Unbelievably, he then wagered and lost the Pandava kingdom, too.

Just after the game, Duryodhana sent a messenger to summon Draupadi to his court. She refused to come to his court, as she was cycling through her menstrual period. Yet, Duryodhana had her dragged into the court. There, Duryodhana ordered, "Younger brother, Duhshasana, disrobe her."

All the male courtiers could not stop Duryodhana. He was now the undisputed king of the entire Kuru kingdom. To show his power and lust, he showed the beautiful Draupadi his bare thigh.

When Duryodhana's younger brother and fellow bully, Duhshasana, was unable to disrobe Draupadi because her *sari* kept on lengthening, he withdrew from the shameful act. In anger at this act of disrespect, Bhima vowed, "I will break Duryodhana's thigh. I also vow to wash Draupadi's hair with the dead Duryodhana's blood."

When the official ruler, blind Dhritarashtra, heard about the game and its outcome, he became furious. He declared, "As the official ruler of the entire Kuru territory, I restore the stolen share to the Pandavas."

Duryodhana became furious at his father's ruling, so they conspired and Shakuni again set up the dice game and, just as before, Shakuni cheated and Yudhishthira lost. This time, the loss earned the Pandavas and Draupadi an exile for thirteen horrible years.

After their return from exile, the Pandavas asked, "Duryodhana, return our portion of the kingdom." Upon having their request refused, the Pandavas decided to fight him. Kurukshetra, near Delhi, was chosen as the battlefield. The elder hero, Bhishma, a granduncle of both the Kaurava's and the Pandava's, led the Kaurava army. Dhrishtadyumna, Draupadi's brother, led the Pandava army.

As Krishna drove Arjuna in a chariot toward the battlefield, the noise of war increased in volume. Arjuna saw the two armies waiting to fight. He saw friends and relatives on both sides, ready to kill each other. Such an atmosphere altered his awareness. He went into a deep depression and dropped his bow on the chariot floor. This war looked to him to be an invitation to destruction as he said *na yotsye*: "I will not fight."

Arjuna meant that, very clearly. Krishna, hearing his soul, bolstered Arjuna's resolve. "Do your duty, or dharma, ignoring loss or gain, pleasure or pain. Arjuna, you are a *Kshatriya* warrior. Your soldier dharma is to engage in the action of fighting."

It was needed at this time. "Action for the sake of action" with "no attachment to its outcome" was emphasized by Krishna during this counsel.

Regarding dharma, Krishna specifically told him that, "Working with this attitude, no sin will be incurred."

I paused to explain the Sanskrit to Jennifer and Marla, "Krishna justified the idea of *holy war.* But this war's rightness or righteousness was fuzzy. At best, it was a war for shaky honor, for enjoyable slaughter—all under the illusion of sinlessness."

Jennifer recalled our earlier classes, "The story of Arjuna's depression and Krishna's treatment of it is discussed in eighteen chapters. These chapters became famous as the *Bhagavad Gita* here. Please, go on..."

After Arjuna's depression ended, he decided to fight. Thereafter, one of his priorities had to become the killing of the leader of the Kaurava forces, his granduncle Bhishma. Shikhandin, the female reborn as a male who was prophesied to kill Bhishma, was chosen as an alternate charioteer for Arjuna.

Even though Bhishma had a soft spot for the Pandavas, he was still their opponent. This was not inadvertent. Bhishma was requested first by the Kauravas to join their side. The Pandavas were late to the battlefield and thus late to choose their allies. Not only Bhishma, but all warriors took sides on a "first come, first served" basis. This policy turned friends into foes on both sides.

I concluded my lecture with one of the strangest details of the saga. "The live war was reported to the blind ruler Dhritarashtra by his advisor Sanjaya. With Vyasa's blessing, Sanjaya had received a psychic gift: Sanjaya could witness things from any distance. Thus, as Sanjaya was sitting in Hastinapura with Dhritarashtra, his master, he could see the war at Kurukshetra. The drummers will tell you the rest."

Right on cue, Tula redirected our attention, "The drummers are warming up; we had better get ready."

They were tuning the *dhol* and *damau* in front of the bonfire. Tula and I waved hellos to our neighbors from up the street who had begun to join the other guests around the bonfire. Marla, Jennifer, and other team members were already with us, so I took a second and reminded everyone, "We'll stop talking and taking notes, but leave the tape recorder on. Our project requires recording of every session, all of which should follow a typical, traditional pattern."

The long *Pandau* song is a series of pieces. Each piece is sung for about a minute with soft drumming. Then the loud, eardrum-piercing playing of the drums follows. Each piece or set of pieces has a key word or sentence.

The *dhol* player is the lead musician. The *damau* player repeats the key word or sentence only after the lead drummer finishes the piece. The audience and the dancers know what the song-piece is about. The repetition of the key phrase functions as the title of every piece. The rhythm or tempo keeps varying throughout the entire session, from two to four hours.

In each session, the spirits of the Pandavas and Kauravas are invoked. This doesn't guarantee there will be a possession in every session. However, when a possession does occur, the possessed person has to prove the spirit is real. The lead drummer frequently tests the spirit by issuing a challenge or some task to be performed.

During the drumming, I found myself also journeying into my own introspection, but before putting my mind into words, I noticed Puran, who, by the look on his face, seemed to be brooding over his own query. He raised an interesting question.

"The *Mahabharata* story begins with Vyasa and Ganapati writing it. There is evidence that Vyasa may have been a devotee of Vishnu, a Vaishnavite. In contrast, Ganapati is a son of Shiva, a Shaivite. Can we be sure about how much the Shaivites altered the *Mahabharata* story that might have been Vaishnavite in its original folk form?"

In response, I elaborated further, "My Sanskrit teacher in college, Shastri ji, had his own question. For him, the *Mahabharata* authorship myth simply implies this: Ganapati had ample opportunities to count and discount the contents here and there while Vyasa was intermittently dozing during dictation! After all, Vyasa means *editor* and Ganapati means *master of counting*. The recognition of these two title holders suggests that at least two outstanding persons, not to mention the other narrators, were involved in the preparation of the *Mahabharata* as we know it. They might have started working on the literary form of the collected *Mahabharata* material after the Vedic period, quite possibly even just before the time of the Buddha. So his central question was this: Who are really the authors of the original *Mahabharata* material?"

Puran took this question lightly, "Whoever they may be, they all believed in robust fun." He blinked and smiled.

Marla would have agreed with him. The war dance begins with the praise of the two main authors. In mythology, Ganesha has two wives. He is a vigorous dancer, too. He also holds a *damaru* or *daunr* in his hand. And Vyasa was even ahead of his time. He was free from the locked box of

43

marriage. He slept with others' wives simultaneously and had children with each of them simultaneously. And yet they found time to prepare such a long epic of the world, the *Mahabharata*.

I guess Puran might have meant all that, but what came out of his mouth was much simpler.

"For the Pahari people, dancing the *Mahabharata* is the greatest robust fun." Then he became serious, "Mythological characters are mythical, hardly logical. Anybody can imagine anything about them. Nobody seems to have any real complaints when it comes to them. But ask any wife how she feels when she finds her son of a bitch husband having robust fun with other women."

Magnu's story reminded me again of the *Mahabharata* story's robust and proud local connection with the Pandava dance. The *Mahabharata* character Bharata was the ancestor of the Kauravas and Pandavas. Bharata was the founder of the country *Bhārata*, the name for India and *Mahābhārata*. His father Dushyanta met his mother Shakuntala on a hunting trip in a lower Garhwal Himalayan region at Sage Kanva's hermitage. Shakuntala became pregnant when Dushyanta slept with her secretly, in Kanva's absence. Dushyanta just didn't care then that he had already other wives back in his capital. His "extra-marriage" with Shakuntala has been celebrated as "true love." The Paharis feel strongly that Shakuntala must have been a local snow-white beauty who bore Bharata here!

# Chapter 5
# Day One of the War

*Arjuna said: My confusion is destroyed. I have gained awareness by your grace, O Krishna, and I am firm, with doubts gone. I shall follow your advice.*

*—Bhagavad Gita 18.76*

About twenty minutes later, we suddenly heard vigorous drumming. The sound drew a dozen men to form a circle around the bonfire. The dance had begun.

"The audience looks excited. I am, too," Tula said as the drummers approached the bonfire. There were about a dozen women in the audience. Like Marla and Jennifer, young girls wore the *shalwar-kurta* suits. All adult women wore *saris*. The women stood together a little away from the bonfire. Most of the men, about thirty, stood around the bonfire. They either danced or were watching the men dancing in the circle.

Bijlu and Daphra, the two drummers, stood in a corner close to the bonfire. Their drums, the *dhol* and the *damau*, hanging around their necks made them literally stand out from the growing crowd. While drumming they sang, "O, praise Narayana!" They did not sing the background story that I had just told to Marla and Jennifer. Instead, they contributed their own touches.

"Narayana is a god with many names. Those names include Vishnu, the pervader. He is in all and all is in him. He is the first person or Purusha. One of his avatars is Krishna: the best among men. He is called Narottama. The *Mahabharata* is about him, about everything. Its original author, the learned Vyasa, says so: *Whatever is in it is out there; what is not in it is not anywhere.* It's not just about a big war. The listener learns wisdom. Hail to the goddess of learning! She is Sarasvati. So, one must begin: *First bow to*

45

*Narayana and Sarasvati. Then pronounce victory."*

Bijlu and Daphra drummed with a fast rhythm. Then, a few minutes later, they lowered the amplitude of the drumming. Puran and Navin sat with their hands folded and prayed to Lord Narayana and Goddess Sarasvati in Sanskrit. They faced the audience while praying. Then they turned their backs. They folded their hands again to salute the drummers.

Puran placed his hands upon the dhol. He addressed the dhol player, Bijlu, the lead drummer, in Garhwali, *"Hey mera dholi dasa!"* (Hey, my dhol's devotee!)

Then he added, "Dance the battle of the Pandavas. Give the true story just as Lord Ganesha took the *Mahabharata* notes from the sage, Vyasa."

Bijlu responded to the request rousingly, *"Nachi jala mera pandau!"* (Let the Pandavas dance!)

The damau player, Daphra, called out the refrain, *"Hey mera Pandau!"* (O my Pandavas!)

"We noticed tears in the eyes of the Thakurs," whispered Jennifer from beside Marla, without taking her eyes off the Thakur brothers.

Keeping my eyes on the brothers, I kept my voice respectfully low. "I have just one simple guess as to the origin of these tears: pride. You see, Ganesha was created by his mother Parvati here in the Himalayas. Both were Himalayan natives. The *Mahabharata* says that Vyasa dictated the epic to Ganesha. The original *Mahabharata*, then, was presented in writing by a Himalayan native! And the great epic bears the name of Bharata, whom Shakuntala bore in lower Garhwal!"

The drummers started the main story with the traditional "Himalayan rap." The Kaurava armies faced the west and the Pandavas faced east. The beginning of the war and the battle was signaled by the blowing of conchs. Each leader had a special conch with its own special sound. Each leader's chariot could be recognized by the flag it bore. Arjuna's banner, for instance, depicted Hanuman, the monkey god.

A tremendous cacophony rang out as the war started. The beating of drums, along with the blowing of horns and trumpets, scared the horses, who added their own frightened neighing to the noise. Despite their bravery, even the men trembled. Nevertheless, the armored fighters advanced on one another, doing as much damage as possible with arrows, swords, maces and spears. Each side was determined to annihilate the other, regardless of the fact that their enemy was often a friend, relative, or teacher. Relationships became blurred in the *Mahabharata*, a war of cousins, all of whom were the descendants of the great Bharata, the ancestor whose name is forever immortalized in the title of this epic.

Beyond Bhishma, who was the most respected granduncle of the warring cousins and the advisor to the Kauravas, Drona and Kripa, two great teachers of military science, also joined the Kauravas, thus pitting them against their favorite disciples, the Pandavas. These are just two examples in this war during which even near relatives fought against each other.

However, most remained loyal to their closer relatives. Each of Draupadi's sons, for example, fought alongside his respective father. Even sons of promiscuous unions turned out to be supportive of their fathers. A divine order was undoubtedly at work.

Krishna's relationship was an interesting one. He was not fighting in the war as a warrior, but giving counsel to the Pandavas. He served as Arjuna's loyal charioteer. This favor of Krishna was enough to make the Pandavas sure of success. Where Krishna is, there also is victory.

On the first day of the battle, the Pandavas suffered major losses. Fighting ceased before dark and both armies retreated to their camps. Some of the Pandavas' leaders were panicked. Krishna encouraged them and a new strategy was planned for the next morning. Shikhandin was already eager to kill Bhishma, in order to eliminate his counsel for the Kauravas. Knowing Bhishma would never kill a woman regardless of his transformation as a man, Shikhandin felt that the goal could be easily accomplished.

Far removed from the battle, the psychic Sanjaya reported on the war to Dhritarashtra, using his abilities to witness things from any distance. His reports were neither objective, nor without criticism of his master, whom he considered to be the cause of the bitter conflict.

The first night of our performance was coming to a close. Signaling the end, the drummers sang, leaving all of the participants with a lingering thought, "Sisters and brothers! Does a woman have to become a man to avenge an ugly harassment from a hard-headed bully?"

This was an especially powerful thought to end the evening on, as this was the night that Goda introduced us to our first possession and asked her question which would burn in our ears throughout the remainder of our time in the shadows of the Himalayas.

# Chapter 6
# Judge's Brother

The following afternoon after we had processed a few lingering thoughts about the incident with Marla and had heard my impassioned pleas to not allow such dangerous behavior, the Thakurs continued with the story of the Tiwari family. Jag had been the oldest. The second was Gobardhan and the youngest was a girl named Bina. Gobardhan was first sandwiched between his two siblings and then between his wives. Gobardhan's story was not a particularly pleasant look at either the life or the customs of the area. As Navin began a recitation of Gobardhan's life, it was obvious the Thakur brothers didn't care for him.

"Gobardhan dropped out of school after failing the high school exam three times. In the last year of the exam, friends advised him that concentration was his problem. He was weak in math and concentration was the key to passing that portion of the test. His classmates convinced him to use *bhang*, the Himalayan hemp that grew wild in the area and was supposed to be good for concentration."

Gobardhan emerged from the test elated, convinced his answers were one hundred percent correct. Unfortunately, two months later, his score card recorded zero in math. It was at that point Gobardhan gave up on education.

"He was a strong hill man and very handsome and was soon married. When classmates asked him about marrying so soon, he told them marriage was far more pleasurable than a high school diploma."

"And just how foolish is that?" Puran queried. "I couldn't understand anyone not choosing to pursue as much education as possible."

"Unfortunately, it's not that uncommon," Marla said. "The high number of teen pregnancies in America is a result of bargaining early sex for early education."

Puran shook his head in disgust, and then took up the story.

"Gobardhan carried an unfortunate burden, due to his name. His Sanskrit name was Govardhana Dhara, meaning 'the holder of the Govardhana mountain.' This comes from the myth that Krishna held a mountain on his finger. The myth is laughable, since the mountain in question is like a mound when compared to the Himalayan mountains here."

Navin took over, "The real problem was the translation from Sanskrit to local Garhwali or Hindi. The consonant *v* changes to *b*. The original Govardhana Dhara is pronounced here as Gobar-dhan Dhar. Gobar means bullshit, dhan means wealth and dhar means holder. His schoolmates often interpreted his name as 'the holder of bullshit as his wealth'. For his part, Gobar didn't always take the abuse lightly. Once he beat up a classmate for calling him a dung holder. In his own village, he was referred to as Gobri, which he accepted as his normal name, knowing none meant any abuse."

Puran muttered, "Gobardhan was bullshit, using *bhang* during the high school exam. I'd have little use for the man, with good reason in some cases."

Shaking his head at Puran's comment, Navin continued, "Gobardhan was a land surveyor. He had money and a horse, unlike many of the villagers. His first wife, Chanda, bore him a daughter named Anandi, then another daughter, named Benu. Gobar wanted a son. Roaming the countryside in his work, he was offered numerous opportunities to meet suitable young women. He soon married Runi, who became the junior wife. Within months, both wives were pregnant. Chanda gave birth to a son, Rewat, earning her husband's respect. Runi bore him another daughter. Nine years later, however, Runi presented him with a son, Lalit, and also earned his respect."

Making faces at Navin's use of the word respect, Puran jumped in, "A year later, Gobardhan brought home a third wife, Mangli. While the arrival of a third wife surprised Chanda and Runi, the new bride was in shock. Gobardhan had presented himself to her father as a bachelor. In addition, he'd falsified his astrological information. Horoscopes for marriage matching are easily manipulated by crafty priests. Mangli was twenty-eight when she married Gobardhan. This is unusual for a Hindu girl, particularly one as attractive as Mangli. However, she'd been born at an odd time, *Mangalika*. For her to marry anyone but a man of the same astrological time was considered very destructive to the husband and the marriage."

"It was destructive all right," Navin muttered, "but not for Gobar."

Puran nodded and continued.

"A year after her marriage, Mangli gave birth to a girl. Unfortunately, her life with Gobar and the other wives was difficult and unpleasant. One day, Judge Sahab sent our father to help grow *lychee* trees. As Father approached, he saw Gobardhan chasing Mangli, shouting, 'Stop, you whore!' When he reached her he hit her on the head with a long stick. She screamed in pain. Gobar's oldest son, Rewat, watched the beating, laughing." Puran said this, shaking with emotion. Seeing Puran like this, Navin finished the story.

"Our father managed to control Gobardhan. He got between the two and took away the stick."

"Our father never laid his hands on our mother," Puran said with disgust for Gobar lacing his voice. "If he had, we'd have thrown rocks at him."

Having gotten this indictment out of his system, Puran continued, "There were rumors the senior wife, Chanda, encouraged his abuse of Mangli. Both of the wives thought her lazy at work, despite the fact she was assigned the toughest jobs and her hands were often blistered from the work she did. One day, Navin saw Chanda beating Mangli with her bare hands and shouting at her. 'You bum slut. How could you forget to shut the canal to the fields?' The cursing continued."

Navin cut in, "I wanted to tell her to beat the hell out of Chanda. After all, she was bigger and younger. It would have done no good. Mangli was a very docile woman and respected Chanda as her *didi*, her senior sister."

"We thought there was hope when her brother came to the village for Raksha Bandhan," Puran said. "The ceremony provides for a sister to tie a protective string around her brother's wrist. The sacred string is to protect the brother. In return, the brother protects the sister."

Navin continued, "I told her brother how she had been abused. I told him of what I had seen. He was college-educated and was appalled at what I said. He wanted to take her and his niece away from Gobardhan and care for them. Unfortunately, she wouldn't listen to his counsel."

Puran's face showed anger as he again picked up the story. "Manu, the ancient Hindu law giver, contended a woman must serve her husband in order to earn salvation. Judge Sahab believed the ancient book of *Manu's Laws*."

Marla looked surprised at Puran's anger at the man he generally considered a hero.

"How come the village couldn't protect her?"

Neither Puran nor Navin answered.

"Eventually, the prediction about the marriage being dangerous to the husband seemed to come true," Puran said, with an ironic satisfaction in his voice.

"As Gobardhan entered his fifties, life became difficult. He quarreled with his senior wife, Chanda, and she left to live with her oldest daughter and her family in Dehradun. There, Chanda cared for the couple's four children."

Navin took over the story, "During his land surveys, Gobardhan became aware of large forest contracts offered by the Maharaja of a neighboring state and he invested heavily in the project. Unfortunately, like the projects of a couple of other contractors, Gobardhan's project didn't prove profitable and he lost all his money. His debts to the Maharaja government caused him mental and physical problems. He developed serious stomach and back problems and for days he was unable to get up and go out into his gardens, let alone leave his house. He died of a heart attack before he was sixty. His death went unremarked. His two remaining wives circled his dead body three times, their final ritual farewell to their husband. Neither did Chanda come back for any of the funeral rites, nor did her daughter or grandchildren. Rewat, his oldest son, should have performed the funeral rites, but he led a troubled life, going from one job to another, often getting thrown out of work. Fortunately, Lalit, the younger son, performed the funeral rites. When Chanda died a few years later, Rewat again didn't show up, but left it to his oldest son to perform the thirteenth-day funeral rite."

# Chapter 7
# Day Two of the War

*The Lord said: If you will not do this holy war then having forsaken your own duty and honor you will commit sin. You will obtain heaven if killed or you will enjoy the world if victorious. Therefore, O Arjuna, stand up with determination to fight.*

*—Bhagavad Gita 2.33, 37*

The sound of the drummers tuning up again drew us away from the discussion of Gobardhan and toward the gathering crowd. "The drummers' story will pick up where it left off the previous day, at the end of the first day's battle," I told my excited students.

The drummers sang, "The scene of the battlefield was a gory nightmare, littered with men and animals alike. Our fabled soldiers fared little better. Disabled chariots were scattered across the battlefield, the wounded and dying charioteers inside them. Injured men cried for water. There was none. Some cried out their family members' names, clearly out of their senses from pain."

"The Kauravas wanted the heads of the Pandavas. The Pandavas wanted the death of each of Dhritarashtra's one hundred sons and the return of their kingdom. Nothing else mattered."

Miles away, Sanjaya related to the king that the Pandavas suffered heavy losses on the first day, but that it now appeared that they'd rearranged their armies and some of their strategies were beginning to work.

The psychic stopped. The blind king had tears in his eyes as he considered the imminent danger for his hundred sons.

"What Sanjaya said was not acceptable to the blind king," sang the drummers, ending the song.

It was a short session. Today was an auspicious day in the

community. Lots of celebrations were taking place in the town. For me, this session turned out to be especially auspicious. This time, instead of a single pair, two pairs of drummers played together. The other drummers playing that evening were the relatives of Daphra and Bijlu who had visited the house with Guru before the performance series had begun. The four men were in complete unison in their drumming. Such synchronization was stunning. Before they left, I quietly gave them a hefty sum of rupees.

Wanting to get out of the house, I came out in the streets for a walk. After a couple of blocks, I heard the sounds of drums and bagpipes. The music compelled me to walk faster and faster until I located the source.

It was a Garhwali marriage procession with two teams of folk musicians, one team from the bride's side and one from the groom's side. All players were typical Pahari men in their forties. Behind each team were standing hundreds of men in rows. Outside, the rows were onlookers – men, women, and children. The men on the bride's side had garlands in their hands, obviously to welcome the groom and his party, which is called a *barat*. The groom was riding a white mare. He was dressed in western clothes with a tie. But his head was covered with a turban and a *sehra* or groom's crown tied in a turban. He was a handsome young man.

The musicians from the groom's side came closer, facing their counterparts who remained in their positions. The two bagpipe players stopped playing, but the four drummers continued playing their dhol-damau sets, taking turns to match each other's rhythmic patterns. After playing for about five minutes, the two teams played the drums together with a fast rhythm, taking the noise level as high as possible for about five minutes. It was a drumming rivalry.

The drummers expertly displayed their skill and energy. Neither team seemed to win or lose. Finally, both teams stopped playing and exchanged greetings with raised folded palms. And then they started playing together with a slow rhythm, now accompanied by the bagpipes, firecrackers, and gunshots. Before I could or would be recognized as Archi Rainwal, I left and headed back.

On my way, I kept asking myself questions, courtesy of my academic habit. Why were such great folk musicians oppressed as Shudras or *dalits*? The rishis or sages of the past were not rationalists; they were theists or godists. I liked to use the simple word "godist"—believers of God or gods. My teacher, Shastri ji, used this word to refer to his and other native theistic religions.

He said to us students things like this: Godists fool people into believing that it's divine decision or the result of past lives' *karma* to be born into your family. The *charvak* philosophers, the earlist rationalists and atheists, failed to change the unproven religious theories of the godists. Even the Godless religions, such as Buddhism, failed to change godist myths. Buddhism is more sophisticated than our Vedic religion.

I guess the IAS man, Guru, targeted the godist religions specifically in his message, *"Dharm hatao; gyan bachao"* (Oust religion; save knowledge)! And, in reflection of Guru's other comments, I had to admit that I was not sure whether those fantastically talented folk musicians I had seen in the wedding party would be allowed to share seats for dinner with the guests.

# Chapter 8
# The Monogamous Sister and Her Progeny

Today, we heard the story of the last of the Tiwari children. We had already heard about Jag and Gobardhan. Bina, the brothers' little sister, married at the age of sixteen. Her marriage was monogamous. She and her husband, Janardan, had thirteen children, four daughters and nine sons. This was as many as Jag and Gobardhan had between them, with their multiple wives.

Navin pointed out, "This refutes a popular folk theory: that a male with many wives contributed to the population explosion."

"Most Chinese and Indians are monogamous," he explained. "Our seven male cousins have only one wife each, yet all have three children or more. Puran has two sons and I have a son and a daughter."

Puran said, "I consider Bina in a very negative light. She was a foul-mouthed bitch, but I cannot deny that Bina and her husband were religious. They recited the *Hanuman Chalisa* daily, which consists of forty verses of praise meant to remove trouble anytime, anywhere, against anyone."

"There was no doubt Bina and Janardan needed protection from friends, relatives and neighbors," Puran said. "They stole what they wanted or needed whenever an opportunity arose. Nobody considered sending them to jail. Who would raise their children? Instead, the victims accused them verbally. With her abusive tongue, Bina wasn't on speaking terms with most of the village people, almost all of whom were victims of her thievery."

Shaking his head, Puran continued, "Bina also devised another form of protection. All of her children held the second name of Prasad. This placed them in the position of being Devi's 'Prasad,' or pleasure. As Devi, she was the mother of the entire cosmos, the children all fell under her protection."

Navin added, "Girija Prasad, the oldest son, was considered the most highly educated of the brothers, although he attempted four times to pass the high school examination. Many people believe the only way he obtained a diploma was to steal the high school certificate of a cousin who died of typhoid just after passing his exams."

Upon remembering the story and hearing Navin relate the old rumor, Puran's face, once again, showed his disgust at the abuse of education. He waved his hand at his brother to indicate that he would continue.

"Following in the questionable footsteps of his parents, Girija took the forged certificate to Simla and became a clerk in the government road construction department, under public works. The salary was standard, but the position offered an opportunity to amass much more money than most clerical positions earn. Like the overseers and engineers, the clerks were not adverse to bribes to ease the contract process. The bribery money assisted in the education of Girija's nine children, all of whom graduated from college."

Smiling from the absolutely shameless immorality of these people, Navin took up the story of Bina's children.

"Girija's brothers weren't so fortunate. None of them advanced beyond middle school education. However, their wishes to be 'big men' were fulfilled by the British Raj. They all joined the military, the easiest employment under British rule. They were often referred to as the 'British Prasads' or 'military Prasads'."

Navin digressed for a moment, offering Jennifer and Marla some context. "The Pahari people, coming from central Himalaya, were preferred soldiers. The Raj created three famous Pahari rifles, which later evolved as the Garhwal Regiment, the Gurkha Regiment and the Kumaon Regiment. With little education, many Pahari soldiers earned big honors during the First and Second World Wars, the highest being the Victoria Cross."

Nodding ruefully, Navin added that the Prasads didn't ultimately succeed in the military. He spun the yarn out, telling us of the second brother who was discharged after he was accused of raping his eldest daughter. His cousin, Durlabh, a police officer, refused to get involved in saving him. The third brother was wounded in an accident and discharged. The fifth was caught stealing supplies from the military canteen and was thrown out of the regiment. The last three were laid off as soon as the Second World War ended and soldiers were no longer needed. Only the fourth brother remained in the military.

"These brothers all returned to their village and shared their parents' house, working the fields. When the parents died, the brothers quarreled over who should own how many fields. Not that it mattered much. The fields were relatively worthless, being full of difficult slopes and filled with rocks. Nevertheless, they battled in court and hatred grew among them."

Then, Puran said, "We don't really want to talk much more about them. Our interest in exploring their sordid history was only to provide an introduction to the horrible blow one Prasad brother would eventually deal to the Judge. We promise to talk about this later."

Curious, Marla then added, "Before we continue, I just have a note based on my experience with the eighth brother, Sirdhar Prasad: I thought that this brother behaved better because of his business needs. His Tantrik guru taught him not only folk tantra but also the art of communication that goes along with it."

Puran explained to Marla that Sirdhar Prasad's highest education was fourth grade level. He didn't know Sanskrit, so he was not fit for the classic tantra practice. In the classic tantra practice, there are very complex sets of mantras, mystic designs, rituals, sex and food, including alcohol.

Like other interfaith believers, this group can be called religiously very liberal and tolerant; some of them believe that all practices of any religion are forms of tantra. Even any holy recitation, incantation, chant or prayer for any imaginary or real entity is considered a part of tantra. The prayers can be offered in any language from any religion at any place. They maintain that tantra is useful to fulfill any worldly desire, but the highest goal is self-realization. Fulfillment is possible if the practitioner does it the proper way or selects the right type of tantra. Two ways, the "left" and the "right," are the most standard ones in classic tantra. For practicing them, everybody needs a guru.

Navin turned to Marla, "Like any mystic guru, Sirdhar had to maintain a good image of himself. As they say, charity begins at home: he was on good speaking terms with all of his siblings and their families. Two of his strengths were his handsomeness and physical strength. His tantra was neither left nor right, just Pahari folk."

Navin knew Marla's position on animal rights, "The Pahari tantra believes in *bali* or animal sacrifice. Its popularity is facilitated because Paharis love meat, beef being the only exception. The meat of the sacrificed animal is respected and eaten as *prasad*. That is sacred food, even though literally and truly it means pleasure."

In big temples, during special worships, this fresh *prasad* is distributed free, so many animals have to be sacrificed—many animals, because there are many gods and goddesses in this land, which is literally claimed by the Paharis as *Deva Bhumi* or the "land of gods." Many Hindus from the plains dispute this claim because of the practice of *bali*.

"Marla," I assured her, "Hardwar is one place in this region where no meat is allowed, let alone *bali*. This town is holy because the sacred Ganges descends down from here to the plains. For the devout, this place is Shiva's door or Hara's dwar, hence Hardwar in Hindi or Garhwali. Thousands of people come here every month to take a dip in the sacred Ganges."

"Millions of people attend Hardwar's famous sacred fair, the Kumbh Mela, so this is the best place to do Hindu religious business," Navin added. "Sirdhar knew how to circumvent the Hardwar tradition for his kind of religion."

Marla replied, "Along with Abdul, I watched Sirdhar in a ceremony in a village between Hardwar and nearby Dehradun. Before that, I didn't believe that *bali* was possible in this area. Abdul wanted to convince me. He made the arrangements for this field trip."

Abdul colored in some of the details, "The ceremony had two shamans, one *daunr* player and a *thali* or metal-plate player. They played these two instruments loudly. On top of that, there were chants in Garhwali, which would be enough to drive even unhaunted persons insane. A ghost had recently been torturing the son of a middle-aged woman, Patti. This was a male ghost. He would haunt Patti, too, when she would go to bed—a big sleeping problem for the poor woman at night."

Marla had a different opinion. In her notes, she had written: *I considered Patti's children—five of them—the real ghosts. The fifth was a son, after four girls. She was already forty-one years old when the son was born. Normally, a son after four girls would bring tremendous happiness in the male-dominant culture of India. This son caused his mother's nightmares; he was born with serious brain disorders.*

Marla considered these parents ethically insensitive to human life. The worst part of their story was that they believed that the boy's frequent epileptic seizures were caused by a ghost, so a cock sacrifice was recommended to bring this problem under control.

Abdul explained the ritual, "The sacrifice ritual began with folk prayers. The possessed Patti began to shake as the noise level of *daunr* and *thali* reached its peak. She screamed a lot and jumped up and down a lot.

Then, she suddenly threw her clothes away. She danced in a frenzy. Then, she picked up the butcher knife and swung it around in the air. Luckily, Sirdhar quickly got up, restrained her, and held her tightly under control. She became calm when he verbally promised to offer the cock to her—or rather, to the ghost. Only then did she put on her discarded clothes. As promised, Sirdhar prepared the cock sacrifice. This was a big cock, so big that first they had to tie his legs. Still, the cock struggled a lot. He tried to shake his head, but could not move it around. Despite ruffled feathers and frustrated twisting, pecking, and clucking, his complaints were ignored. His life was very valuable for the haunted woman. He had no choice. There was no evidence that he understood how helpful he was for that woman. The holy priest strangled the neck of the helpless animal. The cock cried out, but the priest kept twisting his neck. Finally, the oxygen-deprived cock was forced to collapse on the floor."

Marla interrupted, "I wanted to wring Sirdhar's neck." She was in the incipient animal rights movement. "Sirdhar Prasad began to dismember the body of the cock, with chants in Garhwali. I could not stand the bloody scene. Abdul understood my problem as I said to Sirdhar, 'I hope your head is chopped off by this cock in your next life!' Abdul politely asked Sirdhar Prasad to excuse us. We left."

Abdul knew that Marla did not believe in rebirth. He didn't either. But, he pretended to believe. "Marla, maybe the cock was a tiger in his previous life. And Sirdhar was an ass. The tiger must have enjoyed this dumb ass's assassination!"

"Ass, yes," Marla said and paused.

In her notes, I would later read: *I blame the parents of this unfortunate son: India had adopted a big family planning program. Almost anybody could get free birth control advice. This woman and her husband believed that they had the right to have any number of children. After all, India is a democracy. It isn't like China, where such irresponsible parents would be held accountable. For a woman to have a child after forty is very risky for the child. Doctors have been explaining that to the public. Do over-aged parents with children have the right to bring another baby into the world, endangering his or her life? Are there any rights for an unborn child? "To be or not to be" is not a question that an unborn child can answer. The parent can and must, honestly.*

61

# Chapter 9
# Day Three of the War

*The Lord said: One who is unattached everywhere upon receiving good or bad results and does not feel joy or jealousy, his wisdom is steady.*

*What is night of all beings is the time of the self-disciplined to remain awake. The time when other beings remain awake is the night of the seer sage.*

*—Bhagavad Gita 2.57, 69*

Yet again, the evening was met with the sound of drummers tuning up; we moved to join the people arriving to enjoy the performance. Tonight, they sang about Sanjaya's continuing description of the ongoing battle. The events were as gruesome as those of the day before. In any language and at every moment of human history, war lays bare that which lives inside of mankind.

The key event of the day involved Krishna and the vow he'd made when he agreed to participate in the war. He placed a condition on his assistance: Krishna agreed to become Arjuna's charioteer, but he would not fight. And, so, while he vowed to maintain this condition on the battlefield, he faced a dilemma on this third day of the war. Bhishma was clearly targeting Arjuna, creating chaos and trying to force Krishna to break his vow. Even Krishna was hit by the enemy's arrows. At one point, Arjuna was almost killed. Afraid Arjuna had no chance to survive, Krishna picked up his famous weapon, the disk, determined to kill Bhishma and save Arjuna.

Bhishma was delighted to see Krishna rushing towards him, armed and on foot.

"Come on, lord of the gods!" he taunted. "Drop me from my chariot. It would be the highest honor to be killed by you."

Arjuna struggled to his feet, unwilling to allow Krishna to break his vow. He convinced Krishna to retreat with him to the chariot and drive him away from the field.

Bhishma was happy to survive. Arjuna was happy to have helped Krishna keep his vow. Only, Krishna was now in a foul mood.

"Seems we have another possession," murmured a man in Garhwali to my left when the drummers were singing about how Arjuna distracted Bhishma from Krishna.

"The man shows clear signs," another replied.

"Hoot, hoot," a man shouted, dancing in a frenzied state. Screaming between shouts, the man moved quickly toward the center of the circle. His eyeballs were rolling wildly and his hands were interlocked over his head.

"Hoot, hoot," he shouted again, as a warning to all other dancers to stop and move to the sides of the circle.

The drummers played more softly and Bijlu asked him, "O my spirit! Who are you?"

"Hoot, hoot, I am Bhisam," responded the possessed man, using the Garhwali term for Bhishma.

The Pahari man looked strong enough for Bhishma's spirit. He was middle-aged and stood about five and half feet tall. He wore kurta, a tunic shirt, and pajamas and his sandals were likely from the famous Bata Shoe Company.

"Welcome, Pitamaha!" Bijlu said, using the title which showed Bhishma was the granduncle of the Kauravas and Pandavas. The man came close to the drummers and unlocked his hands, then blessed them by touching their heads with his palms.

"Hoot, hoot!"

Was this man really Bhishma in spirit? His word was not enough. It was time for the test.

Puran stood in front of him and asked, "Are you really Bhishma?"

"Hoot, hoot! I am really Pitamaha," the man shouted, sounding quite genuine. His body was shaking and he nodded his head.

"Did you say *ehi ehi devesha* to Arjuna?" Puran demanded.

"Hoot, hoot!"

"What is the meaning of *ehi ehi devesha*?"

"Hoot, hoot."

"I asked you the meaning of *ehi ehi devesha*! If you are truly Bhishma, you will tell me the meaning."

Puran was asking for a translation of the Sanskrit saying for, "Come on, come on, lord of the gods," the taunt Bhishma had issued to Krishna.

"Ask me in Garhwali or Hindi," the man said in a trembling voice.

The crowd around him laughed, turning their attention back to the song. The drummers, ignoring the man, encouraged him to rejoin the audience and ended the song addressing Krishna's behavior: "Arjuna wondered how Yogeshvara, the god of Yoga, could have an attachment problem. But it's all the *maya*, the illusive power of the lord. Fools don't understand it."

The Pahari man who had been so given to hooting just a moment before glared at them, turned, and ran away.

# Chapter 10
# Rewat's Rage

The following day upon joining us on the veranda, the Thakurs continued the saga of the Tiwari clan. Puran began the tale.

"Gobardhan's oldest son, Rewat, was no better than his father, perhaps worse in some ways. His greatest achievement was passing his high school examination with no division, missing only a few points in one subject. Of course, it took him years to do so."

"As we mentioned yesterday, Rewat was married and had two daughters and two sons. When his wife died, there were those who suggested he had suffocated her with a pillow. The eldest child, Sarika, left school and took over the domestic chores. Fortunately, Rewat managed to hold onto his clerical job in Simla longer than his previous jobs, thanks to his cousin, Girija."

"That all changed when Sarika got married. Rewat arranged the marriage. Sarika was a beautiful girl and her husband was only a few years younger than her father. The combination jacked up the bride price considerably. Rewat earned a great deal of cash by selling Sarika to her husband."

"I thought brides provided dowries," Marla said, looking confused.

"Normally, a dowry is customary. It may be cash, but more often it is material goods. However, the bride price is also part of custom and is very useful for her parents, as it's usually cash. A bride is an artifact," Puran explained. "Decorate her until the last day. Everyone has to be convinced about her salability until given away."

Marla scribbled in her notes. Looking over her shoulder, I read: *Commodification of women is worldwide.*

Puran continued the story.

"Sarika didn't get the best of the bargain. Her husband, Manad, had a first wife who'd left him. It was not uncommon for a disgruntled wife to live with her parents instead of her husband. Legal divorce was unheard of in those times. With her mother dead, Sarika had no such option."

"In addition, Manad was neither a Pahari, nor a Brahmin. He'd lied about being from a Himalayan Brahmin family. Still, there was little Sarika could do. At least she had a son, who would inherit the wealth of his father."

Marla made another note: *The husband's salability never in question. He was the customer. The more commodities a male has, the higher he is.*

Puran said, "Flush with the heavy bride price, Rewat quit his job and left his village, promising he'd return for his other three children. Girija had a family of his own, but he was a kind man and reluctantly agreed. So, Rewat opened a little bookstore in Pauri. He was selling popular books, for example, books such as *Kok Shastra, Kama Sutra, Herbs for Manpower, Left Hand Tantra,* etc.— sex-related books translated from Sanskrit into Hindi." He shook his head, showing his clear disapproval of Rewat's base behavior.

Making another face that the story would just get worse, Puran continued, "Girija visited his village and brought Rewat's children along. They all went to Pauri to see the bookstore. They found not only such books, but also bottles—the eight ounce *addhya* bottles made for alcohol. Rewat was a bootlegger; the bookstore was nothing but a front. The next day, Girija left the village along with Rewat's children. He was upset by Rewat's refusal to stop his shameful business. The night before, there had been a terrible verbal skirmish with Rewat about his illicit business of alcohol, books on sex, and neglect of the children. Girija could have used his muscles, but it would not have looked like an act of bravery in front of the children."

Navin joined into the narration, offering some explanation as soon as Puran took a breath, "Rewat expanded his business, in a way. He paid off legally the debt that he and Lalit had jointly inherited from their father's failed contracts. Rewat was responsible only for his half of the debt, but in that case, the Maharaja government was going to take almost all of Lalit's fields for his share of the debt. Lalit was upset because Rewat didn't consult his mother, Runi—or his wife, Pushpa, either. Rewat did tell Lalit that it was a surprise gift. Lalit had just started his new military job in Dehradun. He was just a clerk at the IMA. He had to take care of his two small children, along with a wife and a widowed mother, who all lived in Daya Gad, while Lalit was living here in Dehradun. Their seven year old son, Shans, had just started the first grade in the local primary school. The daughter, Mala, was just three years old."

Puran related the story, again, at his own speed, "The gift turned into a trauma for Lalit's family in Daya Gad. Rewat began to harass Lalit's family. It was now clear what Rewat meant by gift. He wanted to grab Lalit's fields. The village kept watching, but did nothing to help this family. Even Judge Sahab, Lalit's uncle, didn't do anything. The judge's son was a police officer; he didn't do anything, either. All parties had a reason: How do you punish a *pagal*? Everyone considered Rewat a *pagal,* a lunatic."

Rewat's motives were pretty clear to the Thakur brothers. Rithi, the mother of the Thakurs, was very friendly with Runi, Lalit's mother. They would share each other's experiences. Runi had told Rithi that she thought that Judge Sahab could protect her family and asked for their help. Upon his wife's insistence, Bodha, the father of the Thakurs, mentioned Rewat's motives to Jag.

"But the Judge remained completely neutral. So did his son Durlabh, who was already a police officer. Durlabh was afraid of Rewat: Rewat knew Durlabh's Achilles' heel," Puran commented. "Rewat knew Durlabh's deepest secret, which he could reveal in his wild moods."

About seventeen acres of Lalit's land were too cheap for the twelve hundred rupees' debt Rewat paid off. The only property Lalit had was a house with an attached orchard. Half the house—two rooms—belonged to Rewat. The forest was common property of the Tiwari clan. When Lalit's son, Shans, was seven years old, he was in first grade at the primary school, about a mile from Daya Gad, located at the end of the forest. To reach the school, the children from Daya Gad had to cross a creek. During the rainy season, the creek swelled and they had to search for a safe crossing place. One rainy afternoon, Shans saw his uncle waiting for him by the creek, holding an umbrella. Shans was grateful for the favor. Rewat held Shans' hand and led him to an area of deep water.

Shans' grandmother, Runi, hiding in the trees, watched in horror as Rewat put his hands around Shans' neck. She wanted to scream a warning, but no sound came from her throat. No, divine intervention called instead.

Emerging from the forest, boyish shouts forced Rewat to release Shans and step back before he could carry out the murder.

"Here come those *bhainchod* boys," he exclaimed in disgust, referring to them as sister-fuckers.

"Go join them!"

Shans ran away from his uncle and saw his grandmother in the trees. She reached for him and drew him close, sobbing as she hugged him.

After the incident at the creek, Shans avoided Rewat, making sure he was never alone with him. A few weeks later, he was returning home from Pauri and saw Rewat. Instead of taking the open trail to Daya Gad, he ran into the forest. It was some time before a small search party of his friends found him and learned of his fears.

The friends decided Rewat needed a lesson. They approached him and respectfully told him they'd found a large pool in the Daya Gad stream, full of trout. They offered to take him fishing there the following Sunday.

Only one boy arrived to guide him. Rewat settled in with his fishing equipment and spent an enjoyable afternoon catching trout. As it began to get dark, he felt the sting of a rock, then another. Suddenly rocks rained down on him until he collapsed. The next day, he limped home.

A year later, Rewat closed his bookstore and left the village, much to Shans' relief. Lalit's whole family breathed easier. Rewat had continued to bully them and no one had been there to stop him.

Lalit hadn't been home throughout their trauma. With the advent of the Second World War, he'd been transferred to Kohima, near the Burma border. With Lalit gone and no help from villagers, the family had been at Rewat's mercy; they were relieved to have him disappear.

Their relief was short-lived, however. A few months later, Rewat returned looking pleased and, surprisingly, accompanied by a woman. He introduced her to Shans as his aunt. Shans' mother and grandmother accepted her into the family.

With his new wife's help, Rewat reopened his bookstore in Pauri. However, three months later, the woman disappeared, again leaving Rewat alone. Rumors spread through the village.

"He'd abused her, physically and verbally," some said.

"She was a widow," others said, "a woman of about forty."

"Was she an abandoned wife?"

"An unmarried woman?"

"Where had she gone?"

Rewat sought Durlabh's help, asserting that the police office should have been able to locate her. Durlabh not only refused to help, he warned Rewat that pushing this to a conclusion would end badly for all parties.

"Rewat, we're against trying to find her, since she wasn't legally your wife."

With Rewat's return, Shans' trauma came back, worse this time. One evening, Rewat came home. In the middle of that night, he knocked on the door of the room where all four—Shans and his sister with his mother and grandmother—were sleeping. There was only one old wooden chair in the room. The women got up quietly with slightly veiled faces, for the tradition required the veil over the face of Lalit's wife. Rewat was the older brother of her husband, but Runi was his step-mother. Having watched from the forest as he almost drowned Shans, Runi was scared of him; otherwise, she didn't need the veil. She would not even speak to Rewat.

Upon entering, Rewat threw down the big quilt that was on the chair. He sat on it. Then he shouted, "I want my money." He was referring to their twelve hundred rupees' debt he had paid off to the Maharaja.

"I want my money right now. Do you hear me, you two women?"

His black eyes had roamed around the room, questioning them.

"Why did my stupid father need more whores? Why did he need more children from those whores? Here I am, carrying the load of that dead man's bad karma! How long can I carry this load? Give me my money, right now. I am going to burn this place some day. You better give me my money…"

He kept on intimidating them. They kept quiet throughout the entire encounter, about two hours. Fortunately, he didn't lay his hands on anyone.

A week later, Rewat repeated the same kind of session late at night. Runi and Pushpa abandoned the house as soon as he went away. They would find no peace there any longer. They left to seek refuge.

Across the forest was another village. There, Runi's cousin, Balwant, lived with his children and mother. His old mother was Runi's maternal aunt. With Balwant's big family and only two rooms and a small kitchen, there was no space for Runi's family of four. But on Pushpa's suggestion, a portion of their cowshed was made available. On the other half of the cowshed there was just a cow and her calf. A wood panel divided the cowshed into two portions. Despite the smell of cow dung and urine, the family of four was quite happy. They were out of Rewat's reach. Balwant had a Post Office job at Pauri, but every evening he would come back home. They had no fear of Rewat.

About six months after all of this, Lalit got special leave. He came back and took the family back to the Daya Gad home. There, he confronted Rewat, who had no idea of Lalit's sudden presence. Lalit was in his military uniform, to intimidate Rewat. They had some arguments.

Rewat told him, "I never asked your family to leave the house; that was your family's decision. All I asked them about was money. I need money desperately."

Lalit understood, "I promise to return the money as soon as the war is over."

Rewat promised, "I'll not bother your family again."

After a few days, Lalit left for Kohima. Within a few months, the family went back to the cowshed. Unfortunately, Rewat had reverted to his old habits and Runi didn't want any trauma. Pushpa was pregnant. Unfortunately, the cowshed looked unsafe this time. A month earlier a tiger had killed the calf, who was wandering just outside the cowshed. The war was in full swing; Lalit had no chance to get any special leave so soon.

A daughter was born to Pushpa in the cowshed. She was named Gopa, protector of the cows.

Meanwhile, Rewat disappeared again, but not quietly. He showed up in Simla. Girija knew why he was coming. Rewat wanted to make arrangements for his second daughter's marriage. Uma, the daughter, was well aware of what happened with her older sister. Her two brothers were very smart. The older was to graduate from the IMA. Another was just admitted to the same military academy.

Puran explained, "So, Uma had her own independent plans. She fled with her college classmate. It became quite a headache for Girija's family. For one thing, her classmate was a Muslim. Second, the couple could not be located anywhere. Except for Uma's two brothers, everyone in the family was opposed to this marriage. The opposition was not unified, however; some did not like the entire episode. Others thought that religion should have been out. The youngsters, for their part, did not like the name change that Uma would go through upon converting to Islam. Her new name became Ummeed. It translates as Hope."

Navin cut in to add a slightly different point, "Lalit was lucky. He got special leave to see his new daughter. This time, he met Rewat in Pauri and paid off his debt to Rewat: some cash and the two rooms of his Daya Gad house. Additionally, the big orchard attached to the house went to Rewat for free. Lalit wanted to distance his residence from Rewat's. Rewat allowed Lalit to stay in the old house for six months. Lalit was going to build a small new house, to be completed within that period."

Navin's tone indicated we were nearing the end of the story, "Now, Rewat had money. It became obvious when a happy thing happened to him. He disappeared for the next four months. One Sunday afternoon, he appeared at his Daya Gad home. He was not alone. There were four men, two young and two middle-aged. They were followed by two strong young men carrying a *doli*, the carriage for a bride. There was indeed a woman seated in the *doli*. The woman looked the age of Rewat's daughters. As soon as the team entered the front yard Rewat shouted joyfully, 'Shans, dear! Where are you? Come out!' Shans was home. It was Sunday. He came out. Rewat said, 'Welcome your new Tai ji!'"

Puran nodded, took over the narrative from Navin, and concluded the emotional saga of the Tiwari clan, "But this time, it was not like before. This time, the sobbing young woman was greeted by Runi and Pushpa. They understood everything. The couple was odd in terms of age, but they were married legally. She turned out to be complacent. In spite of all her unfortunate circumstances, she began to change Rewat, so much so that Lalit and Rewat never quarreled again. They remained as two brothers should."

# Chapter 11
# Day Four of the War

*In the beginning there was neither non-existence nor existence...*
*Seers searching in their hearts with intellect,*
*Discovered the bond of existence in non-existence.*
                    —*Rigveda, Nasadiya Sukta 10.129*

*The Lord said: There is never presence of nonexistence. There is never*
*absence of existence. Such conclusion of both has been observed by the seers*
*of facts.*
                    —*Bhagavad Gita 2.16*

The battle sung by the drummers on this day was as fierce as any of the preceding days. One of the battles was heartbreaking for Dhritarashtra. And Sanjaya, taking heart from the Pandavas' recent success, felt enthusiastic as he continued narrating.

Duryodhana became angry when he saw his rival, Bhima, fighting with his mace. Bhima hit Kaurava's soldiers so hard that some died instantly. Duryodhana and his brother Nandaka quickly shot Bhima in his chest to parlay his attack. His attention grabbed, Bhima quickly returned to his chariot and ordered his charioteer to move in the direction of Duryodhana. Vishoka, the charioteer, did exactly that.

Bhima came closer, shooting at Duryodhana with sharp arrows. An excellent swordsman, Duryodhana cut the arrows off in mid-air and returned the attack by hitting Bhima's charioteer, Vishoka, with three arrows. Confusion reigned as Vishoka cursed at his wounds and fought for control of the chariot.

Not wanting to loose momentum in the skirmish, Bhima called Vishoka to steady the chariot and notched another arrow into his bow, shooting at and

75

hitting Duryodhana's bow. But Duryodhana, a masterful warrior, quickly took up another bow, aimed at Bhima's chest and shot an arrow which squarely hit him.

Bhima lost consciousness temporarily from his wound. Dhritarashtra's fourteen sons surrounded Bhima with their arrows. It looked like sure death for Bhima, but he was also a powerfully tough warrior who had trained for battle for many years. Upon regaining consciousness, he began to shoot arrows with speed and with skill. Instead, Bhima killed Duryodhana's two brothers, who were also named Bhima and Bhimaratha. Again, as with battle everywhere, confusion reigned: Which Bhima killed which Bhima? Soon, it became clear.

The blind king burst into tears. He had lost two sons. The Kauravas looked dumb and defeated. That was what Sanjaya told Dhritarashtra. Upon hearing this, the blind king complained, "Sanjaya, I believe that destiny alone is above bravery. So the army of my son is crushed by the army of the Pandavas. Look what Bhima did to my sons! You praise when my sons are dead. You always praise the undaunted and overjoyed Pandavas...I don't see a solution by which the Pandavas could be defeated and mine could obtain victory."

Sanjaya said, as if in retaliation, "For this destruction of human bodies, elephants, horses and chariots, you alone are the cause of this mega-disaster. Listen, O King, patiently."

Then he listed Dhritarashtra's misjudgments of the past. In support of the Pandavas, he showed how Duryodhana's vanity was the reason for the terrible losses suffered by the Kaurava forces. To the old blind king, Sanjaya quoted Bhishma's address to Duryodhana thus: "Listen, O King, to the words that I say! I have given advice many times before, but you didn't follow it. I tell you again, make peace with the Pandavas now."

Sanjaya then related to the old king so far from the battlefield that Duryodhana had ignored the advice again. Using his remote viewing technique, Sanjaya saw Bhishma there, surveying the day's dead and wounded, and saying angrily to Duryodhana, "I consider you a damn demon. You are covered with darkness. You hate Krishna and Arjuna. They are Narayana and Nara. Who could afford animosity against these gods?"

After saying this, Bhishma acknowledged that Krishna was the Lord of the creation, sustenance and dissolution of the universe. The great epic quotes him as saying, "He created time, the past, the present, the future. He created the first being, Samkarshana. From him came Narayana. A lotus was born on his navel. From that came Brahma, the creation god. All these creations came from him. He created Shesha, the remainder, which is the infinite Ananta. Thus, Krishna creates and recreates."

Drawing the creed to a crescendo, Bhishma concluded, "Krishna is born here as the son of Devaki and Vasudeva to destroy the wicked. He is named Vāsudeva after his father. He has many names such as Govinda, Janardana, Madhava, Hari, Keshava. He is born of himself. He is the actor and action. He is the guru of all. Where Krishna is, dharma is there. Where dharma is, victory is there."

Sanjaya related that Duryodhana did not really seem impressed with the fantastic praises of Krishna by the old granduncle. He must have seen how the Lord of the Cosmos couldn't kill his old granduncle. Bhishma sensed the disbelief not in his words, but in his eyes. Sanjaya communicates that he proceeded to quote ancient sages as authorities who had proclaimed Narayana's glory. He never quoted the *Rigveda,* which has a different view of the creation of the cosmos. In that moment and on that battlefield, Bhishma punctuated his belief system to Duryodhana, as well as through Sanjaya to the old blind king, Dhritarashtra. There, he made a biting and incisive point.

"Only the persons of wisdom comprehend this mystery in meditation. One of the wisest sages was Markandeya. He has affirmed this mystery. Bhrigu and Devala also praised Krishna like this. Listen! I advise you to make peace with the Pandavas. Krishna is on their side."

It was already evening as this conversation came to a head. Duryodhana, always the stubborn bully, wouldn't listen and insisted on continuing the war. They both left for their camps.

Sanjaya wanted to say more, but the king was too dejected. Sanjaya was not a fair reporter; he was giving his biases. Not able to take anymore, the old blind king requested recess; he wanted to rest.

During that day's session, a man was possessed. He was a total stranger like many present, except that he was in ochre robes—the traditional outfit of a monk. We thought that he was a swami or a temple priest. I had never seen a man in ochre robes possessed in *Pandau,* so I paid very serious attention to this middle-aged man with an average Pahari height. Puran and Navin were equally interested in his possession, so much so that they interrupted the drummers. Puran took the dhol from Bijlu. Likewise, Navin took the damau from Daphra. Both increased the speed of the rhythm. Caught in the tangle of the ecstatic cross rhythms, the possessed man matched them with his swift movements. Then, Puran addressed the man in Hindi, "*Sachcha jogi hoga to sir par khara ho jayega*," meaning, "One who is a true yogi will stand on his head."

Navin matched the rap. "*Sir par khara ho ja.*" Stand on your head.

The yogi really stood on his head—a posture known as *Shirshasana* or "headstand" in Hatha Yoga. While standing like that, he said in Hindi, "I am Arjuna. I know yoga."

"If you are Arjuna then tell us, where are your wives?"

"What wives?"

"You don't know them?"

"Krishna asked me to be a yogi: *tasmād yogī bhavārjuna*. I have no wives. I am Krishna's devotee. Krishna is the Lord of Yoga, Yogeshvara."

"That's why we asked you this question. Like guru: like disciple."

"Ask me another question."

"What is your real name?"

"Arjuna."

"You are not Arjuna if you don't know who your wives are. Get up and find them. Do you know where your children are?"

There was big laughter all around. I should give him credit for quoting the *Bhagavad Gita* and how easily he stood on his head. But the *Gita* has no mention of headstand. It teaches yoga's *dhyāna* or meditation, but no such postures.

More surprising was that I witnessed the two higher caste men playing these drums, and with authenticity. It is possible that someday Bijlu's and Daphra's wouldn't like to associate themselves with *dhol* and *damau*; playing these drums would, after all, perpetuate their untouchable caste. Then, the only hope of saving this fascinating drumming would be through the higher castes, like Puran and Navin, I thought. Obviously, these brothers must have accepted some low caste drummers as their teachers. These brothers were liberated Hindus who, unlike my father for example, ate any food with my drummers.

# Chapter 12
# Hanuman's Heroic Problem

Hanuman Prasad Tiwari, or Ranger, showed up today. The drummers looked very surprised. "He is our hero," Bijlu said loudly as he saw him.

Daphra nodded his head. "He is as great as the Judge."

Judge Jag Tarak Tiwari was Ranger's distant cousin, but they were more like father and son in age. Ranger might have been six or seven years older than Judge's son, Durlabh.

His fame as a hero was quite literally monumental. The continuous flow of bribe money made this monument possible. People called this bribe *dakshina*, the cash gift to a priest for his services. Hanuman Prasad was a Brahmin by caste. There was material evidence for some sort of huge cash flow as a fancy nine-story apartment building emerged in Pauri. This was the tallest building in this entire region. Some of its features fascinated people's imaginations.

The whole building looked spliced to the natural mountain wall in the back. Each story had two apartments side by side. A separate pathway, following the contour of the hilly wall, led to the entrance of each apartment. Sixteen entrances altogether were all linked to a common road ahead. This gave privacy to the owner of each apartment. The most important aesthetic feature was the view. From each apartment, the roof of the world was visible straight ahead. This roof is known here as the Chaukhambha Himalayan range.

"How could you make such an incredible building?" I asked him in astonishment.

He misunderstood me, as he replied, scratching his head, "People around here have a misunderstanding about me and this building. There are rumors that I took bribes from the forest contractors. I never took any bribes. It is true that a contractor would slip an envelope in my pants' pocket because they made good profits. I would scold them not to slip anything in my pocket. But they would insist that it wasn't a bribe. It was just a *dakshina*. After all I am a Brahmin."

I had no misunderstanding. The *dakshina* he mentioned is open to anyone, priest or no priest. It is given to all gods—humans in power.

The other thing he told me turned out to be more incredible.

"You just heard how great Judge Sahab was. He was really a very funny man. The old man wanted me to be his proxy to marry a young woman!" He said this to me in a soft voice, almost whispering.

"What?" I exclaimed.

"It's a long story."

Maybe he was hesitant to continue as he saw Marla and Abdul approaching us.

Abdul came close and touched Ranger's feet. Then, Abdul introduced Marla. She said the usual "namaste." Hanuman looked very pleased. Marla said, "I have heard about you from the drummers. You are a famous hero."

"No, no, I am not. That's very kind of them," Hanuman Prasad said with a smile of humility.

"Ranger Sahab is really like Hanuman—very humble about his achievements," Abdul said to all of us gathered around.

"So, do you recite *Hanuman Chalisa* everyday?" Marla looked very innocent when she asked this, but we all laughed.

"You are like my daughter, very inquisitive. She is finishing her master's degree in psychology. Why people say and do whatever they say or do—that's her interest. Here is what I do as a religious man. I recite the *Bhagavad Gita*, one chapter every day before my breakfast." He began to unfold his background, "I firmly believe Lord Krishna is Bhagavan..."

"Sir, but you are named Hanuman Prasad? Hanuman was Lord Rama's devotee," Marla interrupted with excitement.

"My parents visited a famous Hanuman temple and did recite the famous prayer, the *Hanuman Chalisa*..."

"Like the 'Lord's Prayer' in Christian churches," Marla interpreted out loud mostly for herself.

"And a miracle occurred: my mother had me a year later," Ranger nodded with a smile and a nod toward Marla.

Abdul and the Thakurs, too, were all smiles.

With a look of amazement written all over her face, Marla asked

Ranger, "Were your parents serious?"

"Serious about what?"

"That your mother became pregnant due to Hanuman's prayer?"

"Hanuman is the son of the wind god. Like the wind, he is everywhere. With devotion you can breathe his blessing. That's how my parents expressed their faith in Hanuman."

"Everywhere? Hanuman's wind is not felt in the neighboring Afghanistan." Abdul added his own version of demythification to Marla's rationality.

Ranger took the disagreement in good humor. He seemed interested in entertaining, as well as in educating Marla. "In my primary school days, classmates had fun with my name. They said that I really look like a monkey. Some even challenged me to unbutton my pants; they wanted to see if I had a tail!"

Pausing to let the polite laughter subside, Ranger continued, "But my parents literally believed the *Ramayana* story. It says that Hanuman promised Lord Rama to find his wife Sita. Lanka's evil king Ravana had kidnapped Rama's wife Sita. In revenge, Hanuman burned down the Ravana's capital. Rama defeated Ravana and regained Sita. Hanuman was given the highest honor for winning this war. Unlike modern politicians, he never bragged about his heroic deeds. His prayer is used to overcome any obstacle."

Turning from the ancient to a more modern discourse, Ranger unfurled a little more of his personal history, "My younger brother, Parmesh, was inspired by the great prime minister of India, Jawaharlal Nehru from Allahabad. He was not interested in religion. Parmesh was a student then at Allahabad University. He raised doubts with our parents like these: Hanuman's prayers couldn't burn a single tent of the British East India Company. Maybe English was an obstacle. Did Hanuman really speak Sanskrit? The epic *Ramayana* is in Sanskrit. I can speak English, but not Sanskrit."

Ranger laughed at the irony.

"I like Hanuman. You cannot sacrifice animals to please him," Marla said.

"Monkeys don't eat meat," Jennifer clarified with a sweet smile.

Hanuman Prasad laughed again, punctuating his comment with a serious face at the end, "I eat meat."

"I know. My Hindu friends believe in Ganesha. I told them that

Ganesha was half elephant and that elephant worshippers eating meat seems problematic."

Jennifer seemed to stun Hanuman Prasad.

"Ganesh was born here. Parvati created him here out of her body's sweat. I worship him. He removes my obstacles," he said, evading the meat-eating contradiction.

Abdul supported Hanuman's character even further, "But Ganesh ji has two wives. Hanuman is really great. He was not even married. With India's burgeoning population, we need more Hanumans than humans...and Lord Rama cared for his wife. Sita was the only wife he had."

Maybe Abdul said this because he was not married, at least not yet. Also, he seemed to respect interfaith unity. He should, naturally. After all, he was a Muslim orphan adopted and raised by Hindu parents. They raised him that way, keeping him in his original religion of Islam. Maybe his college education gave him this license: Think critically; express critically. Marla and Jennifer must have liked his critical thinking. Unfortunately, his comment sat poorly with our esteemed guest.

He immediately left the scene. The drummers looked at Abdul with some sort of discomfort on their faces. I was also puzzled.

Abdul obviously noticed the discomfort around. Shaking his head, he offered an explanation as to why Ranger had walked away. He said, "If Ranger was a woman in the Middle East, he would have been stoned to death."

And, as Ranger disappeared from sight, Abdul could do nothing but continue to defend his perspective.

"Why?" Marla asked him, showing her different sort of discomfort.

"You know why: An adultery-committing woman must be stoned to death," Abdul said, clearly unhappy that she would call into question his comment.

"Abdul means we know who these folk heroes are, in and out," Puran interrupted in a sort of confident tone. "There is always a dark side of any hero. Some know it, but don't want to mention it."

I thought that they had told me enough about the Judge. I could not control my curiosity. "What is this proxy marriage Ranger was talking about?"

Both Thakurs nodded their heads as if clear to them.

"Ranger loved money and whatever came along with it. He was already married. But his wife, Sampatti, resented his flirtations. The songs in his praise do mention that he was a romantic man. He was a very handsome man in his young days," Puran elaborated further.

I told him, "Tula was impressed by his handsomeness even now."

"So, it was easy for *poor* women to fall for his money and attraction!" Puran quipped.

I laughed.

"I am serious," he insisted with no smile on his face. "He began to beat his wife, maybe because she spoke against adultery, maybe for not having a child. Regardless, after five years of living in childless monogamy, Ranger arranged another marriage for himself."

"So, Judge Sahab knew that Ranger could arrange a marriage on his own!" I interrupted, jumping to the conclusion.

"It's a long story," Puran said with a sigh.

Of course, we cannot cover anyone's life in short, random notes like ours. But when Puran sighed, I said, "I want to know more. After all, they are my relatives, even though distantly."

Durlabh was the only son the Judge had. That I had known long ago. I also knew how he died.

"The Judge was a traditional Hindu. He never counted his daughters as his progeny. They are married and they belong to their husbands' families. Evidence for this is that their family names change. The Judge didn't care about biology. That is, about his common blood in his son and daughters. He needed a male child in his direct line."

Puran began to unfold the drama.

"I had no idea why Durlabh shot himself. My father knew all the details. He said that Durlabh faulted Nanda Prasad and Rewat. These two cousins knew that Durlabh had a secret son from an untouchable woman."

Puran went on to explain how Durlabh left a note before his suicide. The note stated very clearly: *Never trust my two cousins, Nanda and Rewat.*

They were trying to blackmail him. Durlabh didn't want his father to know about his secret grandson. But these two crooks, Nanda and Rewat, were intimidating him. They knew he had a secret which could be used to control him.

"My father hated these crooks." Puran added, with disgust on his face.

The Judge thought of marrying again, just one year after the death of his son. But he was an old man. No matter how much wealth he had, it was not enough to buy him a bride. So he asked Hanuman Prasad, his own distant cousin, for a proxy wedding. Hanuman Prasad declined. Marry a young woman for somebody else?! He could not do this fraudulent *dakshina* business, even when the Judge guaranteed his legal protection.

The second wife of Hanuman Prasad turned out to be not only docile, but also tolerant. Bimla accepted him as he was. That made him quite happy, so much so that he lived in Pauri with her. He left Sampatti in the village home. Once in a while, he would ride his horse and visit his village. Whenever he would go to Daya Gad, he would invariably beat Sampatti. On a couple of occasions, the father of the Thakurs stopped him from beating her. But the village people made no attempt to rescue her. It was considered a family matter.

Bimla, on the other hand remained safe. She was able to have four children with Hanuman Prasad. As the father of two boys and two girls, he became more serious. When the last girl was born, his famous nine-story building was completed. That's why he named her Purti, meaning "Completion."

A few years later, Ranger became more serious. His oldest son failed again in his high school examination. Mukut was not a bright child from the beginning. The second son was Bhushan. He passed his high school examination in the first division. That's when Ranger decided to leave his job and move to Dehradun with his second wife and the three children. The first wife lived in Daya Gad.

Actually, Ranger had another strong reason to move out. Mukut began to drink with his old buddies. These buddies, about five or six of them, were like Mukut. None of them ever passed the high school exam. They formed a gang. Mukut was the head. They would get drunk and beat anybody for no reason. Mukut lived in an apartment in the famous building of his father. Occasionally he would live in his village. Sampatti, his step-mother, would cook food for him. Yet, he would beat her when drunk.

Once, Parmesh came home from Allahabad. He heard Mukut's bragging. "Look at our building… what a great view… my father's praise is sung… my uncle studied at Allahabad…my brother is going to IMA…"

Parmesh warned him of his vicarious achievements: "You can't go to IMA or any great school of India; you can't buy any real estate; you have no record of having any stable job; you can't even buy a horse. Can you get a wife? Anyone can be successful anywhere—place or time do not matter, our brains do. You could start your own business right here, if you want to. Whatever you do, though, don't talk if you can't deliver. Leave the gang. And, above all, don't drink!"

In the presence of Uncle Parmesh, Mukut remained sober. But as soon as Parmesh left, he went back to his gang. There was no lasting change in his actions.

Eventually, the gang grew a little larger. The new members didn't like Mukut's leadership. At one point, he broke his leg in a fight with a challenger. His father came home and saw him walking with a cane, but it was only when Hanuman Prasad received threats from the gang members that he recognized how out of control his son had become. He quickly left for Dehradun, without Mukut.

"Hanuman didn't count in Dehradun. This town had big military officers, lawyers, doctors, writers, administrators, real estate owners, ministers, and basmati dealers," Puran said.

Ranger, like the Judge, didn't count much for my father, either. My father also had no respect for men with many wives and material possessions. He used the *Bhagavad Gita* word *mithyācāra,* "false ethicist," for them. My father took his position from the verse in which Krishna says to Arjuna, "He who controls the senses and then broods over the objects of the senses is a confused person. Such a person is called a false ethicist."

There is no mention in the conversation of these two polygamists— Krishna and Arjuna—like this: "You are a confused person when each wife wants you at once, so you should consider control of the senses before having the objects of the senses." Dad would not get this. He had only my mother. And he has been very faithful, thus quite confused. I never told him about the serious contradiction he failed to see in his own experience.

I have to bite my tongue whenever I confront devotees. We in academia know that religious and rational approaches are diametrically opposed to each other.

# Chapter 13
# Day Five of the War

*The Lord said: A person's attachment grows on worldly matters as he keeps meditating on them. From attachment grows lust. From lust grows anger. From anger comes confusion, breakdown of memory from confusion, loss of reasoning from memory breakdown. From the loss of reasoning he is destroyed.*

*—Bhagavad Gita: 2.62, 63*

The sound of the drums drew us to the next performance and away from our contemplations of our experience earlier with Ranger. The Pandavas and Kauravas were again arranged against one another for yet another day of battle.

The drummers sang that Bhishma headed a formation that looked like a crocodile. He attacked the Pandavas' formation, which looked like a hawk. Arjuna rained arrows over the soldiers of Bhishma. He almost killed Bhishma. Remembering how some of his brothers were slain earlier, Duryodhana panicked. He decided to talk to Drona, the *acharya* or professor of military science.

"O unblemished Acharya! You are always our benefactor. We count on you and granduncle Bhishma. There is no doubt that we look up to you to win even against the gods in the battle. Do whatever good you can so that the Pandavas are devoid of strength and killed."

Drona reprimanded, "You are stubborn. You don't understand the valor of the Pandavas. The Pandavas cannot be defeated that easily, as they are mighty. For you, we are doing as much as possible with our full energy and strength."

Having said so, Drona forced his entry into the Pandava army formation. The Pandava commander, Satyaki, was watching, but could not stop Drona's onslaught. With everyone engaged in fierce fighting, Abhimanyu and the sons of Draupadi joined together and invaded the troops of the Kauravas as a counter-attack which might drive Drona away.

Shikhandin got close to Bhishma, but Bhishma quickly avoided him. He remembered that Shikhandin was a woman in the past. An attack on a woman was against Bhishma's vow. In order to draw Shikhandin away from Bhishma, Duryodhana speedily engaged Shikhandin in the middle. The fighting was fierce. Yudhishthira, Arjuna, Bhima, Nakula and Sahadeva—all five Pandava brothers—were fighting at their best.

In the afternoon, destruction was constant. It could not be sated or silenced. Wounded soldiers, elephants and horses fell in pain. Some moaned, some groaned, some cried, some were completely paralyzed. Nothing could stop the war until the evening. Every warrior not yet hurt looked for victory.

The drummers ended the evening with these words, "Listen, sisters and brothers! This is a sad story of warriors fighting with the mask of dharma. Morarji Desai should have lost the election. He believes in desi roti. Indira Gandhi should have won election again. She believes in double roti."

# Chapter 14
# Marla

The weather was mild today, so nobody was wearing sweaters or jackets. I told the Thakurs the day before that Marla had trained in Indian music in the U.S.A. Today, Navin and Puran brought with them a harmonium and a pair of tabla drums. Marla stunned them when she sang a Hindi composition. It was in raga *Yaman-Kalyan* with the sixteen-beat rhythm *tin tal*:

*Piya ki najariya jadu bhari*
*Moha liyo mana prema bhari*
"My beloved's look is filled with magic.
Full of love, it has enchanted my mind."

The Thakurs looked impressed while accompanying her. Sometimes they nodded their heads, sometimes throwing up their hands, sometimes widening their eyes and many times saying, "*Wah, wah.*"

"Marla, you did marvelously with the use of F and F sharp," Puran demonstrated on the harmonium.

"What other talents do you have?" Navin asked her.

She just smiled.

Tula, too, praised her for the talent she displayed. She also appreciated the other display—her dress. "Your blouse and sari match is perfect," Tula said with a smile.

"Thanks. It's all Abdul's selection."

Tula had a different opinion a few minutes later, though. We were alone for more tea in the kitchen. She said, "Abdul went too far. I never saw Marla's navel area so much open before. Look at her sari. That six-yard long cloth was manipulated to uncover what should be covered. The blouse was also manipulated likewise—the breasts exposed close to the nipples. She didn't need this manipulation. She is naturally so attractive, like the goddesses in Indian temple iconography. "

Obviously, Tula was too serious. Trying to lighten her mood, I joked, "Thank goodness Marla was not like those goddesses—nude, if it were not for their overarching jewelry."

Abdul had more information about her than others, as he had been organizing her field trips. My father knew Abdul's background very well. His Hindu foster parents were Dad's friends and distant relatives. I gently reassured and reminded Tula, "Abdul came with good references and is widely trusted, Abdul was recommended to Marla and Jennifer by Dad. The Thakurs also trust Abdul. So does Marla. Once in a while she tells us about her experiences. Some of her personal information is already out through Abdul."

For example, Abdul knew who her ex-husband was.

Marla met her ex-husband, Kewal Singh, in Seattle. He was her classmate. Her interest was India. It sounds terrible, but she understood his value for her work. Kewal was from central India, but was not a tribal man from there. He was a medium-sized, handsome brown Indian. Marla was quite tall compared to Indian girls, and very pretty. The two got married.

Marla said to me once, "I knew that several American social scientists had married natives. The native spouses facilitated their fieldwork. Sex was found very useful for scholarship, even outside marriage."

I added, "Many researchers have left behind their progeny out of promiscuity. Anybody could recognize such children by the color of their skin—half Indian and half white. In certain areas, like central India, poor tribal people have been exploited a lot."

Marla's fieldwork involved Hindu temples. "Big temples of India have been studied a lot, but what about small temples?" She added, changing the topic to a more familiar area, "I want to do some research on this topic."

"The Garhwal Himalaya," she was told by locals, "...is the answer. This region is called *Deva Bhumi* or the land of gods. It translates simply to mean a lot of small temples."

Navin praised her. "Marla already studied some Sanskrit, too. She is good at Hindi." The Thakurs were totally impressed by her appreciation of the "Himalaya." She quoted the ancient praise of the Himalaya:

*Astyuttarasyām diśi devatātmā himālayo nāma nagādhirājah* (There in the northern direction is the divine soul named Himalaya, the king of the mountains).

"For such Sanskrit quotes," Abdul has said, "I consider Marla a highly admirable person. I had no idea of Kalidasa's words like these," he himself confessed.

Most temples now do not discriminate against low castes and non-Hindus. But in the early seventies some temples of her interest were not so open to persons like her. Kewal's name was followed by "Singh," so Marla went with him as Mrs. Singh. No temple could doubt such high caste names.

After a year of fieldwork in India she had returned to America. He was not with her. They were divorced soon after.

"Later Kewal married another woman, this time an Indian from his community. A year afterward, he was blessed with a daughter." Marla had told us the story on an earlier occasion when we had first heard of the marriage.

"Why didn't he have any children with Marla?" It was Tula's question later when we were alone, for which I had no answer. Both of us concluded that Marla and Kewal would not have married if they had biases of miscegenation.

One of the other classmates had told Tula confidentially that, "They were not really in love. Kewal married Marla for the U.S. visa. Kewal loved America and Marla loved India. Their relationship was a sort of *quid pro quo*. I help you and you help me: a very normal basis for a working relationship."

Jennifer and Marla were classmates. They had similar interests, but Jennifer was not as open as Marla. She was slim, shorter and looked slightly younger than Marla. Both maintained their vegetarianism here. That made the local women different from these two white American women. However, universal women's rights were the most important common passion shared by Marla and Jennifer.

Because of this passion they took an interest in my project. For them, in their words, "The *Mahabharata* was a work of males for the males. But how did the local women react to the *Mahabharata*? The Himalayan *Pandau* could reveal their true feelings."

When Marla was away, I praised her research to Tula, "What Marla has discovered so far is interesting. Whatever she reveals sounds quite credible. Sometimes Jennifer corroborates, and even Abdul corroborates in part. He often takes them around."

Being a local man, Abdul had easy access to local shamans and priests whom Marla wanted to meet. I joked, "Abdul was happy to arrange such meetings. These two young women have been buying a lot of Indian clothes from Abdul's shop."

But it was more than simple business. Abdul whispered into my ear, "Have you seen Marla's father in any Hollywood movies?" He couldn't say it loudly. I didn't respond in words, either. I just nodded my head. Marla didn't want us to talk about her father.

She never told us directly, but we understood when she said once, "I never want others to know about him and me."

Maybe Abdul also understood. That's why he might have preferred whispering. I hoped Abdul didn't tell the Thakurs or the drummers, either. These men seemed to have very good rapport with one another. They promoted each other's business. Abdul would make publicity for the basmati rice of the Thakurs. The brothers would send their acquaintances to buy clothes from Abdul's shop. The drummers liked Abdul very much. He would give them the local *daru*, liquor. I found that out from our cook, Bhag. What went on between these men was none of my business. And I didn't care what went on between them and Marla.

Again, I don't want to pretend that my information about Marla is very well organized. It's not even my job. Nevertheless, I know a lot about her through our personal interaction or through her notes and anecdotes. And I know why Marla couldn't have said too much about her father to anyone here. He had mistreated her mother. In the movies, he often looked bizarre, but that was probably due to some stereotyped roles. He was suited for them. I never thought of his promiscuous behavior.

One evening we were eating together at our Seattle residence. "My father enjoyed women like the spicy *chat* snacks!" She said this while Tula was pouring hot, spicy *chat* on her plate.

"So your father was *bahubhārya*," I interrupted.

"What is that?"

"That's Sanskrit for polygynous. Want some Mango *lassi*?" Tula asked.

"No…He was never married to any woman. Not to my mother either… she lived with him for three years. He left her when she was pregnant with Simon. And I was just two...But he left enough money for us." She sighed deeply as she said this.

"My brother Simon and I were raised by our physician step-father, from whom I got my full name, Marla Denton."

She said her name as if still trying to get used to it in her mouth. "Later, I had a step-brother, Nick Denton…But I don't know if I have more step-siblings. That is, from the other women my father had."

She paused for a short moment as she sipped *lassi*.

"My father was considered a unique actor, but I have trouble watching him. I have hated him because he exploited women. He died of emphysema —smoked a lot. It's probably a good thing. Otherwise, who knows how many more women he would have screwed up!"

I wanted to laugh, but didn't. Tula was quiet. Then Marla said something that we didn't expect.

"You both may not like hearing this. Some of these people might be your heroes… In America, I met many revered musicians. I mean Indian men. My hunch is that some of them will have children like me and Simon…," she laughed.

Not knowing any other way to respond, we also laughed.

Appreciatively and conscious of the contentious nature of her comment, she abruptly changed the subject.

"Such a delicious vegetarian extravaganza! With your dishes anybody can be a life-long vegetarian!"

"Thanks, Marla. But you didn't eat enough!" Tula said with a smile.

"Are you kidding?"

"You let me know whenever you want this food."

"Thanks. I would like to learn from you, at least some of my favorite dishes."

"Anytime."

This cooking connection in the kitchen removed a barrier between these two women. Speaking academically, the notes emanating from this connection are a real mess.

Marla said, "I'm not a religious vegetarian; I'm an ethical vegetarian."

Noting the look on our faces, she explained further, "I was shocked when I met some meat-eating swamis in an organization in California; it was known as the Vedantic Mission."

We understood from her comment that she saw a duality problem between the *chela,* or disciple, and the *guru.*

"Fish was a favorite delicacy of some swamis. And their American disciples were pure vegetarians. The original guru in India couldn't come out against animal killing for Kali. 'Never offend the Mother' was his ideal. He was afraid of this imaginary goddess. So were his local chelas. Like guru, like chela. The chela swamis imagined themselves liberated like their grand guru, spiritually above all dualities. That's the Vedanta realization...so I stopped going to the Mission."

She also mentioned how a meat-eating Mission swami fell for a blonde. "Kewal used to play tabla with him. I remember one of his Hindi bhajans."

Then, Marla quoted these opening lines of a devotional song:

*Aba mai nāchyo bahuta Gopāla*

*Kāma krodha ko pahiri cholanā, chalata asangata chāla*

"Now I have danced a lot, God!"

Having put on the gown of lust and anger, I am moving with improper rhythm."

With a slight smile, she added, "Fortunately, he did the right thing. He left the Mission and married his companion. Now they can go fishing without worrying about conflicting convictions."

But Marla didn't have such kind words for another Himalayan yoga guru. "Guru ji never told some girls that, back home, he had left a wife with children." She left his ashram, too.

Talking about her wish to write a book against Hindu animal sacrifice, the *bali*, Marla recounted these and other similar experiences to the Thakurs. They were surprised.

"Christians and Hindus talk too much against violence. This is why I am now here in the Garhwal Himalayas," she told them. "Let me tell you, Thakur Sahab, about my encounter with an American evangelical preacher..."

After a momentary pause to allow him to catch her flow of story-telling, Marla continued by beginning a story about a missionary who was emphasizing Christian compassion during a lunch hour in the university square.

"I asked him whether compassion should include not eating animals. He replied that plants, too, have life. Then, he asked me, 'Don't you eat plants?'"

Marla shook her head before pointing out to us what an obvious and over-used argument he was using to silence her. She related to us the tongue lashing she delivered to him.

"Can you eat your dog with your carrots? Can you? And how about your mother-in-law?"

94

We heard the sarcasm dripping in Marla's comments even though this situation had long since passed. This was clearly a memory which still carried much passion.

Then, Marla, remembering how some of the ensuing discussion developed, jumped back into her story by quoting the missionary's reply to her.

"'That's uncivilized,' I remember that he responded in a righteous-sounding tone. 'There are people elsewhere. Their civilizations are much older than ours. Like their ancestors, they enjoy dog meat.'"

She looked around, and added, "But then, he changed his argument. I remember exactly how the exchange went on from there."

"He said, 'I mean compassion for humans. Human life must be respected all around the world. Wars must be illegal internationally. Any leader who wages war must be tried for crimes against humanity...'"

Looking around, Marla had tried to cut him short. She said in response to the missionary, "President Johnson invaded Vietnam. Do you remember how many innocent people were massacred by this man's order? What happened to you preachers then?"

Marla, present in the moment with us, remembered that he had said nothing in reply. She looked around, encouraging a discussion to arise.

So Puran argued with her: "Marla, I am not a vegetarian, but I do believe in human compassion. You asked him about Christian compassion. What about Hindu *ahimsa*? You are here in this Himalayan land. This whole region is predominantly Hindu. The biggest historical holocaust in this region was created by a neighboring Hindu country. This holocaust is known here as *Gorkhali*. The people of Nepal here are known as Gorkhas. Thousands of people, young and old, were massacred by the Nepalese military. Thousands of women were kidnapped and raped. Many of them were forcibly taken to Nepal during occupation. There are Garhwali folksongs to tell what hell this Hindu country created in this region..."

"When did this Nepalese occupation happen?"

"In 1804. But they were slaughtering our people like animals even before and after this date. We were lucky that, finally, the British rescued us. They got Garhwal and Kumaon back to India in 1815 by a treaty with Nepal."

"But you and the Nepalese share the same bad behaviors!" Marla was not smiling at all when she said this.

95

"What do you mean?" Navin looked startled.

She sighed deeply. "You Paharis slaughter defenseless animals and still call your land *Deva Bhumi*. In this land of gods, neither the Shankaracharya nor the yogis have any impact on animal cruelty."

She was obviously referring to *bali*, the common practice of animal sacrifice in the Himalayas.

According to devout Hindus, a visit to Joshimath and the nearby temple of Badrinath on the border of Tibet are enough for spiritual release or *moksha*. In the great Hindu tradition of pilgrimage, millions of devotees come here every summer. The head monk of the Joshimath monastery is called Shankaracharya. He teaches meditation, too. It definitely releases your stress, so even non-believers come here to learn meditation.

For example, the famous Shankaracharya, Swami Brahmananda, taught it to his own disciple Mahesh. The Brahmin swami was charismatic himself, but nowhere close to his non-Brahmin disciple. After the death of his guru, Mahesh took meditation out to the world. He modified its name to include his own: Transcendental Meditation and Maharishi Mahesh Yogi (the Sanskrit word is *Maharshi* "great sage.").

"I learned TM from a disciple of the Maharishi. He never recommended meat-eating. But he was championing the Vedic culture..." Marla added this comment when Puran interrupted her.

"Marla, animal sacrifice is an essential part of Vedic culture."

"I wanted to say that," Marla said.

Then, she introduced her narration of a Garhwali *bali* ceremony near Joshimath, quoting a line of the Vedic hymn *Purusha Sukta* which informs its performance: "That sacrificial Purusha, the one evolved ahead, they watered upon the grass. With him, the gods, the Sadhyas, and the seers sacrificed."

The ceremony in Garhwali is called the *narsing puja*. The Sanskrit name is *Narasimha* or the Man-Lion avatar of Lord Vishnu. That is, the head is lion and the torso is human. Naturally, any lion eats animals. A ram is the favorite food of this avatar. Thus, all humans should eat the sacrificed ram.

Marla was so enraged by this myth.

This was the salutary mantra for the *khunkri* dagger: *Lauhadandāya namah,* (A bow to the sword).

"With this mantra, the priest sprinkled wet red powder over the dagger. He uttered other mantras. Then, he said, 'O Lord of the sword! This animal must be pierced by you quickly. I offer you this animal. My bow to you...'

"Then a man tied a rope around the back leg of the ram. He held the rope tightly in his fist. The ram tried hard to run. It was a big ram. Another man came, and he tied another rope to another leg. The ram was helpless; it couldn't move. Then the priest sprinkled holy water into the right ear of the ram. The animal shook his head. That shaking meant the acceptance of the offering by the avatar." It was at this point that we began to hear some powerful emotions creeping into Marla's words.

"In three strikes the severed head of the ram fell on the ground. The torso was lifted upside down over a large pan. All the blood was collected in it. Some drops were sprinkled in all directions for the deities. Then the entire torso was taken aside and put over a rock oven. The head was given to the priest. This was his *dakshina,* the holy fee. The Vedic Hymn said that the Brahmins were the mouth of the sacrificed Being, so the Brahmin got the head. The torso was roasted right there. Part of it was cut into small pieces. Everybody got a chunk of it as *prasad,* or sacred food."

Marla had tears in her eyes as she narrated this event. Even though a thought crossed my brain, I carefully policed my mouth. I didn't want to make light of her narration or her state of mind. For example, the chunks of the roasted ram's penis and testicles are not given to women. Men compete for them and enjoy chewing them.

Others among us had no tears from Marla's story, but they all looked grim. Puran broke the silence.

"Marla, we need to know your experiences of our culture. Let us hear from you every time you are here."

Marla nodded her head and asked him a question evidencing an earlier conversation which she must have had with the Thakur brothers.

"Did you get a chance to read Peter Singer's book, *Animal Liberation?*"

"Yes. Thanks for giving it to me. Navin is now reading it."

"I want to write my own book on *bali,*" Marla said.

"You should write on women's rights, too. In India, women are not treated as equals!" Tula said.

"That's right. Muslim women are also not treated like Hindu women." Abdul said.

I thought he meant the right of a Muslim male, who has the right to claim up to four wives. It was difficult for me not to laugh at Abdul's nonsense. Not a single Muslim friend of mine had even two wives. Abdul didn't have even one yet.

"Jennifer and I are working on that. But my current focus is on the ethical treatment of animals," Marla said.

The drummers began to tune their drums. Puran said to Marla, "The hides of these drums are from naturally dead animals."

"I have been told so," Marla said.

# Chapter 15
# Day Six of the War

*Arjuna said: O Krishna! Due to increase in immorality, women of decent families commit sin. O son of the Vrishni family! Mixed progeny is given birth by evil women.*

*—Bhagavad Gita: 1.40*

In today's war, the drummers sang the bravery of Drona and Bhima. Drona had almost killed Drupada's son and Draupadi's brother, named Dhrishtadyumna. Lucky for him, a chariot was close by and saved him. The drummers noted Drona's skill in supporting the Kaurava's cause. In the melee of the day, Bhima pressed an especially deadly attack on Duryodhana, who lost consciousness for some time before he was saved. Thus, the balance was struck. Bhima was one of the Pandava heroes.

Consequently, in this evening's dance session on my lawn, a man was possessed by Drona's spirit. This took place when the drummers sang of Drona's slaughter of Pandava soldiers. The dancing man was shaking and screaming, while waving his hands up and down. He didn't look like an ancient *acharya*. He could have been a modern college teacher with his shirt, pants and regular shoes. He looked to be around forty years old. Navin, like Puran in the preceding possession, quickly came near him.

"Who are you really?" Navin asked him in Garhwali.

"I am Drona."

The man answered Navin in Hindi. The medium of instruction in Dehradun's colleges is Hindi.

"Don't you teach in Dehradun's G. R. College?" Navin was smiling. Upon hearing this, the standing crowd laughed.

"I am the teacher of the Pandavas and Kauravas. I sacked the Pandava kingdom," the man said with intensity and seriousness, again in Hindi.

"Is it morally correct for your students to murder you?"

"No."

"Would you like to kill them?"

"Definitely, definitely!" He laughed and went aside.

The dance continued as other bystanders formed the circle again. Marla looked annoyed as she whispered to an agitated Jennifer. Jennifer nodded her head in agreement and then turned to me, and in a low voice, said, "We are really frustrated to witness two fake possessions, especially on the heels of that incident with Goda."

Puran smiled, but remained silent as Navin spoke for both brothers.

"Have patience!"

Soon, everyone left. And, in this quiet space, I was very seriously struck by those cutting words from Jennifer that still hung in the air: Two fake possessions! And what about Goda? Was that one fake too? I wanted to check with the drummers. They were still packing their things.

"Can I talk to you about some fake things?" I asked Bijlu very politely.

"Like what?" Bijlu looked somewhat puzzled.

"Like the fake possession of this evening." I kept a fake smile on my face when I said this.

"Archi ji, you are like Guru. I mean that big IAS man, our relative. He didn't believe in any possessions. Let us tell you a story which he told us."

At this point, I was not prepared to hear any stories. However, during our fieldwork training, we are taught to listen to our informants very attentively no matter even if they are drifting or rambling. So, I nodded very seriously and heard the story.

Right here in a Dehradun suburb every Sunday morning, a man called "Bhakt ji" holds a *darbar* (royal court). He does this because he is a "devotee" of Devi Durga, a queen goddess who is worshiped in a *darbar* by other gods and people.

In the *darbar* ceremony, a shaman sings *bhajans* "devotional songs" in Hindi with a *dholak* (a smaller version of dhol). As the singing stops, Bhakt ji goes into a trance. Every person present shouts in praise "*sanche darbar ki jay*" (victory to the true court). Bhakt ji shakes his head in a frenzy. His whole body trembles.

Trembling means the goddess has arrived in that place riding a tiger and has possessed Bhakt ji. According to Guru, many Indians don't know that her vehicle is a lion, not a tiger. Bhakt ji shouts like a tiger. Nobody in the audience of over a hundred men, women, and children laughs when Bhakt ji sounds more like a cat, rather than a tiger. That means Bhakt ji, or rather Durga Devi, is ready to answer the problems of any attendee in just a couple of sentences. Guru also attended one such session. He asked Bhakt ji or Devi ji a question in Hindi "Will I pass my IAS examination?"

The goddess answered in Hindi, "*ye ho sakta hai agar tum khub trening coching se lo*" (It can be if you get a lot of training by coaching). It is true that there are coaching classes offered by quite knowledgeable experts for any of the top examinations of India. But the simple fact of the matter was that Guru was already a young IAS officer when he asked the question!

We all laughed when Bijlu finished the story. This laugh was cathartic; it marked the end of all of this seriousness.

But Daphra said to me, "Rainwal ji, you are a professor. We know that you don't believe in any possessions anyway!"

"I would have believed it if she spoke Vedic or Sanskrit. When the gods jointly created Durga, there was no Hindi then. And her Hindi contained Persian and English words. Even her vehicle forgot his original roar."

Both brothers laughed.

Since he complimented me as "professor," I added, "Most Hindus cannot understand our holiest scriptures, the *Vedas*. It takes years to study the Vedic language. Just offer a simple test like this when an average Hindu claims that he or she believes in his or her religion: Can you recite or understand a Vedic hymn?"

I thought about this for a moment, but added, "Once, I asked my grandmother this question, but she replied in a very confident voice, 'Son, The *Bed* books disappeared thousands of years ago. Who really knows what the *bed* rishis wrote in their holy temples.' I had to agree with her. I didn't want to offend her. But, there were two problems with her answer."

Our drummers were curious as to what I'd say next, "First, the *Veda* is not *Bed*. Second, the *Vedas* were not written; they were heard or spoken orally. The rishis did not know writing because there was no writing then. No temples existed that early either."

"But she was very religious. Right?" Daphra asked very seriously.

"For her, religion meant a few things. Go to a temple and have '*darshan*' or sit and view one or more idols of Krishna or Ganesha. Take a bow. Perhaps, have some sacred food or *prasad*. Or, participate in singing some Hindi *bhajans*. Probably, do some holy fasting, too. You know what I mean...there's a saying: 'Don't pretend to practice what you don't understand.' But, I can't fault her; even if she was educated enough, she, being a woman, would not have been allowed to study the *Vedas*."

"We *dalits* were not allowed either." Bijlu said.

"If women and *dalits* are not allowed, then how many standard Hindus are there?" I didn't intend to ask a question.

"This is why Guru's advice is *dharam hatao.*"

"*Gyan bachao*," I completed the saying in agreeing with Bijlu to "oust religion and save knowledge."

# Chapter 16
# The Alphas and Others

"Marla and Jennifer didn't show up on time," said Tula. I nodded, "Usually they come early enough to discuss topics of interest, mostly with the Thakurs." Today, we had been waiting for them. The Thakur brothers and the drummers ate some snacks together. Then, my father joined them. I could hear them discussing the various rituals associated with the Pandavas and their dance.

I had joined Tula in the kitchen. Our cook asked her, "You want anything special added to the meal plan?" This was his daily ritual with Tula. He went out to buy things as recommended. Alone now, we began to prepare tea.

Tula asked me, "What are they discussing over there?" She was peeking through the window, toward the lawn.

"I can't figure it out. I'd guess it's something about some ritual." I shrugged as I also peeked.

"And why the name of Marla?"

"Not clear to me." I shrugged again.

"I overheard that Marla was interested in some rituals."

"Her field is folklore. These things are in her territory."

"But you are not covering her entire territory. Right?"

We both laughed.

"In fact," Tula said with sincere finality, "I've covered Marla's territory more than I'm interested in. That would include Marla's extended background: parents, ex-parents, ex-husband, siblings, step-siblings, half-siblings, and other relationships—details like that."

I let the topic end. I did not tell Tula that I was fascinated by Marla's past. The most interesting was Marla's mother, especially how her mother met Marla's celebrity father. I knew a little; I knew that the introduction happened during the fifties. Her mother, Penny, a young college drop-out, was as tall, slim and blonde as Marla. After leaving school, she had moved into a commune in the mid-fifties near San Francisco where some film makers converged with a deep interest. Marla's DNA parents, Penny and the celebrated film actor, met there. When Penny first started living in this commune, she had no idea that she would meet a movie star, fall in love, and conceive an extraordinary, brilliant and beautiful child, Marla.

This was an interesting time and place for me as I had witnessed the arrival of these communes when I was a young student in the Bay Area of California during the fifties. The Bay Area was already going radical, as if preparing itself for the revolutionary sixties, and it was into this turbulent milieu that Marla was born.

The commune consisted of a dozen hippies, evenly divided in gender. Sexual freedom was their common practice, often changing partners with no attachment. It was a renunciation for them, a clebration of detached connection. They had known about *tantra* through translations, so it was a sort of *tantrik dharma* that included sex without marriage, but they called it natural living. In an evolutionary sense our early human ancestors behaved like this.

Like the Pandava boys for one beautiful Draupadi, the big males of the commune would often fall for Penny.

The news of such groups spread around. Filmmakers and news media looked at this place, with its revolutionary sexuality for the time, as exciting material. A Hollywood filmmaker became interested. There was no alpha male in the commune, but the film's script writer wanted to create one. As Marla commented on such film scripts, "Creative writing means creation of non-existent matter."

That's where Penny was introduced to the main actor. He was to play the alpha. And Penny was the most beautiful girl in the commune. Both fell in love. Thus began the begetting of Marla.

As I was lost in Marla's past, I saw both girls speeding toward me.

"Sorry we are late today! How are you?" Marla said in an apologetic tone.

"We are fine. You are not late. The drummers just came early," I said with a big sigh of relief. "Let us join the Thakurs for snacks!"

We all sat together after the Thakurs greeted the girls.

"Marla, I was thinking of the Vietnam War era a few minutes ago," I said, starting this classic topic of conflict.

"My mother was a disgruntled young woman of that era. She had her own war. But the war of ordinary folks does not matter for the bullies. President Johnson and his advisers wanted to be heroes. Just like in the *Mahabharata*, those men were heroes who had no respect for others' lives. Many were decorated and rewarded. What happened to the soldiers who had to live with their traumas, with their lost limbs, with poverty?"

Marla paused, shaping some images "...Imagine some young men of their age playing tennis or going on a honeymoon to these Himalayas; the handicapped soldiers sacrificing their lives for those who would not remember anyone's name...those soldiers were left both during and after that war to carry a heavy load."

Then she delivered her thesis, "The whole idea of patriotism and nationalism is not just narrow, it's cruel. Where is the..."

Jennifer raised her hands and clapped just two or three times. "The drummers," she said, "have been drumming so far the glory of a few persons: the Pandava brothers and their cousins, their children, teachers and relatives. Why only Abhimanyu?" She answered herself with another rhetorical question, "Because he was the son of big Arjuna? What about the children of the ordinary soldiers who died? What happened to the thousands of mothers who lost their young sons? And what about the widows of the poor soldiers? There is nothing about them, as if they were not there. Could they really convince an illiterate widow that her slain husband never died? That she was ignorant if she believed in his death? That his death was just a transition to another life or heaven, while she and her children would, from that moment forward, have a sad life to live?"

Catching her breath, she added her thesis to Marla's. It was a fierce punctuation: "It is easy to rationalize killing."

There was a pause, a recognition of the intensity before Marla jumped back in to add her own questions to those which still lingered, vibrating throughout everyones' consciousness.

"And where is this heaven, by the way? Where those fallen soldiers are having a wonderful time? Who has seen the good Lord meeting them there? Where is the list of all the *Mahabharata* soldiers?"

Puran intervened "And the *Mahabharata* claims what is in it is out there, and..."

"And what is not in it is not anywhere! Those soldiers were in it, but where is the complete list?" Marla completed her query.

"It's just a publicity pitch that the *Mahabharata* contains everything important," Jennifer added.

"But millions of people believe the *Mahabharata*," Navin said.

"That's why we are assembled here!" A common laughter followed as I said this. I meant to mellow down the tenseness, and more than that, the sadness.

Jennifer took advantage of the mellowed air. "Professor Rainwal resembles a *Mahabharata* macho." Marla laughed at her comment. Other members of the audience were neutral. Maybe they didn't understand "macho." But then Jennifer added, "You have a big house with a big lawn, Professor Rainwal. You even have a separate room for the drummers, a separate room for the cook; your parents even have their own room. You and Mrs. Rainwal each have a separate room. Every room has a modern toilet with a bath. There is a spacious living room for visitors. Don't forget the big kitchen with a huge dining room! And the marble floor!"

"I don't think Duryodhana would have considered my home as one even suitable for the Pandavas!" I said in an attempt to keep the mood light.

"You are not like them. You are more like Vidura, a scholar." Marla modified Jennifer's flattery.

Nevertheless, I didn't like to be compared to Vidura. I expressed my discomfort in a subtle manner. "Vyasa took advantage of Vidura's mother... maybe because he was a big author. Even the queens liked him. Vidura's mother was just a maid, a *dasi*, though. Vyasa has mentioned all of this in the *Mahabharata*. After all, he knew he was the father of Vidura. And, by the way, please remember that my mother is neither a *dasi,* nor is my father a sage."

"You are lucky your father is not a big author. You know how big celebrities flirt with women and mess up their lives!" Marla said this with no indication of lightness on her face.

Then I realized that Marla might have meant her own background: her hippie mother and her celebrity father. I really felt sorry.

The drummers moved toward the bonfire that our cook had just started.

# Chapter 17
# Day Seven of the War

*The Lord said: One who knows this self as the slayer or another who considers this self slain they both do not really know. It does not slay, it is not slain.*

*Just as a man abandons old clothes and puts on new ones, likewise the embodied self abandons old bodies and switches to new ones.*

*—Bhagavad Gita 2.19, 22*

Bijlu and Daphra had already sung earlier how Duryodhana was upset. Many of his heroes were full of bloody wounds. He himself was wounded badly through Bhima's masterful attack. Blood was visible all over his body. Other wounded heroes, blaming each other, had left for their respective camps. With a heavy heart, he sought counsel from Bhishma.

"Granduncle, listen! With their fast chariots, those braves of the Pandavas broke our formation. They crushed and killed our fierce and frightening armies. They stunned us all. Bhima has almost slain me with his terrible arrows. He even knocked me unconscious. Even now, I am still unable to get relief from pain. But, with your favor, I still want to win and kill the Pandavas."

Bhishma, the leader among weapon-wielders, smiled. Inside, though, he felt disgusted. He knew that Duryodhana was angry. He replied, "O Prince, with great effort and sincerity, I overtake the opposing army. This is because I intend to give you victory and pleasure. For your cause, I never excuse myself. Their charioteers are ferocious, renowned, brave and well-trained in weaponry. They are undaunted helpers of the Pandavas in the battle. They vomit the poison of their fury in the battle. They cannot be defeated easily or quickly. Yet, take heart! I will fight their army with my full spirit, ignoring my life. I will fight those Pandavas, O King! I will do everything for your happiness. I know all my soldiers will fight for you."

Duryodhana was pleased to hear these words. He ordered all his armies, "Prepare to move out!"

With his command the armies happily marched forward. With their chariots, elephants, horsemen and foot soldiers, they looked awesome.

Then, war cries were heard all around. The Pandavas had attacked. But, Duryodhana was still in pain; he was not ready for war. Recognizing Duryodhana's discomfort, Bhishma gave him some herbal paste to apply to his wounds. The medicine immediately helped him. Ready to fight, he prepared himself.

A full-scale slaughter started on the seventh day. The clothes of the slain soldiers were soaked in blood. They had been inspired by the foolish belief that there was another glorious life for the dead soldier! Duryodhana fought bravely as he showered arrows on all the five Pandavas. On this day, Arjuna was wounded more than the other brothers. Blood stains were all over his body.

Fights between well-known adversaries began again. This time, Drona and King Virata had personal combats. For King Virata, this had become very personal. On this day, he lost another son; two of his other sons had been killed in earlier exchanges. Dhrishtadyumna fought so ferociously on this day that Duryodhana, his defence crumpling from the onslaught, had to come down and fight with his sword. Again, if Shakuni had not taken him away in his chariot, then he would have been killed. The day was filled with much blood.

In another fateful skirmish, Bhishma cut off Shikhandin's bow. That made the senior Pandava brother, Yudhishthira, mad. He addressed Shikhandin, "You told me even before you told your father that you would kill Bhishma. This was your vow. You have not made good on your promise yet. Don't be a liar! Protect your dharma, your family and fame. Look at Bhishma's fierce speed! Like Time the destroyer, he has surrounded my troops with the web of his burning arrows. You are afraid of him. Look, even Arjuna is trying hard to stop him without your knowledge. How is it that you have fear of Bhishma?"

Understanding Yudhishthira's frustration, Shikhandin quickly left him to kill Bhishma. And he would have killed Bhishma if Bhishma's deputy had not intervened. Frustrated, Shikhandin quickly fixed his bow to retaliate for

Shalya's intervention.

After evading Shikhandin, Bhishma engaged Yudhishthira. Yudhishthira shot many arrows at him. But Bhishma seemed unstoppable. He even wounded both Nakula and Sahadeva, who had come to defend Yudhisthira. Not wanting to waste a moment, Yudhisthira addressed the fellow kings, "You all go to kill Bhishma."

The kings followed the request of their leader Yudhishthira. They surrounded Bhishma with their chariots. But, this did not stop the fierce warrior; Bhishma and his assistants destroyed many chariots and cut off the heads of the charioteers. The Pandavas were filled with fear when they saw their fellow kings in trouble.

Emboldened, Duryodhana joined Bhishma in the exchange. They both terrified the Pandava fighters as Bhishma chopped off the heads of many charioteers. It was a battle for the ages, one with an insatiable appetite for death.

As the evening came and all went to their camps, all were tired. Yet no one was interested in a truce. Soldiers took baths and took care of their wounds. Bards provided music for their entertainment.

The drummers ended with this sentence in their continuing rap: "Listen, brothers and sisters! We don't have the names of those soldiers."

In the Himalayan Nights

# Chapter 18
# Phony Vegetarians

"We never asked you this. Hope you don't mind! We have been guessing and guessing. How did you become a vegetarian?" Puran asked Marla.

"I worked in a San Jose restaurant when I was in my last year of high school. It was run by an Indian."

"So, it was a vegetarian restaurant. Right?"

"Right thinking," Marla winked with a smile and then continued, "The owner, Chatur Lal, worked in San Francisco. He was a computer engineer. He wanted full employment for his brother, Madhur. There was a big contrast between Chatur and Madhur. One was an engineer educated in California, the other just a high school graduate from Bombay. One of his relatives tried the motel business and did well enough to live comfortably with his family. He was a college dropout from Bombay..."

"Bombay has the best colleges. Even a dropout is not bad. You can hear people boast, 'Oh, I went to a Bombay University college!' You can even just drive a taxi there and still brag about living in Bombay!" Navin said with a smile.

"His entire family left Bombay. Even a big name of Bombay earns less money in a different world. He was the only earning member. In San Jose, the whole family ran the motel. Full employment. He advised Chatur and Madhur to go for a regular American restaurant..."

"So it was not a vegetarian restaurant!" Navin said with surprise in his eyes and voice.

"Right guess this time!" Marla laughed without winking this time. Others also laughed.

"In this restaurant, customers were actually allowed, even encouraged, to pick up a live lobster or a fish..."

"You mean for cooking live?"

"It was horrible for me to watch the live animal in the cooking pot!"

"Oh no! I don't want to hear any more," Tula exclaimed as she put her fingers into her own ears.

"I understand, Tula! It was becoming painful for me because I would take the orders from the customers. But listen to this part! This man was a high caste, very devout Hindu..."

"What did you say? A devout Hindu?" Tula's hands were down.

"Every Sunday, he would do a puja at his residence. We employees had an open invitation for this residential worship. I went a few times. My weakness for Indian food challenged my resolve! Moreover, it was free. We had to take off our leather shoes at the door. There, in his living room, we sat on leather sofas. Others sat on the floor. He called his puja *Panch Nam Dev* worship. Basically, he would prostrate himself flat in front of the five idols: Sun, Ganesha, Vishnu, Shiva and Uma. His family members would prostrate likewise. He would utter a couple of Sanskrit mantras, then everything else was in Hindi. He didn't know Sanskrit. His Indian English was OK. And every vegetarian dish was just superb..."

"Name some!" Navin asked.

"The best was the sweet dish, *shrikhand*. It tasted like strained Greek yogurt with saffron. Chatur's wife was a super-duper cook. She told us that all her family members were vegetarians. Her parents and his parents were all vegetarians. That was shocking. Money and religion were two separate issues—no conflict for these brothers. But more shocking was their holy priest, the pandit..."

"What pandit?" Puran asked.

"One Sunday, Chatur invited us for a grand ceremony, the *havan*. We went for this fire worship in the same living room. It was jam-packed. Some had no place to sit. Guests were standing in the corners. Too many Indians and non-Indians. But this time there was a priest, Tulsi Ram ji, who was quite a professional pandit. He performed the whole ceremony in Sanskrit. His English was quite good, as well. He explained the ceremony in English, very briefly. He said things like: 'This is a Vedic ceremony. The Vedas are our holy books. Their language is old Sanskrit, but they were never written in any language. The sages saw the mantras in their meditation. They heard the Vedic mantras. That is why they are called *shruti*, the voice that is *heard*.' Up to that part everybody was quiet. Then, when he continued, he said that the

Vedas were heard one million years ago. No sooner had he said this than we could hear some laughter in the audience."

We all laughed. Puran and Navin were leading in laughing!

"I overheard one middle-aged Indian man talking softly to his friend. He was a white American. 'Hey, Mark, this priest is talking nonsense. Looks like he is drunk? You know, his brother runs a liquor store in Santa Clara.' The white man, Mark, was making a confused face. The Indian looked around and responded softly again, 'Mark, don't you get it? Your ancestors heard the Vedas in Africa. And, the best thing is that we now have proof that they were already white one million years ago!' Can you believe that?"

Marla laughed again.

"That pandit should not have said this outside India," Puran said.

"Certainly not in California. The State of California has a great educational system," Marla said.

"And a record number of Nobel laureates live in California." Tula added her support.

"But at least Tulsi ji was in *dhoti*. That six-yard long white cloth made him look like an authentic priest. But Chatur was in his Muslim *pajamas* and *kurta*. Did the Aryans put on that outfit in Africa, Puran ji?" Marla laughed again. "Chatur and Tulsi talked about protecting Hinduism—nothing about animals."

"It's all economics. Animal protection would hurt his livelihood," Navin said.

Marla continued, "Then, Tulsi Ram ji announced a date and place for a big meeting with a Vedic *yagna*..."

"You mean *yajña*, if he meant the Vedic worship," I interrupted.

"That's what he said, as if the Vedas were originated in Bombay. 'You all are invited,' he said as he stretched his hands all around."

"I thought in Bombay they say *yadna*. Anyway, did you attend the big meeting?" Navin asked her.

"I did. The hall was not too big. But there were a good number of Indians. I found most of them were engineers. One of them was a prominent businessman, Mr. Jain. Tulsi Ram ji made him the head of the Vedic temple committee."

"A Jain heading a Vedic temple committee! Two problems. The Vedic culture had no temples. Jainism was opposed to Vedic culture. Wah!" Puran said as he laughed.

"Mr. Jain came up on the stage and gave a pep talk. He said to all present, 'I am originally from Delhi; my family is devout Jain. Jainism and other religions come from the Vedas. The Vedas taught all religions to believe in God. God is everywhere. Without God, there is nothing. God protects us from evils. He has promised this in the Vedas.' When he kept on talking, someone in the audience shouted, 'Jain ji, there are others who want to speak.' The audience clapped. Mr. Jain understood," Marla said, laughing because of Mr. Jain's comments. She completed her story with a final thought.

"Even many American students know that Jainism and Buddhism have no God."

"How in the world do such people manage to reach America!" Navin wondered.

"That shows that Indians can have outstanding careers without the knowledge of their religion! I know another rich Jain who didn't know that the sacred language of the Jain scriptures was Ardha Magadhi. He had no idea that Lord Mahavira preached Jainism in that language around 500 years before Christ. Like the Buddha, he was also opposed to Vedic *bali* and *yajñas*, and, of course, against meat-eating."

Marla continued, "To make the story short, I left that restaurant. It gradually became unbearable, watching the chef picking up live animals from the tank and quickly dropping them over boiling water! I never ate meat again."

"I am against animal cruelty," Abdul said. "I heard our vegetarian prime minister was told by some Americans how Indian monkeys were tortured in American labs."

"Yes. An export ban was in order. Good prime minister, Mr. Desai... I have a friend in Boston, a typical white American. Whatever is digestible is eatable for him. He wanted to eat monkey meat. For him, these are delicacies. I remember how he brags, 'I have eaten dogs, snakes, horses, frog legs, bison, rabbits...'"

"But not monkeys?" Abdul asked.

"Thanks to the prime minister!" Marla said seriously.

Then, Puran went on to tell Marla more about Mr. Desai. "He is opposed to Western culture. He thinks he is a Gandhian. The symbols of *swadesi* or indigenous culture must replace the Western stuff. We are going to lose our prestige symbols."

Puran gave some examples. He talked about how The Doon School of Dehradun has become bad, despite its impeccable legacy. Simply, it encourages Western values; it does not matter if this school has produced some of the greatest leaders in various fields. Saying to us, "Desai wants to reincarnate the highest administrative body in our country at the most backward place," Puran also described how the IAS officers are trained at Mussoorie. The IAS Academy provides that training. But Mussoorie is a symbol of the West.

"The local people felt that these Himalayan hills are the most backward place." Navin highlighted his brother's point by lowering his palm backward.

"Not Dehradun and Mussoorie." Marla counteracted by moving her palm horizontally back and forth.

"The prime minister knows that this area has a very high literacy rate. So he has found another real backward place elsewhere. Some Paharis, I know, are jealous of that place. Mussoorie has no railway line. That place has. Some Paharis told him the railway system came from the West to see what he would say." Puran said with a smile.

Catching the humor, Marla also joked, "Is he really serious about boycotting Western things? I know he is against kissing in Hindi films. That doesn't sound like a bad idea in a culture that produced the *Kama Sutra*."

We all laughed.

Then, Puran commented, "Morarji Bhai moves around in his car as if it was invented by his daddy. Now, he has banned alcohol. So, Paharis are bootlegging."

Remembering what a retired general had told me in Los Angeles, I laughed quietly, but chose not to share. He said to me, "The prime minister doesn't drink. He doesn't have to. When he was young, he drank one bottle of whiskey. Just once. Since then, he is recycling it every morning."

I never thought the general, an old IMA graduate from Punjab, would use this popular joke. Many have ridiculed Prime Minister Desai for drinking his own urine. I had heard that his urine was named after his name: *Morarji daru* or Morarji Liquor.

"How do we get such crackpots as our leaders?" Abdul wondered.

He started to say more, but then the drummers joined us, smiling. Maybe they had overheard our laughing.

# Chapter 19
# Day Eight of the War

*The Lord said: O Arjuna! I create myself whenever there is fall of dharma and rise of non-dharma. I am born age after age for the protection of the gentle-folks and destruction of the evil-doers and re-establishment of dharma.*

*—Bhagavad Gita 4.7, 8*

Daphra and Bijlu started drumming to the story of the eighth day.

The Kauravas and Pandava forces were ready in the morning. They marched against each other according to their formations. The ear-deafening noise of conchs, trumpets, drums and war cries was heard all around again. Bhishma and his assistants rushed toward the Pandavas. Yudhishthira lost no time. He and Dhrishtadyumna challenged Bhishma. A horrible bloodshed surged ahead.

Wounded horsemen and elephant riders fell and were trampled by oncoming chariots and horsemen and elephant riders. Writhing in pain, animals and soldiers made heart-wrenching cries.

In this brutal battle, the worst happened to Duryodhana. His eight other brothers were slain by Bhima. Duryodhana yelled at his deputies, "This Bhima shall be slain in this battle!" He went to Bhishma and cried, "My brave brothers have been killed in the battle by Bhimasena. Other soldiers who tried to fight him were also killed by him. You are with us, but always ignore us. I am walking on the wrong path. Look at my destiny!"

The granduncle became angry as well as sad. "I have told you before. Drona and Vidura also told you the same. And you were told the same by your mother Gandhari. But, Son, you did not care for it. O Crusher of the Enemy, I assure you that neither I nor Professor Drona will outlive the war. Bhima will definitely kill any sons of Dhritarashtra he sees in the battle. I am

117

telling you the truth. So, O King! Be patient and focus your mind on the war. Fight the Pandavas in the battle and go to heaven. The Pandavas cannot be defeated, not even by the gods with their king Indra."

Miles away, Dhritarashtra heard this talk of Bhishma and Duryodhana from Sanjaya through his skill at remote viewing. He asked, "Sanjaya! What did Bhishma, Drona and Kripa do when they saw my many sons killed in the battle? Due to greed that dumb Duryodhana did not understand what was said by me before, as well as by Bhishma, Vidura and Gandhari. Due to that, he obtained this result. Every other day Bhimasena becomes mad in the battle and sends my sons to the abode of the death god Yama."

Sanjaya replied to Dhritarashtra, "You were told by your well-wishers, 'Stop your sons from the dice. Don't despise the Pandavas.' But, my lord, you didn't care for the good advice being offered. Now listen to what happened in the war."

Sanjaya kept narrating the war.

In one specific battle Iravat, one of Arjuna's sons, fought valiantly against a cavalry of the Kauravas. The story of Iravat was incredible. His mother, Ulupi, was a Naga. Ulupi's husband was killed soon after her marriage. She had no children. Her father Airavata, the king of the Nagas, saw her depression. When Ulupi saw Arjuna visiting her father, she immediately felt *kama* and wanted to be Arjuna's wife. Her father noticed her lust, or *kama,* for Arjuna, so he offered her hand to Arjuna. The marriage took place, but Arjuna left Ulupi in the Naga country. From their brief union was born a boy known as Iravat or Iravan.

Iravat's evil-minded uncle became jealous and banished the boy with his mother. Ulupi raised Iravat very well. As the boy reached adulthood, he met Arjuna. "I am Iravat," he said to Arjuna. "Best wishes to you. I am your son, my lord!" He reminded the forgetful Arjuna how he met his mother. Arjuna was able to recollect all that happened between him and Iravat's mother. He hugged his son. He was delighted to see Iravat was just like him.

During that meeting he had promised Arjuna to help him at war time. When he heard of the war, Iravat came and kept his promise, as he was fighting today for his father. Iravat and his assistants created havoc for the cavalry. Alambusha, a giant opponent, was wounded by Iravat several times. Unfortunately, that giant got up again and, though wounded, was able to kill Iravat.

When another giant, Ghatotkacha, the son of Bhima, saw Iravat dead, he yelled at the enemies that he had arrived to take revenge. Many enemy soldiers became terrified and began to run away. Duryodhana saw how the giant Ghatotkacha started devastating his horsemen. He ran toward Ghatotkacha in desperation and showered many arrows on his body, but to no avail. The battle continued with Ghatotkacha slaughtering many of Duryodhana's great warriors.

Thus, Duryodhana's armies suffered heavy losses and, again, he went to see Bhishma. There, he complained, "O hero of the Bharata dynasty! Look how Ghatotkacha has defeated us today so badly. My body parts are shaken. I need your immense support in killing this giant."

"O King! Let me tell you what to do. You should care for your safety in the battle all the time. You should fight Yudhishthira. Or fight Arjuna, Bhima, Nakula and Sahadeva. A king should really fight a king. Let Bhagadatta fight Ghatotkacha."

And this is how Bhagadatta was given the task of slaying Ghatotkacha. Knowing the plan, Bhima, Abhimanyu, Ghatotkacha and other big warriors decided to finish Bhagadatta before the deed could be done.

Finally, when Arjuna was told by Bhima about the death of Iravat, he felt distraught. Arjuna said to Krishna, "O Krishna! So many braves on both sides have been killed in this bloody war. This heinous act is being done for wealth. Shame on this wealth! For this, we are killing our own people. What will we gain by slaying our relatives? The brave Kshatriyas died because of the crime of Duryodhana, because of the mean advice of Shakuni and Karna. We begged Duryodhana, 'Give us the half kingdom.' That wicked man was not willing to offer us even five villages. Shame on me that so many Kshatriyas died for our cause!"

But Krishna praised how those brave warriors fought so gallantly.

There was frustration in the camps of the Kauravas, too. More brothers of Duryodhana were hurt and killed that day. In the evening, Duryodhana, Shakuni, Duhshasana and Karna met together. Duryodhana addressed his deputies, "Drona, Bhishma, Kripa and Shalya fail to foil the attempts of the Pandavas. I don't know what the cause of their failure is. O Karna! Those Pandavas are difficult to kill. They are weakening my strength. Even gods cannot kill them. So I doubt I will kill them in the battle."

Karna responded, "Don't give up hope, O hero of the Bharata dynasty! I will help you in order to please you. Withdraw Bhishma from the big battle immediately. When he stops fighting, I will kill those Pandavas. I tell you the truth. Bhishma is a proud warrior and he always loves to fight. But he is kind to the Pandavas. So, how will he vanquish the Pandavas? You must visit him in his camp right away. Request him to drop his arms. When he does that, then see the Pandavas and their supporters slain by me!"

As Karna had advised him, Duryodhana did go to meet Bhishma. And, as could be expected, Bhishma was very much agitated by Karna's proposal. He admonished Duryodhana saying, "Why are you stabbing me with your verbal weapons? You don't know what is proper and improper to say. Here I fight for your pleasure as much as I can. For your good, I am willing to sacrifice my life in this war. That chariot-repairer's son Karna is incompetent to lead your armies in the battlefield. He has shown many times how he failed in helping you and your brothers. You yourself developed animosity toward the Pandavas. Who can conquer them when they are accompanied by that all-powerful Krishna? But you must fight them like a man. O tiger among men! I, too, will kill all those Somakas and Panchalas who are supporting the Pandavas. The only person I will not kill is Shikhandin. Shikhandin is really Shikhandini, a woman in his past life. I cannot lay my hands on any woman. You sleep soundly. Tomorrow, I will wage a war that people will talk about as long as this earth exists."

The last sentence sung by the drummers was this: "Listen, sisters and brothers! Go home and take care of your children."

# Chapter 20
# Possessed by the Past

"News of my project seems to be present everywhere in Dehradun." I probed Navin's face for clues as we sat outside appreciating the north Indian sunset. Navin enjoyed his cigarette in deep drags as I savored cinnamon, clove and cardamom in sips of hot milk tea. "The listeners had reactions of their own," I continued as Navin and his brother admired the sky. "Even politically-oriented relatives have begun to visit us. Some seem very impressed that I have been doing something to preserve the heritage."

Marla and Jennifer kept their eyes on the horizon.

I got directly to my point. "What I failed to take into account was fundamentalism."

Navin extinguished his Marlboro and nodded. "It has been emerging mainly in the north," meaning northern India. "The Paharis are in the north. For them, below the Himalayas, every state is in the south. Progress comes up here from the south."

But Paharis do not write "North India" in their postal address. All south Indians are "Madrasis" in the north. Many of them write "South India" in their postal address. Puran withdrew his gaze from the sun and finished his tea.

Joining in the discussion, he spoke slowly, "Paharis resent two Indias. They are very nationalist, one-nation believers."

Marla and Jennifer looked at me for clarification, and thus I said jokingly, "Some Hindu leaders were talking about a new political party that should reinstate Hindu values. After all, India's major population is Hindu. The party must represent the main *janta* or public. The word *junta* is etymologically related to *janta* or *janata*."

One leader's wife showed up in today's session. Her husband was locally known as Neta ji or Mr. Leader, so she was called Neti ji or Mrs.

Leader. This was just to ridicule them. They were associated with the formation of some sort of Hindu or Bharatiya party, calling it "janata party." That meant the party of the people.

"It's nice that you are preserving our Hindu heritage," Mrs. Leader complimented me. I thought I was studying folklore of the Garhwal Himalayas. But I didn't want to dispute her praise. She was a guest and also a distant relative. She looked middle-aged. Her height was typical Pahari, about five feet. Her facial features were very Pahari, somewhat Sino-Tibetan —nothing looked south Indian in her.

She went inside to greet my parents. Then, she came out in a few minutes. I thought she would sit with us for snacks, but she left.

I understood later why she must have left so quickly. She saw Abdul coming. He did say "namaste" to her. She responded in kind.

Abdul told us more. "She doesn't like me. Her husband's theme in every speech is 'We are divided. So foreigners invaded us and ruled over us. We have to keep this Hind Bhumi intact.' She believes that Indian Muslims are foreigners, too. If her Chinese-looking husband is Indian, then what's wrong with my brown skin?" Abdul laughed as he finished his playful but sharp parry.

Speaking to her in absence, Abdul went on, "Neti ji, I am not calling myself even a north Indian. Here is my friend Krishnan. He believes he is south Indian. His parents are Madrasis. But Krishnan was born and raised here in Dehradun, not in Madras. His name is from the *Gita.* Was Lord Krishna from Madras?"

All of us laughed with Abdul.

The Thakurs added more commentary. Puran said, "Neta ji has now learned some elementary Sanskrit, and puja, too. He has hired a Sanskrit pandit. Some influence of the pandit is very visible. He recites a *Gita* chapter in his daily puja. He has left meat-eating..."

"And drinking, too?" Abdul asked. But his smile and wink meant there was no question. He knew that Neta ji was an engineer in the Public Works Department before. Shaking his head, he went on, "And Neti ji hasn't learned any Sanskrit. But she thinks she understands the common truth underlying all religious beliefs. She quotes Tulsidas in her talks: 'Whoever has whatever belief, he sees the image of God accordingly.' How does a Muslim or Christian imagine God's image?"

Indeed, Tulsidas' *prabhu,* "God," and *murti,* "idol" or "image," cannot include other religions. His One-God views may or may not impress many.

"It's not her fault. Tulsidas should have known. He was living in the Mughal period. These emperors built mosques. Which mosque had God's icons? Europeans were already in India. Any church they made here had no idols or icons of their God. Tulsidas was recreating a mythical past. The *Bhagavad Gita*'s God had already said, 'Whoever worships me in whatever way, I serve him that very way.' Many people carry that mythical memory as truth," Navin said, in order to clarify some of Abdul's comments.

"And there is a real past in our history. Buddha never gave any indication of God's existence. Mahavira's Jainism, neither. What nonsense is she talking about?" Abdul said, still aiming his vitriol at the political aspirant's wife.

"She seems to have a limited view of Hinduism. Within Hinduism, there are Godless views." Marla broke her silence.

Neti ji's hope of a Hindu party and the use of the word "Hind Bhumi" smacked of fundamentalism. This word is used in the Sanskrit prayer of the *Rashtriya Swayamsevak Sangh*. One translation of it comes from the National Volunteers Association. But it sometimes looks more like a *junta* for a planned *janta* party. It is there to protect Hind. The word "India" is derived from this. Nevertheless, it is a foreign word, Iranian, in fact. There is no such word in Sanskrit.

"Fundamentalists everywhere in the world are history-illiterates," Puran said. He continued, "Civilizations should not be named after a set of superstitions such as Hindu Civilization, Christian Civilization, or Islamic Civilization. Rather, say in terms of earthly parts and times, South Asian Civilization, Early Middle Eastern Civilization, or Medieval Middle Eastern Civilization. I am disturbed when I see fundamentalists naming their political parties after their religion. Alienation by religion must be banned by the United Nations!"

Each of them nodded in agreement with Puran. They all, including the drummers, had something to say about Neti ji and Neta ji.

Puran elaborated further, "Abdul, you are a Garhwali just like me. You were raised in a Garhwali Brahmin family, like Neti ji. But suppose she thinks you are a Muslim. Tell her how her family is influenced by the Muslim heritage of India. Her daughter is very good at the Lucknow-style *Katthak* dance. Her son is a very good singer and tabla player. He learned the Hindustani music at Lucknow's Bhatkhande University of Music. Our singing is so beautiful because of its unique *khayal* style. These are all Muslim influences..."

"And her husband does puja in *pajama* and *kurta*. He even covers his head with a cloth when the sacred mark of *tilak* is being put on his forehead. The daughter goes to school in *shalwar-kurta*, a typical Muslim dress. She buys from me, too," Abdul added. I laughed. Abdul understood the clothing business quite well.

I think my father overheard us. Maybe my loud laugh brought him out. He joined us.

"I overheard your discussion and thought I should say something. We are all children of one and the same Mother Earth. My puja starts with her name: 'Prithivi! I bow to you. All the regions are held by you.' So every region of the world is sacred, not just this Hind Bhumi. When you divide the Mother like this, you insult Her by barking in one part while waiting to urinate in other parts."

I was surprised when I heard my father talking like this. He believed in the caste system, a divisive system. But what he said next embarrassed me.

"Marla, these local people know this. I know you are interested in our local bigamy. Her maternal uncle was a bigamist. He hated his parents because they forced him to marry within our Brahmin community. The girl dropped out of school in the fifth class. But when the young uncle went to study at Lucknow University, he fell in love with a local student. This was the right girl for him, education-wise and career-wise. But bigamy is bigamy. He never divorced the Pahari girl, but married this Lucknow girl. The parents never spoke to him again. They felt humiliated. A married woman living with the parents, not with the husband, is looked down upon."

And, while I understood that Dad was talking about the uncle of Neti ji, Marla seemed lost as she stared into space. The temporary silence was broken as the drummers began to tune their drums.

# Chapter 21
# Day Nine of the War

*The Lord said: Whoever worships me in whatever way, I treat them exactly that way. Humans follow my path in every manner, O Partha!*
                                                    *—Bhagavad Gita: 4.11*

The drummers sang as usual, stirring the crowd into action and attention.

Early in the morning, King Duryodhana ordered his armies to move toward the battlefield under the leadership of Bhishma. He instructed his brother Duhshashana, "Deploy chariots to protect Bhishma. Ask all twenty-two divisions to move along. Today is the time to kill all the Pandavas with their army. Bhishma is willing to fight all of them except Shikhandin, so protect Bhishma from Shikhandin!"

Arjuna saw the armies led by Bhishma marching forward. He said to his general, Dhrishtadyumna, "O Leader of the Panchalas! Today, place that tiger among men, Shikhandin, in front of Bhishma. And I will be Shikhandin's guard."

When Bhishma saw the Pandava armies moving forward, he quickly formed a complex strategic formation called *sarvatobhadra*, "auspicious from all sides." The Pandavas were ready to encounter this formation with their numerous divisions.

But bad omens also accompanied these armies. Noise produced by conchs, cymbals, drums, elephants, horses and war cries foreshadowed the forthcoming bloodshed. The dust produced by the movement of armies clouded the sun. Animals like vultures, crows, dogs, and jackals were visible, adding their own noise. They were looking for fresh flesh.

Suddenly Abhimanyu, Arjuna's son, surged ahead with his forces. He began to shoot the Kaurava warriors. When Duryodhana saw the devastation wrought by Abhimanyu, he became very concerned and started to plan the murder of this young man. On his order, Arshyashringi and Alambusha, the demon-like warriors, went ahead to kill Abhimanyu. There was a fierce battle now in progress. Abhimanyu yelled at them, while they challenged him with their horrible words. But, they were hit hard by Abhimanyu's arrows.

It was Bhishma who had to come to help the two warriors. He showered Abhimanyu with his arrows. Seeing this onslaught from the Kaurava hero, Arjuna ran to cover his son Abhimanyu. He killed several soldiers of the Kauravas in front of Abhimanyu.

Then Bhishma confronted Arjuna. Some Kaurava brothers immediately joined Bhishma to back him up. Likewise, Arjuna was covered by his brothers. The battle became dreadful, intense. Satyaki and Ashvatthaman, Drona's son, fought against each other and Satyaki, despite his injury, was able to hit him hard in the chest with a sharp arrow. Drona saw his son in pain and ran to defend him. He wounded Satyaki badly. Arjuna rushed to protect Satyaki and shot Drona with many arrows.

This melee enraged Drona and he retaliated as furiously. Bhima and Yudhishthira came quickly ahead. Bhima's mace became wet with blood and fat as he broke the skulls of many. Elephants and horses felt bewildered and ran around without their riders. The battle became ugly.

At midday, a battle emerged between Bhishma and the Somakas. Bhishma massacred several of them. Then the Pandava heros closed ranks and hurt Bhishma with many well-shot arrows. Blood began to ooze from Bhishma's body, but he continued to retaliate. Maddened, he would not stop or slow down. Upon having his bow broken in a vicious attack, Drupada quickly grabbed another bow and began to hit Bhishma again. The Pandava brothers worked hard to reinforce Drupada.

Some Kaurava brothers had also moved speedily with their divisions to reinforce Bhishma. Due to the movement of those divisions, foot soldiers and horses were trampled and killed on the way. Mighty elephants began to run around in madness. They destroyed many chariots. Bhishma and Satyaki began to fight again. So did Chitrasena and Abhimanyu. Drona and Drupada, the two senior adversaries, engaged in a raging fight. Shakuni came with his troops to confront the Pandava brothers. Duryodhana sent more troops to support Shakuni. The battlefield became covered with dust.

Chaos emerged. Broken chariots and abandoned weapons were accompanied by mutilated bodies. Body parts were scattered all around.

Wounded soldiers cried for help. Many were trampled by oncoming chariots and elephants. The odor of rotten flesh, urine and feces of humans and animals filled the air. Annihilation looked to be the only victor in the battlefield.

The war made ethics brittle. For example, Krishna almost broke his vow again. During an especially heated exchange, Arjuna was hit hard by Bhishma's arrows. Krishna took up arms and left both his chariot and Arjuna behind. He ran to kill Bhishma.

"Come on, O Lotus-eyed god of gods! Namaste," Bhishma praised Krishna. But Krishna was not moved by all that praise. The two were almost ready to hurt each other, but Arjuna ran after Krishna and shouted, "O Krishna, come back. Don't break your vow. You said you would never fight in this war. Keep your vow. Come back; I will fight my granduncle!"

Krishna did come back and sat down in the chariot of Arjuna.

Bhishma was all fire. He moved forward and slaughtered warrior after warrior of the Pandavas. He would have killed Arjuna, too, except, the criticism was true: he really never wanted to kill any one of the five Pandava brothers.

In the evening, the battle stopped. Yudhishthira was shaken by what Bhishma did today. He said to Krishna, "Look, Krishna, how Bhishma has devastated us today! We cannot vanquish him. I do understand my Kshatriya dharma. As Kshatriyas, our duty is to fight for the right cause. But now I would rather leave this war and go live in a forest. I cannot take any more of this destruction for the sake of a kingdom. My valiant brothers accepted this war for my sake. They are suffering because of me. I consider life much more important than anything else. Please advise me what we ought to do now."

Krishna responded, "Yudhishthira, do not be depressed. You are Dharma's child. You have been always duty-bound and truthful. Your brothers are brave, unbreakable: busters of enemies! Because of our friendship, appoint me to fight Bhishma. For your sake, what is there that I cannot do in this war? If Arjuna doesn't want to, then I will kill that Bhishma myself, right in front of those Kauravas. Your brother Arjuna is my friend, relative and disciple. I can cut my flesh and sacrifice it for the sake of Arjuna. So appoint me, O King! If Arjuna allows me, then I will slay Bhishma in front of all the armies. Arjuna himself is capable of vanquishing any warrior, including Bhishma. But only Bhishma knows what else we can do."

They planned mayhem for tomorrow.

The drummers were having a fine day relating to us the horrors of this war long since erased except in the memories and stories of this famous book from this place. Today's session was disrupted for a while by yet another moment of strangeness. A man claimed to be possessed.

"I am...hoot...I am...hoot," he shouted.

The drummers ignored him. They kept drumming. But, then, he came close to them. He put his hands over the dhol. His hands were trembling. So were his lips. "I am...I am...," he shouted again.

"Just say your name!" Bijlu asked him loudly.

"Arjun!"

"You are not Arjun. You are a drunk," Bijlu snapped at him.

He lifted his hands from the dhol and grabbed Bijlu by the neck. Bijlu pushed him away with his dhol. Daphra hit him on the head with drumsticks.

Abdul and Navin understood the situation. They quickly came to the rescue and dragged him away.

The man yelled at them in Hindi, "*Bhainchod...tum sale...dhakka mat do*!" (Sisterfuckers, you bastards, don't shove!)

They continued dragging him until he was out of the lawn.

Navin was smiling when he came back to join us. Jokingly, he looked at each of us with an exaggeratingly serious face and said, "Arjuna never behaved like that."

Abdul looked upset. He told me later, "There is no way to stop such drunkards. The prime minister has declared our state dry, but the Paharis have their underground *bhattis* to distill cheap liquor everywhere."

I understood what Abdul meant. I was shocked when I saw my first *bhatti*, liquor distillery, near Pauri. I was barely thirteen then.

# Chapter 22
## Conversion of Lust

*The Lord said: One's own dharma, even if less qualitative, is better than another's dharma, even if superior. Dying in one's own dharma is better. The dharma of others is frightful.*

—*Bhagavad Gita 3.35*

During the session, yesterday in the evening, Aryanand, the male Arya Samaj missionary, looked fishy to me. He was talking softly to my drummers, aside. They looked unresponsive. They seemed more interested in tuning their drums. The dance session was about to start. That is why, I guess, he turned to Puran. Just before leaving, he said to him, "Be sure you tell them how I did his *shuddhi* conversion."

"I will tell them, but tomorrow. We leave after the *pandau* dance is over," Puran said.

So today, when I reminded him, Puran told us. Marla, Abdul and Navin joined us. We all were sitting out in the lawn. As usual, the delicious tea helped us all to relax.

Puran began, "Oh, this Aryasamajist Aryanand claims a conversion. He thinks it was a great success. This is about one of your relatives' sons..."

"Yes, Durlabh's son," I said.

"No. It is a long story. You know Arya Samaj has very little appeal here. But it is about your relative Manohar Chacha. First, let me start with Aryanand and Arya Samaj."

There is a D.A.V. high school in Pauri. It has even some local converts in its faculty. The abbreviation of Dayanand Anglo-Vedic, however, rightly suggests its emphasis on modernity. Swami Dayanand, the founder of Arya Samaj or Aryan Society of the nineteenth century, would have been very happy with Aryanand's success story. Here Aryanand is claiming a

129

conversion or *shuddhi*. Actually, it's a case of re-conversion. It could be considered fortunate or unfortunate, depending on one's point of view.

Aryanand is his adopted name. His Pahari name was Sat Vir Pant. The name Pant is Brahmin and suggests a follower of the traditional Hinduism, *sanatan* (*sanatana dharma*). Sat Vir was happy, as Puran told us today, that he became Aryanand. Otherwise in his village of Pabau, he was more known as Sattu. He didn't like this name.

The ancient roasted wheat powder *saktu* is called *sattu*. Paharis sometimes use roasted barley powder instead. It's horrible when you feel its coarseness in your throat, but for any poor person it's a wholesome food in many parts of northern India. It becomes slightly more palatable if mixed with *gud,* or solid molasses. Sugar is a common substitute for *gud*.

The village people called Aryanand "Sattu Maharaj." That was in fun. How could he be Maharaja if he is associated with poor man's food? His wife, Chaiti, also used his powdery name in disagreement.

Her disagreement was because her religion was *sanatan*, not Arya Samaj. Her religion is timeless. Its Sanskrit name *sanatana,* or "perpetual," implies that. Unlike her husband, she didn't change her religion. The Arya Samaj is based on the *Vedas*. This implies its beginning with the Indian Aryans around 1,500 years before Christ. The Vedic religion has no idolatry. The *sanatanis* can believe in anything, almost. Idolatry is the backbone of *Sanatana Dharma*.

The amazing thing was that Chaiti continued worshipping idols, but not in her husband's presence. He was teaching history at the D.A.V. of Pauri, so he had to pretend that his wife had become rational, like him. The Arya Samaj was very much impressed with him. They made him a local crusader of conversion. That is, he left the teaching job and became a missionary.

"In a way, it was good that he left teaching," Puran said. "As is well known, missionaries distort history. In his history class, he would be euphoric about the Aryans—all sorts of fabrications. Aryans originated in India, most probably these Himalayas. The snow-cold of the Himalayas produced their white pigment. He even counted the seven local Himalayan rivers. 'This *sapta sindhu* region was the original home of the Aryans.' There are more than 'seven rivers' in this region. But he would count the big seven like Ganga, Yamuna, Alakananda, Mandakini, etc..."

"But it's true that the white people became white because of cold. Go further up and the Himalayan cold is as damning as any European," Marla interrupted, with a smile and a wink.

"Of course. But would you believe that any white community made vegetarianism its religion?" Puran asked.

"None. The white people liked steak then. They like steak today," Marla responded.

"Like the Pahari Brahmins. Meat then, meat now, meat any time," Abdul said while tapping Marla's shoulder, just one tap. We all laughed.

Puran continued, "But Aryanand would prove you wrong. Indo-Aryans were always vegetarian. They didn't even use the psychedelic *soma* drink. And they believed in one God. These are his firm opinions about the Vedic people…Abdul and Marla! How do you think Swami ji got this 'one God' idea? Certainly not from his parents. They were worshipping the idols of so many gods!"

"Swami ji wanted to show his religion ahead of Christians and Muslims. My parents worship all major gods and goddesses. Why would they spend so much money in buying the statues and different puja materials if they believed in one God? Many gods cost a lot. You can come in our home. You will see many beautiful pictures: Lakshmi ji, Sarasvati ji, Parvati ji and their husbands. I bow to them. I need big wealth, intelligence, and power and many other things. I don't think one god can do all these favors," Abdul said.

We all laughed again.

"Such a devoted Muslim!" Navin joked.

That was the point of Aryanand. He claimed success in converting Nitya to Nitya. The middle part in between Nitya and Nitya bothered Aryanand. He changed that historical reality. Puran told us all about this history.

Nitya's father Manohar had no choice. He had to marry Nitya's mother. Nitya's step-mother Bhanumati was responsible for it. Bhanumati abused Manohar. People in the village made fun of this abuse. Manohar was a sergeant called "hawaldar" in the Garhwal Rifles, yet he would take the abuse. How could a man who was one inch over six feet bow down to her? Bowing here would have been much easier for a woman, who was about five feet tall.

Even kids would imitate his harsh and hoarse voice. He would chase them with a stick. That would make the kids more confident of their strategies. Neither his voice nor his size nor his profession intimidated them.

The kids knew he would never use any stick on his wife. They knew how Bhanumati would become mad and call him, "Hey, Manohar!" A woman was not allowed to utter the name of her husband. If she did, it would be highly offensive.

Their pronominal abuse of *tu* and *tum* was also entertaining.

These two pronouns mean "you." But the former is singular as "thou." The husband uses the former to address the wife. The wife uses the latter as "honorific you" for him. Educated individuals sometimes use the "extra-honorific" you, *ap*.

The kids knew that Bhanumati used *tu* for Manohar. They would act out a debate between the couple. One kid would be Manohar, another Bhanumati. Sometimes they would do it in front of Manohar. It was enough to wound this soldier. The pronominal switch in the debate sounded off like verbal gun shots.

"This would not be a problem in English. Just one 'you' for all. Husbands and wives are equal in America. Doesn't it mean that, Marla?" Navin looked at Marla.

"You are dead wrong. American women are ruled by men. And most of them like to be ruled. Our women are living like in a harem. Each woman wants to love that man. These women cannot unite to kill the son of a bitch." Marla was not laughing, but we all were as she said this.

Puran kept on telling about Manohar, anyway. One positive effect of being a British soldier was visible on Manohar. He wanted to educate his daughter, the daughter he had with Bhanumati. But Bhanumati wanted no higher education for Rani. So far, Rani had completed the fourth grade.

Higher education meant first being admitted to the local Christian school. It was within walking distance. Some Christian girls went to this school. They passed the high school exam successfully. If these converts can do that, then why not Hindu girls? If Brahmin and rajput boys can do it, then why not Brahmin and rajput girls?

But Manohar could not convince Bhanumati. She won because no Hindu girls were going there. Nobody seemed to be bothered about her winning.

Then other rumors began to circulate about how Bhanumati and Manohar abused each other. Remarkably, the abuse was limited to words and gestures. She would call him *ma ko khasam,* "mother's husband." He would call her *babu ki swain,* "father's wife." Sometimes it became a comic scene.

Once in a quarrel, she was seen spitting at him. He closed his fist below his belly, popping out his thumb. This vulgar gesture was used among men only. But on the battlefield, any fake weapon is worth using. So, she mimicked him. He could not stop laughing. The fight ended.

One day a different fight took place. She grabbed his military cap. Then she hit it against his boots, repeatedly. She couldn't care less what it meant to him. Dishonoring Garhwal Rifles! This military unit was established in the British tradition. It was a pride of the Indian armed forces.

Apparently his pride was hurt, so he beat her. He used the same boots to hit her. Finally she fainted. She was bleeding. As they say here: for a soldier, bloodshed is no scary thing. She had to be taken to the local hospital. The case was registered as critical. It was a small government hospital. Somehow it saved her, but not his job. He was discharged after the case was reported with medical evidence.

After the discharge, he did not return to the village. Instead, he went to Delhi. There, he became a cook in a *dhaba*, a street restaurant. He came to understand this business. He started his own dhaba in Chandni Chauk, a busy bazaar of Delhi. He made good money. Now, with the help of a local relative, he was able to marry again.

In pre-independence India, "divorce" was more of a lexical than a legal term. In Manohar's case, who was going to check in his village? Even a famous Pahari political leader married again like this. That leader did this in New Delhi, just a couple of years before 1947. That was the year of India's Independence from the British rule. Moreover, Manohar had no chance to become a leader. Politics was not his forte.

However, in the village he left, Manohar was known as a hero.

It was 1947. This year, on the 14th of August, India was to be partitioned. Pakistan, a new country, emerged that day. India was declared free on the 15th. During the partition, Hindus and Muslims rioted against each other. Delhi became bloody. Refugees began to flee from both countries, Hindus to India and Muslims to Pakistan. Hindu fanatics demanded that all Muslims leave India. The new country, Pakistan, was created for them. But Jinnah, the founder of Pakistan, failed to understand the fallacy of partition. The majority of Muslims considered India their home. Even Jinnah's daughter and her son remained in India.

One evening, some Hindu fanatics chased a Muslim neighbor of Manohar in Delhi. It was dark already. Ibrahim quickly ran into Manohar's house. Manohar's wife was pregnant. She was going through some unexpected discomforts and Manohar's attention was very important for her. Nevertheless, the couple very cleverly hid Ibrahim inside. A couple of fanatics did enter their home, but Manohar flatly denied seeing any fleeing Muslim.

During the whole night Manohar couldn't sleep. What if fanatics came again and killed Ibrahim? What if Ibrahim killed Manohar and his wife in communal revenge? Manohar was certain Ibrahim's relatives must have been murdered already. Ibrahim's wife and daughter were staying with those relatives. Ibrahim was strong enough to harm them. He was a few years younger than Manohar and quite tall.

Fortunately, his fears were unfounded.

The next morning, it was quiet. Ibrahim went back to his own house, but in an hour he was back at Manohar's. Manohar was shocked to hear his story. A Hindu refugee family from Pakistani Punjab had occupied his house. The refugees told Ibrahim to leave for Pakistan. Ibrahim could occupy their house there. The partition justified their occupancy. And so on. They wouldn't leave Ibrahim's house. In fact, they gave him a key to their house in Lahore, Pakistan. Ibrahim had never seen Lahore in his life. He spoke standard Delhi Urdu or Hindi. Panjabi was not even his mother tongue. For centuries, his forefathers lived in Chandni Chauk. How would he belong in Lahore?

Manohar was outraged by Ibrahim's nervous condition. Literally, his sense of an old soldier of Garhwal Rifles became active. He put on his old military uniform. It was clean and well pressed. He covered his hairy head with his cap. That gave him additional height, about two inches more than six feet. He took Ibrahim to his house. The refugee family did not expect that Ibrahim would come back with a soldier—a huge one.

"I have an order for you. You leave this house, right now. Give me the key," Manohar said in an authoritative voice, in Hindi. The refugee family handed over the key right away.

To Manohar, this looked like a cooperative gesture. He understood their desperation. He gave the key to Ibrahim. The family came out on the front street corner. They had no home. They looked lost.

He surprised them by saying, "Come along with me. I will take you to the Refugee Office. You will have a home."

Puran paused and looked at me. He finished his tea to wet his throat, poured another cup, and lit a Marlboro, smiling.

"I need a pause. This is really a long story, so we're lucky to have enough of this excellent drink to see us through to the conclusion."

Marla, Jennifer, and the rest of us cheered him, appreciating his superb storytelling, and we encouraged him to continue with our sincere smiles and compliments. Puran offered his cigarettes to anyone who wanted to smoke before he resumed Manohar's fascinating history.

"Then, a few weeks later Manohar's wife gave birth to a healthy baby. He was named Nitya. Ibrahim became Nitya's godfather. This friendship had one positive effect. Ibrahim persuaded Manohar to bring his daughter out. They both decided to go together for Rani, Manohar's daughter."

Even the young boys and girls of his village knew the Delhi story. Ibrahim might have told them when he suddenly appeared there with Manohar. They had planned carefully how and when to take Rani out. Her mother, Bhanumati, was not home. She had gone to visit her old parents. Surprisingly, Rani was attending the local school.

Manohar was not a deadbeat daddy.

He convinced his daughter to join him. She was impressed with the glamour of Delhi and its schools. The team left secretly for Delhi.

There, the step-mother welcomed her. She was admitted to the same Delhi school where Ibrahim's daughter was going. And, wonderfully, the two girls became very close to each other.

Manohar's son, Nitya, grew up as Manohar's son, but he also grew up to be a very different man. After all, he emerged into a very different world from the one which had developed his father. For example, Nitya was born in free India. And, he grew up in Delhi, not Garhwal. He spoke Hindi, not Garhwali.

Eventually, he passed high school. Unfortunately, the following month, just after this resounding success, Nitya's mother passed away due to TB. This was a tragedy for the whole family which would linger for years.

While most of the relatives of Ibrahim lived in Delhi, one uncle lived in Bombay. This uncle, Mr. Ismail, had several grocery stores which needed a manager. He was a widower who needed assistance as he was also involved with raising his daughter, Fatima. With Ibrahim's recommendation, Nitya went to Bombay. Nitya had already studied some accounting. It was taught under the subject "Commerce."

There, bookkeeping was Nitya's main job. He was doing this job very well. But on top of that, he was attending college, too. Soon, Nitya found that he could make good money without a college degree. His teachers had an average of three hundred rupees' salary per month. He was making more than one thousand rupees. That was his per month salary, not counting other hidden benefits. He dropped out of college.

That year, Rani's marriage was arranged. Unfortunately, the marriage took an unexpected turn. The groom and his parents lived in New Delhi; they were Pahari Brahmins. At the wedding, the father of the groom insisted on more cash. Manohar objected. Ibrahim also objected. After all, Ibrahim was Nitya's godfather. Unfortunately, the argument became heated. In spite of Manohar's objections, Nitya gave the groom's father some cash. They refused to take it. It was not an adequate amount for a dowry.

Ibrahim took Manohar in the other room. In minutes, Manohar came out. He was in his military uniform. He told the groom's father that he was going to report them to his CO. A Pahari like the father of the groom couldn't understand that this was fabrication. He begged them not to bring any police. Most probably he didn't even know that CO meant Commanding Officer. Manohar had no CO. But the trick had worked in Ibrahim's case before, and in this case, the ruse was equally successful.

The wedding ceremony was completed.

Two months later, Manohar's dhaba caught fire. Was it an accident or arson? No one knew for sure, but Manohar left Delhi for home after this incident. He went back to the village. With partial help from Nitya, he didn't need a job.

Soon, he received a telegram from Ibrahim. Rani was dead. She had committed suicide. Was it really a suicide? Or had she been murdered because the dowry wasn't enough? That too remained a question.

But Manohar and Nitya didn't want to remain in limbo. One day, they came to Delhi. They stayed with Ibrahim. He gave them some details and they hatched a plan. The next night, Nitya and Ibrahim's nephew entered the home of Rani's in-laws. Rani's husband opened the door. Apparently, he failed to recognize them. They beat him until he was unconscious. Suddenly, his old man woke up and came to the rescue. He met the same fate, and both were admitted to a hospital. They had a long recovery. Rani's father-in-law was never able to walk again without a cane.

Nitya continued his job in Bombay. His father actually didn't want him to go there. He advised Nitya to open a posh restaurant in New Delhi.

Manohar went back to his village.

Nitya ignored his father's advice, but not out of disrespect. There was a hidden benefit in Bombay for Nitya. It was the daughter of the owner, Mr. Ismail. His daughter, Fatima, had just passed high school. She wasn't going to college. Nitya was training her in bookkeeping and other things. One main thing he was teaching her was how to speak standard Hindi or Urdu. Her Bombay Hindi or Urdu was primarily good for creating comedy. North Indians like her Delhi relatives would laugh and laugh at her Urdu.

All this worked in Nitya's favor. His earnings increased. So did his love for Fatima. For Nitya, the greatest reward of this love would be Fatima's wealth. She was Ismail's only child, the heir-apparent of Ismail's entire business. Why wouldn't Ismail like Fatima's admiration of a tall handsome Nitya?! Not to mention his clean bookkeeping record.

Also, Nitya was not a poor, low caste Hindu from the north Indian plains. He was a Himalayan Brahmin with the high ego of his caste.

After four years of faithful service, Ismail told him very clearly that Fatima must marry a Muslim. No ifs, ands, or buts.

And within a year, Fatima did get married. More importantly, the marriage took place with her father's blessings. Not only cash, but several shops were included in the blessings. The lucky groom was an apparently successful young Muslim man named Mubarak. This was Nitya's new name: He had converted to Islam.

The tragedy of the situation was that not a single relative of Nitya attended this marriage, not even Ibrahim, his godfather.

But life goes on and is filled with twists and turns. Fatima's father was diabetic. Five years after Fatima's marriage, he died. He was not even fifty. Nitya, now found himself the owner of Ismail's flourishing businesses. Everything was going fine for Nitya, except that one thing: He had no communication with his father.

Not only for a Pahari Brahmin but for any high caste Hindu, a conversion like the one this family had experienced was deplorable. For Manohar, his son was Nitya, not Mubarak. He would not respond to Mubarak's letters.

About ten years later, though, he did write a letter to Nitya. He informed him that he had TB. Tuberculosis scared the couple, not only Mubarak but Fatima, too. She insisted that she would accompany her husband to his village. She had never seen this part of India. Her reason moved Mubarak: She wanted to help her father-in-law. She wanted to tell her father-in-law that Mubarak would always remain his son, and that she had been given a loving husband in Mubarak. Through the efforts of his father. Mubarak and Fatima reached the village after three days' journey.

As soon as she saw Manohar, she touched his feet. "Abba, I am your Parvati. You are my father, Himalaya. Nitya and I have been praying for your health."

These words of Fatima brought tears to Manohar's eyes. She knew so much. She did so much. He put his hand over her head.

"Yes, beti, you are our goddess, our Parvati!"

Their rapport started cordially. She touched his feet and called him what loving daughters call their fathers, Abba. And, he called her Beti, the pet name for a daughter. Such mutual interactions were ideal for any daughter-in-law and father-in-law.

The following week, Manohar arranged a welcome reception for them. A *havan* ceremony by this Aryasamajist, Aryanand, preceded the feast. Aryanand used their Hindu names, Parvati and Nitya, in the ceremony, but then these had become their names already in this place. Manohar was using these names, as his daughter-in-law wanted him to.

Before finishing his story, Puran brought the point back from the beginning, reminding all that this long story had much more context than the priest liked to recognize.

"On that last evening, Aryanand was taking credit. He did do the ceremony. He thinks the fire of *havan* purified Fatima and Mubarak."

The decision to use a Sanskrit name on that day came, not from a religious impulse, but from a deep and human love, a connection among family members. The recognition of the deeply moving moment which these two young people, Nitya and Parvati or Mubarak and Fatima – whatever one wants to call them – fomented spoke to all there in our circle listening to Puran's story.

"I am proud of my parents. They never thought I was ever impure."

Catching the meaning of the moment, Abdul was the first to speak. His voice sounded choked.

"Abdul, do you think these drummers are impure? This Aryasamaji was trying to convince them last evening. They ignored him. That is why he came to me. He was expecting me to convince them," Puran explained, sadly shaking his head.

The hollow sounds of untuned drums finding their pitch, and the laughs of our wonderfully talented drummers answered Puran's question in a way which words can never begin to.

# Chapter 23
# Day Ten of the War

The drummers started the evening singing about how the tenth day of battle culminated in more chaos. Through Sanjaya's strange psychic gift, an unexpected doom was unfolded for Dhritarashtra. As the old blind king was already very suspicious of Shikhandin, he asked the psychic Sanjaya, "How did Shikhandin proceed in the morning?"

To pleasure him, Sanjaya described the day's events.

It started when the battle was begun with the sounding of horns, conch shells and drums. The Pandava army was arrayed in a special formation today. It was headed by Shikhandin. His chariot was protected on the sides by Bhima and Arjuna. The plan was clear: finish Bhishma's onslaught.

Behind them were Draupadi's sons and Subhadra's son in their chariots. Satyaki and Chekitana protected these sons. Dhrishtadyumna followed these two. He was protected by the Panchalas.

Yudhishthira and his twin brothers, Nakula and Sahadeva, left for the battle, giving orders loudly. They were followed by Virata with his army. Drupada was behind Virata. The Kekaya brothers and the five Dhrishtaketus, each of them valiant, protected the rear of the Pandava army.

Likewise, the Kauravas left for the battle with Bhishma, the great chariot-warrior, heading the entire army. Bhishma was covered by the powerful sons of Dhritarashtra. Following them was the great bowman Drona, along with his mighty son Ashvatthaman. Playing his part, Bhagadatta followed them with elephantry. The two supporters of Bhagadatta were Kripa and Kritavarman. Behind were the two mighty kings, Sudakshina of Kamboja and Jayatsena of Magadha. They were accompanied by the stalwart son of Subala. Similarly, other great royal bowmen led by Susharman protected the rear of the Kaurava army.

The battle started in the killing field of Kurukshetra. There, the

Pandavas began to decimate the Kaurava troops.

Their success enraged the great Kaurava war lord, Bhishma. With no regard to that which lay in his path, he began to slaughter Pandava's elephants, horses, infantrymen and charioteers. On this day alone, his merits in battle would enter this great warrior into immortality.

Seeing this slaughter, Duryodhana and his brothers felt much surprise and praise for Bhishma.

Shikhandin moved closer to Bhishma. He began to hit the old hero with arrows. Bhishma smiled and said loudly, "Whatever way you may try, I will never fight with you. You are the same Shikhandini, the woman the creator made you before!"

Shikhandin was mad at these words. He licked his lips and responded, "Bhishma, I know how you destroyed many warriors. I don't care if you fight or not, but I will fight you and do good to the Pandavas. I swear I will kill you today, O conqueror of armies, so have a last look around."

Arjuna heard these words of Shikhandin. He said to him, "Shikhandin, I will cover you and kill the enemies. You keep on fighting the mighty Bhishma. I will protect you from behind. I will stop the enemy chariots; you take care of my granduncle. If you don't kill him the world will laugh at you and me!"

The Pandavas and their generals converged upon Bhishma as the day proceeded. The Kauravas knew that Bhishma could face serious trouble on this day.

By the late afternoon, both sides were ruthless. Soldiers used even mallets, clubs and mortars in hand-to-hand combat. Bhishma killed many soldiers with his sharp arrows. Cries were heard: "Shove! Grab! Fight! Stab!"

Finally, Arjuna moved closer to Bhishma. Shikhandin was in front of him, continuously targeting the old man with his arrows. Bhishma understood why Arjuna was covering Shikhandin. He threw some spears and arrows to scare away Arjuna, but Arjuna relentlessly kept on hitting the grandsire. With his special arrows, he was able to make holes in Bhishma's armor. Some of his arrows tore Bhishma's flesh from his chest.

Bhishma thought that only Arjuna could do this kind of feat. With this realization, he decided to stop fighting. He dropped his arms and pretended that he was descending from his chariot. The arrows of Shikhandin and Arjuna kept coming to hit him. Those arrows stuck to the old man's body. So many arrows had fallen around him, they made a sort of bed for him when he fell. Thus, Bhishma lay down over the bed of arrows, not on the ground.

The news of Bhishma's fall spread like wildfire. Warriors from both sides ran to see him, some out of respect, some in amazement, some with sadness and some due to this war's worthlessness.

The battle stopped. The sunset lit the skies.

During this lull, Bhishma, whose mother was Ganga, asked for water. Everyone was astonished to know that he was still alive. Instantly, Arjuna shot the ground with his powerful arrow. Water came up bursting beside Bhishma. The son of Ganga drank water and blessed Arjuna.

Bhishma pleaded with Duryodhana to make peace with the Pandavas. Duryodhana could not respond. Like others, he was overwhelmed. For him, this feeling at this moment was filled with the unbearable loss of a leader.

But Bhishma felt contented and wanted to wait to die until the Northern Solstice in a few days. That sacred day of *Uttarayana* or after, he thought, would be an auspicious date to transition from this life to the next. With no discrimination, he welcomed all the warriors present there. Then he added these words, "My head is hanging too low. Please give me a pillow."

Several kings offered him fine pillows, but Bhishma, the son of king Shantanu, rejected those pillows. He looked at Arjuna. "Arjuna! My head is hanging down. Son! Give me a proper pillow. You are the knower of the dharma of a Kshatriya."

Hearing these words of his wounded granduncle, Arjuna burst into tears.

"Yes," Arjuna replied. He made instantly a pillow out of his bow and arrows that were woven.

The granduncle accepted that pillow and praised his grandnephew for that favor. Physicians came with an assortment of medicines. Bhishma didn't accept any treatment at that time.

As the night approached, the formidable Bhishma wished all to be at peace with each other. Then, with his permission, all left for their camps.

Bijlu and Daphra ended the night's song with two lines that disturbed me.

"*Bhisam kukarmi chhayo*," Bijlu chanted. "Bhishma was an evil-doer."

"*He kukarmi Bhisama*!" Daphra concluded. "O evil-doer Bhishma!"

I frowned as I considered the context. The compound word, *kukarmi*, made me uneasy. Its words *ku*, meaning "bad," and *karmi*, meaning "karma doer" were out of order.

The day's session had lasted longer than usual and the drummers were hurrying to pack up their instruments and equipment. I didn't want to delay them. Puran and Navin looked tired, but I did question them about the ending of the song.

The two men laughed.

"These drummers feel free to improvise their music," Navin reminded me.

"I understand that. My question is about the text, not the music—the contents of those last two lines."

"Professor Sahab, you know how the *Mahabharata* texts differ from each other. This is improvisation, is it not?"

With sleepy smiles, the Thakurs left.

As I'd watched, the thirty dancers had drifted away, none of them stopping to ask the drummers why they appeared so angry with Bhishma. The fact that many Hindus name their boys Bhishma with pride further confused me.

Alone, I began speculating on the bad feeling I sensed in the drummers' attitudes and their final lines.

Shikhandin had been a princess in his past life and very much in love with a young prince of her own choosing. Bhishma had cruelly dragged her away, intent on marrying her to his half-brother Vichitravirya. Although Bhishma was angered by her refusal to wed his half-brother, he let her go. Her beloved prince, however, rejected her when she returned to him. For this, Bhishma was responsible.

He'd carried a woman away against her will. Yet, he wouldn't lay his hands on women. Bhishma was confused about dharma in practice, and that confusion sowed the seed of his misery.

As granduncle of the Kauravas and Pandavas, he should have stood for peace. Instead, he engaged in a war that meant the killing of his own people, his own relatives.

Thinking about the story of the *Mahabharata*, I began to wonder if the drummers considered Bhishma a phony hero. I certainly started wondering where I stood on the question.

# Chapter 24
# The Folklore of Equality

Swami Sanatana was trying to impress Marla. She was trying to impress him. The game looked like that. Abdul was not here today; he sent this young swami instead. Marla seemed a little bit dazed, maybe by the handsome figure and age of the swami. He was tall, tan-brown, and in his late twenties--an unusual Pahari swami. At such a young age, he was known as a swami, a monk with self-realization. He came here for her help.

Marla was well aware of the general swami psychology. Tula and I had heard her views on several occasions. "Since the success of Swami Vivekananda, many missionaries want to come to America," she said once. "One common slogan of the aspiring gurus has been 'America needs peace.' Yes, America needs peace and the swamis need dollars. The swamis see no peace problem in neighboring Pakistan, not to mention the Middle East and Africa."

Marla held the belief that the almighty dollar was the ultimate motivating power for the human impulse towards God-realization.

"The dollar is God's sweet fruit. That is why we see this line on it: *In God we trust*! But gurus know better about God. Americans don't. So these God-knowing gurus are needed in America. They try to prove that Hindus believe in one God. Many Christians wonder about that claim when they see a line of gods and goddesses in the homes of their Hindu friends."

Tula was familiar with these expressions of Marla, so she looked skeptical when she saw Swami Sanatana today in discourse with Marla. This swami spoke better English than Swami Dukha Mukta (the swami "free from pain") of Hardwar. At his ashram, he teaches foreigners Hatha Yoga like this: "Bring your hands down and touch fingers of your foots with your paws. Then lift one of your hands up with open paw. Then lower it and touch thumb of your foot of same side."

Some called him Swami Mukta English (the swami "with free English"). By his good luck he found a young disciple, Shila. She corrects him in order to help him to not speak Hindi in English. Thus no *panja* "paw" for palms, no *anguli* "finger" for the toes, and no *angutha* "thumb" for the big toe. She firmly claims that he aroused her *kundalini*, the "coil" sleeping inside invisibly at the bottom of her spine.

Marla hated the kundalini-seers and the missionaries—the big myth-makers. But Swami Sanatana made it clear, "I don't believe in kundalini, because it is not in the *Bhagavad Gita*. It is not there because it is not in any body. And I am not a missionary, because the *Bhagavad Gita* accepts any path. It says: *samatvam yoga ucyate*. Equality is called yoga. My yoga is to be the identifier of one's identity in all beings."

Marla momentarily closed her eyes, soaking in his comments.

"I understand," she said, opening her eyes, "Your name Sanatana implies that your religion is the oldest. The other religions from here are recycled books or reinvented wheels. The devout followers may claim that their religion is different from *Sanatana Dharma*, but they all carry the elements of *Sanatana Dharma*. Why was there a need for other religions when *Sanatana Dharma* already existed? Wasn't one book enough, the oldest book of religion, the *Rigveda*? Why do you need the *Bhagavad Gita*? Or any book of any religion? I like the *Rig Veda* for one reason. It doubts at the end the belief of a creator's omniscience, a creator with intelligence. It sounds so scientific. But Krishna claims to be the creator of the cosmos and he is all-knowing; he sounds like the Biblical creator, all-knowing, all-intelligent."

"You said that very well. I can tell you, very few Indians know about the 'Creation Hymn' of the *Rig Veda* you just mentioned. Try this evening with the people you meet in the dance," he complimented her remarks as he spread his palms toward her. "You are right. The views of *Rig Veda* and *Bhagavad Gita* are in opposition. Very few would believe that here. But, the *Bhagavad Gita* is not a book; it is a summary of all the paths that already existed. That is why I am not going to change anyone's religion. Abdul told me about that Arya Samaj preacher. He believes in the *Rig Veda* and other Vedic books, but he wanted to convert you, Marla."

Marla laughed, "I am Aryan already."

"How did you become that?" The Swami asked, with no discernible guile.

"My parents converted me. They were white. I had no choice." We all laughed at Marla's meaning that she was white by birth, hence Aryan.

"Did they have God's vision?" The Swami asked after everybody stopped laughing.

"You mean my parents?" Marla asked.

"Yes."

"No. They were looking for other things."

We laughed again. Apparently, the Swami had no knowledge of her background.

"God's vision must be the single goal of everyone." The Swami raised his index finger as he spoke.

"You mean God's realization!"

"No. God's vision is what Krishna and Arjuna saw in the Bhagavad Gita."

"They saw many things. Many women, too."

That comment of Marla's seemed to throw him off balance, but he paused for only a few seconds, "Professor Robert Oppenheimer was serious about that vision when he saw the Atom Bomb experiment. It was his vision. Let me make it clear. Krishna and Arjuna are just metaphors. They are philosophers' characters. Their goal is to see a vision of cosmic proportions, or *vishva rupa*. There is no such thing as a granddaddy God. It's a metaphor for grand vision. How do women enter here?"

"I am sorry. I didn't mean to offend you," Marla said. Then, she elaborated her view. "I just wanted to tell you that everybody has different visions. My vision is to see a woman president of America. India's democracy was less than two decades old when you got a woman prime minister. Our democracy is over two centuries old, and no woman leader yet. When John Kennedy became president, the American Catholics felt equality. Catholics and Protestants, Native Americans and Hispanics, Blacks and Whites, Asian Americans and Jewish Americans are all folk names—social or cultural communities. Many are ignorant, however. They consider some of these communities as various *races*. Anthropologists have failed to convince them that there is only one human race. These communities are not natural like *men* and *women*... American voters are stupid. They will vote for a male no matter what community he is from. They will vote even for a crook if he is male."

"You will have a woman president."

"When?"

"Whenever the women of America are ready; whenever they have this grand vision: a grand vision of a woman candidate, a grand vision of staying behind her, a grand vision of voting for her as a whole. If the American women cannot come together for this grand vision, then they will be whining only. You are very fortunate that you have democracy. You can freely tell all about the meaning of your grand vision, soon and loudly. Time does not have a mouth, just wings. Don't let men make meaning for women. If women can give birth to men and women, then they can give birth to new meaning too."

Navin and Puran had just arrived and sat quietly, raising their folded hands as a general "namaste" to all of us. The swami said, "I will not take your time. You all forgive me. I have to go."

Marla looked serious, awed. Just as the swami got up, she said, "You are a man of wisdom. Do you have any set of rules or steps to achieve that grand vision?"

"Thank you. Is it possible that we meet again? But before I go, let me tell you I have no steps or rules like 'eight steps for peace' or 'seven ways of success' or 'six rules for sex' and all such cheap popularity stunts. I have just three reinforcements that help me along the way. Keep looking at your vision; keep looking at your vision; and keep looking at your vision. In the process you will see your rules, your ways, and your steps. Remember, it has to be your vision, your rules, your ways, your steps, your meaning."

The Thakurs were smiling.

The swami got up and folded his hands with a smile as he said, "Namaskar to you all."

Marla responded likewise as she said, "Namaste. Let us have Abdul arrange our next meeting. Maybe we should discuss whether it is necessary to have a government with a leader. Remember, leader means inequality. Leader is a vestige of alpha male. The rest of us make up his harem...we will talk later."

After the Swami left, Marla asked me, "Is he a social philosopher or a swami? How much do you know about him?"

As I shook my head with my lips pressed together, Navin said, "Bhaiya and I know a lot about him. Quite a character, he is; somewhat different from his parents. We understand his parents, but not him."

Navin and Puran also warned Marla about *bhang* when they told us about him.

"This plant of cannabis grows here everywhere. It has many uses here.

One is for altered vision. Anybody can pick up fresh leaves from the plant, eat its fried *pakoras*, drink its cold *thandai*, smoke its hot *chilam*. And guess what? You have some sort of vision!" Navin said as he broadened his smile and eyes. "Vision varies in Hinduism." Then he talked about Swami's father.

During a *Shiva Ratri* celebration in Daya Gad, Puran and Navin saw Swami's father completely hallucinating—nothing abnormal, traditionally. For celebrating the darkest and coldest winter night of Shiva, the god of destruction, *bhang* was used quite commonly. He smoked it. Soon, he saw Lord Shiva coming into his front yard. He prostrated. His several flat prostrations on the ground were evidence of his vision. The kids were laughing at his *dandvat pranam*. In Sanskrit, a *dandavat pranama* meant laying like a log. It was considered the highest devotional "bowing," or *namaskara*.

Puran and Navin were also present as guests who refused to bow. He asked them again and again to prostrate. They, like others, failed to see any lord. They said so. But he wouldn't believe them. He went inside. In a minute, he came back with his hunting rifle. He aimed it at Puran and Navin. Who knows? They could have been destroyed. That would have been the Lord's will. He yelled, "Those who don't believe in the Lord must be destroyed." The kids prostrated at once. Others ran away.

Swami Sanatana's older brother became a doctor. The doctor discovered another use for *bhang*. Their mother developed cancer. Its pain was unbearable for her. The doctor gave her *bhang*. She felt good. But once in a while she would take too much. Then she thought of herself as a *gopi*. The cowgirls or *gopis* were Krishna's lovers. That is what the mythology says. She believed it literally. If she took too much, then she would dance in front of Krishna's picture or icon, sometimes naked. A few years later, she was found drowned. Some say she was not treated well by her husband.

Maybe that changed the older brother's, the doctor's, view. He had other serious problems with his father even in therapy. The doctor's newborn daughter fainted. No medicine would wake her up. The father ridiculed those modern medicines. He forced the doctor to let him treat the baby. After all, it was his granddaughter's life that was at stake. The doctor let the grandfather treat his granddaughter.

Grandpa held her in his arms. He sprinkled some powder on her face. The doctor was suspicious of it. "Don't use *bhang*. Please!" But it turned out to be a pinch of ash. It was not ordinary ash. It came from an ashram. The devout grandpa used it with a small booklet, *Hanuman Chalisa*. No sooner had he finished uttering the first two couplets from it very loudly than the baby opened her eyes. The doctor ridiculed his father's claim of a miracle.

"I agree with the doctor. Hanuman couldn't save Indian monkeys in American labs," Marla said.

"The swami, like his doctor brother, did not believe in miracles like these. He was a philosophy graduate from Banaras Hindu University. His main interest was to present the *Bhagavad Gita* in rational terms. That is why he mentioned the American nuclear physicist Robert Oppenheimer. Professor Oppenheimer uttered the famous verses of the *vishva rupa*. This 'cosmic picture' as described in the *Bhagavad Gita* is dramatic. This scientist's story shows that." Puran kept on explaining what the swami claimed. "The experimental explosion of the atom bomb was human choice. But the scientist thought it was like the *Kala* or Time of the *vishva rupa* that had come to destroy. He was correct. The atom bomb did destroy."

The Thakurs seemed to like the swami. They told us that this swami was intellectual, quite different from other swamis. He knew that the *Gita* was added to the *Mahabharata* story centuries later, that it was the creation of some philosophers who were influenced by Buddhism, that these philosphers had used Krishna and Arjuna as pegs upon which to hang their discourse.

But why did Abdul send Swami Sanatana by himself? Why was he absent himself? He had never missed any session before. In the preceding session, he looked unhappy. The Aryasamajist was not his ideal. But it was not enough explanation.

While we were discussing Abdul's absence, we saw him coming. He looked very happy. Jennifer was also with him.

"Jennifer did a lot of shopping in Paltan Bazaar. I personally know some shopkeepers there who became very curious. I brought Jennifer to their shops. Oh, didn't they ask us so many questions! But Jennifer enjoyed it so much. Right, Jennifer?" Abdul put his hand on her shoulder.

"Very much. Marla, you would like to buy from them. Very reasonable prices," Jennifer said.

Not only I, but the Thakurs also felt good. Abdul was in a good mood. He still had his hand on Jennifer's shoulder.

"Abdul, we thought you were upset with Aryanand, so you sent Swami Sanatana today," Navin said.

Abdul took his hand off Jennifer's shoulder. "In a way, yes. Our family knows Aryanand very well. It bothered him that they adopted me without the Arya Samaj conversion of *shuddhi*. My parents are traditional Hindu *sanatanis*. His Vedic conversion is not acceptable in my parents' *Sanatana Dharma*. My parents don't even believe that Hinduism started with the Vedic religion. Their religion is much more ancient dharma. It was long established before the Aryans came to India. They told Aryanand not only this, but they also told him that the Aryans sacrificed animals, ate meat, and drank *soma*. But Aryanand argued that these were false interpretations spread around by the European scholars. Why would Europeans say bad things about the Aryan scriptures? They are the real white people, not us, certainly not Aryanand," Abdul elaborated. "Isn't that true, Puran ji?"

"Without European scholarly research, we would not have known about our history. True, those European missionaries distorted Hinduism. But aren't any missionaries supposed to distort other religions? Swami Dayanand did the same with Christians and Muslims. The idea of *shuddhi* implies that," Puran said.

"In some cases," said Navin, "the *shuddhi* conversion idea could be good. Judge Jag Tarak Tiwari died wretched. He had no son to perform his funeral. He had grandsons, but they were his daughter's children. He had his son's son, though, Durlabh's son from that untouchable woman. The problem with the Judge was he wouldn't accept an untouchable as his grandson. This Aryasamajist would have purified him."

My father knew that Durlabh's son *was* purified. As purified he was called Ved Prakash Tripathi.

The first two words of his name meant the "Veda's Light." It brought more darkness in his future. The last word was more mockery. The Brahmin who recited the three Vedas was called a Tripathi, "Reciter of the three." Ved Prakash was expected to study the three Vedas: *Rig Veda, Yajur Veda, Sama Veda*. The fourth Veda, *Atharva Veda,* was optional. As an Aryasamaji he was free to study any Vedic scriptures, hundreds of them.

Under *Sanatana Dharma,* he could not have this freedom. The *Manusmriti*, a major *Sanatana Dharma* scripture, forbids women and untouchables to study the *Veda* "knowledge." Ved Prakash was a male, and now a Tripathi. The word *Tripathi* is a pure Sanskrit root version of the word: "Tiwari."

This family name disqualified Durlabh's son for free education. India's new policy of "reservation" or affirmative action allowed free education for all low caste and tribal children. There was no such privilege for higher castes, no matter how poor some of them might be. There were several other privileges for the "scheduled castes and tribes" under this affirmative action. Purified, and with his new name, Ved Prakash Tripathi qualified for none. Now, he could not afford to go beyond middle school. He could have previously, but he was now not a "scheduled caste" anymore, at least under the legal definition.

The Tripathi name haunted him until his wedding evening. Just before the wedding ceremony, the priest asked for his *gotra*. The priest had to announce the *gotra* of the bride and bridegroom. Tripathi's "Aryan ancestry" had to be uttered loudly. But Tripathi didn't know his *gotra*. His parents had died. But he knew he was a purified Arya. He told the Brahmin priest that he was Arya.

"In Garhwal, everybody knows that Arya means converted untouchable," the priest scolded. The bride's caste was unquestionably Brahmin. The priest refused to conduct the wedding ceremony.

Then two young male relatives of the bride came to his side. "We are *sanatani* Brahmins. How could you *Arya* cheat us? You have to pay for all the expenses or we will sue you. Do you understand, *Dom*?" one of them shouted. The *D* word for the untouchable caste had been made illegal, but, the higher castes didn't give a damn. They had continued to use this derogatory and illegal word.

Words, though, were not enough to hurt him.

"I have no money," he responded.

They dragged him out and away from the party. He was beaten badly. Some of the guests heard his cries and went out there to see what was happening.

"Leave him alone!" my father and the others yelled until they let him go. Fearing more retaliation, he ran away, and to date, no one knows what happened to Ved Prakash Tripathi, the purified Aryan.

# Chapter 25
## Day Eleven of the War

As the day's dance began, the drummers started singing the dilemma of the Kauravas. Who would be their supreme commander now that their great leader had been mortally injured? Karna heard the news of the battle and Bhishma's fall. He had always wanted to lead Duryodhana's armies, but Bhishma had kept him out. Now, Karna's ambition rekindled. He went to see Bhishma.

There, he saw Bhishma lying on his death bed. He bowed and touched the old man's feet. "O greatest of the Kuru dynasty," Karna introduced himself, "I am Radha's son. You have looked down upon me whenever we met."

Like a father, the old man stretched his arm out and put it around him very affectionately. "Come on, my rival! You have been competing against me. Had you not come to see me you would not have seen your greatness. Your father is not that chariot-repairer. You are Kunti's son. Your real mother is not Radha. Narada and Vyasa told me all about your secret birth. You are a Kshatriya, not a low caste. I have no animosity for you. This is the truth I am telling you, son. I just wanted to keep your pride within bounds. I just wanted you not to look down upon the Pandavas, so forgive me for being tough on you. You are a man of vows. You keep your promises, and nobody can equal you in valor. You have defeated many mighty kings and warriors. Even the toughest Girivrajas and Kiratas of the Himalayas have been no match for you. So, go to help the Pandavas. Join them with no animosity. In truth, they are your blood brothers."

"I know, O mighty-armed! There is no doubt in what you say. I am Kunti's son. But when I was abandoned by Kunti, that chariot-master Adhiratha and his wife Radha raised me. Later, how fortunate I was to share with Duryodhana his prosperity! It is not possible for me to deny the honor I

153

received from Duryodhana. Like Krishna is dedicated to the Pandavas, I, too, am dedicated to Duryodhana's cause. Granduncle, I will fight Arjuna. I am determined to vanquish the Pandavas in the battle. Now that you know my just determination, I deserve your permission to fight them. Please forgive me if I badmouthed you with rivalry, rashness, and immaturity."

"Karna! I permit you if you are unable to abandon this awesome animosity. Fight with a desire to attain heaven. Lead without anger and pride."

Karna received profound praises and blessings from Bhishma. He left for the battlefield. There, he cheered up the depressed Kauravas and their commanders. They were jubilant when he said, "Today, our battle has lost its leader. Our side is in bad shape. Its enthusiasm is killed by the enemies. It is leaderless. The Kauravas will be protected in the battle by me, like that great Bhishma did, with true might. Yes! I will kill those Pandavas; my mind is set and firmly focused to drive the enemy away. Today, I will go into battle to defeat those armies. I will kill the troops of the enemy and restore the whole kingdom to Dhritarashtra's son. Now arrange for my armor."

Duryodhana, the son of Dhritarashtra, was mighty happy to hear Karna talk like this. "I now believe in myself with a leader like you. Please decide what is sensible and helpful, here and now."

Karna responded to Duryodhana, "O tiger among men! You are the most intelligent king. All present here are eager to hear your words, O king! This I know: you will not speak unjustly as you have been moved, as we all have been, by this moment."

Duryodhana raised his hand up and said, "Bhishma was the leader of our armies because of his age, bravery and knowledge. And he was respected by all the troops. That great soul earned fame by slaying my enemy's troops. For ten days, he protected us with a good fight. When that man of excellence in action is gone to heaven, who do you believe should be the next leader?"

Karna said, "All these mighty men are fit for the job of supreme commander. There is no room for doubt here. But only one of them can have that job. If you appoint one, then the other will be disinterested and not fight for your cause. The senior teacher of all these warriors is Drona. He is your teacher, too, Duryodhana. He excels among all the arms-bearers. It would be appropriate to make him the supreme commander."

Duryodhana nodded his head and looked all around. Everybody seemed to approve Karna's recommendation.

Duryodhana went to see Drona. He said to the honorable guru, "By the superiority of all qualifications including varna, family origin, learning, age, intellect, bravery, dexterity, invincibility, practical wisdom, ethics, victories, austerity and graciousness, you are above all. Among these kings, no one can be equal to you as protector. Under your leadership, we want to conquer our enemies, O topmost among the twice-born varnas! O tiger among men! In the battle, I will definitely vanquish Yudhishthira and his brothers if you are our supreme commander."

All the warriors present loudly seconded this.

Drona responded, "O Duryodhana! I know you wish to win. With all the qualifications you just mentioned, I will fight the Pandavas."

With Drona's acceptance of the job, there was jubilation among the Kaurava armies. The celebration was marked by benedictions, best wishes, songs, and cries of victory.

After assuming the position of supreme commander, Drona began to prepare for the battle. Karna was also ready to assist him. Seeing the two mighty men, the warriors felt as if they had already won the war.

On the battlefield, Drona organized the armies in a special formation called *shakata,* or "cart." The Pandavas countered with a formation called *krauncha,* or "crane." Krishna and Arjuna were at the front of the Pandava armies.

Before the battle, Drona asked Duryodhana, "Now, tell me what best action you want me to take!"

Duryodhana replied to the indomitable professor, "It would be a great favor if you could capture Yudhishthira alive and hand him over to me."

"That Kunti's son is lucky to be captured alive. That is what you are looking forward to. You don't wish him dead. That's wonderful! I guess you know that Yudhishthira is a man without enemies. You must want to hand over part of the kingdom to Yudhishthira and then live in peace with your cousins. You do this in order to protect your entire clan."

"O Preceptor," Duryodhana began to betray his real motive, "if Yudhishthira is murdered, there is no victory for me. Upon his death, Arjuna alone will kill us all. But if Yudhishthira is brought here alive, he can be defeated again in another dice game. And he will keep his promise. We will defeat him at the dice. His brothers will remain loyal to him. They will go to the forest with him again. Everything will be just like before! That will ensure my victory for a long time. This is why I don't want that fair man's murder."

Drona, a guru of polity, understood the intention of Duryodhana's speech. He gave the disciple his blessings. "Consider Yudhishthira's capture as an eventuality, if Arjuna does not protect him in the battle. There is no doubt that Arjuna is my disciple, but he is young and possesses very special weapons. This is why I don't dare to capture Yudhishthira. So, first we must somehow divert Arjuna somewhere else. Once he is away from Yudhishthira, you will have your king captured."

Duryodhana was so naïve that he became overconfident in Drona's strategy. Nevertheless, he was cognizant of the soft spot that Drona had for the Pandavas. So he made the strategy public to all the troops. The soldiers welcomed the news. They shouted in excitement and blew on their conch shells. Many threw arrows around in appreciation of this strategy.

The news reached the Pandavas. Yudhishthira quickly had a meeting with his brothers and others. He spoke to Arjuna, "O tiger among men, you have heard Drona's intention. Let us draw a plan so that his intention is foiled, so that you keep fighting within distance."

Arjuna responded, "Duryodhana shall never obtain his wish from Drona. And I cannot murder my teacher. This is my vow. So long as I am alive, O king, Drona cannot kidnap you. You ought not to fear."

Then the sounds of the conch shells, horns, drums and cymbals filled the camp of the Pandavas.

The Kauravas responded likewise with their conchs and other instruments. Moments later, the two sides began to clash. In no time, the battle became fierce. The Pandavas were shaken by the swift destruction caused by Drona's reorganization.

Then, Yudhishthira told his general Dhrishtadyumna and brother Arjuna, "Drive Drona away from all sides."

The warriors followed Yudhishthira's order and surrounded Drona. As soon as they came forward, Drona and his soldiers beat the hell out of them. There was blood all over. The Pandava reorganized their armies. But too slowly, Drona caused more devastation. At one point he came close to Yudhishthira, but he was showered with arrows and had to withdraw. Then, all of a sudden Arjuna attacked Drona's troops. He and his soldiers created a bloody scene for Drona.

Eventually Duryodhana and Drona were forced to withdraw from the battle. The evening was close; darkness was quickly creeping over the camps. The Pandavas were delighted. Drona's plan to capture Yudhishthira alive had failed.

There was a meeting in the Kaurava camp about how to kidnap Yudhishthira the next day. All agreed to take Arjuna away from Yudhishthira. Full of shame, Drona suggested a new strategy. He said to Duryodhana, "As I have said, O King, even gods cannot grab Yudhishthira so long as Arjuna is beside him. If someone challenges Arjuna at the battlefield to fight elsewhere, then he would go there to engage his challenger. He will never return if he doesn't win. During his absence, I will grab Yudhishthira, even when their general Dhrishtadyumna is watching."

The king of the Trigartas heard these words of Drona. In the presence of his brothers, he addressed Duryodhana, "O King! Arjuna has humiliated us many times for no reason. For us this is the right occasion to challenge him in our territory. I assure you we will lure him there for a fight. There, we will kill him and make this earth happy."

All the brothers of the Trigarta king supported his idea. Their warriors also agreed. They made a promise by a ritual of self-cremation. Each of them lit a fire and sat in front of it on a grass mat. Everyone smeared his body and armor with ghee. Then, together they took an oath. Each *samshaptaka,* or oath taker, gave gold coins as *dakshina* to Brahmins. All these commandos uttered the oath loudly, "We shall not return to the battlefield if we don't slay the enemy there."

In today's session a small disruption took place. Two middle-aged men came with a ram. They were in a frenzy. The ram was not, except for being forced to follow these men. In this, the ram had no choice. One of the men was holding him by a rope around his neck.

The drummers asked the men as usual, "Who are you?"

One of them said, "We are Nakul and Sahdeb. This ram is for our brothers Bhim and Yudhisthar. We will sacrifice him."

Then, two other men rushed into the dancing circle. Everybody stopped. These two identified themselves, "We are Bhima and Yudhishthira!" They were really big-built compared to the so-called Nakula and Sahadeva duo with the ram.

"These four look virtually unstoppable," I said.

The drummers replied, "They all are fakes, but they are Paharis; their features look partly Tibetan and partly non-Tibetan."

"Our problem is how to get them out."

Suddenly, one man from the crowd came out with a gun in his hand. He looked like a retired military Pahari soldier. He fired a shot in the air and shouted, "I am Duryodhan! I have come to kill you four brothers! You are my cousins! I hate you Pandavas!"

He fired a shot at the ground, close to the ram. The poor ram bleated and tried to run away. The man holding him looked scared. The rope slipped from his hand; suddenly loosened, the ram ran away. All four ran after the poor animal.

The Thakur brothers and I shouted, "Thank you, Duryodhana!"

"Thank you for your divine intervention!"

And, Duryodhana just laughed.

## Chapter 26
## Deranged Marriages

"Welcome, Chacha ji," I said as I touched his feet. Professor Shib Dutt Dyuranee was standing at the door.

He said, "I brought a basketful of *tairu*," a Pahari root vegetable, and "I've just returned from my ancestral village," which was also near Pauri. "Where are the drummers and the Thakurs?" he asked.

For years, he and his family have lived across from our family's house. Being Brahmins, they are distant relatives. I addressed Shib Dutt as "Chacha ji." In relation, he was a distant uncle or Chacha ji; he looked a few years younger than my father. He had retired from the University of Allahabad. Since then, he has been living across our street here.

I steered him outside saying, "Let's move out in the lawn," and so he slouched on an easy bamboo chair I had brought especially for him from inside. I pulled up another chair for myself beside him. As we waited for the session team, we started tea.

For a few minutes, he kept sipping tea and didn't say a word. I guess he was waiting for me to start a topic. I thought he would start a topic. He did say, "Besides the *Pandau,* I'm interested in meeting the American girls." Finally, we both opened up with several topics. He asked me, "Have you met my nephew in the States?"

"What is his name?"

"Ashwini Kumar."

"Oh, yes. He came to visit us with his wife. If I remember correctly, his wife is a clinical psychologist."

"You know, he is an aerospace engineer. He is more in the air and less on the earth. It was good for him to have a doctor wife like her."

"Wasn't the doctor already divorced? She frankly told me that she had two teenagers with her previous husband, but she said she couldn't live with

159

that man, her ex-husband. Then, your nephew Ashwini Kumar came into her life."

"And Ashwini had already a son from his second wife."

"I thought that the doctor was his second wife."

"Let me switch to a different woman. I have been told that a woman in one of your dance sessions screamed a lot. She did many 'hoo, hoo's' and 'ha ha's.' Then, she picked up an ax and swung it around. I heard that she threw this ax and it hit a stray dog."

It took me a second to realize that he was referring to Goda, whose story had developed an ax from the original ladle through the assistance of the town's gossips. I decided to play along, rather than correct Shib, however. No doubt, Tula and our team would find this little twist fascinating.

"Ah, yes, the ax woman, I thought she was faking possession."

"She doesn't fake. She imagines."

I laughed a little bit, appreciating his distinction, before responding to him in such a way that it was clear I had rationalized the possessions we had observed.

"Many dancers fake. After all, the dance is fun."

Switching gears on me again, Shib became serious, "This is similar to the story of Ashwini's ex-wife. She imagines a lot for about six months. And then, she becomes more or less normal. Just for about six months, then everything starts again. We didn't know that she had these phases when her marriage was arranged with Ashwini. This made for quite an awakening to the married life for him. After the marriage, she said that she slept with his brother. Then, she added his father, too—all her wild imagination."

"Very strange. Ashwini never told us about this first wife of his and what had happened. One of my Indian colleagues in America divorced his Indian wife for the same reason. One day, she disappeared. Finally, he located her and called her. She refused to come home; she told him that she was going to marry President Kennedy. Apparently, she was looking for a great handsome lover."

We both laughed, perhaps inappropriately.

"I introduced your nephew to this colleague at a dinner with us. The next day, Ashwini called and asked if we could come for a dinner the following Saturday. He was very curious about my colleague's family. I did say that my colleague had grown children. Then, Ashwini asked me about the mother of the children. He was determined that I talk about my colleague's wife. First, I declined to talk about her. All I told him was that they were separated. He kept insisting that his doctor wife could help him. 'My wife is a marriage counselor,' he said..."

"She couldn't help her own marriage with Ashwini. You know, she is not with him any more… but go ahead."

Shib apologized for stopping my story.

"The following week, my colleague called me. He was upset. 'It was none of your business to tell Ashwini about my private life,' my colleague admonished me. That was so embarrassing to me. I wanted to slap Ashwini right away."

"Ashwini Kumar means literally 'mare's son.' But I tell you he is a son of an ass," Shib said with raised eyebrows.

While laughing at Shib's play on words, we looked up and saw the Thakur brothers coming. As we exchanged greetings, we teased them.

"We were talking about fake dancers," I said.

Puran and Navin laughed.

"You don't mean us!" Puran managed to say in the middle of their joint laughter.

"Bhendari ji is exposed now. In the first session, he faked a possession. Then, he quietly told Abdul, 'Bring my wife here.' Abdul told the drummers and they laughed. Bhendari also laughed and quit," I said.

"Perhaps you don't know this. Mrs. Bhendari doesn't believe in spirits. She is a college professor. But, Pretam Bhendari is very superstitious. Here is a proof: A *baba* from Rishikesh told him that the letter *e* was very auspicious for his name and also for his children's names. His name was spelled Pritam Bhandari, and pronounced that way, the standard way. His two sons have these names: Nermal and Semant, not the normal spelling of Nirmal and Simant. He was going to do the same with his wife's name, Vimla to Vemla. She refused. I heard he keeps nagging her, but she continues to pronounce his name Mr. Bhandari, never Mr. Bhendari. The same for her. You know, he is a Congressman. He didn't need to change his Party's name. It already has an *e*. But the Congress Party lost the election last time. Prime Minister Indira Gandhi was replaced by Morarji Desai."

"Ah, Desai has an *e*. Didn't his *baba* suggest changing Indira to Indera?" Navin asked Shib. We all laughed at the ridiculous situation.

The drummers had arrived in the meantime. Shib engaged them, asking Daphra, "Wasn't Bhendari trying to impress his wife by his possession?"

Both drummers laughed.

"He drinks a lot. He curses Morarji for making our state dry," Shib said.

Puran added, "Bhendari claims that his wife believes his spirit possession. She told him so. Poor politician Bhendari takes her statement literally. It is just like I told our priest about the *Satya Narayana* worship. Our wedding was considered complete when the priest finished the worship. I told the priest that I passed my high school exam because my parents had performed this puja two months before the exam. I told them this as a joke, but nobody was laughing. I think those people believed me literally. But I did tell my wife later that the *Satya Narayana* worship was a hoax."

# Chapter 27
# Day Twelve of the War

*The Lord said: He who does not envy nor desire should be known as an ever-renouncer. He, free from conflicts, is released from bondage with happiness, O mighty armed Arjuna.*

*—Bhagavad Gita 5.3*

The drummers continued singing the story of the last evening's *Pandau* dance.

The Trigarta commandos challenged Arjuna the following morning. Arjuna heard their promise. He said to his big brother, Yudhishthira, "I am challenged. I shall not turn back. My vow is spoken. O King! These commandos and their leader Susharman are calling me for a big battle. I deserve your permission to complete their obliteration."

"Brother! You already know what Drona desires. He is mighty and brave. Loaded with weapons, he fights untiringly. He has vowed for my capture."

Saying this, Yudhishthira looked disturbed, weary from the constant stress of battle. Respectfully, Arjuna reminded him of his most loyal and fierce protector.

"Satyaki will be your protector in the battle. The teacher will not succeed in his goal while Satyaki is alive and active."

Yudhishthira hugged Arjuna and gave his permission to fight the commandos. He wished him much success.

When the Trigarta commandos saw Arjuna moving toward them in his chariot driven by Krishna, they were delighted and began to yell at him, while organizing into their moon-like formation.

"Look at these Trigartas. How happy they are! The day will be good for them. Soon, they will reach heaven." Saying this to Krishna, Arjuna turned and blew his conch, thus announcing his arrival.

The commandos began to shower the chariot of Arjuna with their arrows. After a brief skirmish, Arjuna cut off the head of Sudhanva, one of their leaders. The severed head and torso were crushed by oncoming cavalry. The sight of their fallen hero created terror among the Trigarta commandos. Many began to flee. Seeing this desertion, the Trigarta king became mad. He screamed, "Stop running away, warriors! To be afraid is not worthy of you. You took a formidable oath by the sacred fire in the presence of Duryodhana's army. What will you tell them?"

Many stopped their retreat, turned again, and fought back. They covered Arjuna's chariot with so many arrows that it looked nonexistent, but the heroes were untouched. The bewildered commandos paused to figure their next attack. In their confusion, Arjuna slaughtered them without mercy.

On the other side of the battle yet still early in the morning, Drona spoke to Duryodhana, apprising him of Arjuna's absence. Their armies moved swiftly to attack the Pandava ranks protecting Yudhishthira.

Looking upon the field as Drona swept towards him, Yudhishthira ordered his general Dhrishtadyumna to devise a plan to ensure that the king would not be captured. The general responded to the king's concern with a resolute voice.

"O man of promise! You will not come under Drona's control, no matter how hard he tries. Today, I will drive him away with his troops."

And he moved swiftly with his horsemen toward Drona. Durmukha, one of the brothers of Duryodhana, instantly moved to the front to encounter Dhrishtadyumna. There, a fierce battle, full of noise and dust, followed. Dhrishtadyumna held Durmukha back with heavy rains of arrows. Duryodhana came forward to defend his brother, but Dhrishtadyumna's masterful strategy forced Drona to avoid him.

Later, Drona found a way to move closer to Yudhishthira. Satyaki, the Panchala prince, quickly noticed Drona's move. He rushed to protect Yudhishthira. There was a fierce fight between Drona and Satyaki. In spite of Satyaki's toughness and defence tactics, Drona hit his head hard and quickly moved to grab Yudhishthira. But before his capture could be completed, Drona was immediately given heavy resistance by Yudhishthira's defenders. Wisely, Yudhishthira used the opening and pulled back. The Pandava king understood that, on this day, even great warriors like Shikhandin and Satyaki might fail to stop Drona.

Highly impressed by Drona's amazing feats, Duryodhana said to Karna, "O Radha's son! Look how Drona has devastated the Pandava forces! I don't think they will come again to fight. They are all fleeing away in fear. Look at that fat, mad, humiliated Bhima surrounded by our troops! He is watching Drona's extraordinary performance. Today, abandoned by his defenders, that evil-minded Pandava looks with no hope for his life and kingdom."

Karna responded to Duryodhana's exaggerations, "O tiger among men, as long as this mighty-armed Bhima is alive, he will never leave the battlefield. He will not tolerate the lion-like roars of your warriors. Equipped with dreadful weapons, the brave Pandavas cannot be defeated in the battle. They are determined to fight back. They remember how you tried to destroy them by poisoning, playing dice, and imposing a forest exile. You will see how Bhima will decimate our top chariot warriors. He will slaughter our troops, one after another, with sword, bow, shafts, horses, elephants, chariots, mace and whatever else he can get hold of. He will be aided by Satyaki with the armies of the Panchalas, Kekayas, and Matsyas. They all will surround Drona. I believe without doubt that soon they will pressure the unprotected Drona, so we had better go quickly to where Drona is situated. Let us not allow them to kill Drona like the wolves ganging up to kill a big elephant."

Duryodhana heeded the counsel of Karna and moved with his brothers to protect Drona. There they heard a tumultuous noise. It was caused by the movement of the armies of the Pandavas. They were converging upon Drona.

Kaurava armies lost no time in defending Drona. A formidable battle took place. The sky over the battlefield became even more noisy and dusty. Arjuna and Krishna could hear and see from a great distance where they were battling the Trigarta commandos. Krishna was amazed by the huge slaughter of the commandos at the hands of Arjuna.

Regardless of their success there against these commandos, their attention was now diverted back to the main battlefield. Feeling apprehensive about the possible capture of Yudhishthira, they left the defeated commandos. The commando leader, Susharman, and his brothers chased Arjuna, but to no avail. Arjuna simply drove them away with his sharp flying arrows as Krishna drove back to the major battle centered on Drona.

Krishna quickly drove Arjuna's chariot to the main battlefield. His brothers were delighted to see the two of them. Reenergized by Arjuna's renewed presence, they gave a tough fight to the Kauravas.

Bhagadatta, a formidable senior warrior of the Kauravas, was fighting

Bhima. Besides a Pahari ruler of the Pragjyotishas, he was well-respected by both the Kaurava and Pandava warriors for his prowess. Today, Bhima was trying to topple him from his elephant. They had been locked in a protracted conflict.

As soon as Arjuna arrived at the battlefield, though, Bhagadatta withdrew from Bhima and attacked the newly arrived Arjuna, who retaliated with sharp arrows. The arrows flew true and wounded the giant elephant. In pain, the animal created a stampede and crushed many soldiers and horses. Bhagadatta hurled a powerful weapon at Arjuna, but Krishna quickly covered him with his shield, otherwise Arjuna would have been laid out for dead.

Then, Arjuna aimed at Bhagadatta's eyes. His arrows made him blind; now, the sightless Bhagadatta felt nothing but darkness and pain. He could not hold his bow steady. His turban fell down. He, too, fell down from his elephant and was killed by one of Arjuna's arrows.

The news of such a mighty man's death sent waves of fear among the Kauravas. Vrishaka and Achala, the brothers of Shakuni, attacked Arjuna. Arjuna fatally shot both of them. Outraged by the deaths of his brothers, Shakuni rushed at Arjuna with various weapons, but Arjuna kept parrying all the weapons targeted at him. He hit Shakuni hard enough to force him to run away from the battlefield.

Arjuna quickly moved to where Drona was situated with his troops. Arjuna, with his assistants, began to then methodically decimate those troops. On this day, Arjuna channeled lightening. The Panchalas yelled loudly, "Drona, Drona over there!" Duryodhana shouted back, "Not Drona, not Drona!" Thus, a kind of dice game for Drona took place. Dhrishtadyumna, the head of the Panchalas, chased Drona, but Drona turned back with full fury and retaliated heavily.

A game of offense and defense was going in all directions. The battlefield was soaked in blood. Dead bodies lay all over. The Kaurava armies were defeated by sunset.

Finally, all retired to their camps. There was gloom and confusion in the Kaurava camp on this night, while the Pandava camp bristled with confidence. Yudhishthira was not only safe, but victorious. Arjuna's successful fight, with Krishna's help, against the Trigarta commandos and in the battlefield today was highly praised.

The drummers ended the story with unkind words for Drona: "Listen, sisters and brothers! This Drona is an example of a teacher with no ethics.

May we never have in our schools such crooks as ones who would take up arms against his or her own students. May we have teachers who would teach any children of any caste, religion, or region of our birth—rich or poor."

# Chapter 28
# Hero, Who?

Today, Shib Dutt brought two packets of Pahari sweets, *bals* and *singoris*, from the Bengali Sweets House. This shop's name is "Bengali." Of course they sell great Bengali sweets, but the owner is a Pahari. He knows the Pahari people consider the *bal* and *singori* to be the best milk sweets.

After our usual greetings, he said with a smile, "In our last meeting we didn't talk much about your American students. All I heard was that they are interested in our polygamy. Tell them, far more interesting are many other things. For example, our food—sweets, especially."

"The two girls like almost any Indian food. The only food they are opposed to is that which is obtained by violence against animals," I said. "They take their position against *bali* very rationally: animal sacrifice is based on a simple falsehood—there are no gods, nor God's representatives."

"And, through rationality, a huge number from the West will turn to a vegetarian diet. These girls show the signs. They should know that human *bali* is worse than animal *bali*. Even rulers have resorted to violence to save and promote religion...I wanted to tell you...as you already know that... uh...uh..."

I got the impression that his utterances began to show signs of rambling and stumbling because he saw Bhag, our great cook, coming toward us. Actually his eyes were glued to the big tray that Bhag was holding in his hands. The tray was full of crisp warm *golgappas* and two glasses of hot spicy *jaljira* drink. As soon as Bhag put the tray on the small portable table, Shib picked up a couple of *golgappas*. In each *golgappa*, he poked a hole with his spoon and poured a couple of spoons of *jaljira* into each of them. As he cracked them in his mouth, he apparently felt great gusto and philanthropy. "Give some *golgappas* to your American girls and tell them my real experience with an American vegetarian friend, total atheist but great admirer of Mahatma Gandhi and..." he said. With a bit of pause he took a sip of the *jaljira* drink and continued. "This American friend translated *gol* and *gappa* as 'round puff'. He considered them bad for his digestion. Their deep-fried bleached wheat flour bothered him, gave him gas, flatulence. Still, he liked these round puffs. His field was mathematics. But, with ordinary people, he would talk ordinary, even deliberate nonsense. I can't quote him directly, but he put it something like this: after the zero, the greatest thing India discovered is *golgappa*—the *granddaddy* of all Indian snacks."

"Yes, the *Dada* of all snacks," I reinforced the mathematician's myth in Hindi as I selected a few more *golgappas* and started poking holes in them with the tip of my spoon.

Shib Dutt laughed and then he, too, picked up another golf ball sized *golgappa*. While crunching it in his mouth, he mumbled.

"He said this too: 'So many people enjoy *golgappas*. I guess you have eaten them in the millions and yet have zero farts. As a number theory teacher, I tell my Indian students: don't count on *golgappa* talkers for advice. Always seek counsel from people with a high number of successes."

Shib laughed again and I could see in his wide open mouth a number of crumbled *golgappa* pieces as if waiting to be flushed down with *jaljira*.

In spite of his random selection of discourse topics, I found Shib Dutt very engaging. His views about some local men as heroes were quite interesting. In our last meeting, just before he left, I told him how I considered Puran and Navin my project's heroes. He must have understood my intention as his response was clear.

"The Pahari drummers must be genuinely impressed. Mentorship or money does not impress them. Otherwise, Puran and Navin could have been heroes, like the lawyer Jag Tarak Tiwari. These two brothers were his protégés."

Then he winked his eyes with a funny smile. Did that suggest the rumor that the famous lawyer had a sort of *quid pro quo*? He had a secret relationship with their mother Rithi. These two brothers went to the university with his money. I didn't have the gall to ask Shib Dutt why he winked and smiled.

But today, Shib Dutt looked a little disappointed. I thought he wanted to meet Marla and Jennifer. I cheered him up.

"This morning Gurmeet delivered fresh milk after a hiatus of a month. We were thinking of making *kheer*," I said. "But we don't need other milk sweets. You have already brought our favorite sweets."

Gurmeet Kaur is the widow of Kishan Singh. Her daughter and son-in-law have come to help her.

"Sardar ji was an honest milk seller. No customer ever complained. He never mixed water in his milk. That is why we never complained about his residence in our neighborhood. We will miss him," Shib said

The death of Kishan Singh just a month before had been sudden. He had a heart attack while he was washing the cowshed. It was still early morning. His next-door neighbor was a doctor in the Doon Hospital. Kishan was already dead by the time the doctor came to see him.

Kishan was born in Pakistan into a Sikh family of farmers, the jats. During the partition his family fled to India. On the way, all the others were murdered. He arrived in India penniless. But he felt lucky, Gurmeet told us this morning. I can understand: he was a live man who had survived the modern *Mahabharata* of the partition.

As a young man Kishan Singh came here to Dehradun. He bought a small house on our street. At that time, there were no houses on this fork. It was a good place to raise she-buffalos for milk. And that is what he did. First, he had one she-buffalo. Then, he was able to afford a couple more. He made good money by selling milk.

Two decades later, new houses were built on this fork, all of them big, posh houses. Nobody questioned, "Why is this buffalo business in this rich neighborhood?" Nobody minded smelling the dung on the way. Kishan was not very religious, but neighbors addressed him as Sardar ji, or "Mr. Headman," the customary way to address an elderly Sikh male respectfully. He and his wife provided pure milk to the rich neighbors.

"They had only one child—just one daughter, but they donated regularly to the Guru Ram Rai schools in Dehradun. He had genuine respect for Mahant Indresh Charan Das ji," said Shib Dutt with sadness in his tone.

Mahant ji could be considered a genuine folk hero. This highly educated monk was from the Kukreti Brahmin family of Garhwal. His village was not too far from Pauri. Some of his relatives were our relatives by marriage. I have met his Brahmin priest Uniyal ji. The Uniyal Brahmins are very high in the Garhwali hierarchy of priests. Some of them have been the priests of the Nehru-Gandhi family. Thus the name Indresh Charan Das ji was striking. How could a Brahmin become "holy headman" or Mahant of a Sikh sect?

This sect's history is very well known in Dehradun. Its name comes from one of the last Sikh gurus, Guru Ram Rai. The Mughal emperor Aurangzeb was a Muslim fanatic, unlike his liberal ancestors from Akbar to Shah Jehan. Under the influence of hardcore mullahs, he had his older brother Dara Shikoh assassinated. That cleared his way to claim the throne of Emperor Shah Jehan. The old emperor was his own father, whom he imprisoned. It was an irony to place under house arrest the man who built the Taj Mahal. He was capable of monstrosity. For Aurangzeb, it was no big deal to bring holocaust to Hindus and Sikhs. One of the gurus and his children were murdered by this emperor, not to mention countless others. Many Sikhs vowed to fight Aurangzeb. A few didn't.

Guru Ram Rai was one of those few ones. He knew fighting the emperor of India meant inviting more persecution. Instead of fighting, he showed peace gestures to Aurangzeb.

"Guru ji called for peace with this idiot."

During our discussion, Shib Dutt clearly showed his disgust for Aurangzeb when I asked him what he thought of Guru Ram Rai as a hero.

"As we say here, *kabhi kabhi ariyal khacchar ko tez ghora kahana parta hai,* meaning 'Sometimes you have to call a stubborn mule a smart horse.' That call cost Guru ji leadership. The majority of Sikhs didn't accept him as the guru."

He gulped another *golgappa* with *jaljira.*

Shib had been looking first at me and then at the tray throughout. I anticipated that he might elaborate on the Sikhs and Aurangzeb's time. Most probably he would say what my high school history teacher, a Christian by religion, told us in the class. Luckily, there were still enough *golgappa* on the tray to keep him focused for a while.

Aurangzeb could have united Hindus and Muslims and, thus, would have saved one of the greatest empires of the world—the Mughal Empire. His great-grandmother was a Hindu. But he could not unite even the Muslims. He thought he was a genuine Sunni Muslim and hated the Shia branch of Islam. Yet, he had a big ambition to spread Islam—the Islam of his mullahs. Late in his life, this murderous missionary confessed how he was wrong. Our history teacher had recited in the class some letters of Aurangzeb's confession to his son.

The letters made it very clear how much remorse the old emperor was feeling on his death bed. He apparently realized how his mullahs had

172

misrepresented Islam. He deeply regretted heeding their counsel. They had ignored the great understanding of Islam which had come from his great-grandfather, Akbar. Emperor Akbar had respected all religions. His ancestor, Emperor Akbar, had even developed a new religion of fusion, *din-e-ilahi*, with no pressure on other groups to accept its tenets. Sikhism, for example, had complete freedom to practice its beliefs during Akbar's reign. In contrast, Guru Gobind Singh, the last Sikh guru, had been forced to raise an army to stop Aurangzeb's atrocities. This new army of saint-soldiers became known as *Khalsa,* "Pure."

To have a country based on a religion is a painful superstition. Sooner or later, others will revolt to fix the pain.

Aurangzeb's rule implies that lesson, the history teacher had summed up in the class.

My dear neighbor, old Shib, started again.

"Aurangzeb would have been the greatest Mughal hero. However, he realized too late the suffering of the people he tortured. His letters show that he had the potential to be a Buddha. The Buddha was guided by the yogis. But..."

"You must be joking!" I couldn't hold my spontaneous reaction.

"Yes, Aurangzeb would have been a hero had he not chosen to be a mullah mule. He was able to run like a horse, fast and far. His mullahs never advised him to conquer the nearby small continent of Australia and convert the natives over there. These mullahs claimed to know God and heaven, but had no idea where the hell Australia was located. They saw a real threat to the Mughal Empire, not in themselves and not in the fast-moving East India Company of the British traders, but rather in the small Sikh army of saint-soldiers." He paused for another *jaljira* sip before continuing.

"Aurangzeb could have sown the seeds of some sort of progressive conversion like the British East India Company did—for example, the introduction of English to Indian education. Today, India is the largest English-using country after Great Britain and the United States of America. No Mughal emperor could have imagined the power of such a conversion. English made it possible for the college-educated Indians to run far and fast."

Responding and adding to this idea, I jumped in, "...incredibly fast conversion. It also accelerated the *double roti* culture. I mean the East-West mix. My high school history teacher, too, thought so. The conversion of Indians into English-users took India out of the Brilish world and yet kept her in the English world. He used to call the East India Company an ever-expanding Banyan Tree. The British planted the small East India Company in 1600 A.D., just about eighteen years before Mughal Emperor Aurangzeb's birth, and it grew into the largest India ever on the world map. That's what my teacher must have meant when he made his cryptic comparisons. One of his comparisons was very striking and has rumbled through my brain for years. He had said something along the line of, while Aurangzeb's *Mahabharata* failed, the British *Mahabharata* succeeded."

"Did your history teacher know that Aurangzeb's title was 'Alamgir'?"

He looked at me and I understood he was not asking a question. I was quiet and just nodded my head. He continued after he took another sip of *jaljira*.

"You cannot call yourself 'world conqueror' while you are dividing your own people and turning them into rebels. No Mughal could conquer and unite India, but the British did. And then we divided the united India again using the same old destructive primitive tool that Aurangzeb used—religion. The partition of India along religious fault lines in 1947 is the open record of our replicable stupidity. We thought we would go forward, not backward after we gained freedom from the British Raj! We still have polygamy. For votes, crooks in the political bazaar are still gobbling up women's rights, like *golgappas*..." And, switching gears in mid-thought, Shib dropped a topical point right into our discussion.

"Did I tell you one of my ancestors kept several wives?"

"When did it happen?"

"During Aurangzeb's time. About three hundred years ago. That is why I say that we should not go backward, to Aurangzeb's times again." He smiled, enjoying that he'd brought the point back around and pinned it to our research topic.

This was a strange thing to say, though. Personally, I never thought of Aurangzeb as a possible local hero. He was neither a resident of this region, nor was he an exemplary ruler of India. Maybe dear Shib had another reason to include Aurangzeb's time in our *golgappa*-hour. Feeling the tickling of an intuition, I thought that this was a good time to ask Shib a question which would bring us back to the point of our research questions and our motivation for having come to this place in the shadows of the Himalayas. So I asked him with a broad smile, "Was your ancestor considered a local hero?"

He took another sip of *jaljira* and pouted.

"I don't think so. But Jag Tiwari is. He is our relative from my mother's side. That polygamous ancestor was from my mother's side, too. My wife considers Jag Tiwari a gutter lawyer whose practice of polygamy was nothing more than organized prostitution."

"Details of your old story of polygamy should be interesting for my American students, Marla and Jennifer." I dangled the invitation hoping to convince Shib to stick around and allow for some time with my students.

Perking up, Shib looked excited and said, "I hope they come this evening. We can ask them to interview my wife, too."

"Ah, that sounds like a very good idea. But keep it hush-hush. Don't make it too obvious. Apparently, not everybody likes the *double roti* mix. You and I are educators. We try our best to engage in rational discourse and advancement, look for new ideas no matter where they come from and no matter how the mobsters react. We train our students in view of these objectives. But some people here are very upset with these students. Marla and Jennifer have been interviewing educated women a lot, but quietly, very quietly. In every *Mahabharata* dance session, Krishna and Arjuna look like holy heroes to our locals, but like big polygamists to Marla and Jennifer. These American students think the *Mahabharata* dance is an extraordinary window to peek through into the black hole of holy polygamy."

"Yes, the devoutly religious among us would not like to look into this window. They would rather ignore it and look the other way—the 'haa haa hoo hoo hoot way,' the no-way."

"So the American girls asked many devout Indian women, 'Are polygamists holy?' Most women said no; however, when the girls asked, 'Are Krishna and Arjuna holy?' most said yes. At the same time, though, the same women responded with a flat-out *'No'* when asked: 'Would you like to see your daughter in a harem?' these women went on to tell the girls, Marla and Jennifer, of the many horrors of the harems."

I was trying to make it implicit how these girls, both very smart and observant, see some holy men as womanizers.

"By the way, Jennifer is British and Marla is American. They both go to the University of Washington. I can say they fairly represent the general opinion of college-educated women in the West," I added further.

"My wife is college educated. Your students will find in her no trace of Indian mob sentimentality."

"On this, I partially disagree with you. I know many first generation

175

immigrant Indians in America. Many of them have degrees from American universities and they are no different than the devout mob in India. Modern critical thinking has no impact on their beliefs. For example, one lawyer woman in New York wanted her school children not to know about the evils of the caste system, especially the mistreatment of the *dalit* castes. Can you imagine the lawyer suppressing the well-known evidence from her children? The kids knew that educational discrimination was practiced in India since ancient times. They knew how Drona refused to teach Ekalavya..."

"And millions of Ekalavyas here can tell those children what dumb things were done to their ancestors. Telling your own people that they are born untouchables is a heinous crime. The lawyer should tell anyone about the logical regression that was used by the higher castes for the suppression of lower castes. Even today, the higher caste people resent the *reservation* system adopted by India." He took a breath before punctuating with a sharp thought. "Affirmative action by *reservation* is the highest atonement of higher sinners."

"That's true," I agreed. I wasn't about to tell him how my parents avoided eating with my drummers.

Instead, I added a humorous case, "Another example, a woman doctor in Phoenix firmly believes that Ganapati wrote the *Mahabharata* for Parashara Vyasa. A doctor should know about human anatomy. Elephants lack a human speech mechanism. Yet this doctor was going to invest her money in a Ganesha temple. She would have, too, if her American-born college-going son had not ridiculed her." I said this with a smile.

With a roaring belch, Shib reverted to other interests of Marla and Jennifer, such as *bali*, animal rights, and vegetarianism in Hindu belief systems. My comments about critical thinking were still lingering in the mood between us.

"Yes, there are exceptions, quite a lot of them. Tell your students to visit some of the holiest Himalayan temples where *bali* is not allowed. Guru Gobind Singh declared Hemkund literally the highest pilgrimage place. He meditated here. I am sure your students know that Buddhism and Jainism were opposed to *bali*. Sikhism has no *bali* either."

He emphasized his next thought on the matter with a raised index finger, "They must note how the tenth Sikh guru is honored in this meat-eating region. My favorite example is Gobind Ghat, which is named after Guru ji."

176

"I have seen Gobind Ghat on the bank of the beautiful Alakananda."

"It still functions as a holy bathing place leading to Badrinath and Hemkund Sahib."

"And even a big number of non-believers visit these two temples because of their high altitude and natural surroundings."

"To date, I have not heard that there has ever been any *bali* in the Hindu Badrinath."

When he said this, I wanted to interrupt him with my delayed reaction. I had listened carefully and now some of my own perspective was beginning to work towards an emergence. He had tried enough of what other critics had already done before: demonization of Aurangzeb for his religious intolerance. My intent was to play a little bit of devil's advocate.

After all, Aurangzeb could have leveled Badrinath and raised a mosque there. He had done that kind of conversion elsewhere and not necessarily in the spirit of retaliation. But the local Pahari Maharaja had sheltered Dara Shikoh when Aurangzeb was hounding him. Hindus liked Dara and looked forward with hope to see him identified as the legitimate owner of the Mughal throne.

I also wanted to check with Shib to find out if he knew of any inclusion of an *asavarna* or untouchable member serving on the Badrinath Temple Committee. In accordance with the tradition, all the members had to be *savarna* or high caste; not a single low caste man or woman was admissible.

By this time, though, I began to fear that our bittersweet digressions might continue *ad infinitum*, so, I let Shib Dutt continue, hoping that the *golgappa* tray would be the limit. Instead of focusing on what I would like to challenge him about, I settled and peeked at the dessert tray to see how far we had come. To my relief, he had emptied it.

"The *prasad* and other food dishes have always been vegetarian in this temple," Shib Dutt continued, in the absence of the wonderful *golgappas*, "It is true that Dehradun is not known as a town of vegetarians. It should have been. Guru Ram Rai considered Dehradun as a holy valley and called it his Dera."

Thus, he confirmed one of the etymologies of Deradun or Dehradun—Dera means "home" and Dun (spelled also as *Doon*) means "valley."

"Then the name Dehradun is enough to recognize Guru Ram Rai as a hero," I added, hoping that he would agree with me.

"He would have been the topmost had he not regarded that mule..."

"A horse." I echoed the rest.

Shib's remark about Aurangzeb's potential of being a Buddha kept reverberating in my head. "The only Indian that received the international adoration of the Buddha is Mahatma Gandhi." I recollected my history teacher's historical evaluation when he read in the class a local politician's interview against Gandhi's mission of *ahimsa*. "Not everybody in the world is as stupid as this politician," the teacher said with a laugh. But I can seriously see now solid support for his point. The numerous statues of the Buddha and Gandhi visible around the world provide the material evidence of their successful missions (neither of them adored idols). Maybe Shib Dutt has a point, too!

Emperor Aurangzeb kept helping Guru Ram Rai. He gave him several land grants here, so much so that the organization of this guru was called Guru Ram Rai Darbar. The word *darbar* was usually reserved for "Royal Court." The Darbar was headed by Pahari Brahmin gurus successively.

Mahant Indresh Charan Das was the current guru. His focus has been mainly on education. He got support of not only the Sikhs but other local Hindus, too. The Flag Fair, or Jhanda Mela, alone generated a lot of funds. The Fair is the largest annual celebration here. It unites the local people to honor all the Sikh gurus.

I asked Shib Dutt, "Have you heard any folk song in praise of Mahant ji?"

"No. It's a shame. No Garhwali can match his contribution to education. Dehradun is one of the most literate cities of India. I think part of the credit goes to Indresh ji."

The drummers were already here. They were accompanied by two middle-aged men, Matru and Jodha; they were relatives of the drummers. All of us sipped tea with snacks, together. The two relatives looked very happy. They were very respectful to me, even though I didn't like to be addressed as "Pandit ji."

I told them with a smile, "I am not Pandit ji. You are not Das ji."

They both laughed. Matru was clean-shaven. Jodha means warrior (from the Sanskrit *Yoddhā*). He did look like an awesome traditional rajput with his big moustache. I could have addressed him as Thakur Sahab.

It is not clear to me if they understood the semantic variability of the word *das*. For Mahant ji it meant "devotee." For them, it meant "devotee of the drums," quite respectful. But its Vedic source, *dasa,* meant "Shudra, slave" which is why I object to it on occasions like these.

Before the drummers started tuning the drums, I asked them a similar question, "Are you familiar with Mahant ji?"

"Who?"

"Mahant Indresh Charan Das ji of Dehradun," I said with emphasis in my voice.

"We are not from Dehradun. Our village is near Pauri. Too far from Dehradun. Never saw him," Bijlu said.

I turned my gaze at Jodha and Matru. They were shaking their heads.

I understood.

The Mahant's native village was not too far from Pauri.

# Chapter 29
# Day Thirteen of the War

*The Lord said: Treat pleasure and pain, gain and loss, victory and defeat all the same. Then move on to fight. Thus you will not incur sin.*
*—Bhagavad Gita 2.38*

The drummers began to sing the battle of the thirteenth day. The story quickly unfurled with the dawn of the day following the success of the Pandavas on the battlefield.

Duryodhana looked despondent and dazed early in the morning. With other warriors, he met Drona. He was full of anger. Nevertheless, he politely asked Drona, "O supreme Brahmin! You are versed in speech. For you, we are on the side of death. You didn't capture Yudhishthira yesterday. He was so close to you. The enemy has no way to escape once he is in front of your eyes. You had given me your blessing because you had favored me, but later you backed off. Decent men never destroy the hopes of their favorite persons."

Drona, the son of sage Bharadvaja, was displeased by this utterance of Duryodhana. "It is not worthy of you to talk like this. You know I am constantly working hard for your pleasure. No one can win in the battle so long as Arjuna is accompanied by Krishna. Son! I assure you: Today, I will drop a great warrior dead. I will devise a special formation that cannot be even broken by the gods. But first, O King, Arjuna must be removed from the battlefield by some strategey that cannot be known to anyone involved in the battle who has received complete military training."

Duryodhana understood what Drona suggested. Immediately, the Trigarta commandos, again, challenged Arjuna. He went to fight them, away from the battlefield.

On the other side, in the main battlefield, Drona placed his army in a special formation. It looked like a concentric circle, hence it was called *chakra vyuha*. This was really mind-boggling. No one in the Pandava army knew how to penetrate through this concentric circle. It was defended by such stalwarts as Duryodhana, Karna, Duhshasana, Kripa, and Ashvatthaman. Other surviving sons of Dhritarashtra joined the army of Jayadratha, the king of the Sindhu region and son-in-law of Dhritarashtra.

This huge circular array was encountered by the Pandava forces. They were headed by mighty warriors like Yudhishthira, Bhima, Nakula, Sahadeva, Satyaki, Dhrishtadyumna, Ghatotkacha, Uttamaujas, Yudhamanyu, Dhrishtaketu, Shikhandin, Virata, and sons of Draupadi with her father Drupada.

Soon, the battle started. Drona's strategy began to work. The Pandava troops began to suffer heavy losses. They failed to penetrate the concentric circle. Yudhishthira was scared of certain defeat. He found no one who knew how to break this formidable circle. His armies began to withdraw.

Abhimanyu, a son of Arjuna and Krishna's sister Subhadra, came forward to accept this responsibility. With such a lineage, this young warrior looked undeterred and confident. Yudhishthira knew that Arjuna would have broken this Kaurava circle. What about Abhimanyu? He approached Abhimanyu. "Son, do something until Arjuna comes back. We don't know at all how to penetrate this circle."

"My father," Abhimanyu responded, "has taught me the method of breaking into this circle. But I don't know, yet, how to come out of it."

Yudhishthira said, "Son! Break it and make an opening for us. We will follow you through that door."

Bhima also said, "I will do the same with all other generals. Once we are in, we will quickly destroy it and kill the top warriors."

"I promise, today both armies will watch bodies after bodies being bruised by me, or I am not the son of Arjuna and Subhadra," Abhimanyu said in a reassuring voice.

Yudhishthira gave Abhimanyu his blessings. Then, the young boy instructed his charioteer, Sumitra. They both proceeded to the battlefield. On the way, Sumitra kept praising his young master. He knew today would be the day his young master would stand among the immortal warriors.

The Kauravas saw Abhimanyu's chariot coming toward them. They also saw the huge Pandava army behind him. Abhimanyu lost no time. He quickly moved ahead against Drona and his deputies. A fierce battle erupted.

Abhimanyu broke the front part of the concentric circle while slaying the defenders. He continued breaking ring after ring of the circle.

Seeing him crush the powerful leader of the Ashmakas, Karna, Kripa, Drona, Ashvatthaman, Shalya and many other warriors led by Duryodhana rained arrows upon Abhimanyu's chariot. Without slowing or showing any fatigue, Abhimanyu shot back with his own arrows. He swiftly killed three of their big defenders.

Karna also got hurt, but still continued shooting. Ashvatthaman and Kritavarman came to aid Karna. Abhimanyu rained his arrows on them. Shalya came forward in his chariot to attack. Abhimanyu shot him so hard that he fell on the floor of his chariot and lost consciousness. Shalya's brother, intent upon revenge, was also slain swiftly. The incredible killing speed of Abhimanyu jolted the Kaurava troops. Many soldiers began to run away out of fear. Some of them defiantly shouted at Abhimanyu, "Even if we don't live, you will not be left with life." Abhimanyu kept slaughtering them. Duryodhana himself failed to stop Abhimanyu's march.

After a while, Duhshasana became mad and rushed to attack. Abhimanyu shouted at him, "Fortunately, I see in the battle an arrogant warrior who was merciless, who has abandoned dharma."

Duhshasana had done unethical things both before and after the fraudulent dice game. Also, Duhshasana had been the one who tried to disrobe Draupadi. Abhimanyu remembered all those wrongs as the two engaged in a fierce fight. Abhimanyu wounded Duhshasana, who was quickly carried away by his charioteer. Karna was outraged and began to shoot his arrows toward Abhimanyu. Yet, the attack was thwarted; Karna's bow was cut off by Abhimanyu's arrows.

Stepping into the fray, Karna was defended by his deputy, whom Abhimanyu quickly killed. Karna was forced to back off from the battle. Abhimanyu ran after him while slaying a lot of his protectors. Abhimanyu kept entering ring after ring, leaving layer after layer of dead defenders. A wave of terror spread in the circle. Soldiers began to run away for their lives.

Jayadratha, Dhritarashtra's son-in-law, saw the chaotic disorder. Seated in his chariot, he moved ahead with his troops. He reorganized the army and deployed defenders in places vital for the circle. The Pandavas thought that they were on the verge of routing all the Kaurava forces out, but then they saw Jayadratha and his troops coming toward them. Jayadratha had already blocked all the exits of the circle.

In this quickly changing ring of fate, Drona, Kripa, Karna, Ashvatthaman, Brihadbala, and Kritavarman came back and surrounded Abhimanyu. They could not intimidate Abhimanyu, even when they made their best effort to kill him. Instead, Abhimanyu fatally hit Brihadbala. Other warriors joined Drona's team to fight him, but he methodically slew each of them. Just as his charioteer had fortold, Abhimanyu was, on this day, unstoppable.

The Kaurava regrouped again and ganged up against Abhimanyu. Since Jayadratha had closed all the exits, Abhimanyu could not find any escape route. He kept on fighting these warriors. They cut his bow and disabled his chariot. The bloodied Abhimanyu came down and picked up his mace. He went after Lakshamana, Dhushasana's son. Lakshamana fought back and was thrown down by Abhimanyu. Rising to the moment, though, Lakshmana got up and killed Abhimanyu with his mace. Many of Duryodhana's warriors were jubilant when they saw Abhimanyu's dead body on the ground. The remaining Pandava forces inside the circle were surrounded and bore the punishment for all of the Kaurava dead that day. The blood was so thick that even the Kaurava soldiers, those brave soldiers who had lost so many of the peers that day, began to sicken from all of the death.

In the evening, all returned to their camps. Yudhishthira was totally distraught with grief. Rocking himself, he lamented on questions such as: How will I tell Arjuna that his son was killed? How will I inform Subhadra?

In the meantime, sage Vyasa came there. Yudhishthira told him how he was responsible for encouraging Abhimanyu to break the circle. Sharing with him great counsel, Vyasa consoled him and gave him courage.

On the south side, Arjuna and Krishna punished the commandos with a heavy death toll. They returned as the night approached. On the way, Arjuna felt uneasy. He was concerned about the safety of his people. Krishna assured him that everything was going to be all right.

Both suspected something when they came closer. Their camp appeared silent. Nobody was out to greet them. When they entered the camp, everyone looked depressed. Arjuna's brothers were there, but no Abhimanyu. Arjuna felt very uncomfortable, as he had heard earlier about the circle. He became wary. He had taught Abhimanyu how to break it, but not how to come out of it. Did his son die in the circle?

When Arjuna's concerns were confirmed, he became uncontrollably sad and cried, "How did he fight? How did they kill him? What will Subhadra say to me when she does not see Abhimanyu with me? How do I tell Draupadi, who is already grief-stricken?"

Krishna consoled him.

Yudhishthira's condition looked pitiful. Somehow, he composed himself and told Arjuna about the extraordinary deeds Abhimanyu performed in the battle.

"We requested him to lead us into the circle. He led us and began to devastate the Kaurava forces, but Jayadratha reorganized them to trap us. He shut all the exits of the circle. Drona, Kripa, Karna, Ashvatthaman, Kritavarman and a few others supported him. They surrounded us and disabled Abhimanyu's chariot and cut his bow. Undaunted, he kept fighting with his mace until his death."

Arjuna heard all the details from Yudhishthira. He vowed to kill Jayadratha the next day. With his oath, Krishna blew his conch. Arjuna got excited and he also blew his conch. Other musical instruments and victory pronouncements followed the conchs.

The Kaurava camp heard these sounds. Their spies soon found the cause—the oath taken by Arjuna. That oath terrified Jayadratha. He addressed the assembly of the Kauravas, "That evil-minded Arjuna wants to kill me. Good luck to you all. I want to live, so I am going home."

Duryodhana gave him courage, "O tiger among men! Fear not. Who can challenge you in the battle when you are standing in the middle of Kshatriya warriors? With help from Drona, Karna, and all these mighty warriors, I will cover you."

Jayadratha bowed to Drona and asked, "Sir, please tell me what is the difference between my military skills and Arjuna's military skills?"

His teacher replied, "Your training and Arjuna's training is equal. Arjuna has an edge over you because of his performance. But that should not bother you in the battle. Son! I am your protector from fear. Don't doubt it. I have a formation which Arjuna cannot overcome. Therefore fight. Don't be afraid. Do your duty. Follow your forefathers' path, O great chariot-warrior!"

Hearing Drona's inspiring advice, Jayadratha made a fateful decision that evening to join the battle the next morning.

The night was cool, the bonfire bright, and the story of Abhimanyu's fight and murder was emotionally charged. A perfect ambiance was set for us to encounter another strange possession.

This time, Matru, the drummers' relative, began to scream with hoots.

His hands were interlocked on his head and his eyes rolled up and down. All the dancers went aside. Everyone was focused on Matru's expressions.

"Who are you?" Bijlu, the dhol player, had to ask him. Matru came close to him, shaking.

Using the local pronunciation of Bhishma, he said, "I am Bhisam."

The spirit of Bhishma had come to possess Matru. But, what was the proof?

Waiting for a response, Matru reached into the fire, grabbed some red hot embers with his bare hands, and chewed them. As he chewed the embers, smoke steamed out of his mouth. The sight of a man pulling burning embers from the fire with his bare hands in a nonchalant way and eating them had stunned everyone present. We were all as statues watching Matru.

The drummers sang, "You are true Bhisam."

The drummers changed the rhythm, slow and soft. Bijlu, as the lead drummer, began to sing his rap. Matru moved closer.

"O Bhishma, on your deathbed you described the path of dharma to Yudhishthira after the war," Bijlu said in his rap.

"You spoke so in the *Shanti Parva*."

With this last comment, Daphra had referred to the *Shanti Parvan,* or "The Peace Chapter," of the *Mahabharata*. There, Yudhishthira paid his final respects to Bhishma. The old, dying wise man explained dharma, or right conduct, to his grandnephew.

The possessed Matru nodded his head and screamed "hoot" twice.

"These *das* drummers bow to you. *Namaste, namaste.* The dharma of the *dasa* is to serve the Brahmins, Kshatriyas and Vaishyas?"

Bijlu asked the spirit for test.

"You spoke so in the *Shanti Parva*," Daphra sang his part.

The possessed Matru nodded his head while dancing.

"The Shudra should never collect wealth. Otherwise, he will control the upper classes and thus become a sinner," Bijlu said.

"You spoke so in the *Shanti Parva*," Daphra repeated the same rap.

Matru, or the thing inside him, danced and said, "Yes."

"The Vedic worship is only for the three higher classes. The sacred fire ritual is not for the Shudra class," Bijlu said.

"You spoke so in the *Shanti Parva*," Daphra sang again.

"No!"

This time Matru, or the great warrior Bhisma possessing him, could not agree. Yet, the drummers were not about to let go.

"The Creator made the Shudra as the *dasa* of the upper castes." Bijlu sang.

"You spoke so in the *Shanti Parva*," Daphra sang.

Silent, Matru said nothing, not even a hoot. He simply kept on dancing. The drummers kept on drumming, waiting for the answer. Then, the mood broke.

"You are not that wise man; you fake! You are confused."

With this indictment, Bijlu changed the rhythm.

"Hey, fake of the *Shanti Parva*!" Daphra echoed while matching the dhol player.

The drummers failed this supposed appearance of Bhishma. It was clear from their words.

After this moment had passed, we asked our cook, Bhag, to offer Matru some hot spicy *chat*. He finished the entire bowl. That was a big sigh of relief for me. The sizzling *chat* would have produced excruciating pain in his mouth if he had been burned.

You see, Tula and I had concocted our own test with the cook as our accomplice.

# Chapter 30
# Heroes, Why?

"I have not met your American students yet," Shib Dutt said as he handed me a packet of *arsa* sweets today. "Share these *arsas* with them."

"I will give them the whole packet. They may think these are Indian donuts." I meant it.

"How about *singori* and *bal?*"

"They may like them. They didn't show up at the last two sessions. Maybe Abdul took them out for field work. If not, you will see them today."

We moved out to the lawn. The tea came quickly. "Ah, this is Pahari tea. No water, just milk," he commented as he sipped.

"Courtesy of Gurmeet. She brought more milk today."

"Gurmeet and Kishan are real heroes. They came from Pakistan barely clothed and never complained."

I switched the direction of our conversation to Mahant ji.

"Bijlu and Daphra didn't know Mahant ji. Can you believe it? They all are from the vicinity of Pauri!"

"I was surprised that many in Allahabad didn't know Indresh ji. They should. He studied at the University of Allahabad," Shib Dutt said.

"How about Maharishi Mahesh Yogi? He also graduated from that university," I asked him on purpose. It turned out that he knew quite a lot about him.

"Everybody knows him as the guru of the Beatles. Even the Paharis know him. He lived for years in the monastery of Joshimath, and then he established the meditation colony between Rishikesh and Dehradun."

"You mean the Shankaracharya Nagar?"

"Yes, after his teacher's title. Only the Garhwal Maharajas founded new towns or *nagars* after their names: Srinagar, Kirtinagar, Narendra Nagar...It's amazing how the Maharishi got that kind of money!"

"That's an interesting question," I said, because I saw one of his interviews. An American talk show host wondered about his big money. The Maharishi was quick to answer, "You can see. I have no pockets!" He spread his hands from his chest downward. He meant his *dhoti*, the plain long white cloth he had on his body. The entire audience laughed. The host saw no pockets on his clothing and did not ask again about money.

"But he did have a lot of money," Shib Dutt said. "Usually most people need more money, especially if they have children. The Maharishi has no children. He is a monk. A monk who is a non-meat-eater, non-drinker, non-night-lifer, non-suitor-booter does not need that big money. He spent that money in propagating his TM. His wording, 'Transcendental Meditation,' for *dhyana* turned out good for publicity. Quite a smart move…I mean, meditation or *dhyana* is the seventh stage of the standard yoga, and the eighth and last is *samadhi*. The eighth definitely transcends the seventh. He mixed both under TM. Altogether, Maharishi was very good at the guru business. Rishikesh-Hardwar area has the biggest baba-bazaar of the world. Here you can shop around for big babas. Don't you think he beats all those holy men? "

In my head, the same question was reverberating, so I asked him, "The Maharishi lived in Garhwal for so many years. He would have been the Shankaracharya at Joshimath."

"No. He was denied that title. He was not a Brahmin. His Kayasth caste disqualified him. He would have been a better Shankaracharya than either of those two quarrelling Brahmin Shankaracharyas, though."

"Yes, I heard of the two Shankaracharyas who went to the Allahabad High Court to settle the claim," I said to show my familiarity with the court case.

"The Maharishi could have claimed that position," Shib Dutt said, slapping his thigh for emphasis.

"But then the Maharishi could have challenged the caste system. Some even believe that the Kayasth caste does not fit in the traditional *varna* system."

"It is an irony that the Maharishi accepted the worthless caste system. The *Gita* was his favorite scripture. He never challenged its support of the *varna*. He was a student of physics. Shouldn't he have debunked the claim of Krishna as the head of Nature as simply a myth created by the Brahmin men?"

"It's not easy to overcome the male chauvinism of thousands of years. I understand what you mean. Krishna is masculine and Prakriti is feminine. This feminine Nature does everything by His will. So it implies that the ultimate boss of any woman has to be a male. Krishna could have said, 'All of us, including me, are governed by Nature's laws.' He didn't. His voice is male."

My mind flitted to what Marla and Jennifer would have said if they were part of this conversation, while Shib Dutt laughed. I breathed a little sigh of relief and turned my attention back to him as he said, "Mahesh Yogi would have lost his popular appeal in India if he had questioned the *Gita* chauvinism. He was a clever man. His opinions resonated very well. How could he fool people into believing that mass meditation with mantras causes world peace? Devotees in huge numbers have been praying for ages in temples. Many of them were killed when the fanatic invaders demolished the temples. That historical evidence did not diminish people's belief in mantras. Mahesh Yogi knew that very well. Meditation by mantra resonated. And it worked in his favor. He sold one mantra per customer of TM."

I understood.

"Anyway, I am going to check with the drummers. 'Any *git* for Mahesh Yogi?' I am going to ask them."

When the drummers showed up, I did ask them. First, they smiled. I thought that they had no idea.

"So, you don't know him," I teased. They must have guessed from my smile.

But then, Bijlu turned serious.

"We know him," he said, "but why should we have a *git* for a *desi*?"

I understand the dichotomy of *Pahari* and *Desi*. A person of Himalayan ancestry is *Pahari*. Anyone else from another part of the *Des* (Sanskrit *Desha* "country") is a *desi*. This is the belief here.

"Any drummer will say this. The Paharis are not Desis. Every Pahari knows this: that the Desis speak Desi or Hindi, we speak Pahari," Shib Dutt said to me after I walked away from the drummers and asked him about Bijlu's response. He dove further in to give me a better understanding.

"You are still a Pahari even if you live in America. But the Maharishi is not Pahari, even if he has his own town near Rishikesh. His language is Hindi. He came here from central India. His caste is Kayasth. There is no Pahari Kayasth caste. No drummer will sing his song."

"I don't think anybody from Garhwal could be compared to him." I said.

Shib Dutt nodded his head. "He put our region on the world map. Do you think any Pahari could have brought the world's greatest musicians here?"

"No." I said in complete agreement, "The Beatles came here because of him. They even stayed in Dehradun."

"Many Hindus stay here for years. For ages, they have been practicing meditation here. Mahesh Yogi, too, practiced meditation here. But he was the only one who took it out from Joshimath to millions, globally. Has any Pahari monk done that?"

I said nothing. He was not expecting an answer from me. Silence, in this instance, was the greatest homage.

Bijlu and Daphra started tuning the drums. They went near the bonfire and began to sing the list of the famous warriors: "The famous warriors assembled on the fourteenth day…"

None of them sounded like a Pahari.

# Chapter 31
## Day Fourteen of the War

*The Lord said: O Arjuna! One who by comparison of himself sees equality everywhere in happiness or sadness, that person is regarded as a transcendent yogi.*

*—Bhagavad Gita: 6.32*

The dance session started on time. On this evening, I saw more newcomers for the dance. They were all men. Matru and Jodha were not seen, however. And the drummers did not explain their absence.

The drummers began to describe the battle. After the night was over, the Kaurava and Pandava armies were arrayed in new formations. The Kaurava soldiers could not see Arjuna in the front. Some of them began to shout his name. "Where is Dhananjaya, the booty-winner?" The Pandavas also could not locate Jayadratha. Drona had placed him far out, well-protected by powerful warriors.

Again, the gory battle began, with the sounds of conchs, gongs, trumpets, and drums. Arjuna, driven by Krishna in the chariot, appeared from behind. He began to massacre the soldiers of Durmarshana, another brother of Duryodhana. They were unable to stop Arjuna. They fled. Duhshasana was upset. His forces attacked Arjuna, but Arjuna repelled them. When Arjuna came close to Drona, he addressed his teacher loudly with folded hands.

"O Brahmin! Give me your best wishes. You are equal to my father. I respect you as much I do Yudhishthira and Krishna. Protect me like your son Ashvatthaman. With your blessings, I want to kill Jayadratha today. He is responsible for my son's murder."

Drona quickly responded to Arjuna, "Warrior! Without winning me, you cannot win Jayadratha."

Drona laughed as he said this; he focused his bow and began to shower

Arjuna with his arrows. Arjuna retaliated, but he could not move Drona out of his way. Sensing the futility of the attack, Krishna addressed Arjuna.

"O Partha, we better not waste time. Leave Drona behind. We have a bigger job to do."

Arjuna followed his advice. Quickly sneaking past Drona's right side, he moved away. Behind him, Drona shouted, "Where is this Pandava going? Is it not true of you that you don't retreat in battle without winning the enemy?"

Arjuna shouted back, "You are my guru, not my enemy. I am your disciple and like your son. This world has no man who can defeat you in battle." He sped away in search of Jayadratha.

For their part, the Kaurava forces fiercely resisted Arjuna's advance. Drona, too, chased him. He attacked Arjuna and Krishna. Avoiding Drona, Arjuna charged at Shrutayudha and Sudakshina, two other renowned enemies. Wanting to kill Krishna with his deadly mace, Shrutayudha hurled it as Arjuna charged by him. The mace hit Arjuna's chariot with such force that it bounced back, falling upon Shrutayudha's head and cracking his skull, fatally.

With lightning speed, Arjuna reeled around and cut Sudakshina down, while, from another direction, Ambashtha tried to flank Krishna and Arjuna and defeat them by controlling the angle. They struggled twith Arjuna, in the end, slashing his head. Thrown down, Ambashtha was mangled by the elephants coming from behind.

With the murder of such stalwarts, Duryodhana came to speak to Drona. "That super warrior Arjuna has bypassed us after suppressing our big army. O Brahmin! Please use your ingenuity. Tell us how to kill Arjuna so that Jayadratha is not killed. You are our ultimate resort. Jayadratha's protectors are now anxious."

And then, twisted Duryodhana began to speak poison yet again, "You do not favor us, even when we have always been your devotees. You favor the Pandavas, who are devoted to our displeasure. I was dumb enough to be assured by you for our protection, so I gave Jayadratha assurance for his protection. But due to this confusion, I have given him to death."

With elegance, Drona responded, "O brave lord of the people! Go now; let me devise some plan for young Jayadratha's protection. Fear not. Go to fight in the place where Arjuna has gone."

Duryodhana asked, "How can I stop Arjuna who has even overcome you, the topmost bearer of arms?"

"You speak the truth, Duryodhana. Arjuna is undefeatable. But I will do something so that you will overpower him even when Krishna is watching over him. Here is a new armor for you. Let me tie it on you so that you remain unscathed in the battle."

Drona gave him his blessings after he helped Duryodhana don the impenetrable armor. Accompanied by his trusted troops, Duryodhana proceeded to where Arjuna was fighting. There, Drona was attacked by the Pandavas, with help from the Somaka troops. A raging battle took place. There was a one-on-one fight between Drona and Dhrishtadyumna. Drona's army came under intense pressure. Divided into three parts, it began to retreat. Drona tried to reorganize them, but the Pandava troops wreaked havoc whenever they modified their strategy.

A massacre was about to take place. The Kaurava troops were simply unable to stop the march of Arjuna and his troops toward Jayadratha's location.

Jayadratha was sighted by Krishna and Arjuna.

Duryodhana ran with his troops to defend Jayadratha. Krishna said to Arjuna, "O Arjuna! Look, Duryodhana has just bypassed us. It's lucky time. You have been waiting for this opportunity. You can fight this evil man, now!"

"It shall be so," Arjuna responded. "I will chop his head off today. This crook humiliated Draupadi by pulling her hair."

Soon, Duryodhana appeared in front of them, fearless in his new armor. He tried to stop them. All the other warriors watched Duryodhana challenging them. Arjuna was full of anger. Some from the Kaurava side cried in fear, "The king is dead; the king is dead."

Duryodhana addressed his troops, "Fear not, you all! I will send these two to die."

Then, he addressed Arjuna as son of Pritha and Pandu, his mother and father, "O Pritha's son! If you are Pandu's son, then show me quickly the miraculous weapons that you use, as well as also the power and valor of you as well as of Krishna. We want to see your manhood, here and now."

With these words, Duryodhana began to rain arrows upon the two. Arjuna did the same, but to no avail. Krishna was surprised. "Arjuna, what's wrong with your bow and arrows? Are you using them skillfully?" he asked Arjuna.

Arjuna replied, "I guess Drona has tied a new armor on him. No weapons can penetrate it. But watch how I defeat this Kaurava."

Arjuna killed the horses of Duryodhana's chariot. Then, he killed the two charioteers. He quickly cut Duryodhana's bow and gloves. Now with sharp arrows, he hit Duryodhana's palms. The disabled Duryodhana was quickly withdrawn from the fight by his guards. Other warriors of Duryodhana ganged up on Arjuna, but Arjuna decimated them. Krishna blew his conch. Hearing its sound, the soldiers of Duryodhana fell down in fear. Arjuna's chariot passed through them and saw the line of guards protecting Jayadratha. Despite their attempt to stop Arjuna's advance, he methodically swept through their lines, slaughtering them.

Then the big warriors like Bhurishravas, Shala, Karna, Vrishasena, Jayadratha, Kripa, and Ashvatthaman came to fight Arjuna. A raging carnage ensued.

Across the battlefield, the Panchala warriors, along with Yudhishthira, surrounded Drona. There, Drona fought fiercely. He was so masterful, in fact, that he almost captured Yudhishthira before being surrounded by the Pandava heroes. Drona's brother rescued him, quickly taking his brother away from that melee.

Yudhishthira was concerned about Arjuna's safety. Seeking to reinforce him, Yudishthira called Satyaki back and said to him, "Satyaki, you are as brave as Krishna's son, Pradyumna. You are equal to Arjuna. You have even surpassed Bhishma. I urge you to go where Arjuna is fighting at this time."

Understanding his leader's concern, Satyaki responded wisely.

"King, you can give me orders as you would like regarding Arjuna, but Arjuna has instructed me to protect you. Who can vanquish my teacher Arjuna when he is with Krishna? I cannot go without securing your safety."

Yudhishthira said, "O great son of Madhu's clan! It is as you have said. But I am unable to overcome my concern for Arjuna."

Satyaki realized how anxious Yudhishthira was, but also didn't want to let anybody feel that he was afraid to go in the battle for Arjuna's assistance. For a moment, he weighed his response.

"All right, my lord," he agreed, "I will go at your command."

Duryodhana's army was taken by surprise when Satyaki was seen back in the battle. On his way, Satyaki encountered Drona and, like Arjuna, bypassed him. Karna failed to stop him, as well. Kritavarman chased Satyaki, but Satyaki threw him down from his chariot.

Drona also chased Satyaki towards the massacre that was Jatadratha's defense, but Satyaki threw Drona's charioteer down. With Drona's horses disorganized and wild, Drona waited to reorganize his troops. With his goal in sight, Satyaki headed towards Arjuna.

On the way, he was challenged by King Sudarshana. Ending the challenge quickly, Satyaki fatally shot the king. The Kamboja and Yavana soldiers attempted to stop him, but Satyaki forced them to quickly withdraw. Unstoppable, he surged onwards despite his challengers' attempts to slow his advance.

Suddenly encountering Shakuni and other Kaurava warriors, Satyaki pushed all of them back and forged his way ahead. Duryodhana and Duhshasana came forward to fight him. He hit Duryodhana's charioteer so hard that he fell down. Duryodhana had to be taken away in another chariot by his brothers.

After beating them all, Satyaki proceeded further. He was blocked by the Pahari soldiers. Satyaki violently routed them out of his way.

Drona was surprised when he saw Duhshasana in panic. Drona exhorted him to fight again. Leaving him there, Drona went forward to fight the Pandavas. Duhshasana quietly moved in the direction of Satyaki.

Drona attacked the Panchalas headed by Dhrishtadyumna. After a fierce fight, he beheaded Dhrishtadyumna's charioteer. Dhrishtadyumna ran away for his life.

Duhshasana was not so lucky. He attacked Satyaki, but Satyaki shot his charioteer and horses dead. He was about to kill Duhshasana, but he left him to be killed by Bhima. It was his wish to allow Bhima's prophesy to come to pass. When Draupadi was being disrobed at Duryodhana's court, Bhima had promised to wash Draupadi's hair with the dead Duhshasana's fresh blood.

Despite his injured hands, Duryodhana came to fight the Panchala troops and Yudhishthira. Reinforced and reorganized, Drona wrought havoc. The pace of the battle raced, causing panic in the Pandava army. Yudhishthira became concerned. What happened to Satyaki? How are Arjuna and Krishna? All these questions began to make him very anxious.

Bhima encouraged him, "King! I will go and locate them. Be careful about your safety. I trust Dhrishtadyumna will protect you."

Bhima left him there wondering of the fate of Krishna, Arjuna and Satyaki.

On his way, Bhima slaughtered Kaurava soldiers. He also had a fight with Drona. And, again, Drona failed to stop the advance of a Pandava hero. Bhima located Arjuna and Krishna where they were engaged in a fierce battle to kill Jayadratha. He sent the information to Yudhishthira to encourage him, to rouse his spirit.

Then, coming together, Krishna and Arjuna, as well as Bhima and Satyaki, proceeded to advance in the direction of Jayadratha. They were engaged by big Kaurava warriors such as Kripa, Ashvatthaman, Bhurishravas, etc. After a merciless fight, Bhurishravas lost his life.

Finally, Arjuna and Krishna confronted Jayadratha, who was protected by big warriors. Krishna said to Arjuna, "O Partha! Jayadratha is in the center surrounded by six mighty warriors. Without defeating them, you cannot reach Jayadratha." Arjuna understood.

Guided by Krishna, Arjuna created a ruckus. The enemies looked confused. Arjuna hit Kripa, Karna, Shalya, Vrishasena, Ashvatthaman, and Duryodhana with sharp arrows. Then, he aimed at the terrified Jayadratha. In the blink of an eye, Arjuna's arrow flashed towards the head of Jayadratha. A severed head fell to the ground.

It was already late afternoon. Yet, the news of Jayadratha's death became sensational for both sides. Vengeance spread all over. The ethics of warfare became elastic. A fierce battle continued even after the sunset. Each side was bent upon winning this war tonight. Torches were used for clear light. Nevertheless, it was not possible all the time to recognize foe from friend. Inadvertently friends hurt friends, sometimes fatally.

It was in this bloody confusion that Drona killed the sons of Dhrishtadyumna. Distraught, Dhrishtadyumna promised to mutilate the body of Drona so that he might feel pain in the same manner. Bhimasena fatally crushed two more sons of Dhritarashtra—Durmada and Dushkarna. It was a fateful night for the old man.

Drona and his forces engaged Yudhishthira, Nakula and Sahadeva. He began to slay the Pandava soldiers in huge numbers. Arjuna came to support his brothers. The battle swelled and many warriors lost their lives on both sides.

By midnight, the giant, Ghatotkacha, and his demon troops had created complete chaos in the Kaurava ranks. Nobody had the courage to fight him. Karna challenged him, but was injured. Then, he decided to use a special deadly weapon against Ghatotkacha. The weapon was called *shakti*, a power dart.

Having saved this sure-shot dart for Arjuna's assassination, the Kauravas urged him to use it now against Ghatotkacha. With it, Karna pierced the giant body of Ghatotkacha. Unable to sustain the damage it had created in him, Ghatotkacha fell and was quiet.

# Chapter 32
## A Famous Pahari

So the drummers will sing *gits* of a Pahari. But why will they also sing of the *Mahabharata* warriors of *Pandau*? Most of those big warriors may not have seen the big *pahars,* these mountains which have become known as the rooftop of the world. The word *Himalaya* must have been just a lexicon for them. Snow or *Hima* may have been an imaginary stuff for them, just like for many Indians of today. Some Indians never see snow until they go to Europe or America.

Should heroes have any borders? I thought of testing this hypothesis with the drummers again.

One of my heroes was my school principal, George Choufin, at the Christian school where I had first grown up. Because of its missionary tendencies, it was commonly known as Mission School. Behind its foundation was the big name, Mr. Messmore.

Shib Dutt might feel the same about Choufin. He also studied in that school under Choufin. I waited for Shib Dutt. He had said yesterday in the evening that he would come today; he was eager to meet Marla and Jennifer.

Finally, he showed up, followed a few minutes later by the Thakur brothers. During our tea, I mentioned George Choufin and watched all of those who knew him get excited. Some heroes might be unsung, but the heart recognizes their importance.

In this case, the drummers should have sung Mr. Choufin's praise. There is a story that his male ancestor was Chinese. His family name suggests this. Whatever his lineage, he settled in Garhwal as a Christian. He married a Garhwali girl, an untouchable.

Christians are above the caste system, so why does it matter what caste his wife was? While her lineage was that of an untouchable and this didn't matter to George Choufin or other Christians in the area, it certainly mattered to all others among whom they lived.

It mattered for the drummers, for example. They are from an untouchable caste, just like Mr. Choufin's wife. Through her, George Choufin's presence and behavior shifted the order of things. Shouldn't they be proud of him? Shouldn't they accept him as one of their own? Principal Choufin became the greatest educator of Garhwal. When he died, all the schools of Garhwal closed for a day.

Many of his students were afraid of this short guy. He measured slightly over five feet in height. He was like Napoleon of France in height and in discipline, too. In almost every class, there was at least one bully, always a boy, a local Hindu boy. Choufin was great about identifying who that boy was each year. For their part, the bully boys would get their ego and skin bruised once Choufin found out about their behavior. The boys would be whipped with *the Choufin hunter*, our nickname for Choufin's shiny thick beating stick.

I remember how he once whipped a big bully boy. This boy was a terror for younger boys. We were jubilant about the whipping news. A senior boy informed us in Hindi, "*Choufin Sahab ne sale ka murga bana diya.*" It translates nicely: Mr. Choufin made the bastard a chicken.

Otherwise, the principal was a kind man. He believed in the Bible. The school would start with the meeting of all the students in front of the main gate. On the steps to the main gate would stand four to six boys, mostly Hindus. These are good memories, as I was also included in that elite group of singers during my time at the school. We would start a prayer in English or Hindi. Then all students would repeat after us line by line. Finally the principal would come out and stand on the top step. He would look all around. That was his order to be attentive. He always read his favorite passages from the Bible, including the occasional excerpt from the "Sermon on the Mount." This was his routine. After that morning meeting, once school began, he had nothing more to do with the Bible.

Above all, Principal Choufin was a kind father. His wife died after the birth of his fourth child. He remained a widower and single father until his death. Not only his two sons, but his two daughters also went to college. Gender equality in education was his prime objective. His first daughter was the first female student of this school. She was also the first female teacher. In fact, she taught me in my fifth grade in this school.

Shib Dutt cried when he shared with me a cherished memory of this great man from when he was in sixth grade. For over a month, he disappeared from the school; he had typhoid. Because of his long absence, the principal was worried and sent the class teacher to check on his health. Shib began to run and hide when he saw his teacher walking down to his village. He knew that truants had been whipped by teachers. But, before he could hide, this class teacher called to the young Shib.

"I am here to help you. Don't go away. Mr. Choufin has sent me to help you. How are you?"

Shib understood and surrendered to the class teacher.

He finished the story with a poignant thought about leadership in education: "How much more caring a principal could he have been? He knew my father was out somewhere fighting in the Second World War. My mother and my little brother were alone in our village."

I could see tears in Shib's eyes. He wanted to say more, but he stopped. Puran, seeing the Shib touched with emotion, added to our collection of memories of George Choufin.

"Of course, he was a hero, a fearless man. My father told me that he had even killed a man-eating tiger. He had often seen him with a rifle, riding through his family forest."

After Shib was able to compose himself, he said, "When Choufin Sahab died, an unpleasant thing happened. The Choufin family allowed anyone to touch or carry his coffin. My cousin and I also touched his coffin. We bowed, like others. In the evening, my cousin told his grandmother how we paid our final respects. She forced him to take a cold bath outside before entering the house. That was not enough: He had to drink a few drops of fresh cow urine to purify himself. I remember that she admonished him, 'You didn't have to touch his coffin. Christians are untouchables.' I also had to do what my cousin did for purification. Later, we were told that a few other high-caste boys, too, experienced similar purification for the same reason!"

The drummers arrived on time. I didn't want to bore them or make them not feel connected with the group, so I asked them the same type of question. "Bijlu and Daphra, do you know how famous Principal Choufin was? Your village was close to his village."

"We know his two big *kothis* and big jungle," Bijlu replied. "I have met his sons. They are so humble."

Undoubtedly they knew that he owned a big estate, not one *kothi* but two *kothis,* or mansions. The huge forest he owned covered the whole canyon; it included pines on the hilltop and oaks in the middle; a creek marked the entire length at the bottom.

"Yes, the Choufins are known for humility. So wouldn't you consider a *git* in memory of Principal Choufin?"

"The *baddis* should do that," Daphra intervened.

"Why not you?" I asked.

I was curious as to why Daphra would make this suggestion. After all, the bards, or *baddis,* usually sang romantic songs. Principal Choufin was anything but a romantic man, though he did have a great sense of humor. He even created a new language, a mixture of Garhwali and Hindi. He used it for jokes. His mixed language was enough to make listeners laugh.

"We never played drums for any Choufin," Bijlu said.

It was clear to me that they were disinterested in my proposition, but I wanted to remain persistent. Then, the Thakurs and Shib Dutt joined our discussion, shedding some light on a different perspective.

"His *git* will not be popular. He was a principal of a Christian missionary school. Anybody who converts untouchables is disqualified," said Navin.

"But he was not converting anyone. Look, many Hindu students of this school have made a future for themselves. Some are now doctors, judges, generals, university professors, administrators and even politicians of national stature. Ask them and they will have the same feeling as I have for him."

"You are talking about the elite that came out of this school. The masses are a different matter. The scheduled castes and tribes are small minorities. Their clients are high castes. The drummers are not the obstacles; mass appeal is. They are as clever as Maharishi Mahesh Yogi. He was also converting people of different faiths, but in a subtle way. Remember the principal read the Bible every morning in front of all the students! People here don't consider missionaries as heroes," Shib Dutt said. His analysis would apply to the Aryasamajist and Mahant ji, too.

Such was the end of my promotion of any *git.*

# Chapter 33
## Day Fifteen of the War

*Arjuna said: Here in this world it is better to enjoy even by begging than to kill the teachers who are venerable. Having killed the teachers, even if they had lust for wealth, enjoyments become blood-soaked here.*

*The Lord said: You are grieving for those who ought not to be grieved and yet you are speaking apparent wise words. The wise don't grieve for the dead or living.*

*—Bhagavad Gita 2: 5, 11*

The drummers continued singing the continuation of last night's battle as soon as they had warmed up and found their rhythm.

A big gloom covered the Pandavas and their troops when the news of Ghatotkacha's demise reached them after midnight. Bhima was totally distraught at the loss of his son, but Krishna looked happy. He uplifted their spirits.

"This death is a blessing in disguise," he said, "That *shakti* weapon was reserved for Arjuna's murder. Now, Arjuna's life is spared. He will defeat these culprits. Let us not waste time in mourning Ghatotkacha's death. We had better be prepared to take revenge."

With this advice of Krishna, the Pandava heroes resolved to continue the fight and fell asleep with quietly confident hearts. It was a short night for all, though. The sleepy soldiers on both sides had to get up early in the morning. The moon was still shining in the sky.

Upon the start of the day, the Pandavas were wary of Drona and decided to address his continued success on the battlefield. Yudhishthira spoke to Dhrishtadyumna quietly, asking him, "Let us stop Drona. Ask our leading warriors to surround him."

Shortly after, Duryodhana saw the Pandava forces marching toward

Drona. Approaching Drona with a conflicted spirit, Duryodhana spoke to Drona, again using accusatory language. He said, "No sectors of ours should have been left relaxed. We thought the Pandavas were overwhelmed with grief and fatigue. You have been kind to the Pandavas. They were your favorite students. Otherwise, nobody in the world can be your equal. I am telling you the truth. The Pandavas dread you. Now, they are coming to get us."

Drona responded calmly, "Even though I am getting older, I do my best in the battlefield. I assure you I will fight for your cause. But you have to remember that Arjuna has no fear, no fatigue. No one can intimidate him in battle. No one can defeat him."

Duryodhana hated this praise of his rival. It turned his stomach.

"All right. Today, I will first divide the Pandava army. Then we will all go to kill Arjuna."

Drona smiled and said, "Good luck! Sure, you should go to fight Arjuna. You and your fellows are the source of this battle through your manipulation of the dice game and your disrespect of a woman. You fellows have been bragging about killing the Pandavas. Now show it!"

Having said this, Drona moved away from Duryodhana.

By this time, the battle was already in progress on several fronts. Bhima had become determined to kill the killer of his son, so he confronted Karna. There was a fierce fight between them. Bhima was very close to hitting Karna with his mace, but Karna destroyed Bhima's chariot. Saving himself, Bhima quickly jumped in Nakula's chariot.

Arjuna confronted Drona. The teacher and the student displayed their deadly skills, but nobody looked like a winner. Then Drona raised his bow and was ready to discharge the deadly *brahmastra*. The troops of Arjuna were horrified to see the raised bow. Before the shot was carried through, though, Arjuna cut off Drona's weapon with his own *brahmastra*. Arjuna's troops exhaled and thus regained their confidence.

Not far away, Duhshasana and Dhrishtadyumna were engaged in a big fight. Dhrishtadyumna began to overpower Duhshasana, but Kritavarman came quickly to attack Dhrishtadyumna. Then, Nakula and Sahadeva came from behind and attacked Kritavarman. Confusion was, again, the only real owner of the battle.

Duryodhana and Satyaki went on trying to kill each other, but both were saved by their respective warriors, the great nameless ones who ended without being sung. In these confrontations many soldiers were murdered, many animals mutilated, many chariots disabled.

Drona was successful in moving the Kaurava armies ahead. The Panchalas and Srinjayas, supported by Bhima, Nakula and Sahadeva, attempted to stop Drona's advance. Their confusing stratagems, however, failed to stop Drona's carnage. After such a strong start to the day, the Pandava armies were becoming quickly and totally demoralized.

Krishna watched the loss of the Pandavas' confidence. He counseled Arjuna quickly, "Arjuna, no one can overpower Drona in the battle. You have to trick him. You have to break the standard conventions of warfare. If Drona is convinced not to fight, if he lays his weapons down, then shoot him. The only way to convince Drona to drop his guard is to announce the death of his son Ashvatthaman in front of him. Drona has vowed to fight unless Ashvatthaman is slain. All we have to do is ask Bhima to kill the elephant of Malava's king Indravarman. That elephant has the same name as Drona's son, Ashvatthaman. Yudhishthira should announce this news to Drona. He knows Yudhishthira doesn't lie, so Yudhishthira must announce just this much, 'One Ashvatthaman is killed. It is an elephant.'"

Arjuna instantly rejected Krishna's advice, but all the others assembled there supported Krishna's suggestion. Yudhishthira was told about the plan and, with great reluctance, accepted it. Bhima and Arjuna decided to work out the plan.

Bhima returned to the battlefield. He faced Drona and announced, "Ashvatthaman is slain."

Drona was startled for a few moments, but came to doubt what Bhima said. He firmly believed his son was invincible, so he resumed his fight.

Krishna was greatly agitated by Drona's carnage. He spoke to the hesitant Yudhishthira, "If you don't announce the elephant's death to your teacher, you are all going to be finished by him. One is not committing a sin if he has to tell a lie to save his life. But you are reporting to Drona a fact: Ashvatthaman is dead. It is an elephant, not a man."

Krishna didn't make it clear that the part, "It is an elephant, not a man" would be drowned in the noise deliberately produced by the Pandava people.

Playing his part, Bhima convinced Yudhishthira that he had really killed an elephant named Ashvatthaman, and that all Yudhishthira had to do was to announce this in front of Drona. Yudhishthira understood their intention, but still felt deeply conflicted over the act. He did want, though, to bring the war to an end. Moreover, he wanted to stop Drona's total annihilation of the Pandavas.

Yudhishthira, heavy in heart, faced Drona and reported loudly exactly that. But Drona, exactly as planned, didn't hear the last words and couldn't know that the announcement was not about his son, but about an elephant. They were inaudible because the crooks on the Pandava side produced an ear-deafening noise of conchs and other instruments.

Drona never distrusted Yudhishthira. He looked dumbfounded and shaken. Dhrishtadyumna took advantage of his weak moment. The two fought each other. Drona grew more and more dejected. Still, he forced Dhrishtadyumna to retreat. Then Bhima came ahead and began to insult his own teacher.

"You are a Bharadvaja Brahmin, yet you practice bigotry. Sure, you were a teacher of military science, but you abuse your knowledge. A Brahmin's duty is not to engage in a fight. He is expected to observe *ahimsa* in all beings. You fail to observe that lofty dharma of non-killing. Instead, look what thoughtless carnage you have wrought upon us and others. The person in whose name you are doing this immoral act has been killed. The truthful Yudhishthira told you that Ashvatthaman was dead."

Drona dropped his weapons aside and addressed his warriors loudly, "Karna! Kripa! Duryodhana! Keep fighting. My best wishes for you. I am abandoning arms."

He cried out his son's name and sat on the floor of his chariot, wailing. Soon, he became quiet, as if in meditation. Dhrishtadyumna saw him from behind. He quickly came forward and climbed into Drona's chariot. Arjuna cried out when Dhrishtadyumna raised his sword to Drona's head, "Don't kill him!"

Thirsty for glory and revenge, Dhrishtadyumna had already slashed Drona's head. He laughed loudly and slashed it more and more until it was severed completely. Then he threw the bleeding head toward the Kaurava warriors. Shakuni, Karna, Kripa, Shalva, Kritavarman, Duhshasana, Duryodhana and the others fled away with their troops. The Pandava warriors were jubilant; Arjuna was deeply upset.

Meanwhile, Ashvatthaman was returning after a fight with Shikhandin. On his way, he saw the fleeing troops and warriors. He met Duryodhana and Kripa. They told him the reason. Ashvatthaman was distraught and outraged. He promised to avenge his father's murder.

Calling them to him, Ashvatthaman rallied the fleeing troops to fight back. All the warriors supported his decision. They all felt the outrage course through their systems, triggering a renewal of their hunger for death.

In the evening, all the armies retired to their camps. During the night, the Kaurava warriors, especially Karna, Duryodhana and Duhshasana, could not sleep well. They feared the fury of the Pandavas, whom they had wronged in the past. One wrong that bothered them most was the humiliation of Draupadi. They each knew that this act inflamed the Pandavas' desire for vengeance.

The drummers ended with these lines of doubt: "Listen, sisters and brothers! How could a man call himself God when he could not save his own friend's son? He didn't have even the human decency to express sympathy for such a loss. Instead, he was happy and stopped others from mourning."

After the drummers left, I raised an issue with the Thakurs. Puran and Navin had influenced the drummers' narratives. I knew this as the drummers had told me so. My suspicion was about Bhima's insults. "Did Bhima really say to Drona, 'But you practiced bigotry'? Or is this your modification?" I asked Puran.

"No," replied Puran. "It is the drummers' resentment in Garhwali, *Par tin bhed-bhau kare*. It's because of Ekalavya."

Puran made it clear. The pre-Aryan natives of India, like the *nishadas*, were not the members of the higher *varnas*. Young Ekalavya wanted to learn military science from Drona, but Drona refused to teach him because he was a *nishada*, a black man, an untouchable. Bhima could not have spoken against Drona's refusal. Why would he? He was a *kshatriya*, an Aryan. Drona taught him and his brothers. Arjuna considered Ekalavya his rival in archery. Drona had Ekalavya's thumb cut in order to keep Arjuna ahead of Ekalavya. That made the Pandavas happy. Of course, Bhima had no reason to accuse Drona of depriving a bright untouchable of higher education. So it was obvious why Arjuna, unlike Bhima, objected to Drona's humiliating murder, the murder of a venerable teacher, the murder of an unarmed man. But I was curious: why hadn't I heard in the drummers' rap any comments on Arjuna's objection?

"These drummers firmly believe that Drona deserves many more insults from millions of untouchables," Navin said. "Drona was murdered by a kshatriya, not by an untouchable. The untouchables had deeply respected him."

In other words, the Thakurs were not responsible for the drummers' additions. Navin made it clear further. "Storytellers like these drummers add occasionally to unload the unbearable humiliation. Retelling any story over centuries makes it heavier and more disgusting. Now you see why the *Mahabharata* literally translates as a mega-burden!"

# Chapter 34
# Marriage Counseling

"Are those American girls coming today?" Shib Dutt asked me as soon as he entered our house.

"I have no idea," I replied.

"Before they come, I would like to disclose more about my nephew." He took an envelope from his pocket. "I already told you that his doctor wife left him. Actually, he left her...see this envelope. We are invited to attend his new marriage. It's just a formality. He knows we can't attend. Or rather, we would never like to. Not his son, either...I heard that children from the previous marriage can also attend the current marriage. Isn't that right?"

He handed over the envelope to me.

"His son can even act as his father's best man. And her daughter as bridesmaid, if this is what they want." I said this, holding the envelope in my hand, but unsure as to what I should do with it. "Should we sit outside on the lawn? The tea should be ready anytime."

We sat on the lawn. There, Shib encouraged me to look at all the contents of the envelope.

"Wow, his new bride is American. Am I right?"

"Yes, she is white; here is a photo of her with him." He showed me one of the pages of the letter. Shaking his head, he made a negative proclamation: "I can tell you this marriage will not last. She is also a divorcee."

"Maybe he and she will be counseled by his ex-wife."

He understood my joke. He was laughing.

After a pause, he said, "I am glad those American girls are not here yet. His ex-wife slept with another man whom she was counseling. The man was an American. I never thought that she would be so much Americanized!"

"Spouse cheating is an old thing. Sanskrit literature has stories of extra-marital relationships."

Cheating is everywhere in literature throughout the ages. Not wanting to stir the pot further, though, I held my tongue and said nothing about the real local men like Durlabh. Instead, I waited for Shib to steer the conversation.

"Ashwini found that out."

"And then Ashwini divorced her. He had no choice. He is lucky, though. It could have been worse. An Indian gynecologist went through a bigger mess than this. He teamed up with an American gynecologist, who began to call himself a sexologist."

"What is a sexologist?" Shib Dutt asked me with a funny expression on his face.

"An expert on sex."

"A *Kama Sutra* specialist!"

"More like a tantric sex specialist. That's what Dr. Lalit Kaushik told me when I asked him the same question. But it was more than that." I smiled as I explained, "Since they were gynecologists, their clients were women."

Then I told Shib Dutt about the mess of Dr. Lalit Kaushik.

Lalit had a pretty wife. I met them at the party for their son's first birthday. Later, they invited me on *Krishna-Janmashtami*. They were doing a puja to celebrate the sacred birthday of Lord Krishna. I didn't know that they were so devout. Around the puja altar, they had hung several colorful pictures related to Lord Krishna's life.

On one picture, baby Krishna assumed cosmic form in a prison with his parents. Kamsa, the evil king of Mathura, had put his parents, Vasudeva and Devaki, in prison. It had been prophesied that their eighth child was going to be his killer. Fate would have it that Krishna was the eighth child.

Another picture had baby Krishna sucking the breast of a screaming demoness, Putana; she was sent by Kamsa to kill Krishna with her poisoned milk. Instead, Putana died as Krishna sucked her entire life through her breasts.

Another picture had a young Krishna stealing butter with his boy friends, the *gopas* "cow boys."

Another large picture was the dance of Krishna and his *gopi* girl friends.

Another large picture was Krishna counseling Arjuna in a chariot surrounded by two armies; this was related to the famous *Bhagavad Gita* discourse at the battlefield.

At the end of the worship, Lalit and his wife Kalyani prostrated. When they got up, they exclaimed loudly, "*Jaya Shri Krishna.*" (Victory to Lord Krishna). Other attendees echoed.

Everybody was given the sacred food, *prasad*: punch, sweets, and fruits after the ceremony. All of us enjoyed the full vegetarian meal that followed the *prasad*. It was a great feast. As we left, we wished the Kaushiks well.

"Did they have any picture of Krishna with his eight wives?" Shib Dutt meant this as a joke, as he was laughing, "My wife remembers only two wives—Rukmini and Satyabhama."

"My mother, too. She loved the picture of Krishna playing the flute for Radha." I just wanted to see his reaction. Radha was married to some other man, but loved Krishna secretly.

"You just mentioned about spouse cheating in Sanskrit literature. The *Mahabharata* itself suggests women's exploitation for sex. Some of Arjuna's marriages look like that. His marriages to Ulupi and Chitrangada took place when he was traveling alone. Do you think he telephoned his first two wives that he was going to marry again and again?"

"You mean Draupadi and Subhadra didn't know?"

"They must have known only when they found about his two sons, Iravan and Babhruvahana."

"But the nice thing about Arjuna is that he recognized them. He didn't lie that Iravan was not his son from Ulupi or Babhruvahana was not his son from Chitrangada."

"He needed brave warriors for free, didn't he? He didn't pay a penny to raise those two sons. The *Gita* does not say anything about Arjuna's exploits with women. Not Krishna's, either." He laughed again.

"I am sorry; I am laughing too much. I am happy that those American girls are not here. What would they think about our heroes?"

I laughed, but not because of his jokes. I thought of Marla's background. She also knows that some American heroes were no different from Indian heroes. American heroes, I wanted to tell Shib Dutt, included American presidents, senators and congressmen.

"Some American religious leaders were very much like Krishna. Their followers thought that their gurus were world teachers."

Shib Dutt immediately understood my point. He quoted a Sanskrit *shloka,* or an octo-syllabic verse, *Krishnam vande jagadgurum* (I bow to Krishna the world teacher).

"Don't we pray something like that?" Shib Dutt asked, folding his hands with a smile as he quoted the prayer verse.

"My father says that *shloka* very often as he bows to Krishna's icon," I replied. Dad really believed that Krishna was Jagad Guru, "World Teacher," and that the *shlokas* of the *Bhagavad Gita* were really meant for the entire world.

"I am sure your father knows that Krishna's world was limited to India." Shib Dutt stretched his palms horizontally about a half foot.

"Some American religious world teachers have sent their missionaries all over the world. They have converted many, giving them hope for a true salvation."

"And in India, too, our jagadgurus' teachings couldn't stop conversion. Every big or little guru claimed that only his religion's teachings were true and some day his religion was going to rule the world. If this is true, then how come these religions couldn't rule even India?"

Shib Dutt would have continued his skepticism, but the Thakur brothers had arrived. After our mutual ritual of greetings, I thought of eliciting their reactions. "Navin," I said, "We were discussing the marriages of Arjuna with Chitrangada and Ulupi. What do you think of the right of Draupadi and Subhadra to be consulted before?"

Both brothers began to laugh.

"What?" I asked.

"My wife asked that question. Actually she was not asking even though she was asking. She was objecting, not only to Arjuna's decisions, but also Krishna's decisions. It must have been very painful for Draupadi when Subhadra was added to the list. And then both must have felt pain when Arjuna added more. That was my wife's main point," Puran said.

"What was your answer?"

"I simply told her that, for men, women are like sweets. You see a candy and you can't control your craving. You see a *jalebi* sweet and you salivate. And you already have your own *lassi* drink to sip in your home. But your mind gets fixed on those beautiful women wherever you see them. Big Jagadgurus are open to the whole world. A woman is a woman anywhere. The world teacher can dance with any woman."

"You thug! Was she convinced?"

Shib Dutt gently slapped him on his back with a smile.

"I am not sure," Puran replied waving his palms circularly. "But she knows my view. I know her view. Krishna and Arjuna were totally insensitive to women's rights. That's the issue for her—women's rights. Why would Krishna counsel Arjuna on marital fidelity? Arjuna would have laughed at a polygamist's counsel. I will bring my wife along one of these days. She will tell you herself."

"I wish those American girls were here. Pahari women are the most backward women for many. Asking questions—questions that have been ignored by the dumb devotees." Shib Dutt punctuated his thought in a strange manner.

"Devotees deodorize their religious shit and keep using it as sacred stuff."

The drummers arrived.

"I am going to ask those drummers, too," Shib Dutt said.

Meanwhile, I went inside to bring snacks. When I came out, they all were laughing. "We were wondering," said Shib Dutt to me, "if the drummers could sing a *Gita* where Rukmini and Subhadra counsel their husbands on the dharma of marriage."

I also laughed with them.

# Chapter 35
# Day Sixteen of the War

*Arjuna said: O Krishna! Mind surely is fickle, excitable, and very powerful. I consider its control as hard as that of wind.*

*The Lord said: O mighty one, mind is undoubtedly uncontrollable and fickle. O Arjuna, by practice and detachment it is controlled.*

*—Bhagavad Gita: 6.34, 35*

The crowd was larger than usual. I counted fifty people, but more arrived after the drummers began their rap. Today's verses began with the morning after Drona's death. The Kauravas had lost one of their best leaders. Drona's son, Ashvatthaman, spoke highly of Karna's skills and abilities, and Duryodhana and his brothers appointed Karna the new chief of the Kauravas. Karna assured them he would lead the Kauravas armies to victory.

The next day in the early morning, after necessary ceremonies, both sides prepared for the battlefield. This time, Karna organized the armies in a different formation. Ashvatthaman, Shakuni, Uluka, Kritavarman, Sushena, Chitra, Chitrasena and a few other warriors were given special positions in the battlefield. Then, Karna blew his conch.

Yudhishthira saw the Kaurava armies. He said to Arjuna, "Look at the Kaurava armies. Karna has arrayed them very differently. Look how those big warriors are stationed! We must quickly adjust the formation of our armies."

Arjuna immediately readjusted the positions of Bhima, Nakula, Sahadeva, Yudhamanyu, and Uttamaujas.

As the sun's rays spread, the noise of conchs, drums and other instruments was heard. A gory battle began. Some big warriors like Kshemadhurti and Chitra lost their lives early in the morning. Bhima and Ashvatthaman came almost face to face. After a rough fight, both were injured. Their charioteers quickly took them in opposite directions.

Arjuna encountered a group of the commandos. He slaughtered a good number of them and forced the rest to retreat. Then, he saw Ashvatthaman coming to fight. Both gave each other a tough time. Ashvatthaman was hurt severely and taken away.

Across the field, Karna and Nakula confronted each other. After a tense battle Nakula had to run away.

The bloody battle continued the whole day without any one side or the other making a definitive blow or tipping the scale either towards the Kauravas or Pandavas.

# Chapter 36
# My Side Concerns

The dance of the Sixteenth Day of the War started slightly early. In the middle of the dance, a man showed the signs of possession. All others left the ring. I could see the man a little better. He must have been in his late fifties, medium height, and clean-shaven. Clad in loose *kurta* tunic, *topi* cap and tight pajamas, he looked like a very traditional dancer. Puran quickly situated himself between the two drummers. Nobody among the audience was talking. Normally the drummers were supposed to do the talking, but Puran poised for the role during this encounter. This promised to be an interesting exchange. Playing their part, the drummers kept drumming softly as the dialogue between Puran and the dancer started in Garhwali.

"Who are you?" Puran asked the possessed man.

"I am Krishna, O my devotee!"

"*Uddharet ātmanā ātmānam*. Where is this from?" Puran asked.

"That's Sanskrit," the man replied and danced.

"If you are true Krishna, then what does it mean?"

The dancer came close to Puran and screamed, "One should liberate himself by himself."

"Did Krishna say this in Sanskrit?"

The dancer kept dancing.

"Did Krishna say this?" Puran repeated.

The dancer said, facing the audience, "Some Brahmin said this in the *Gita*. He took it from the *Dhammapada*."

"What is it in the *Dhammapada*?"

"*Attanā codayattānam*."

"Say it again!"

"*Attā hi attano nātho*."

I was stunned. The first quote in the Pali language means "One must

219

motivate himself by himself" and the second "One himself is the master of himself." So he knew both—the *Bhagavad Gita* and the Buddha's *Dhammapada*. He also implied that the former is influenced by the latter.

"Amazing! This man is definitely a scholar," I whispered to Tula. She nodded her head. We went aside to have a better look at that man. Tula and I had an earnest desire to meet him.

I wanted more elaboration of his thoughts on the Buddha and the presumed Brahmin author of the *Gita* verses. The Buddha preached nonviolence and never encouraged anyone to fight. The author of the *Gita* liked the Buddhist non-violence. His Krishna, too, preaches non-violence. Why, then, does Krishna encourage Arjuna to fight? This is one of the inconsistent messages of the *Gita*.

The devotees or the cult followers insist that the *Gita* is consistent. They beat around the bush and become sentimental instead of logical. But they know what the story says. Not only Arjuna, but even Krishna engaged in the bloody war of greed. Actions speak louder than words, as they say.

Tula liked his view that the author of the *Bhagavad Gita* was a male Brahmin. This Brahmin had culturally-generated xenophobia. He had the audacity to put women, the business castes and the untouchables in one category: born sinners or *papa yonis*. This is very similar to *heathen* in Christianity or *kafir* in Islam. Tula is absolutely clear on the matter; like Marla, she wants religion out.

"It is stupid to consider the majority of people in the world unholy. All Brahmin males, like any males, are born of women. This idiot considered his mother's *yoni* a *papa yoni*."

I laughed out loud when Tula said this.

She didn't like my laughing. I could see her frown. Actually, I didn't laugh at her repudiation of religion; it was her semantic extension of the word *yoni* that caused my laughter. *Yoni* means vagina.

Both of us waited to see that man later. I joined the men's group. Tula, likewise, sat with the other women. When the dance session was over and I didn't see the possessed scholar in the crowd, I asked Puran about him.

"What happened to Krishna? I don't see him around. I had some questions for him."

"He quietly left with his reporter."

"Reporter? What kind of reporter?"

"A regular professional reporter. A very reliable reporter."

I laughed.

"Why are you laughing?" Puran asked me with a dry smile.

"I am thinking of Sanjaya. He is considered a very reliable reporter of Dhritarashtra. There is no doubt that the *Mahabharata* war described by him is one of the most fascinating stories of the world. But that war is full of fantasies. Like Krishna's cosmic form. Armies of millions and millions of soldiers. Gods and goddesses coming to watch the war. You know, lots of figments of author's imagination. You have to be blind like Dhritarashtra to believe all of these strange elements."

"But the situation of Dhritarashtra and Sanjaya in the epic looks very appropriate. The king was blind, helpless and hopeless. Sanjaya was nice; he gave company to the desperate king. If the king were not blind, he might have questioned Sanjaya's fabrications. He could have asked Sanjaya, 'Sanjay! Were you not hallucinating when you saw a man assuming cosmic form instead of driving the horses? Don't tell me that joke of cosmic proportion! Be more factual!'" Now, Puran laughed.

"Precisely, that is my point and concern. Not only the cosmic form of Krishna, but any part of the *Gita* may never have belonged to the epic. Let us assume that a big war took place and someone named Sanjaya did report it to a blind king. Sanjaya looks like some reporters here, with no degrees in journalism or mass communication and no professional training. What training is needed to report a controversial topic? Just blow it out of proportion. Fuel the controversy. Include your own biases even when you are a reporter. No objectivity. No accountability. So I am rightly concerned that this reporter is going to put my project in a bad light."

"I agree," said Navin. "There is no doubt about cheap journalism. Dhritarashtra occasionally criticized Sanjaya for taking the side of the Pandavas. Sanjaya had no qualms in blaming even the king for such a horrible war. As a reporter, Sanjaya was very much prejudiced. He took advantage of the king's blindness. How would the king see for himself? In your case, we all are seeing what is happening here, so what could this reporter say against your educational project?"

"Let me say what he can imagine to besmear me," I answered without mentioning Marla and Jennifer. "Suppose your reporter implies that my project is indirectly supported by the American CIA and that they found this out from an American source. Of course, they will say that they won't reveal that source. Remember, the CIA's network is real and worldwide, if not of cosmic proportions. You can find this agency's agents right here, in these Himalayas, from Dehradun to Nandadevi; maybe they work for India; maybe they are just working against China. The readers will believe your reporter. You understand what I mean?" I asked as I looked at Puran.

I assumed that the Thakur brothers were aware of some scholarly projects in the past funded for the purpose of spying. After those projects were exposed and cancelled, other such projects occasionally became suspect. My project's fieldwork was taking place in an area that bordered with Tibet, which was annexed by Communist China. The entire Himalayan border was militarily and politically tense. Dharamsala, the headquarters of the ousted Tibetan leader Dalai Lama, was not very far from Dehradun.

I was really concerned, but didn't want to elaborate. Nevertheless, I reiterated, "You know what I am referring to?"

"I do. By the way, he is not our reporter," Puran said with a wide smile. "You know you are not going to make any political career. The possessed man is. There is a rumor that he wants to run for our Parliament seat. The reporter is with him to make him popular, so he has to associate himself with some popular stuff. Your event is very hot heritage material! Many are going to believe his possession."

"There you go. Who is he really?"

"You will find out that in the news!"

"No, no," I raised my index finger. "I just told you he might put my project in a bad light. Could you please tell him not to use my project for his political popularity?"

"No need to worry. He is not only an astute politician, but also a fine scholar. He will do nothing to harm your work. He liked your work. Otherwise, why would he participate in the dance actively? He is now in your project. You took his picture, right?"

"Yes. I did."

"And you will write about his possession. Right?" He nodded his head in expectation.

"That's right." I nodded my head.

"I can assure you, he will buy your book. I doubt any individual in the entire Pahari region has a personal library as big as he has. He wouldn't like to spoil his royal image in your book."

"What royal image?"

Navin came forward and spoke quietly, "He is from the family of the late Maharaja."

I wasn't sure that I had heard right.

His disclosure flabbergasted me. "Wow. Why didn't you tell me before? That's wonderful. Our drummers might sing a *git* in his praise."

"They will never," Puran said. "That is why I intervened when he was possessed." Puran paused and scratched his head. I saw some hesitation on his face. Maybe he didn't want to say anything further, but he must have seen my eager eyes.

"He comes from a bad family. The maharajas exploited women and untouchables. Lots of wives, lots of concubines, lots of maids…And then lots of children. The untouchables were regularly forced into the *begar* labor."

Puran gave me a very strong reason. The *begar,* or forced labor, was a disgrace in this region's history.

"But this man should not be held accountable for what those maharajas did, Puran."

"Average people generalize categorically. That is what these drummers are…average people. Otherwise, that man really is a hero. We call him the Vidura of the Himalayan *Mahabharata.* He has wisdom, but only one wife!" Puran laughed. Navin and I joined him wholeheartedly.

Then, I became serious. I told the brothers why I wanted to meet their Vidura.

Puran continued, "Let's see how the news comes out. We can contact him easily. He lives here. But I can tell you my opinion. I suspect he has the same opinion…"

"Puran, I am very much interested in your opinion. Navin's too. What do you have to say?" I got excited.

"Navin first." Puran looked toward Navin.

"The subtle message of the *Bhagavad Gita* is behavioral. Humans are not consistent in thoughts and deeds. This inconsistent nature offers a fascinatingly rich look into the volatility at the core of human nature. The Buddha, rightfully and appropriately, reminds us that nothing is static."

In the Himalayan Nights

# Chapter 37
# Covert Converts

Today my false understanding was removed. In my boyhood days, I knew all the Christian converts of my school. They were either students or teachers. Every one of them came from a local untouchable caste. Some of their relatives are still classed as "scheduled castes." Such a classification grants them a privileged status, but the converts are not entitled to such a status. I thought they would be classified on the basis of their ancestry instead of their new religion. I was wrong.

Jay Singh and I sat on the lawn. We waited for the tea and snacks. Meanwhile, we started chatting about local forests. Jay knew about some forests where game animals were easily available. He was almost shocked to hear that I was a vegetarian and believed in wildlife preservation. The wildlife preservation stand did not surprise him so much as my being a vegetarian.

"Any medical reasons?" He asked me when I told him so.

"No. It's a matter of ethics."

"You mean the rest of the Himalayan Brahmins are unethical?"

We both laughed.

"Pandit ji, one of my reasons to meet you was to offer you fresh pork. I thought you would like that. Just last week, I shot a wild swine. I was passing through a dense forest and there I saw a huge swine, very strong. He ran even after my first shot. Then, I shot him again. He fell down. By the time I reached him, he was not dead yet. Wild swine are thick-skinned animals. I shot him again. All my family members enjoyed that wild pork. Wild pork tastes much better than market pork. In America, it would be difficult for you to get natural pork. I would be very happy to hunt for another swine if you wish to go back to your ancestral diet. That's very funny that you converted to vegetarianism."

He must have seen my face. I didn't enjoy his mercilessness. It was nice that neither Marla and Jennifer nor Abdul showed up today. As if Jay wanted to convert me, he said, "I see nothing wrong in hunting," with a funny look at me.

"You are a rajput. Hunting is the sign of bravery and royalty. Rajputs are the bravest of the Hindu castes. You know those Victoria Cross winners of the World War!" I said.

"Pandit ji, I am not a Hindu. I mean, I was a rajput. But, I converted to Christianity."

"That's interesting. You are the first Pahari rajput Christian I ever met. I was under the impression that only the untouchables were willing to convert. Tell me why you left Hinduism for Christianity."

"That's a matter of ethics."

This time, he didn't laugh. I didn't, either. I guess we had different reasons.

"As a student through high school, I remained Hindu. During those years, I saw some of my class fellows insulting the untouchables. Then, I went to college. I thought we would become more enlightened as college students. But, I found that many high-caste class fellows resented the quotas reserved for the scheduled castes. Personally, I didn't care for the caste system. Since I was attending Lucknow's Christian College, I converted. High castes always want both ways in their favor. They don't want the untouchables to convert, but they also don't want to give them special opportunities to develop. The high castes say that everybody should be given equal opportunity. They are saying that now. Why didn't their forefathers say that two thousand years ago, one thousand years ago, or just before the Muslim rule came? What's wrong if Christians are saying that? You understand my point?"

"Yes, I do. I am a product of a Christian school, too. But I wish you had become an atheist!"

He laughed.

I don't know why he thought I was joking. But, I didn't want to continue this topic. New converts are more fanatical. We have a saying in Hindi: a new mullah reads the *namaz* ten times. The Islamic requirement to read the prayers is five times a day. It would have been fruitless to try and convince Jay Singh that religion is not the way to enlightenment in academics.

He must have sensed that as I kept my mouth shut momentarily. The tea and snacks came. That gave us time to change the flavor of our interaction.

"This is a hundred percent Pahari tea. No water. Just pure buffalo milk. Courtesy of our neighbor." He understood my explanation of the tea.

He sipped a drop or two of the tea. When he realized it was too hot, he tried to cool it the Pahari way. He was creating cool waves on its upper level by blowing his breath into it, repeatedly. Then, he sipped a few drops again.

"I suggest that you should market this tea in America. Buffalo milk can be replaced by cow's milk…In fact, my other reason to see you is to market my own invention. I want to discuss its possibility in the States."

"I have no skills in marketing anything. New inventions, however, turn me on. Tell me about it."

"You can tell your American friends. It is very useful for everybody. I have found a Pahari plant. Its fiber is fire-resistant. You can make clothes of it. It's quite soft on your body. Very safe even for children…"

"I presume for fire-fighters, too," I inserted my comment. "Do you have a sample of it with you?"

"I will bring it tomorrow. You have a bonfire here. What I will do is wrap it around my hands like gloves, then place my hands over the embers."

"Yes, nothing like that test. It's a more useful test than those Pandau spirit tests."

We laughed, but I wished he would never see me again. What if his hands are burned and I am in trouble? Big Himalayan trouble?

"I hope I didn't offend you," Jay said, sounding somewhat apologetic. "Hunting wild animals is very risky. The government has very tough rules against it. In a Dehradun street, if you were to find a dead human body, then you would have to call the police. You call again. And again. You are lucky that you have finally succeeded in reporting. The man is dead, anyway. The police may or may not show up for hours. Now, if you kill a sparrow in your backyard, then in minutes you will find two police jeeps around you, as if you are a hard core criminal. You know you are in a deep mess."

"No kidding!"

"I am serious. Humans have become the less important animals inhabiting this country."

This time, I was laughing. He wasn't, though.

After a pause of a few seconds, I asked him for his perspective on a different issue, "You just mentioned your hunt in a dense forest. What do you think of the deforestation problem?"

"For my plants and hunting, I am personally dead against deforestation. Also in the interest of our planet, we need to consider the preservation of forests. And I am delighted to say that this awareness has become a movement. The leaders of this movement are Sundarlal Bahuguna and Chandi Prasad Bhatt..."

"You are talking about the *Chipko*, the 'Hug!' movement started by Garhwali women?"

"That's correct. Who would have believed it then!? Just a few years ago, the local women began to hug the trees when the axmen of the forest contractors came to fell them. And look what happened! The axmen couldn't touch the tree huggers. The trees were saved. These women gave birth to a radical movement. They converted many. Two major missionaries started a new enlarged movement! Keep the planet green. Thanks to Bahuguna and Bhatt!"

"These two men are Pahari heroes."

"World heroes. They will convert the whole world to green!"

I concurred with him. "I was thrilled to hear their names and their new lofty movement in the news. Otherwise, even many Indians don't know where the heck Garhwal and Kumaon forests are! Now the Hindi command word *Chipko* has reached an encyclopedic level with its new revolutionary semantics. Those ordinary women started the story of *Chipko*. And then more sophisticated men joined. Those two Pahari Brahmins improved and evolved the *Chipko* story. This is just like the *Mahabharata* story—from ordinary bards to brilliant Brahmins. I know these Brahmins got well-deserved recognition, nationally and internationally. Do you remember the names of those women?"

I noticed that he wasn't looking at me. His eyes were moving in the direction of Puran and Navin. The Thakur brothers were moving toward us.

Our dialog about these world heroes stopped as Puran and Navin joined us.

After the usual greetings, Jay Singh said, "I will see you later. There is some business I have to attend to this evening." And he left abruptly.

I told the Thakurs about his conversion. "I never imagined that a Pahari rajput would convert to Christianity."

"Well, historically many rajputs became Muslims. Why not Christians? But Jay Singh is a mason. Some converts do claim they are from high castes.

All they do is twist some high caste names like Singh, Tiwari, Juyal. But this twist turns out to be false when you meet their untouchable relatives," Puran explained.

"So, it's like the Pahari Brahmins claiming their Vedic ancestry!" I quipped.

"Or, the rajputs claiming their Kshatriya ancestry!" Navin said.

Thus, with all of our own mythical genealogies exposed, we laughed heartily.

# Chapter 38
# Day Seventeen of the War

*The Lord said: O Arjuna! They who have taken refuge in Me, even if they may be sinful species such as women and Vaishyas including Shudras, reach the highest state. Not to mention the meritorious devotee Brahmins and likewise the royal sages who have come to this impermanent and joyless world. So worship Me.*

*—Bhagavad Gita: 9.32, 33*

The drummers started singing and drumming and quickly conjured the tale we had left in the midst of a devastating war.

It was sunrise. Both armies came face to face. Karna announced loudly, "I will give awards, huge riches, to anyone who kills Arjuna today."

"You will see Arjuna today," Shalya, his new charioteer, retorted sarcastically. While Shalya was required to guide Karna's chariot, the Pandavas were his relatives and his feelings about the war were deeply conflicted.

The two continued verbal attacks on each other for a while. Then, the warriors of each side signaled the battle. Sounds of conchs, trumpets, drums and other instruments filled the sky. Noise and dust was all around.

Arjuna was seen moving his forces toward Karna. There, the war broke with frenzy and fury which spread throughout all the sectors of the battle. In one sector, Karna and Yudhishthira encountered each other. After a gory battle, the Kaurava armies fled in several directions. Bhima and Karna met each other face to face. A tough fight started between the two, ending with Karna defeated. He retreated.

At noon, all forces engaged in another fierce battle. Arjuna slaughtered a huge number of commandos. He had navigated this kind of slaughter in earlier days.

Ashvatthaman attacked Yudhishthira. Others joined the fight. As it became worse, Yudhishthira had to retreat. There was a fight between Ashvatthaman and Dhrishtadyumna, who had killed Drona earlier. With vengence for Drona at hand, Arjuna came to rescue Dhrishtadyumna. Ashvatthaman had to be taken away from the battle, as Arjuna wounded him.

In another section, Karna fought Shikhandin and forced him to run away. Dhrishtadyumna rallied and fought Duhshasana. Again, Dhrishtadyumna had to be rescued, as Duhshasana wounded him heavily. On the whole, however, the Pandava were quietly successful; Duryodhana's troops were forced to withdraw as Nakula pressed them hard.

In another fight, the Kaurava troops went forward to stop Yudhishthira. Nakula and Sahadeva accompanied Dhrishtadyumna. This time, Duryodhana was wounded by Sahadeva. Karna came to his rescue. Among the Pandavas, Yudhishthira backed up Sahadeva. Karna forced Yudhishthira to retreat with his charioteer, but Bhima cut through the middle and had engaged Duryodhana. Karna was going after Yudhishthira, but Shalya advised him to protect Duryodhana from Bhima. Nakula and Sahadeva joined Bhima as Karna engaged him. Suddenly, Ashvatthaman appeared there. The battle became fiercer.

Later, Duhshasana joined the fight around Bhima. He injured Bhima with a sharp arrow. That made Bhima mad. He yelled at him, "I am hurt so soon by you. Now, feel the blow of my mace."

When Bhima struck Duhshasana with his mace, Duhshasana fell down. Bhima remembered what Duhshasana had done to Draupadi and knew that revenge was at hand. He addressed him while he was surrounded by Duryodhana, Ashvatthaman, Kripa and Kritavarman.

"I will kill this sinister one today. Come ahead, you all! Try to defend him!"

Bhima put his foot upon the throat of Duhshasana. He grabbed his arm and said, "This is the hand that dragged Draupadi by her hair which she had just washed clean."

Bhima severed Duhshasana's arm from his body and crushed his throat, depriving him of breath and life. Enraged, he opened the dead man's chest and drank his blood.

"This blood is sweeter than mother's milk, sweeter than honey, butter and yogurt or any juice. I have fulfilled my promise."

Many warriors ran away when they saw Bhima in this frenzy. They shouted in fear, calling him an animal. Bhima laughed with his bloody mouth open. In his frenzy, he killed ten more sons of the old blind king of the Kaurava, Dhritarashtra.

Karna fought back against the Pandava warriors. Karna's son, Vrishasena, and the great Pandava warrior, Nakula, had a big fight. When Nakula was in trouble, Arjuna came to his rescue and later, killed Vrishasena. Karna was distraught to see his son dead. In a fury, he decided to slay Arjuna immediately. Shalya spoke to Karna as he drove him to fight Arjuna.

"Karna, if Arjuna kills you today in the battlefield, then I will kill both Arjuna and Krishna."

Krishna saw Karna coming toward them. He said to Arjuna, "Arjuna! Karna cannot kill you. But if he does, I will kill Karna and Shalya together."

Arjuna replied, "Krishna! Today, you will hear the sweet talk. Karna will not be there anymore. You will console Abhimanyu's mother. Today, you will make your aunt Kunti very happy."

Karna was flanked by Ashvatthaman, Duryodhana, Kritavarman, Kripa and other big warriors. Ashvatthaman took Duryodhana aside and said very politely, "Duryodhana! Be pleased and calm. Enough of your opposition to the Pandavas! Shame on this war! Great warriors like Drona and Bhishma have been finished. I and my maternal uncle Kripa cannot be killed. It is better to jointly rule the kingdom with the Pandavas for a long time. Arjuna will be pacified if I dissuade him. Krishna does not intend opposition, either. Yudhishthira is interested in the well-being of his people. Bhima, Nakula and Sahadeva follow him. If you reconcile with them, then it would appear that you are interested in the well-being of the public. Let all the fighters leave the war. If you do not listen to my words, then you will regret it and be killed in the battle. Please consider my words!"

With a deep sigh Duryodhana responded, "My dear friend, you have said what you wanted to say. Now, listen to me. It is not hidden from you and me how the evil-minded Bhimasena killed Duhshasana. How is peace possible? Arjuna cannot control Karna in the battle. The Pandavas will not trust me. They will keep thinking about my deliberate opposition to them. Listen, you, my teacher's son, Arjuna looks overcome by fatigue today. Karna will kill him very easily."

Saying this, he ordered his troops to move forward, urging them to engage in the bloody fight.

The battle between Karna and Arjuna had already begun. After a fierce fight, Karna's army began to retreat, but Karna kept fighting Arjuna. Having saved another special weapon for this moment, he decided to use a special snake-arrow to kill Arjuna. Shalya warned him, "Karna, this arrow will not get to Arjuna's neck. Think again before you shoot!"

His advice angered Karna. "Shalya! Karna never attempts the same arrow on second thought." He shot the arrow as he said, "O Arjuna! Here you are killed!"

The shining arrow made a noise. Krishna heart it and saw it coming. Knowing it could hit Arjuna's head, he pitched their chariot down, so that the arrow hit Arjuna's crown instead of his head. The crown fell into pieces, but Arjuna remained safe. The battle continued.

Krishna advised Arjuna to go closer to Karna. Arjuna understood and entered into better shooting range. With a powerful shot, Arjuna disabled a wheel of Karna's chariot. Karna was angry, but began to cry as his chariot sank down in the ditch.

"Wait, Arjuna! Don't shoot until I come up to fight. You are not a coward. Brave men like you don't shoot at a weapon-less fighter. You know the dharma of battle. You are in your chariot. It is not worthy of you to kill me while I am fixing the damaged wheel. Remember the dharma of a Kshatriya. O Son of Pandu, forgive me at this time!"

Krishna responded from his chariot, "O son of Radha! Luckily you remember dharma. Often, low men immersed in crisis blame destiny, not their own ignoble acts. Your dharma did not shine when Duryodhana, Duhshasana, Shakuni and you brought Draupadi into the Assembly Hall when she was clad just in one garment. Where was your dharma, when in the Assembly Hall, Shakuni cleverly won the dice game against honest Yudhishthira? O Karna! Where was your dharma when you would not return their kingdom after they completed the thirteenth year of forest exile? Where was your dharma when that king, on your advice, planned to kill Bhima with snakes and poisoned food? O Son of Radha! Where was your dharma, when at Varanavata, you burned the wax-house inside which the Pandavas were sleeping? Karna! Where was your dharma when you laughed at Draupadi, who was having her period, when she was being dragged by Duhashasana? O Son of Radha, where was your dharma when you ridiculed the beautiful Draupadi, telling her at that time, 'O Draupadi! Your Pandavas are finished and gone to permanent hell. Choose another husband!'? Where was your dharma when those big bully warriors surrounded the young boy Abhimanyu, and killed him? Why is your mouth drying up now if this dharma was not present there? And now you want to practice dharma here, but I tell you, you will not leave here alive!"

Karna heard all this and felt shame. Nevertheless, his temper flared up. He picked his bow and started fighting Arjuna. Both used sharp arrows to try and kill each other. Finally, Arjuna used a deadly arrow called *anjalika*. With it, Arjuna beheaded Karna. Blood oozed from Karna's severed head. Krishna and Arjuna joyfully blew their victory conchs.

It was already late afternoon. The Kaurava soldiers began to run away as Arjuna chased them. Duryodhana cried. He and other Kaurava warriors surrounded the dead body of Karna that was left behind by the Pandavas. Then, he ordered his charioteer, "Move on to join our troops. Arjuna will not escape me with his bow. I will avenge Karna's death by killing Arjuna, Krishna, Bhima and other enemies."

On the other side, Arjuna kept chasing the Kaurava troops. Dhrishtadyumna, Bhima, Nakula, Sahadeva and Satyaki fought Shakuni and other warriors. Catching up, Duryodhana came back and challenged them. He cheered up his fleeing troops. There was fierce battle again, but by the evening the Kaurava army could not withstand the forces of the Pandavas. They fled to their camps.

Then, Krishna said to Arjuna, "Let us go to inform Yudhishthira that you have killed Karna."

Arjuna accepted his advice. Krishna requested the troops and big warriors, "You all remain alert for any attack from the Kauravas until we return."

The two went and woke up Yudhishthira, who was sleeping in the camp. He sensed that they were there to give some great news. They both looked cheerful to him, even though there were visible bloody marks on their bodies. Krishna told Yudhishthira about how Arjuna destroyed Karna and forced the Kaurava armies to flee.

"…that man of low character who laughed when Draupadi was won by the dice game is dead. The earth is drinking his blood. O mighty-armed Yudhishthira, now you rule and enjoy with us all this earth when your enemies are killed."

Yudhishthira thanked Krishna. "O Krishna, it is due to your grace that this son of Pandu has vanquished the enemies without turning back. Our victory is definite. There is no defeat for us as long as you are the charioteer of Arjuna."

Yudhishthira continued praising Krishna and Arjuna as he sent the warriors back to the waiting Pandava troops and leaders. They cheered both, showering praises upon them. Then, they all happily went to rest.

Across the lines of battle, Kripa knew that Duryodhana would fail now. He approached Duryodhana and advised him to make peace with the Pandavas. He said emphatically, "Son! I consider this move safe. No more fighting with the Pandavas. I am not saying this with weakness or with the fear of losing life. I am telling you the remedy. You will remember this when your life will be at its end." The old teacher began to sob heavily.

Duryodhana replied, "O Brahmin! This is very friendly advice you have spoken. You have done your best to fight for us without any fear for your life. But your words do not make me happy, just like the right medicine does not make a patient near death happy. O great warrior! Why do you think that the Pandavas will trust us? King Yudhishthira was defeated by us at the dice. We banished him from his kingdom. So, how will he trust us? How will Krishna, their adviser, trust us? He has seen how Draupadi cried in the Assembly Hall and how I asked my brother to drag her by her hair. We deprived the Pandavas of their kingdom. Krishna sleeps every day with the pain of his nephew's death at our hands. We have done so many wrongs to him. Why will he pardon us? Arjuna has had no peace since he lost Abhimanyu. Why will he be favorable to me now? Bhima has taken a terrible vow. He will break, not bow. Both twins, Nakula and Sahadeva, are hostile to us like gods of death. Dhrishtadyumna and Shikhandin remain hostile to us. The Pandavas still remember the defenseless Draupadi disrobed by Duhshasana. And how will I enjoy my kingdom after the pardon of the Pandavas? How will I, who have ruled over kings, follow Yudhishthira like a servant? I cannot accept your advice even though it is affectionate and beneficial. This is not the time to behave impotently. This is our time to fight."

The troops heard Duryodhana's decision. They supported it. Then, Ashvatthaman said to Duryodhana, "This Shalya is great by his family, form, fame and fortune. He has all the qualities for being the commander. He has left his own sister's sons Nakula and Sahadeva to reciprocate your courtesy. O great King! Please make him our commander. We will be victorious."

Upon hearing Ashvatthaman's recommendation, all the warriors assembled there surrounded Shalya and cheered. Duryodhana addressed Shalya with folded palms, "O Uncle! You are so brave that the Pandavas will become dumb when they see you in front of our army. Their hopes will be shattered. I select you as our commander-in-chief."

"O King! If you regard me so, then I will do whatever you want me to," was Shalya's reply.

The drummers ended up with lines: "Brothers and sisters! May we have praiseworthy women. May we have mothers who raise good children, not like the violent Pandavas and Kauravas."

In the Himalayan Nights

# Chapter 39
# No Hero

Marla and Jennifer showed up after missing a few sessions. Marla joined our discussion. Puran strongly disbelieved public opinion. "Masses have very little knowledge of history. It's not easy to correct their myths."

He was saying this in the context of Hitler. Many north Indians consider Hitler a hero.

I just joked, "Can Hitler be praised here in Garhwal? Some local Brahmins say that Garhwal is the origin of Aryans."

The Thakur brothers were laughing, but the two girls remained quiet. Navin looked at the drummers. "Did you know Marla's ancestors were Paharis?" Then Marla and Jennifer couldn't resist laughing.

"I have to tell you about Bhupal Yamadagni," Marla said after composing herself.

Marla knew Bhupal's family. Bhupal and his wife lived in Chicago. He was originally from Delhi. Their two daughters and a son were born in Chicago. The family background was considered very important in his home. Bhupal's mother was from Jaipur and his father from Amritsar. Both towns were not too far from Delhi. The parents were married in Delhi in the Brahmin tradition. So were Bhupal and his wife Urvashi.

Bhupal was very proud of his parents. They changed their name from Jamadagni to Yamadagni. In Sanskrit, there is no such name as Yamadagni, but they must have known that the correct name for the river was Yamuna, not the modern Jamuna. They believed that India must follow the ancient traditions correctly. Hypercorrections are not uncommon among elite Indians.

The Yamadagnis were elite. Bhupal was a student of St. Stevens in New Delhi. There, he was one of the best students. Interestingly, he was also a regular member of the RSS. The Rashtriya Swayamsevak Sangh, or the

National Volunteer Society, strictly believes in the value of serving the Hind or Hindu nation. Their Sanskrit prayer is meant for ancient values.

"So it is like many white Americans believe: America is founded on Christian values. The native Americans, who were the first inhabitants, lacked such values," Marla added her analogy.

"All Brahmins here will tell you how they are descendants of the great Aryan sages. What is your Aryan *gotra*, Pandit ji?" Puran asked me.

I didn't open my mouth. Of course, I know what my Vedic ancestry is. It is written in my horoscope, unquestionably in Sanskrit. Drona of the *Mahabharata* and I share the same *gotra*. That is, however, my mythogenesis.

Marla continued her discussion of Bhupal, "Bhupal considered Hitler a hero. For him, the Holocaust never happened; he believed that the Jews, Americans, and the British fabricated it."

Marla told Bhupal about the Gypsies, showed him some pictures. Some of them looked very much like him. Bhupal learned from her how the Gypsies were Indians. They originated from the region that was between Punjab and Rajasthan, from the place where Bhupal's parents, too, came.

After leaving India in the medieval period, Gypsies reached as far as Europe. There they were misunderstood as Egyptians, hence Gypsies. But one of the words the Gypsies used for themselves was *Doma*. The retroflex *D* sound of *Doma* was difficult for the non-Indians, like Europeans. So, they pronounced it with the closest sound, *R*. Thus came about the word *Roma* for the *Gypsy*. Their major language became known as *Romani*. Unfortunately both words, Gypsy or Doma, were derogatory.

Those words became costly.

"Hitler spent considerable resources to eliminate anyone who was not pure Aryan. He tried to wipe the European Gypsies from the map. For him, they were a disgrace, a people of inferior race. He never thought of purifying them. They looked like you." Marla said this deliberately to Bhupal, just like that without soft edges.

Bhupal was well aware that Hitler was not doing anything new. The Indian high castes had a long tradition of discriminating against the Doma people, therefore the modern Indian word *Dom*, derived from *Doma*, was now illegal to use in India. He knew that in Sanskrit *Doma* meant "untouchable."

The Gypsy information provided by Marla impacted Bhupal's view.

Hitler was no longer his hero. But, Marla had also another reason for telling him this story of the myth of "races."

Bhupal's older daughter, Bharti, married a black American. Bhupal, like many Indians there, used the Hindi word *kallu,* "black," for them. This is a derogatory word. The black son-in-law had a Muslim name, too. His Christian parents had converted to Islam. Bhupal hated Muslim names. He did not like Shakeel. His daughter didn't use her Hindu name anymore, either. She didn't exist. Her marriage never happened.

When she and Shakeel got married, no religion was involved. Theirs was a court marriage. More importantly, any Indian father-in-law would normally look for a professional son-in law. Shakeel happened to be a college-educated man and a lawyer.

Shakeel was raised in the south side of Chicago. In this section of the city, the majority of folks were blacks, very poor blacks. Shakeel practiced in the neighboring town of Gary, Indiana and, like Dr. Martin Luther King Jr., was under the influence of Mohandas Gandhi. He was convinced that the Gandhian way was the way to integrate the world. He had criticized President Johnson for wasting over 600 billion dollars on the Vietnam War.

It was his reasoning that less than one billion dollars would have lifted the poverty of the south side of Chicago, from where Shakeel came. Johnson's slogan "war on poverty" was actually, in Shakeel's mind, "war on the poor," especially the poor of Vietnam. Johnson could have learned human compassion from Gandhi.

But Bhupal, the father of Shakeel's bride, hated Gandhi. Like many Hindu fundamentalists, he maintained a strong bias. It was Gandhi who agreed to the partition of India. Bhupal had facts to support his misinformation. Gandhi persuaded India to send millions of rupees to help the new country of Pakistan. Some of Bhupal's relatives were displaced from the Pakistani Punjab to the Indian Punjab—one for Muslims and the other for non-Muslims, like the Kauravas and the Pandavas with two separate capitals. That money should have been spent for the refugees from Pakistan. But Gandhi, in Bhupal's mind, favored Muslims, not Hindus. So Bhupal had no regrets for Gandhi's assassination by a Hindu fanatic. Hitler, too, would have been very happy. He had given advice to the British against Gandhi. The British Raj dreaded any attempt on Gandhi's life. Bhupal hated the British, too.

His second daughter, Kirti, followed her sister Bharti. She fell in love with David. He taught transcendental meditation in a Chicago Yoga center. That should have made Bhupal happy. Yoga, including TM, was an ancient Indian discipline of health.

But David's ancestry was Jewish—David Weinstein. The Yamadagnis were burnt this time worse than before. Kirti told them that she was already married to David. Theirs, too, was a court marriage. It was attended by Shakeel and Bharti. Shakeel had convinced Kirti and David that that was the only way to stamp their marriage. The question of Bhupal's approval was moot. The Yamadagnis repeated history. They abandoned all contact with Kirti.

Two years later, their son Yashpal's turn came. His fiancée made the Yamadagnis very happy. Maitreyi was a Hindu girl born and raised in Chicago, a very friendly girl. Maitreyi meant "friendship." Unfortunately, a problem arose when the time of their marriage approached. Yashpal and Maitreyi agreed to be wed with the traditional Vedic ceremony on one condition. Shakeel and Bharti, as well as Kirti and David, must be invited with all due respect.

There was a debate in the family. According to Marla, it was an educational experience for the Yamadagnis. The young groom, Yashpal, used the Gypsy experience to persuade his parents. The Gypsies made a mistake; he reasoned. They remained "Roma" people. Maybe they didn't try hard enough to integrate with non-Gypsies. Or maybe others didn't welcome them. Whatever, they remained a visible minority, so it was easy to target them anywhere.

Yashpal warned his parents. He considered them and other Indian immigrants as modern Gypsies. Marla mentioned a few of his warnings. Do not make a "Little India" in America. That would be like partition: One with the caste system, another without it. The children born here will opt for the casteless. That is the way. It is in everyone's interest.

Such warnings entailed his straight request: Invite Shakeel. Invite David. They are members of our family.

The Yamadagnis did. They all came.

The drummers started tuning their drums.

# Chapter 40
# Day Eighteen of the War

*The Lord said: I am Time. I destroy the world as I progress. I am busy here to annihilate all lives.*

—*Bhagavad Gita: 11.32*

The eighteenth day's music was not as sweet as the Yamadagni story. The Kauravas and the Pandavas were adamant about winning the war. Shalya now headed the Kaurava armies. He had vowed, "I will kill the Pandava warriors, or be killed by them."

All the warriors met Duryodhana. They decided together to make a unified attack on the Pandavas. The Pandava armies, headed by Yudhishthira, came forward for the encounter.

The battle began early in the morning. After a while the Pandavas began to gain over the Kauravas. The Kaurava armies were retreating. Shalya ordered his charioteer, "Drive the horses faster toward Yudhishthira!"

The charioteer moved the horses ahead. Shalya began to devastate the Pandava troops. The fleeing Kaurava soldiers saw the feats of Shalya. They returned to fight and joined Shalya. It was a bloody fight. Again, many warriors lost their lives. There was a fight between Shalya and Yudhishthira. Shalya engaged Yudhishthira.

Jumping to their king's protection, Satyaki, Bhima, Nakula and Sahadeva challenged Shalya. Bhima hurt Shalya. There was a fight between Arjuna and Ashvatthaman. Dhrishtadyumna fought Duryodhana. The worst was that, at times, Nakula and Sahadeva were forced to encounter their own maternal uncle, Shalya.

But Shalya was more interested in killing Yudhishthira. He moved ahead and engaged the king. Bhimasena and his twin brothers, Nakula and Sahadeva, came to back up Yudhishthira. Nevertheless, Shalya hurt

Yudhishthira. Yudhishthira lost his chariot in Shalya's violent attack, his charioteer and horses disabled. This made King Yudhishthira angry.

The king, in desperation, picked a blazing arrow and aimed at Shalya. The dart hit Shalya. It tore his armor and burned his organs inside. Shalya fell in pain and died. Shalya's brother tried to kill Yudhishthira, but he, too, was shot dead by Yudhishthira. Thus came the end of the commander-in-chief of the Kauravas. The Kaurava armies were in disarray again.

Duryodhana was sad and mad. He went after Yudhishthira. On his way, he struck many warriors with his arrows. Shakuni also urged his warriors forward, to go after Yudhishthira. Most Kaurava soldiers, though, began to flee, sensing that the situation favored the Pandava once more, and perhaps definitively.

Arjuna noticed the losing signs among the Kaurava army. He said to Krishna, "O Krishna! Today is the eighteenth day of the war. I will finish the enemies with sharp arrows. Drive my chariot and enter the flood of the Kaurava forces. Look at the armies already gone to waste. The stupid and arrogant Duryodhana failed to make peace when Bhishma fell. He failed to listen to Bhishma's advice. So many wise men urged him for peace. So many relatives are already dead. Even when Drona, Duhshasana, Karna and now Shalya are dead, this evil man has not stopped fighting. After his entire camp is empty of warriors, he would still look for a fight and his end. That will be the end of enmity. Today, after destroying this powerless Kaurava army, I will do right by Yudhishthira."

A big fight erupted between Dhrishtadyumna and Duryodhana. With a fierce attack, Dhrishtadyumna disabled Duryodhana's chariot. Duryodhana quickly jumped onto the unyoked chariot horse and rode away. Ashvatthaman and his maternal uncle Kripa could not see where he had gone. Other warriors also tried to locate him, but failed.

Some went to help Shakuni, who also didn't know the whereabouts of Duryodhana. Not seeing him anywhere on the battlefield, the Kaurava armies began to retreat. While searching for Duryodhana, Bhima killed Dhritarashtra's other sons. After his attack, there were only two from the original one hundred. The other surviving son now, beside Duryodhana, was Yuyutsu. This Yuyutsu was a fair-minded and brave man. He was opposed to the mistreatment of Draupadi and the manner in which Abhimanyu had been killed. The Pandavas were therefore interested in sparing Yuyutsu's life.

Sahadeva in the meantime slew Shakuni. It was already late afternoon.

With a careful search, Kripa, Ashvatthaman and Kritavarman located Duryodhana. They were shocked to see him sleeping behind a pond. They yelled at him, "O King! Get up and fight Yudhishthira! With our help, the enemy will not be able to face you!"

Duryodhana replied, "Fortunately, I see you safe from this killing field of Pandavas and Kauravas. We will win the war after we are well-rested and refreshed. The strength of the Pandavas is on the rise. I don't want to fight them at this time. After a restful night, I will fight them tomorrow—in the morning."

In the meantime, some hunters heard them talking behind the pond. The excited hunters quickly went back and reported to Bhima. He rewarded the hunters and informed Yudhishthira as to the location of these Kaurava leaders.

The Pandavas, accompanied by Dhrishtadyumna, Shikhandin, Uttamaujas, Yudhamanyu, Satyaki, five sons of Draupadi and many other warriors, immediately moved toward that pond. They found Duryodhana hiding there. Ashvatthaman, Kripa and Kritavarman had already left Duryodhana alone.

Yudhishthira challenged Duryodhana to come out of hiding and fight. "O brave warrior, where did your manhood go? Where is your honor? Where is your perfection of weaponry? Why are you hiding in the pond? To fight is your dharma. Fight us and become the sole king!"

Duryodhana replied, "I am not here because of fear. I just want to rest. I still hope to defeat you. But now Drona, Karna, Bhishma and my brothers are finished. My armies are weakened. What will I do with this kingdom? I would rather go to the forest as an ascetic."

Yudhishthira said loudly, "Get up, get up. Fight me, O son of Gandhari! Pick up your mace and have a duel with me. Fight like a man! Or you shall be slain today."

"None of you is equal to me in mace fighting. I will kill you all now with my mace."

Krishna knew the great mastery of Duryodhana in mace fighting. He took Yudhishthira aside and suggested that Bhimasena fight the duel. Among the Pandava, Bhima was the best at mace fighting. Bhima said to Krishna, "I will terminate the life of Duryodhana with my mace, right now."

Fatefully, Duryodhana accepted Bhima's challenge and came out to fight him. The sun had already gone down.

At that moment, Krishna's older brother Balarama appeared there. Balarama had finished his pilgrimage to the Himalayas. Yudhishthira honored him and explained the event.

Duryodhana and Bhima insulted each other before the fight at the selected spot. Their tempers flared up. Bhima remembered all the wrongs Duryodhana had done to the Pandavas. It was then that the dreadful duel started.

The fight was fierce and bloody. Neither of them looked to be winning. Arjuna asked Krishna who he thought had a better chance. Krishna told him that Bhima would not win if he fought fairly. Arjuna understood Krishna's intention. He tapped his thigh. Bhima also understood. Duryodhana hit Bhima so hard that he began to lose blood. That made Bhima stop momentarily. Duryodhana waited for Bhima's attack. While Duryodhana was waiting, Bhima hit him on his thighs. It was really a powerful and unfair blow. It was below the belly, not allowed in a mace fight. It fractured Duryodhana's thighs. He fell down in terrible pain. All the bystanders were aghast. The Pandavas were jubilant.

Bhima kicked Duryodhana while he was trying to get up. He reminded him, "You, idiot, called us animals. Here is the fruit of that insult. In the Assembly Hall you laughed at Draupadi, who had just one garment on her body. You wanted to see her naked. These are the thighs you wanted to show her. We had no deceit, no weapons, no fire at the dice."

He laughed as he looked in the direction of Yudhishthira, Krishna and other brothers and warriors standing there. He witnessed to them by saying, "See today Dhritarashtra's sons slain who dragged helpless Draupadi to shame when she was on her period!" Then, he placed his left foot on Duryodhana's head.

Many did not like the behavior of Bhima. Yudhishthira scolded Bhima, "You have fulfilled your promise by fair or unfair means. Stop your action now. Don't crush his head with your foot. He is king. He is our own kin. He is down. O faultless Bhima! This is not fair."

As Yudhishthira spoke these words his breathing became heavy; he broke down.

Suddenly Balarama raised his hand, warning Bhima, "Shame on Bhima! He hit Duryodhana below the navel in a fair fight. Such an act has never been seen before." Then, he angrily addressed Krishna, "Duryodhana was not unequal to me. He is weak now and he is being reviled."

Krishna lifted Yudhishthira's depression, too. "Yudhishthira, now the earth is yours without enemies. O King, rule it. Follow your dharma, O Lord of the Earth! The man who was the creator of enmity and lover of evil works lies on the earth here. Foul-mouthed men like Duhshasana and others, including Karna and Shakuni, are all dead. You have no enemies alive now. Today, this rich Earth is yours. You are fortunate that you are free from the debt of your mother. You are free from your hostility. O mighty man, fortunately your enemy has been struck down. Let us go to the capital to announce you as the new king."

Duryodhana praised himself that he would go to heaven for the good deeds he did, and cursed them as they were leaving. Later in the evening upon their return, Ashvatthaman, Kripa and Kritavarman found Duryodhana struck down. He was still alive. They were infuriated when they heard of his unfair downfall.

The drummers sang the end of the war like this: "Sisters and brothers! Thus the bards finish the big war. They began the story. They told it as the famous Pahari wrote it. That Pahari was Ganesha. His mother was a Pahari. So her name was Parvati, the daughter of Nagadhiraja, 'the king of the mountains.' His father was Nataraja, 'the king of the dancers.' May you all continue this great dance initiated by Ganesha. May Shiva be good to all, as he was to his son Ganesha."

Before the drummers left, I asked them if they were familiar with the famous verse of the Gita: *The Lord said: I am Time; I destroy the world as I progress. I am busy here working to annihilate all lives.*

Bijlu promptly replied, "Is it about when Sanjaya tells the blind king how Krishna showed Arjuna his big godly form?"

"Yes. The big form is known as *Vishva Rupa* or Cosmic Form in English." (We were talking, as usual, in Garhwali).

"Archi ji, there is a big lie about it." Bijlu said.

Daphra explained, "Sanjaya says there that this godly form was seen only by Arjuna and that no other person saw it."

"Yes. So, what's the lie about that, Daphra?"

"Krishna claims to know everything everywhere, but he didn't know Sanjaya, too, saw his big godly form."

"You mean Sanjaya had no courage to say that Krishna was not really an all-knowing God?"

"Yes, yes!"

It was at that moment I clearly understood to which lie they referred.

I just laughed and joked, "Sanjaya was untrained in journalism. Like many untrained reporters in our times, Sanjaya may have made up stories to create sensation. It is easy to fool a blind person."

"Our Guru thinks Sanjaya was lying."

Bijlu said this with a smile.

"Maybe Sanjaya was not lying. He sounds like my grandmother. She used to see ghosts. These are actually tricks our brains play. Some are really grand illusions. For ages, very nice people have claimed to see or hear God. Forget my grandma. She could barely read or write. Even Mahatma Gandhi was under this kind of illusion."

"Yes, he called us *harijan*. That means God discriminates against others. We alone are 'God's People.' Then, what are the rest?"

Bijlu was, of course, trying to make fun of Gandhi. I could see that in his eyes and smile. At the same time, I could feel his burden.

"Gandhi wanted kind feelings for you from the disciminators. Gandhi was a great kind man, as much one as the world has ever seen." I paused momentarily. "Anyway, my point is that many could not see Sanjaya as a true reporter. His reporting is full of his personal judgments. He is the first one in history who tells us that God reincarnates as a human, time and again as needed. He says that God himself has told us this. That's how a cult is created and grows into a big religion. Our religion is not alone."

I wanted to stop as I thought I was behaving like a guru, like an academic guru! But I resumed talking.

"By the way, Marla and Jennifer have their opinions on *avatars*. Let me tell you about what they say. Many famous gurus are adored by well-educated folks as *avatars*. There are a couple such *avatars* from these Garhwal Himalayas and a couple from Dehradun, too. The *avatar* business is booming now across Indian borders. Even women have entered into this business. Some have been found as magicians in holy clothes and hair styles. And some of them put on regular Western clothes with Western hair styles included...for more opinions, check with those American girls."

The drummers were laughing. Nevertheless, after a quick glance at them, I warned them, "But don't tell any PUDI about their opinions. A PUDI will only doubt you, not his or her own beliefs. "

"What is that man's name, PUDI?" Bijlu asked.

"That's a person under devout influence." I replied, "But check about this with those girls, as well."

Just before leaving, Daphra looked at me. "Rainwal ji, they really mean *avatars* from Dehradun?"

"That's what those girls told me." I responded with a smile.

"So, Dehradun is a holy land!" Bijlu laughed.

"All parts of Mother Earth are holy." I said, remembering my dad's daily puja prayer.

"All people?" Bijlu inquired.

"Yes, except oppressors." I had said this on purpose. The drummers are oppressed, the *dalits*.

Regardless, I was in awe. These drummers could question and change. Maybe, the IAS Guru taught them how to question such fantastic claims or reports. That's what I had learned in my higher education from my Indian, American, and European teachers: question everything and then develop change. Shastri ji was my first college teacher from whom I learned to challenge the unjust established order and do things differently.

I began to hear a faint sound of bagpipes and drums. The drums didn't sound like dhol-damau. Turning to our drummers, I asked Bijlu, "Do you hear the bagpipes and drums?"

"*U miltiri ku baind cha.* (That is the military band)."

Of course, Dehradun is the India's "West Point."

# Chapter 41
# Crown after Terror

*Time creates beings and Time destroys their progeny. While burning the*
*progeny Time extinguishes the fire again.*

— *Mahabharata*

The following evening more than a hundred people came to attend the dance session. The drummers looked very happy. With a bow to all, they began to sing the remaining part of the preceding session.

Ashvatthaman affectionately held the wounded Duryodhana's hand in his hand. With tearful words, he addressed him.

"My father was murdered by those crooks with their heinous act, but I am not pained by that as much as by you, O King! Listen to my promise as I speak truthfully, my lord! I will kill all the Panchala friends of the Pandavas in the presence of Krishna. O Maharaja, you ought to give me your permission."

Upon hearing that, Duryodhana requested Kripa to bring water in a pitcher. Kripa, who was the teacher of Duryodhana and Ashvatthaman's uncle, brought the pitcher and came close to the king. Duryodhana said to Kripa, "O supreme Brahmin! With my permission, please sprinkle the water over the son of Drona. By the virtue of our new commander, let there be your good and mine too, as you wish."

Ashvatthaman hugged the wounded king when Duryodhana declared Ashvatthaman to be the new Kaurava chief. Kripa and Kritavarman hailed the new chief. The three Kaurava warriors left Duryodhana, who was bleeding and in pain.

The next day, after the 18-day war was over, at sunset the three warriors rested under a big tree. When it was dark, they fell asleep. At the noise of birds, Ashvatthaman woke up to see an owl killing several big,

251

sleeping crows.

He got an idea. He woke up the other two and told them his plan to kill the Pandava while they were asleep during the night in their camp.

Kripa objected to his plan. He said, "What you are planning is a sin. Look, Duryodhana was greedy. He ignored the advice of his best friends. His corrupt advisers led him on the wrong path of animosity with the Pandavas. Right from the beginning, he has been cruel to the Pandavas. Now we should go to Dhritarashtra and Gandhari and also to the wise Vidura. Let them tell us what is good for us. We will work with their advice."

Ashvatthaman felt sorrow and anger at Kripa's opinion. He said to both, "Every man has different understanding. Each of them considers his position better. I am convinced with my position."

Then he explained further the reasons and details of his plan. His position was that Duryodhana was mortally wounded by Bhima with an unfair hit. His father, Drona, was butchered like an animal by the Pandava general Dhrishtadyumna.

So, the three agreed to follow the plan during the night.

They all reached the gates of the Pandava camp. Ashvatthaman quietly entered inside and located Dhrishtadyumna's sleeping place. He cut off the head of the sleeping general. Then he proceeded to find Shikhandin. He found him and beheaded him instantly. After a while he killed the five sons of Draupadi. Many others woke up to fight Ashvatthaman and lost their life at his hands. When he saw others coming after him, he quickly came out and met Kripa and Kritavarman. They placed fire at three separate places and soon the entire camp was on fire. The three heard the painful noise of other burning humans and animals inside. Ashvatthaman was overjoyed as he watched the hellish bonfire.

The three warriors went back to give the great news to Duryodhana. When they came upon him, Duryodhana was still conscious. They told him that they were successful in avenging the injustice the Pandavas had done to them. Duryodhana understood and thanked them before he died.

Dhrishtadyumna's charioteer managed to survive the fire. He ran to Yudhishthira and informed him about the tragic deaths. The senior Pandava brother was distraught. When Draupadi found out about the deaths of her sons, she was in grief and anger. She wanted to burn the culprit alive or burn herself. The Pandavas promised to bring the perpetrator to her.

The Pandavas found Ashvatthaman hiding behind Vyasa. Ashvatthaman threatened to go after Uttara, the pregnant wife of Abhimanyu. He wanted to destroy her child, Parikshit, in the womb. This child, the heir to the Pandava kingdom, had to be saved. With Krishna's help, a solution was found to save Parikshit. The Pandavas would not kill Ashvatthaman. In return, he would surrender his precious crown jewel.

Ashvatthaman agreed. The Pandavas took his crown jewel and presented it to Draupadi. She was pleased and placed it on the head of Yudhishthira.

The drummers sang their final words. "Brothers and sisters! Ashvatthaman was a Brahmin, but he bore arms. He was wrong. He cared only for his position. He was wrong. This war would have been averted if the Kauravas had understood the position of the Pandavas and the Pandavas the position of the Kauravas. Follow the path of peace: Swap your position with your opponent's and then speak to each other. Namaste."

# Chapter 42
# The Aftermath: Her *Gita*

Today's session was the last—the concluding review of the 18-day war and anything else relevant. It was going to be short, so we planned to assemble at 3:30 p.m. There was enough sunlight left over. Some people had already started to come. Everybody was served snacks and tea as they came.

The actual dance began at 4 p.m. We had not yet had the pleasure of seeing Marla and Jennifer. The Thakurs were eager to ask them what they thought of the last remarks of the drummers.

"It was a statement from people who never went to college," Navin said.

"I know, my parents never went to college either. They were upset by what the drummers implied throughout. Dad thought these drummers were dummies. They went overboard," I said. "What do you both think of my father's views?"

Puran scratched his head and then said, "I wish your father could check with any untouchables. They would tell him that the Brahmins went overboard for ages; the time has come to get used to listening to the voices of the suppressed folks. Some, like Abdul, would tell him why his ancestors were Muslims. And some, like Jay Singh, would tell him why they converted to Christianity. Let us ask Bijlu and Daphra why they did not convert?" Puran looked toward the drummers.

Bijlu surprised us when he replied that he and Daphra were separately interviewed by Marla quite often. He added, "Marla also asked us if any in our family converted to Christianity or Islam. When we told her 'No,' she said she was not recommending those religions or any religion. If Hindus created untouchables, then they, too, created their *heathens* or *kafirs* and killed them and occupied their lands..."

Bijlu stopped as he saw Marla appearing at the gate of the lawn. She slowly walked toward us. As usual, we all exchanged greetings.

Then, she moved toward Tula, who was standing at the kitchen door and waving a hand for her. But Puran asked loudly, "Your shoes are missing, Marla?" This time she had put on an American skirt instead of the Indian *shalwar*.

She shot back, "They are not missing. A few days ago Jennifer and I went to see the snowfall at Mussoorie. On the way up, we saw many Pahari women carrying big loads of fuel woods, bare-footed. I want to feel how they feel."

"But you are not vowing not to put on shoes from now on, are you?" Navin asked as he laughed.

It was clear to Marla to whom Navin was referring. She responded, "Not at all. I am not a Gandhari!"

Marla paused as Tula brought tea for her. Tula also looked at her bare feet. "Your feet are naked," Tula said with a surprised smile. Marla thanked her with a laugh. After having a couple of sips, she said, "Navin ji, Gandhari wanted to feel the pain of her husband, the blind man's difficulties. Even a few hours would have been enough. But she bandaged her eyes forever. She was stupid."

The two drummers laughed when they heard her saying "She was stupid" (*wo bewakūf thī*). Bijlu had to cover his mouth with his hand to stop his laughing.

"Did you fellows say much about Gandhari in your songs later? I understand you agree with me about her," Marla addressed Bijlu and Daphra as she looked toward them.

"No, we said nothing. But we do agree with you," Daphra said.

Bijlu also nodded his head, as he was still unable to speak.

"Maybe you should tell us a little more, Marla. Why would you not consider Gandhari a hero?" Puran asked.

From earlier discussions, Tula and I knew why and what Marla said here.

Marla did give her explanation. She said, "I thought Gandhari was a foolhardy woman. She had too many children. No wonder why they turned out to be so stupid. This mother gave them birth. She didn't even want to see them. You bring children into this world and then leave them to others' care! This social-welfare attitude is so unethical. Her husband was unfortunate enough to have so many other responsibilities. With eyes open, he could have been more active, more responsive, less dependent on Sanjaya, less dependent on his brother Pandu. That woman could have made his life much easier. Instead, she became a burden on others—by choice. She opened her eyes once only. This happened just after the eighteen-day war was over. Yudhishthira, the designated king of the Kurus now, was lying at her feet. He wanted her forgiveness. He told her how he was responsible for her sons' destruction. She saw Yudhishthira's toe only with a slight slide of her eye bandage. In her rage, she hurt his toe. And then she closed her eyes again forever."

"And just before that hurtful event, Dhritarashtra wanted to hug Bhimasena. He wanted to crush Bhima to death. As the mythology maintains, Krishna's tricks triggered triumphs. Krishna slipped into an iron statue instead. The blind man hugged the statue, not Bhimasena. The statue was shattered. Had Gandhari opened her eyes it would have been no problem for Dhritarashtra to recognize Bhima. The strong man couldn't avenge the cowardly killing of his son Duryodhana. Gandhari is to be blamed for that failure. She was supposed to be her husband's eyes."

Diving deeper, Tula gave Marla several hypothetical scenarios in their discussion, "After all, the *Mahabharata* must have originally been a folk story, created by men. Any scenario is possible in a folk story. Here is a hypothetical scenario. Gandhari and Dhritarashtra are not blind. After their marriage, Gandhari goes blind. What's the guarantee that Dhritarashtra, like his other male relatives, wouldn't go with other women? With a blind wife, adultery is a piece of cake. Non-blind Gandhari wouldn't be an obstacle, either."

This was Marla's answer: "If he was not blind, he would have seen lots of pretty women and who could have stopped him? Gandhari, blind or not-blind, couldn't have done that unless forced like Draupadi. A woman can be manipulated into fidelity while her husband is adulterous. For holy men, adultery is an added virtue. The ritual of marriage makes man's adultery sacred and praiseworthy. Just see how often boys are named after such holy men here and there!"

The drummers looked very serious now—not a single laugh from either. Bijlu interrupted, "Marla, we think that Kunti was a hero. We will tell you later which other women are heroes. Right now, we leave to tune our drums for the dance." Both drummers did leave, saying "*Namaste*" to her.

Surprisingly, Marla had a bitter attitude toward Kunti, too.

"Kunti deceived the Pandavas throughout. Bhishma knew her secret through a reporter, fictitiously named Narada. But, when Karna died, Kunti told her sons who he was. How affectionately that brother was raised by his kind adoptive parents, Adhiratha and Radha! Karna told Kunti how he pined for his natural mother's love, his brothers' company. Yet, it was Duryodhana who treated Karna like his own brother. This all happened because of a biological mother's insensitivity. Karna kept his promise to Kunti, his biological mother. He would never kill more than one of her sons. In that case she still would have five sons, including him. If Karna were alive he would have been the king now instead of Yudhishthira. How much agony Yudhishthira suffered when he learned all this! Kunti's sons from Pandu were as problematic as Gandhari's sons. Duryodhana never hurt, let alone killed, any of his brothers."

Tula and I know Marla had other *Mahabharata* characters she hated or loved. She had no problem in expressing her sentiments.

Jennifer was different, however. She seldom expressed her opinions, but Marla had noted Jennifer's differences with her. One interesting note was about Marla's query: "Why was Kunti respected as a Devi?"

Jennifer did respond: "Kunti, like anyone else, is not one thing. She is a bundle of things, relationships. Relationships arise in contact, in interaction. Why only Kunti? Every other character is a complex of fleeting relationships. The whole war is a set of relationships. Underlying it are several sub-sets of relationships, all in motion. It's not the kingdom in conflict. It's the conflict of relationships. The kingdom is there, but only in the relationships of the participants. The *Mahabharata* story is basically a mega-breakdown in relationships."

Marla had her own version: "Relationships are a capital—*relational capital*—that everyone has; its losses or gains vary according to its investment, which is needed for the security of the investor. Any fight is the result of bad investment of relational capital. The *Mahabharata* warriors were unwise investors of relational capital."

Just at the end of the dance session our cook, Bhag, came out with a package in his hand and handed it to Marla. She was alone with me at that time. We were talking about our notes.

"What is it?" Marla asked the cook.

"This is a packet of Pahari sweets someone brought for you," he replied with a smile.

Marla took the packet in her hand. "Can we repack it in the kitchen? The wrap is oily," she said.

I knew why it became oily. This was the packet of oily *arsas* from Shib Dutt.

Marla and Bhag began to walk toward the kitchen. I noticed that on her way she gave some paper to Bhag. He put it in his pocket and folded his hands. I understood that Marla must have given him a tip and he was doing *namaste* to thank her. Both looked very cheerful as Marla put her hand on Bhag's shoulder.

In a few minutes, Marla came out, apparently to join us. She looked pretty grim. I had no idea why her face was showing tenseness. Maybe the cook told her about the *arsa* recipe and its cumbersome preparation. Or maybe she tasted an *arsa* piece and she didn't like it. Whatever, she appeared uncomfortable. And then she returned to the kitchen.

Just then, the drummers started drumming and singing Marla's praise.

*Yo cha hamaro gita Marla ko*! Bijlu sang in Garhwali, "This is our song for Marla."

*Hey Marla*! "O Marla!" Daphra as the damau player echoed the praise title after the dhol player's line.

*Marla ko cha yo sachcho gita.* "This is true song of Marla," The dhol player sang.

*Sachcho gita.* "True song," The damau player echoed.

*Hey Marla, tu chhai hamari debi.* "O Marla, you are our goddess."

*Hey debi*! "O goddess!"

*Teri bhuli cha pyari Janiphara.* "Your sister is the lovely Jennifer."

*O Janiphara*!

*Jai jai bola hamari debi Marla.* "Let us speak victory to our goddess Marla."

The drummers continued.

To my surprise, I saw Abdul darting toward me. He had not been seen in the session for quite some time. I hadn't the foggiest idea why he held my hand and took me aside. Then, with a frown on his face, he whispered into my ear, "Rainwal Sahab, stop the drummers."

"Why?" I instantly asked.

"They are not sisters. They are lovers."

"What?"

"I swear I saw them naked, together, in bed."

His intense breathing was clearly audible to me. Nevertheless, I gave him a laugh instead of a rapid response. I wondered about his free access to their rented flat (apartment) on Rajpur Road.

He looked challengingly at me as he whispered again, "If you say nothing, then I am going to say loudly to the Thakurs, that there should be no praise for Marla."

"Go ahead. They will sacrifice you instead of the rams. And more mantras for Marla, *puja* from the players, and *bali* from the brothers."

He slapped his hands in the air and stomped the ground with his shoes. He briskly ran toward the drummers.

They kept drumming and singing. Bijlu smiled as Abdul approached him. Abdul leaned toward Bijlu and laid his hands over the dhol. Navin pulled Abdul back and lifted him onto his shoulders. Then, he danced with others in the circle. The audience clapped. Abdul laughed and clapped his hands up in the air rhythmically, matching the 4/4 common time drumming. Obviously, he was gesturing that he wasn't possessed. The sun had just set. The red hue in the sky brightened everyone's faces: the Thakur brothers' typical Pahari faces showing Sino-Tibetan mix, red-brass copper; the drummers' dark faces looking like burning coals; and Abdul's ember-copper face on the top. The drummers kept singing and beating the drums.

A few minutes later, Abdul dismounted and the drummers stopped. Immediately, he whispered into Bijlu's ear. The excited dhol drummer also laughed. The damau player was unable to react yet. He was scratching his head. Abdul whispered into his ear. Did Daphra laugh enough!

He then whispered into Puran's ear. And, again, into Navin's ear. Neither of them reacted, except nodding their heads. All I overheard was one sentence. It was Abdul's. He had said it loudly.

*Allah ki qasam*, "I swear by God."

In a way, I felt relieved. I didn't overhear the buzz word: CIA. Thank goodness! And also thank goodness I haven't heard Marla labeling Abdul as a PUDI: Person Under Devout Influence. She did label my father in this manner, though.

The drummers went away to take their drums off their necks. A few yards and minutes away from the gate they began drumming again, and Bijlu shouted "*Dharam hatao, gyan bachao!*"—"Oust religion, save knowledge!" Daphra repeated it louder. I kept hearing these words until they became inaudible. These words I had heard before as a warning for change. I clearly felt their warning was more than the voice of the victims of "dharma." They were drumming up for *gyan* (*jñāna*) "knowledge" instead. That's what Guru, the government administrator, wants.

Marla came out of the kitchen and gave me a sandwich. "So you were preparing *double roti* for me. Thanks a lot," I said.

"You're welcome," Marla responded. She paused for a moment and said in a serious tone, "Can we talk to those guys over there?"

I took a couple of bites and forgot to tell her how all of them went overboard. Both of us moved toward them. Their heated discussion suddenly came to a standstill. Nobody was looking at us. They must have heard the flow of our breath as we stood in front of them.

Marla dropped her voice into their pool of silence. "Thakur Sahab! So the celebration is ready?"

"What celebration?" Puran asked her.

"What about the rams?"

"What rams?"

"I heard you both talking about the sacrifice of rams at the end!"

"You heard nothing from us."

Both Thakurs looked tense, as did Abdul. I also became serious, "What is this talk of sacrifice?"

Marla looked suspicious and surprised, not to mention depressed. This was ironic, since she was just given a heroic recognition, a totally unexpected honor. Unlike me, Dad would have cheered her up with this *Gita* verse:

*Treat pleasure and pain, gain and loss, victory and defeat all the same. Then move on to fight. Thus you will not incur sin.*

Dad considered depression a sin. Whenever he would know of my depression, he would quote this verse.

That was the last session Marla attended. Apparently the girls left Dehradun, without saying goodbye or telling anyone their plans, as they didn't show up at the farewell meeting—just Tula and I were there with the drummers at our residence. After the meeting, Daphra and Bijlu began to pack up their belongings. At the time of their departure, Tula gave them a black and white photograph as a special gift. It showed them with the two girls. They both looked at the photograph but didn't say a word.

"*Photo ka pichhnai dekha* (See the back of the photo!)" Tula said in Garhwali with a smile. They both saw what was written in Hindi, in red ink: *Mahabharata ke sachche gayak—vadak: Bijlu aur Daphra ke liye hamara pyar* (The true singers-players of the *Mahabharata*: Our love for Bijlu and Daphra). Both girls had signed their names in Hindi as well. Both the drummers were crying. We both hugged them.

When we returned to Seattle, Marla and Jennifer were not seen there, either. To date, to the best of my knowledge, I haven't seen anything published by Marla. Jennifer was at least involved with note taking.

I wish I had seen them leaving Dehradun with a good impression of the Thakur brothers and Abdul. They all liked Marla and Jennifer very much, despite even Marla's odd research question: "Are polygamists holy?" Marla's face, as I last saw it then, is still difficult to remove from my memory.

I am sure she told Jennifer about the aftermath. Jennifer, too, must have gone into depression. I am reminded of their depression when I listen to the cassette mix-tape they made for me as a gift, especially the incredibly sad relationship-breakdown song they played on our house stereo so often called "Landslide" by Fleetwood Mac.

Tula upholds the metaphor of the *Gita*, "The two friends should have fought it together, in and out. Their *git* needs to be sung aloud; their battle conch needs to be blown." Dad insisted on the *Gita* line *"Tato yuddhāya yujyasva"*—"Therefore move on to fight." He considered this advice just a musical sentence, not a missionary act. Who knows who said it and sang it first? Certainly not one of those two imagined characters, Krishna and Arjuna!

But I know what I am saying here. My notes are influenced by Marla's copious notes. As a professional academician, I am obliged to acknowledge her contribution. I haven't erased anything.

This book is her song for anyone out there.

***END***

# Glossary

*Abhimanyu*
Arjuna's son from his wife Subhadra

*Adhiratha*
A chariot-maker who was Karna's foster father

*Adi Purusha*
The first person in the Universe, God, Vishnu, Narayana

*Agni*
God of fire

*Ahimsa*
Non-injury, non-violence

*Arjuna*
The third Pandava brother

*Arsa, arsu*
A Himalayan pastry

*Arya*
Aryan, a noble person

*Asavarna*
Low caste

*Ashvatthaman*
Son of Drona, sided with the Kauravas

*Avatar, avatara*
Divine incarnation

*Baba*

In the Himalayan Nights

Holy man

*Babhruvahana*
Arjuna's son from his wife Chitrangada

*Balarama*
Vasudeva's son from Rohini, Krishna's half-brother

*Bali*
Animal sacrifice

*Bhagadatta*
A king who sided with the Kauravas

*Bhagavad Gita*
The 18-chapter discourse between Krishna and Arjuna at the Kurukshetra battlefield, lit. "godly song"

*Bhagavan*
God

*Bhajan*
Devotional song

*Bhakti*
Devotion

*Bhang*
Indian hemp, *cannabis indica*

*Bharadvaja*
A Brahmin sage, father of Drona

*Bharata*
Son of Shakuntala and Dushyanta and founder of the empire Bharata (Bharat, India)

*Bhatti*
Liquor distillery

*Bhima*
The second Pandava brother

*Bhishma*

Son of Shantanu and granduncle of the Kauravas and Pandavas, sided with the Kauravas

*Brahma*
The god of creation

*Brahmacharin, Brahmachari*
A man with a vow of austere life including celibacy and study

*Brahmana*
Brahmin, priest or any person from the priestly class in the caste system

*Chat*
A spicy snack

*Chekitana*
A king, sided with the Pandavas

*Chilam*
The pot for smoking tobacco or narcotics

*Chipko*
A 'green revolution' slogan to save forests with this command word "Hug! " or "Cling!"

*Chitrangada*
One of the wives of Arjuna and mother of Babhruvahana

*Dada*
Grandfather

*Dakshina*
Sacred cash gift

*Dalit*
Hindi word for untouchables or low castes

*Damau*
The small timpani-shaped drum used in the *Pandava* dance

*Das, dasa*
Slave, devotee

*Dasi*

Maid, female devotee

*Daunr*
A modern folk drum, related to the ancient drum *damaru*

*Debi*
Goddess, same as *Devi*

*Dehradun*
The town where the dance takes place, the capital of the Indian state of Uttarakhand

*Desi*
Any person from India, indigenous, lit. "a native thing or person of a country"

*Devaki*
Krishna's mother and Vasudeva's wife

*Devi*
Goddess, same as *Debi*

*Dhammapada*
A book of Buddhist sermons in verse, "dharma song" (cf. *Bhagavad Gita* "godly song")

*Dhananjaya*
A name of Arjuna, lit. "winner of wealth"

*Dhanyabad*
Thanks! (same as *dhanyavad*)

*Dharam, dharm*
Religion, same as *dharma*

*Dharma*
Duty, law, righteousness, religion, behavior, fairness

*Dhol*
The big bass drum used with *damau* in the *Pandava* dance

*Dhrishtadyumna*
The commander of the Pandavas and Draupadi's brother

*Dhritarashtra*
The blind king and Duryodhana's father attended by Sanjaya during the 18-day war

*Dom*, *doma*
A low-caste person, an untouchable

*Draupadi*
King Drupada's daughter and the common wife of the five Pandava brothers

*Drona*
Sage Bharadvaja's son and Ashvathaman's father, taught military science to Kauravas and Pandavas, sided with the Kauravas

*Drupada*
Draupadi's father and king of the Panchalas

*Duhshasana*
Duryodhana's second brother

*Duryodhana*
Eldest son of King Dhritarashtra and Gandhari, leader of the Kauravas

*Ekalavya*
A low-caste man, whom Drona refused to teach archery

*Ganapati*
The elephant-headed god of success and scribe of the *Mahabharata*

*Gandhari*
Wife of King Dhritarashtra and mother of the hundred Kaurava brothers

*Ganesha*
Same as Ganapati, son of Parvati and Shiva

*Ganga*
The river Ganges, Bhishma's mother and Shantanu's wife

*Garhwal*
An area of the central Himalayas in the Uttarakhand state of India

*Garhwali*
One of the new Indo-Aryan languages spoken in the Garhwal Himalayas

*Ghatotkacha*
Bhima's son from the demoness Hidimba

*Git*
Song

*Gita*
The *Bhagavad Gita*, song

*Golgappa*
A spicy deep fried round snack

*Gotra*
Clan, lineage

*Gyan*
Knowledge, Hindi word for *jñana*

*Hanuman*
A monkey character in the *Ramayana* regarded as the greatest devotee of Rama

*Hanuman Chalisa*
The forty verses authored by Tulsidas in the Avadhi language in praise of Hanuman

*Hari*
God, Krishna's epithet

*Harijan*
God's person, Gandhi's term for the low-caste people or untouchables

*Hastinapura*
The capital city of the Kuru Empire

*Havan, havana*
Vedic fire ritual, (cf. *homa* "burnt food")

*IAS*
Acronym of "Indian Administrative Service," an officer in this administrative service

*Indra*
King of heaven and gods

*Indraprastha*
The ancient capital city established by the Pandavas on the site of Delhi

*Iravan, Iravat*
Arjuna's son from Ulupi

*Ishvara*
God

*Jai, jay, jaya*
Victory

*Jalebi*
A sweet

*Jayadratha*
Son-in-law of King Dhritarashtra, sided with his brother-in-law Duryodhana

*Jhirna*
A wild variety of asparagus

*Kali*
The black goddess, wife of Shiva

*Kalidasa*
Goddess Kali's devotee, a prominent Sanskrit poet and playwright

*Kama Sutra*
A treatise on love authored by Vatsyayana in Sanskrit

*Karna*
Kunti's son born when she was unmarried, sided with the Kauravas

*Kaurava*
The hundred sons of Dhritarashtra and Gandhari, named as a group after their ancestor Kuru

*Kothi*
A big residential building, mansion

*Kripa, Kripacharya*
Ashvathaman's maternal uncle and teacher of the Kauravas and Pandavas, sided with the Kauravas

*Krishna*
Krishna, son of Vasudeva and Devaki and one of the human avatars of God who instructs Arjuna in the *Bhagavad Gita*

*Kshatriya*
The second class in the caste system, the warrior people, the royal class Rajanya

*Kunti*
Pandu's wife and mother of Karna, Yudhishthira, Arjuna, and Bhima

*Kurta*
Tunic or any long loose Indian shirt

*Kuru*
The male ancestor of the Kauravas and Pandavas

*Kurukshetra*
The battlefield named after Kuru

*Lassi*
A drink made with yogurt, usually sweet but can also include other flavors including salt

*Madri*
Pandu's second wife who gave birth to their twins Nakula and Sahadeva

*Manusmriti*
The ancient law book in Sanskrit attributed to sage Manu, lit. "Manu's Law"

*Mata*
Mother

*Moksha*
Salvation, release from the endless cycle of life, death and rebirth

*Naimishsa, Naimisharanya*
A forest in north India where the story of the *Mahabharata* was narrated to the sages

*Nakula*
A Pandava brother, Pandu's son from his second wife Madri, the twin brother of Sahadeva

*Namaskar*
Act of bowing, salutation, greeting

*Namaste*
Greeting for welcome or farewell, lit. "A bow to you!

*Narada*
An ancient sage and devotee of Vishnu

*Narayana*
God, Vishnu

*Nishada*
The dark-skinned pre-Aryan people, the Austric ethnic group of India

*Om*
The sacred syllable, most commonly attached to holy mantras in Sanskrit and other languages

*Pahari*
A native of mountains

*Pakora*
Spicy fritters deep fried in a batter

*Pandau*
The Garhwali name for the Pandava brothers, the Garhwali dance related to them

*Pandava*
Pandu's five sons named after him

*Partha*
Arjuna's name after his mother Pritha (Kunti)

*Parvati*
Mountain goddess, Shiva's wife and Ganesha's mother

*Prasad*
Sacred food

*PUDI*
Acronym of "person under devout influence"

*Puja*
Worship, religious service

*Radha*
Karna's foster mother and Adhiratha's wife after whom Karna was called Radheya

*Rajanya*
The royal or warrior class, the second class in the caste system, the Kshatriya people

*Rama*
The hero of the epic *Ramayana* and an avatar of Vishnu

*Ramayana*
The ancient Sanskrit epic about Rama originally authored by the sage Valmiki

*Rishi*
Sage, saint

*Rohini*
Another wife of Vasudeva, Balarama's mother

*Roti*
The round flatbread

*Rukmini*
One of the wives of Krishna whose son was Pradyumna

*Sahab*
An honorific term for a man, officer, boss (spelled also *Sahib*)

*Sahadeva*
A Pandava brother, Pandu's son from his second wife Madri, twin brother of Nakula

*Samshaptaka*
A commando, suicide squad, oath-takers to do or die

*Sanatana Dharma*
The eternal and perpetual religion of Hindus

*Sanjaya*
Sañjaya, the psychic who narrates the 18-day war to his blind master King Dhritarashtra

*Sarasvati*
Goddess of learning, Brahma's daughter and wife

*Satyabhama*
One of the wives of Krishna

*Satyaki*
A warrior and general of the Pandavas

*Savarna*
High caste

*Shaivite*
Follower of Shiva the God, related to Shaivism

*Shakti*
Energy, the female deity instead of the male God, Shiva's consort

*Shakuni*
Gandhari's brother and Duryodhana's uncle, sided with the Kauravas

*Shalwar*
Women's loose pants

*Shalya*
Brother of Madri, uncle of Nakula and Sahadeva, sided with the Kauravas

*Shantanu*
Father of Bhishma and great grandfather of the Kauravas and Pandavas

*Shikhandin*
King Drupada's daughter who changed her sex to kill Bhishma for spoiling her marriage in her immediate past life, fem. Shikhandini

*Shiva*
Parvati's husband and Ganesha's father, God in Shaivite view, lit. "good"

*Shiva Ratri*
Shiva's Night, an annual worship of Shiva

*Shuddhi*
Purification, religious conversion

*Shudra*
The fourth and the lowest class in the caste system, an untouchable

*Sita*
Rama's wife and heroine of the epic *Ramayana*

*Tantra*
An esoteric philosophy and practice, *Tantric* or *tantrik* religion of ancient India

*Thandai*
Cold drink with or without *bhang*

*Tulasidasa, Tulsidas*
The author of the epic *Ramacharitamanasa* in the medieval Avadhi language

*Ulupi*
One of Arjuna's wives whose son was Iravan or Iravat

*Vaishnavite*
Follower of *Vishnu*, philosophy and practice centered on *Vishnu* as God

*Vaishya*
The third class in the caste system, the business caste people

*Varna*
Class, color, distinction, the term for the four Hindu social classes

*Vasudeva*
Father of Krishna and Balarama

*Vedas*
The first four Vedic scriptures: *Rig Veda, Yajur Veda, Sama Veda, Atharva Veda*

*Virata*
A king who protected the Pandavas during their exile and later sided with them

*Vishnu*
God, Narayana, lit. "pervader"

*Vyasa*
A sage and original author of the ancient *Mahabharata*

*Waham*
Superstition

*Yajña*
Vedic fire ritual with or without animal sacrifice

*Yama*
The god of death

*Yoni*
Life, being, vagina

*Yudhishthira*
The eldest Pandava brother

# About the Author

**Anoop Chandol**a, an American linguist-anthropologist, was raised in a priestly Brahmin family in India near the Nepal-Tibet border. Dr. Chandola, a graduate of the Universities of California-Berkeley and Chicago, has taught Indian literature, culture, and religion at S.V. Patel University, M. S. University of Baroda, University of California-Berkeley, University of Washington-Seattle, University of Texas-Austin, and University of Wisconsin-Madison. He is a member of the American Anthropological Association, Association for Asian Studies, Linguistic Society of America, and Linguistic Society of India. Dr. Chandola, now Professor Emeritus of East Asian Studies at the University of Arizona, lives in Tucson with his wife Sudha. He is a frequent guest lecturer on Hinduism and related religions.

If you enjoyed *In the Himalayan Nights* consider these other fine Books from Savant Books and Publications:

*Essay, Essay, Essay* by Yasuo Kobachi
*Aloha from Coffee Island* by Walter Miyanari
*Footprints, Smiles and Little White Lies* by Daniel S. Janik
*The Illustrated Middle Earth* by Daniel S. Janik
*Last and Final Harvest* by Daniel S. Janik
*A Whale's Tale* by Daniel S. Janik
*Tropic of California* by R. Page Kaufman
*The Village Curtain* by Tony Tame
*Dare to Love in Oz* by William Maltese
*The Interzone* by Tatsuyuki Kobayashi
*Today I am a Man* by Larry Rodness
*The Bahrain Conspiracy* by Bentley Gates
*Called Home* by Gloria Schumann
*Kanaka Blues* by Mike Farris
*First Breath* edited by Zachary M. Oliver
*Poor Rich* by Jean Blasiar
*The Jumper Chronicles* by W. C. Peever
*William Maltese's Flicker* by William Maltese
*My Unborn Child* by Orest Stocco
*Last Song of the Whales* by Four Arrows
*Perilous Panacea* by Ronald Klueh
*Falling but Fulfilled* by Zachary M. Oliver
*Manifest Intent* by Mike Farris
*Mythical Voyage* by Robin Ymer
*Hello, Norma Jean* by Sue Dolleris
*Richer* by Jean Blasiar
*Charlie No Face* by David B. Seaburn
*Number One Bestseller* by Brian Morley
*My Two Wives and Three Husbands* by S. Stanley Gordon
*In Dire Straits* by Jim Currie
*Wretched Land* by Mila Komarnisky
*Chan Kim* by Ilan Herman
*Who's Killing All the Lawyers?* by A. G. Hayes
*Ammon's Horn* by G. Amati

*Wavelengths* edited by Zachary M. Oliver
*Almost Paradise* by Laurie Hanan
*Communion* by Jean Blasiar and Jonathan Marcantoni
*The Oil Man* by Leon Puissegur
*Random Views of Asia from the Mid-Pacific* by William E. Sharp, Jr.
*The Isla Vista Crucible* by Reilly Ridgell
*Blood Money* by Scott Mastro

Scheduled for Release in 2012:

*Perverse* by Larry Rodness
*On My Behalf* by Helen Doan
*Rules of Privilege* by Mike Farris
*Light Surfer* by David Allan Williams
*Traveler's Rest* by Jonathan Marcantoni

http://www.savantbooksandpublications.com
http://www.savantbookstorehonolulu.com